Active's Measure

Pennywhistle Series
Book I

D1572281

John McClellan Danielski

"Ambushed by the charming, charismatic, and complicated character of Royal Marine Captain Thomas Pennywhistle, the reader of *Active's Measure* becomes a willing captive to his grand adventures in this riveting nautical adventure. *Active's Measure* commands one's attention and respect from Pennywhistle's first act of personal heroism to the final act of magnificent selflessness. The writing is as strong, forceful, and compelling as the handsome marine himself. Thrilling, heart-warming, and intense enough to hold the novice's attention as well as the most demanding connoisseur of period military detail, the intrigue and action will leave the reader breathless for Pennywhistle's next adventure."

– Thomas George, Antiquarian

"Meet a truly remarkable hero, Captain Thomas Pennywhistle. In *Active's Measure*, John Danielski brings to life the world of warfare at the time of the Napoleonic Wars in vivid and detailed writing based on exhaustive and intelligently informed research. Alongside this, his skill in inventing and telling a rollicking good tale makes turning of the next page inevitable. This first novel brings a new and remarkable author to the world of naval fiction, one to be watched with keen interest in the future."

– George Odam, Professor Emeritus Bath Spa University

"An exciting, fast-paced, naval swashbuckler with vivid writing that makes you feel you are living every broadside, sword slash, and musket shot. The action is strong and unremitting, the plot twists are sharp and surprising, the characters robust and strongly realized. The central character, Thomas Pennywhistle, shows traces of Sharpe, Hornblower, and Darcy, yet emerges as a distinctive, complex personality worthy of your full attention. This is a real page turner; be prepared for sleepless nights."

– James Taylor, Ph.D. Southern University

"This is not just a wild, edge of your seat nautical tale for men, but a powerfully passionate and captivating love story that women will enjoy from start to finish. The hero, Tom Pennywhistle, while certainly brave, resourceful, and constantly captivating you with his feats, is also a surprisingly deep, reflective, and somewhat cunning character with a dark side. Carlotta, the object of Pennywhistle's admiration, is a strong, capable, independent female who exemplifies great sensitivity to a woman's point of view. It is refreshing to see a heroine who is competent and not a mere damsel in distress who exists simply to be put in jeopardy and then rescued. The endearing chemistry between hero and heroine leaves you in constant fear for the survival of their future. Unable to stop at the end of each chapter, I decided the author must have employed as yet undiscovered reading pheromones!"

– Sandi Lindstrom

"This is a wonderfully well told story, with great imaginative flair and well-researched detail. It combines vividly dramatic action with sympathetically drawn characters on all sides of the battles. Although the hero, Captain Pennywhistle, says 'I am a marine officer, not a spinner of rattling sea yarns,' John Danielski takes us right into the heat of the action and spins a rattling good yarn of the Napoleonic War."

– John McRae, author of *The Routledge History of Literature in English*

Active's Measure by John McClellan Danielski

ISBN: 978-1-61179-345-1 (Paperback)
ISBN: 978-1-61179-346-8 (e-book)

BISAC Subject Headings:
FIC032000 FICTION / War and Military
FIC014000 FICTION / Historical
FIC047000 FICTION / Sea Stories

Address all correspondence to:
Fireship Press, LLC
P.O. Box 68412
Tucson, AZ 85737
info@fireshippress.com

Or visit our website at:
www.fireshippress.com

Dedication

This book is dedicated to James, Thomas, and Sandi for their kind and constant encouragement.

Author's Notes

Active's Measure is unequivocally a work of fiction, yet key elements and people in the story were real. The book was inspired by a painting now hanging in the National Maritime Museum in Toulon, France, titled *Pomone versus Active, Alceste, and Unite*, painted in 1837 by Pierre Julien Gilbert. It is a stunning work that features the naval battle portrayed at the end of the book.

Although Tom Pennywhistle is fictional, three of the important figures in the book lived and left a mark on history. Sir William Hoste was one of Britain's most underrated naval heroes and is the subject of a fine biography, *Remember Nelson* by Tom Pocock. James Alexander Gordon later figured prominently in the British attack on Washington in 1814. Bernard Dubordieu earned a place of honour in French naval history for being one of the few Napoleonic captains to capture a British frigate in single ship combat. I have endeavoured to reconstruct their personalities as accurately as possible.

All of the ships and their captains featured in the book existed. British lieutenants Moore, Meers, Haye, Dashwood, O'Brien, and Slaughter were real figures as well. Sadly, research uncovered only the vague outlines of their personalities.

HMS Active no longer exists, but one well-preserved English frigate does. *HMS Trincomalee* in Hartlepool, England was constructed in 1817 and never saw battle, but was built to almost exactly the same Leda class specifications as *Active*. Other than being built of Indian teak instead of English oak, she could be *Active's* twin. She is well worth a visit.

Acknowledgments

I would like to thank Ms. Bernadette Wright for checking the French phrases.

I wish to extend my undying gratitude to Chris Wozney, my editor, whose erudition, kindness, humor, and generosity gave me both an education and wonderful support throughout a process that can sometimes be painful. She constantly saw little things I missed and made suggestions that were as informed as they were useful. Thanks, Obi Wan!

Active's Measure

Pennywhistle Series
Book I

John McClellan Danielski

FIRESHIP PRESS

"In obtaining for them the distinction of 'Royal,' I but inefficiently did my duty. I never knew an appeal to them for honour, courage, or loyalty that did not more than realize my highest expectations. If ever the hour of real danger should come to England, they will be this country's sheet anchor."
—Admiral Sir John Jervis, 1st Earl St. Vincent, 1802

One

"Yes, it's dangerous, but we need all the speed we can muster! Run up the driver and push her for all she'll take!"

Royal Marine Captain Thomas Pennywhistle's shouted order was barely audible in the fierce wind. A flash of lightning illuminated the anxious face of Master's Mate Hudson, whose long experience at sea told him he should actually reduce sail, but he nodded, stowed his doubts, and obeyed.

The rain struck in slanting sheets, drenching everyone, and it was difficult to see more than a few yards in front of the bow. Thunder boomed and the angry sea rose in high peaks followed by plunging troughs. These miniature hurricanes, spawned by a temperamental wind that locals called *the Bora*, were short-lived, but as violent as they were unpredictable. This one had appeared without warning: one minute heavy overcast, the next minute the Bora in full fury. The wind was at least force ten on the new Beaufort Scale. Pennywhistle's brain calculated the sail area, weight distribution, ballasting, the bow's angle of attack relative to the waves, and a host of other factors against the dangers of high wind and roiled sea. The launch was well-designed, tough, and sturdy; she could handle the extra sail. Nevertheless, he knew even a slight miscalculation could doom the boat. The men of his command looked to him with great confidence; he fervently hoped it was not misplaced.

The launch corkscrewed violently as it ploughed through the phosphorescent green sea. Waves smashed furiously against the

1

bow, blasting the interior with spray, and the rain turned everyone's clothing sopping wet. The ferocious rocking made it difficult for the forty-one passengers to retain their seats.

Pennywhistle ignored his surroundings, squinted slightly, and pressed his pocket watch close to his angular face. The hands on the expensive Swiss timepiece were large, but barely discernible. Almost half past three: not more than thirty minutes until dawn. He fought down a driving impatience and willed his expressive face into a stoic mask of command. The men in the launch would take their cues from him. It was imperative he make it all seem unremarkable routine. It was his job to do the tactical worrying, not theirs.

The clouds parted for an instant and he directed his gaze to the saltwater trail ahead. The brilliant swath of the Milky Way pointed straight toward the landing site, almost as if nature were providing a beacon for the expedition, and the launch ran before the shrieking wind. His support of the main assault was vital. He needed to make up time, even if it entailed extra risk.

"By the deep, twenty-seven!" The boat's leadsman bellowed the depth. There was a very real danger of grounding or gutting the hull on an outcrop of jagged rock. The charts had proven useless; the sea beneath was a maze of unmarked reefs and shoals.

Bam! The launch glanced violently off a hidden reef and shook heavily. Men bounced upward from their seats, hats flew off, and jaws rattled. Pennywhistle controlled his alarm and kept his face neutral. He glanced over the port gunwale and saw a large dent in the hull. Thankfully, the bowed planking remained firm and watertight, but a second hit could prove fatal: most of the sailors and marines could not swim.

Suddenly, the wind dropped to nothing and the rain ceased. After the blasting winds, the silence felt oppressive. The Bora was fickle, behaving like a wronged lover seeking revenge on a man who sought to use her. Pennywhistle ordered the two sails furled and the twin masts stowed. From here on, it was up to sheer muscle power. One way or another, he *would* land before dawn!

Sailors seated seven pairs of oars in the muffled oarlocks,

inserted thole pins, then silently slid their blades into the night sea. The rowers dipped and lifted in purposeful, practiced rhythm. He estimated the boat was making two knots, far slower than when under sail, but good for a world where no craft moved faster than fourteen. Coxswain Markham moved the tiller slightly, his hard, calloused hands taking the measure of the current. The only sound was the steady *woosh, woosh, woosh*, as the sea reluctantly parted in front of the bow.

A swirling mist obscured the landing site ahead. No hardship, this: Pennywhistle's navigational skill furnished him with a clear mental picture of the launch's exact position relative to the beach. The snow-topped peaks of the Alps behind the broad, coastal plain were clear, a pleasing assurance that they were on the right heading. Far less pleasing was the fact that he could see them at all. The hint of flint grey in the eastern clouds told him the cloak of darkness was starting to lift. He checked his watch again. Still behind schedule, but not by much.

"Come starboard two points," he quietly ordered Markham. It took a small movement of the coxswain's hand to make the correction. The two companion boats, thirty yards astern, made similar adjustments. The launch sped up. Good, he had picked up the swift, offshore current that paralleled the beach.

The men in the tightly packed launch maintained a disciplined silence. It was unnatural, given the tension, but this way even a whispered command would be clearly heard. Sailors and marines watched and nervously waited.

The fog dissipated with dawn's approach, revealing pin-points of light where no light should be. Alarmed, Pennywhistle unshipped his spyglass and picked out the distant, muted lanterns of scattered French sentry boxes. Blast! Those had not been there two days ago. The boats were close enough to be spotted, but the lack of shouts or hails suggested that the French soldiery was less than fully alert. Picket duty was tedious, and Pennywhistle knew men often shirked it.

Pennywhistle's launch was part of a wave of British boats that had left the frigate HMS *Active* two hours earlier. Lieutenant Steven

Meers commanded the first twenty-five foot cutter. His plain, boyish face wore a look of anxious concentration, at once far away and deeply present, and his china-blue eyes sparkled with tension. Excitement and a lupine smile lit up the handsome, worldly face of Lieutenant James Moore, who commanded the second cutter. He was naturally combative and always eager to have a good bash at the French.

Pennywhistle's twenty-seven-foot launch contained most of the complement of *Active*'s 39 Royal Marines. His marine rank was equivalent to the naval ones of Moore and Meers, but he was the senior officer both by experience and date of commission; hence, he was responsible for the mission's success. He felt a simmering unease, as if a low-level current of electricity was being pumped through his body. He knew he was being over-analytical and willed his brain to slow down. He failed, as usual. As he thought of the fighting to come, he began to flush a deep, hot crimson. Blood coursed through his body and his lips grew dry. He knew the signs well, and they comforted him. It was simply his body preparing for battle.

Marine Private Ian MacLeod felt the rising tension. He fancied that the three boats of the landing party were three barracudas gliding through the night. Lacking something better to do, he fidgeted with the leather stock around his neck, then checked the flint of his musket for the tenth time. He was confident of success but his body thrummed with energy, at odds with having to sit still and do nothing. He was a long way from Glasgow and the mill that had rendered his job as a weaver obsolete. He didn't feel obsolete or unwanted now, but rather a proud member of a good team. He was sure they would bag the entire enemy convoy and thought excitedly of the prize money. He hoped to save enough to leave the Service someday and open an inn of his own.

MacLeod shifted his position on the thwart and looked across at Captain Pennywhistle's tall frame for reassurance. The captain appeared calm, detached; almost bored. MacLeod knew from experience what that signified. He had been with the captain in plenty of fights and his face always underwent the same eerie transformation. It was Pennywhistle's "battle face," and meant that combat lay just ahead. It inspired confidence in him because it would drive fear into the hearts of the enemy. The captain was well-mannered, courtly even, but now seemed something other than human: a feral, hungry predator, eager to mete out death to his prey. His eyes added to the effect. They burned with the fire of incandescent emeralds.

MacLeod checked his cartridge box and was pleased to discover that the gale had left his paper cartridges untouched. He noted Private Maxwell performing the same ritual; anything to keep occupied.

Pennywhistle unshipped his long spyglass and methodically swept the beach ahead, panning side to side and back again. Meers and Moore did the same.

Pennywhistle's boat led the triangular formation. The plan was for Pennywhistle to land first, with the two cutters taking flanking positions on either side. He had reconnoitered the area incognito two days before and realized an attack here would provide a perfect diversion for the main British assault on the anchorage. Conversely, if the main thrust ran into spirited or prolonged opposition, this attack could be turned into the primary offensive. Either way, the French would not see it coming.

"Damn!" Pennywhistle mouthed silently. He snapped his glass shut in frustration. The sparkling lights of hundreds of campfires lay ahead. What had been a corporal's guard now appeared to be a force approaching battalion strength, perhaps as many as six hundred men, and far more troops than his small landing force: a dangerous and unwelcome development. An encyclopedia of actions flashed through his mind. No! He would *not* call off the attack. He would improvise quickly and trust to the shock value of surprise.

The scent of decaying vegetation assaulted his nose; they were fast approaching land. Not long now.

"By the mark, three," called Able Seaman Whitson, the leadsman. He read from a twenty-five-fathom weighted plumb line marked with coloured strips at regular intervals to indicate depth.

The launch sped swiftly along with the current, but Pennywhistle mentally commanded it to go faster. The French would not remain unaware for long.

They were three hundred yards from the beach. He again unfurled his spyglass. The grey sky slowly marched toward pink, the breaking surf drew closer, and a French sentry box with no active inhabitant became clear in his glass. He focused on a disheveled military cantonment some distance to the rear. A French tricolour fluttered lazily to the top of a slightly askew flagpole. Smoke rose from scattered campfires and a few men in white shirts emerged unsteadily from improvised tents. The scene was one of torpor and boredom, but reveille was not far off.

"Load carronade!" Pennywhistle commanded in hushed but imperious tones. "Double shot, canister only. Run out!" Gunner's Mate Rowlinson soon had his hand on the lanyard, ready to fire at the command.

The 12-pound carronade fitted to the launch's bow was stubby artillery on a slide, rather than wheels. It was simply called the "smasher." It had a lighter, compact barrel and was designed specifically as a short-range weapon. It could not send projectiles as far as a cannon, but at close range it packed a deadly punch. Loaded with two charges of canister, over four hundred musket balls, it was a supreme close-range, man-killing weapon—essentially a giant, wide-mouth shotgun. Terrific for clearing enemy decks of boarders, it would work equally well for clearing a beach.

Two hundred yards to go.

"By the mark, twain," the leadsman called out.

"Check flints," commanded Pennywhistle. He wanted to make sure no marine's musket had a misfire due to a loose or bad flint.

"Check bayonets." He was nothing if not methodical. Cold steel was a necessity with a one-shot musket. He wanted to make absolutely certain each bayonet was firmly attached to the nub that doubled as the musket's sight.

Stratton twisted his bayonet on just a little tighter. He had a strong feeling it would see plenty of action today.

"Check cartridges." Pennywhistle knew the men had already done so, but in combat there was no such thing as too much preparation. Each man needed sixty rounds in his cartridge box; twenty-eight held in the main tray slots, the rest stowed beneath. Private McCarthy did as ordered; his cartridges were as dry as the dust from a pharaoh's tomb. Good—even a hint of moisture would render them inert.

One hundred and fifty yards to the beach.

On land, Fusilier Chouteau emerged from his sentry box and cast a long look toward the sea. To his surprise, he saw three boats approaching. He was new to the French Army and frightened, but remembered his orders. He leveled his Charleville at the boats and fired. The shot went wild, but the British had been sighted, and he had given the alarm.

"By the mark, one, shoaling fast," the leadsman called in his distinctive cadence. Six feet, still too deep for marines to exit the boat. Almost there, patience!

In the French camp, Lt. Flambard heard the report of Chouteau's musket. He and another officer rushed forward to see if it was a real threat or just another jumpy recruit.

Two minutes later, Pennywhistle heard the drums start to pound *La General*, the French call to arms. Surprise was gone. Things would happen quickly now.

One hundred yards to the beach. The other two boats fanned out so that they were roughly six hundred yards off the larboard and starboard beams.

"Boat oars!" At Pennywhistle's command, sailors silently retracted the oars inside the launch. Momentum and the current would do the rest.

French soldiers in full uniforms and packs stumbled from the lean-to tents and formed a crude line on the camp's parade ground. It never occurred to them that in an emergency they could have dispensed with some of their kit. They wanted to look smart and military and were too new to have any sense of discrimination. Regimental drums thundered, officers shouted, and men squared their shoulders and stood to attention.

Ten yards out, Pennywhistle heard the blessed words.

"By the mark, half!" Three feet. Time to go.

"Marines, follow me! Form skirmish line on the beach." Pennywhistle drew his cutlass and plunged over the gunwale into the surf. The shale was uneven, slimy, and slippery. He stumbled, very un-heroic. He grimaced briefly, then his boots found purchase on the rocks and he slogged toward the beach. MacLeod, Stratton, and McCarthy followed.

In the distance, two blue rockets arced over the sky, signaling that the primary British attack was underway. A diversion was necessary. Immediately.

Once ashore, as he waited for the rest of the marines to muster behind him, Pennywhistle took a long, careful survey of their opponents through his spyglass. The French troop assemblage, slightly less straight than a ram's horn, amateurishly struggled to form a real line. The soldiers were confused and lackluster, hesitant in their parade ground evolutions. They bumped, tripped, and jostled each other, as though they were not fully awake. An officer in blue and gold violently waved his sword with his hat atop its tip and shouted what were either words of anger or encouragement.

Pennywhistle's practiced eye told him these slovenly soldiers were minimally trained recruits. Good. Probably conscripts, little experience with drill, none with battle. All of his men were experienced veterans. That would go a long way to compensate for the disparity in numbers. Satisfied, he closed his glass slowly.

From the French camp, enervated, hollow cheers rippled through the morning chill. *"Vive l'Empereur! Vive l'Empereur! Vive l'Empereur!"* Officers hectored men, flourished swords, and moved up and down the line.

Pennywhistle carefully walked forward through the beach sand, looking for some kind of natural barrier, stopping three hundred yards out. There were dunes, swales, driftwood, beach grass, and large rocks. Good cover; the men could improvise a low line of obstacles to serve as an anchor for a picket line, handy for troops trained to exercise initiative and use terrain to advantage.

8

Unlike conventional soldiers, marines had to fight on pitching decks, alone or in small groups. They were trained to duck down when reloading, use any cover available, and fire from almost any position imaginable. This gave them a marked advantage over conventional land soldiers.

Sergeant Dale, who had once been a silent and skillful poacher, quietly appeared at Pennywhistle's side, like the chief *ghillie* on a Scottish estate reporting to his laird.

"Sarn't, we'll make our stand here. Spread the men out, have them take cover and lie down. Put Maxwell and his men on the left and Corporal Wainwright's people on the right. Tell them to use stones, brushwood, gorse—anything they can find for concealment. Each man can scrape away a few feet of sand with his bayonet and create a makeshift hide. Let's keep them protected as long as possible. No sense in making it easy for French scouts. They can't shoot what they can't see. I don't want any firing until the French are within thirty yards. Remember, patience. Don't waste ammunition on distance shooting. We need to get the enemy in close. Johnny Crapaud will be upon us in short order."

"Aye, aye, sir!" Dale acknowledged enthusiastically.

Pennywhistle endeavoured to put a bright face on what he loathed: standing on the defensive and waiting. He was a patient man only by training and discipline, never by inclination when action was at hand. Attack suited him better than defense, yet he was also prudent and disdained recklessness. He was eager to come to grips with the enemy, but it was far more effective to keep his numbers hidden from the French until he judged the moment right. There was no sense in letting the French know in advance how few they faced. Green troops often wildly overestimated the number of their foes. He wanted them to have time for their imaginations to work and make that estimate as high as possible. Once they engaged, he would trust to a show of confidence and superior fighting skill.

"They know we are here, but we are going to give them a surprise they won't forget, Sarn't," said Pennywhistle. "We're outnumbered badly, but as long as we act as if the opposite were true, we can prevail. We just need a stratagem." He was always brutally honest with Dale. A good NCO was an officer's best ally in battle and deserved to be told the unvarnished truth.

Dale touched his round hat in salute and acknowledgment. "Aye, sir! You have more tricks than a conjurer, sir, that's no lie, and I am sure," he gestured in the direction of the French, "you have something in mind for that lot." Dale knew his commander was a trickster and his ideas were subtle, their ultimate purpose hidden. He trusted Pennywhistle implicitly.

"Sarn't, I think the enemy is composed of conscripts who have little or poor training. They form up and march like amateurs. I am sure you have seen that for yourself. Unfortunately, they look to have a full battalion of six companies out there, far outnumbering us. I did not expect those numbers, but ingenuity and experience can always prevail over brute strength. We're going to play on their rawness and give them what all green troops want: the pride and the thrill of success. Then we are going to yank it away." He looked at Dale with the eyes of a scientist who had just discovered a new and exciting chemical reaction.

Dale, a stalwart soldier and a bluff, uncomplicated man, eyed Pennywhistle with an amused curiousity. "How are we going to do that, sir?" asked Dale, confident a clever explanation would be forthcoming.

"You remember you told me once the experienced poacher never rushes things and takes great pains to line up the killing shot?"

Dale responded with unrepentant pride. "Aye, sir! I do! I miss those days out in the woods."

Pennywhistle smiled knowingly. A good poacher's instincts were worth their weight in gold to any military organization. "I recall you mentioned a woman got in the way."

Dale's expression turned rueful. "Still be at it, sir, had it not been for my damned cousin. That bugger and I liked the same lady, so he sold me out to the assizes. Found out later that my sweetheart had a very loose tongue and wasn't really so sweet on me after all. Bloody shame people are not so easy to read as animals, captain."

"Isn't there a saying among poachers," inquired Pennywhistle, "if you want to catch the lion, tether the goat?"

"Aye, sir. If you want to bag big game, use smaller stuff as a lure. Let the large animal pick up the scent, watch the smaller beast struggle, and make him come to you," replied Dale.

"Our marines are going to be the bait," Pennywhistle explained. "It will be a bit like a game of hide and seek. Lure them in, play on their over-eagerness, then stop them with a few volleys. Reduce their numbers and fall back. They are too inexperienced to see it's a *ruse de guerre*. They will rush us, flushed with their first success. We lie down and pound them with canister at point-blank range from the carronades. After that, we rise up, give a huzzah, and give them the bayonet. Lure them in close, then hammer them quick and fast. They won't stand!"

Dale beamed as the cleverness of the plan hit him. "And let me guess, Captain, as soon as we charge straight head, Lieutenants Meers and Moore will hit them on the larboard and starboard flanks?"

"Exactly correct, Sarn't. You know my methods. Make every man count and do the unexpected. Beaten enemies simply do not turn and attack, and fresh troops do not suddenly materialize on the flanks. Send Addison and Leicester as messengers, Sarn't. Tell them my compliments to Lieutenants Meers and Moore, and have them meet me here at the double quick. Martin has the best eyesight of the company. Assign him to help Rowlinson with the carronade. We probably have time for only one shot before they realize they've been duped. That shot has to decide the game."

"Aye, aye, sir." Like a wraith in fog, Dale departed.

Pennywhistle extended his glass to its full two-foot length and examined the on-coming French. The powerful Ramsden scope was an exceptionally precise instrument and he could see uniforms and faces clearly. The French line had formed itself into a column with a two company front. It had taken them far longer than it should for real professionals; amateurs, just as he suspected. Columns were a simple but powerfully effective method of attack against soldiers of little experience. The sight of a solid marching block of determined men generally inspired terror. Most troops broke before the column got very close.

Most troops, but not British ones. The line always trumped the column, firepower over shock. All you needed was a trained, disciplined line and resolute officers to lead it. The British had both.

Billowing pillars of choking, acrid dust rose as the column lumbered forward. It was roughly a thousand yards distant.

Private Maxwell looked into the gradually lightening distance, but continued his digging. There were alarming numbers of Crapauds out there! Still, he had no doubt that he would be on the victorious side in the fight ahead.

Private Blandon took a sip from his canteen and waited. He had great confidence in Mr. Pennywhistle and felt the French were in for a nasty surprise.

Pennywhistle glanced at his Blancpain; 3:55 a.m. The fast-expanding pink horizon confirmed the time. It was officially dawn; objects could be seen clearly at the quarter mile. The enemy had the scent. They would come to him. He just needed to wait.

Two

Colonel Pierre Dupleix watched the British landing with irritation. The English goddams were like roaches, always popping up where you least expected them. On closer reflection, he decided the landing was all to the good. Nothing put fire into green troops like meeting a small number of the enemy and driving them off in triumph. From atop his favourite mount, Bucephalus, named for Alexander the Great's famous horse, he swung his heavy brass spyglass in a slow arc, noting the British movements on the beach. He was not absolutely certain how many British were out there; they seemed to have taken cover, but it appeared nothing more than a reinforced scouting party—after information rather than a fight.

He debated sending out a few skirmishers to investigate, but impulsively decided it was unnecessary. With new recruits, it was important to act with swiftness and decisiveness. He had plenty of men. They knew only the rudiments of drill, but a strong column was easily formed and guaranteed the requisite solid cohesion to turn novices into an unstoppable battering ram. Complex maneuver was unnecessary. The sheer mass would be sufficient to intimidate sensible opponents. The British would naturally withdraw in haste. He did not anticipate any real shooting. It would be a cheap and easy success for his men.

*****

Meers breathlessly pounded up the beach to Pennywhistle's position. Meers' cutter had landed a third of a mile to the right. Moments later, Moore, who had landed in roughly the same position on Pennywhistle's left, breezed in. Not anything close to running, mind you; he positively sauntered, as if he had nothing more on his mind than a pleasant Sunday promenade in Brighton. He was the picture of ease and relaxation. Pennywhistle found the contrast between the naval lieutenants striking.

Steven Meers was of medium height and sturdy build, long of torso but short of leg. He possessed limited social graces and gave the impression of an excitable yet earnest beaver: enormous buck teeth set in a moon face, topped with an explosion of rebellious platinum blond hair. No one ever called him clever or imaginative, but he invariably displayed a quiet, unshakable determination that caused him to doggedly persist long after others had given up. He would be brave enough at executing a set piece battle, but poor at an improvised one. He would need very specific orders, covering several contingencies.

The Honourable James Moore, tall, well-proportioned, was the second son of an impoverished Irish peer. He was unfailingly charming, blessed with a quick wit and glib tongue. His chiseled, square face was framed by curly, jet-black hair, which contrasted nicely with his perfectly shaped white teeth. His smile was frequent, his laugh infectious; both suggested he took neither himself nor life too seriously. Women always took him seriously.

Pennywhistle discounted the handsome features and mannerly veneer. The man's true essence showed in his eyes. They were the keen, restless, predatory eyes of the natural born hunter. Moore was a killer cloaked in gentleman's guise who gloried in the chase and rejoiced in the blood of the slain. A very tough customer, highly useful in a fight.

A strange pair and an odd couple, but he trusted them and they reposed perfect confidence in him.

Moore, who was senior to Meers, 3rd Lieutenant of *Active* to Meers' 4th, spoke first and radiated good cheer, confidence, and *bonhomie*. "Tom, good day for a dust-up, don't you agree? Those French buggers out there look keen on some mischief. A bit unnerving that they seem to have invited more fellows to the party than we expected, but no matter. They don't look very skilled. Time for Jonny Toad to meet a reception from people who know their business. A damned good hiding! My people are in position and ready to go, but we have mostly close-quarter stuff—pistols, pikes, edged weapons, not many muskets. I can't do much unless they are very close."

Pennywhistle nodded and patiently reiterated the plan he had discussed with Sergeant Dale. "They outnumber us, but they don't have any artillery support. We do, and we'll use it to even the odds. They are betting everything on sheer, blunt force. They see only easy prey and are barreling toward the closest alluring and shiny object. Amazing they have deployed no skirmishers, conducted no reconnaissance. They think they have the initiative; all the better for us, we will soon disabuse them of that notion.

"You and Steven keep your men hidden on the flanks. We'll allow them to approach, like a thief who puts his hand in your purse to purloin its contents, but once the hand is fixed in its larceny, we will cut that hand off at the wrist."

"Use our experience and artillery to cancel out the advantage of numbers. Very good!" said Moore with a twisted grin.

"Precisely," replied Pennywhistle. "I want you and Steven to detail a few men to bring your cutters back down the beach and place them twenty yards on either side of the launch. Double shot your carronades with canister. Three 12-pound carronades will give us a battery. These Frenchmen probably have never taken a real volley in combat, so it's a good bet they have no idea of the destructive power of a naval broadside against human targets. But we need them very near, say, fifty yards. Thirty would be even better."

Meers enthusiastically bobbed his head in assent; he was eager to prove himself, and the plan gave him a key role. "Captain, what will be the signal for me and Lt. Moore to attack?" Meers tended to be formal in address, even though all three dined together daily in *Active*'s wardroom.

"Attack thirty seconds after the carronades fire. Let the shock sink in. Every battle has a tipping point, where men make the decision to stand or flee. Aim your attack at the rear of the column; that's where it will start to break apart. Men who can't fire are the first to run. Keep the pressure on. Have your men yell like demons and keep on them like a pack of Irish Wolfhounds worrying a wounded bear. Don't let up! Until then, keep your men out of sight and quiet behind the dunes. Any questions?"

Meers touched the brim of his bicorn hat in salute. "None, Captain. This will be a glorious day for *Active*, glorious!"

Pennywhistle smiled inwardly. Meers did run on a bit, but at least he was game!

Moore allowed a half-smile to play about the edges of his mouth. It was not in the least merry, but dangerously combative. "It's a good plan, Tom. I have no doubt it will be a bloody marvelous show. I think we can smash the lot of them." As Moore spoke, his icy grey eyes lit up with an unnatural, unnerving light. He relished the idea of a fight, whereas Pennywhistle merely saw it as a necessary evil to be performed with dispassionate efficiency.

"All right, gentlemen," said Pennywhistle calmly, "remember, surprise and skill lie with us. Good luck. Let's get to it!"

The two officers departed for their commands. Pennywhistle opened his Ramsden spyglass for an exacting observation of the approaching column that was now several hundred yards closer. He had been right: a battalion, though under strength, roughly five hundred men.

Counting Dale and himself, he had thirty-eight. Meers had twenty-two, and Moore twenty-five. Eighty-five officers and men against five hundred. Not ideal odds. But he had a plan and a singular skill at assessing an opponent. This opponent was rash.

The French column stopped, six hundred yards out. It had begun to lose marching integrity, common enough with recruits, and clusters of sergeants with halberds hovered about the sides trying to dress ranks. The sergeants dashed to and fro like angry water beetles, swearing, pleading, and threatening the recruits back into order. A lone gold-encrusted officer pompously pranced up on a white charger and began giving some sort of speech. Pennywhistle could not hear, but guessed it was one of those flowery-set pieces of battle oratory favoured by Napoleon's acolytes. "For the Emperor, for God, for France!" was the general idea.

The column straightened and lumbered forward. The mounted officer zigzagged in front of the column, urging it forward. He enthusiastically waved his sword about, then brought it to a decisive point in the direction of the British.

As the mass of men moved closer, Pennywhistle heard the words plainly. His guess had been right. In addition to the usual triumvirate, the French officer invoked appeals to honour, glory, and the success of the 5th Regiment. The words struck him as canting blather and rank sloganeering, yet he knew it was unwise to underestimate their effect on green troops. The force and fire behind the words always carried more weight than the words themselves. He translated easily, but even to someone unschooled in French, the raw emotion would have made the meaning clear.

The British had a different take on such matters. His marines laughed at such flummery; they preferred quiet leadership from the front to officers' speechifying.

"Sergeant Dale, assemble the men!"

"Aye, aye, sir."

In short order, thirty-six marines were drawn up in front of Pennywhistle. Their faces were deeply tanned, almost bronze, the skin on their hands darkened to the colour of old leather; their bodies lean and hard; their coats were threadbare and patched; heavy exposure to sea and sun had faded the brick-red colour to a dusky reddish-brown. The red and white plumes on their black, round hats looked thin and tattered, but their line was admirably formed and presented an appearance of lean, sinewy strength. Their carefully polished Royal Marine cross-belt plates reflected dappled sunlight into the eyes of the approaching French. Their calloused hands held meticulously oiled Brown Bess muskets hard by their sides in the perfect "Attention" position. Not bandbox or parade ground soldiers, true, but they would fight hard and well. His plan depended on their ability to execute his orders swiftly and without hesitation, no matter how dangerous they might seem.

He explained his plans. "Remember, three volleys, three shots from your hides, make for the beach and the shelter of the carronades. Aim low and no heroics."

"Aye, aye, sir!" The marines responded in lusty unison. Then they stood silent, implacable, but a few sported broad, non-regulation grins. He instinctively returned the smiles. "Gentlemen, the French may have the numbers, but we have the discipline! To your posts!"

The marines broke ranks, moving quickly and unobtrusively forward fifty yards to re-form into a line barricade of red. The advance was intended as an additional provocation to the already over-excited French. The men dressed ranks silently and Dale methodically checked the alignment with the flat edge of his cutlass. The line was perfectly straight, as usual; everyone at toy-soldier attention, and the only sound was the whipping of a rising wind. No voice spoke save the silent one of training. The stoic quiet of the British line was deafening in its way, compared to the noisy, oncoming French. The men's immobile faces showed neither anger nor fear, merely rock-solid determination.

Near the middle of the line, Stratton worried as he watched the approach of a column with numbers eight times greater than his own, but trusted his officer and his training. He would stand steady, resolute, and reserve his fire until he saw the mustaches of the French.

The French column continued its slow, intimidating advance. Swirling clouds of dust rose.

On the right flank of the small line, Dale checked the action of his Baker Rifle. He liked the Baker both for its accuracy and its sturdiness. If he'd had something similar during his poaching days, he might just have eluded the constables who'd brought his highly successful deer-hunting career to a close. The .62 calibre piece was good out to three hundred yards, although two hundred was a much better range. It was more labourious to load than a smoothbore musket—a trade of speed for accuracy. He looked toward the French line and spotted an officer who would make a fine target. Not quite in range yet. He started his preparations.

No great fan of officers, save Pennywhistle, Dale always targeted the commissioned officers first, then switched to the non-commissioned ones. He borrowed his philosophy from Pennywhistle: "Kill the brave officers and the cowards will carry the men away." Rankers had no power; they were mere playing pieces on a battlefield chessboard: drones trained to fight, die, or surrender, as commanded by the officers in charge.

The menace of the approaching French battering ram would frighten any sane man, but Pennywhistle would not be rushed. "Fencible Fever," the driving urge of unblooded officers to fire at the enemy as soon as they came in sight, was no part of a professional's outlook. Madly heroic dashes might thrill the public, but battle was about minute details, thorough preparation, and timing.

Pennywhistle believed in scientific efficiency. Killing at a distance without giving him a chance to respond was the best way to eliminate your opponent. He carried a sword—that was expected of officers—and was skilled in its use, but he disdained to carry a pistol. They were point blank weapons and useless after one shot, save as clubs.

His weapon of choice was a rare Ferguson Rifle. Ordinary rifles were accurate, but could barely manage two shots a minute. The Ferguson was accurate and fast. Six-shots-a-minute fast. It loaded at the breech, or back end, rather than the muzzle. It needed no ram-rod, could be reloaded even at the walk, and functioned admirably in rainstorms which rendered muzzle loaders unusable. The piece was good to three hundred yards, years ahead of its time, and unmatched by anything in either country's army. He made one last inspection to make sure the Ferguson was ready for the ordeal ahead. He changed the flint and verified the edge was sharp and crisp. The frizzen felt right to the touch, having been hardened by the armourer under his exacting eye the day before. It would deliver an avalanche of sparks when struck by the flint. He applied a coat of light beeswax to facilitate the action of the breech screw. He massaged some extra gun oil onto the lock plate with a soft chamois cloth and checked the action of the cock, or hammer. Fluid and easy, good. He whisked the pan clean and wormed out the touch hole with a vent pick. He ran an oiled patch impaled on an old ramrod down the barrel to make sure the seven lands and grooves of the rifling were in pristine state. He fingered the patches for his rifle balls to be certain they were suitably oiled and supple enough to grip the rifling tightly. Meticulously, he filled his small brass priming horn with super fine powder that ensured faster ignition of the pan. He examined each of the sixty paper cartridges he had painstakingly fashioned two nights before: dry and ready to go. He left nothing to chance or to others when it came to his weaponry.

He would do his level best to kill Frenchmen today, yet he admired the French, both for their contributions to civilization and their customary courage under fire. He felt no necessity to demonize his opponents. That was for amateurs. Combat soldiers, whatever flag they favoured, had more in common with each other than with the civilians on whose behalf they fought. Homebodies who had never seen a shot fired in anger were much more likely to be bloodthirsty, unforgiving devils than were soldiers in the field.

Many British officers disdained the personal infliction of death. They believed themselves to be the directors of battle, not its agents: men who heroically bellowed the right stage directions at exactly the key moments, yet were somehow morally insulated, above the gory fray. They were leaders who inspired the men, showed them how to die, but left the actual killing to the "other ranks."

Such delicacy of spirit had no place in his universe. His soul might be hard, dark, and misshapen, but it was scathingly honest. War meant fighting and fighting meant killing; there was no way to disguise it. War soiled the souls of everyone and it was fatuous to pretend that officers could emerge from a fight without any moral dirt on their hands. He never beguiled himself about what he was, just did his job the best way he knew how.

He tried to forget after each battle, but horror was resistant to extirpation. Unlike men, memories of caked blood, smashed bodies, and broken lives never died. You simply learned to live with them.

The time would someday come when he could not, and then it would be time to leave the field to younger, more morally naive officers. But that would not happen today. He viewed his duty as Henry V had, showing himself the greatest warrior among his men. His men would never know of his sleepless nights.

He breathed in and out, slowly and deeply, and emptied his consciousness of everything but one task: beat the French. Husband the lives of his own men and kill the French quickly and efficiently. His breathing steadied, regularized, and a deep calmness flooded him. He considered the French column as a jeweler would a diamond before cutting it. He coldly calculated its vulnerabilities.

The French were now three hundred yards out. They marched deliberately and carefully, as if trying to recall drill they had only recently learned. Their faces were pale and their blue and white uniforms looked newly issued, the colours lively and un-faded. Tunics and breeches were free of patches and the rigid, yellow collars and stiff, crimson cuffs showed only crisp, unfrayed edges. Their high, black gaiters displayed no layers of deeply ingrained dirt. Their bell crown black shakos—undoubtedly smelling strongly of new leather—featured the latest sunburst-patterned brass plate.

The kettle drums boomed the advance: *ba bum, ba bum, ba bum bum bum.* The French column slipped in and out of good alignment and snippets of "La Marseillaise" drifted toward Pennywhistle's position. He was surprised the column included a small band, but music was always a convenient way to put heart into frightened men.

The sun was barely above the horizon but it was already an unforgiving molten red orb and the day promised to be sultry. A whisper of the Bora caused the column's colourful regimental and national flags to snap gracefully. The drummers' marching cadence was primal, savage, hypnotic. Shouts of what sounded like, roughly translated, "Death to the goddams" rose from the column. Others shouted "*Vive la France!*"

A second officer on horseback joined the first at the head of the column. Like his companion, he was dressed in an impeccable, tight-fitting midnight blue uniform with a crimson sash. The splendid uniform flattered his slim figure and looked as if it had just come from an expensive tailor. The gold in the buttons, epaulettes, and shoulder knots dazzled the eye. His charger pranced and reared with eagerness. A colonel probably, maybe even a *général de brigade*. He seemed ready not so much for combat as to be painted in heroic attitude by Napoleon's favourite painter, Jacques-Louis David.

Pennywhistle thought of his own appearance and made a face. After months at sea exposed to salt spray and blistering sun, his brilliant scarlet coat had faded and its gold buttons were dull. The bullion epaulettes had tarnished and the crimson sash around his waist was frayed. The arms of King George on his gold gorget were scuffed almost beyond recognition and a patch covered a bullet hole on his right blue cuff. His blue-grey trousers displayed no patches but were thin in the knees. It was the working rig of a well-blooded combat officer, not an over-fed member of some palace guard.

The French column continued its advance. *"Vive la France! Vive la France! Vive la France!"* chorused hundreds of young voices, with enthusiasm as tremendous as their collective naiveté. The rhythmic chanting helped to steady nerves. *Ba bum, ba bum, ba bum bum bum*, counterpointed the drums.

Pennywhistle estimated that the distance to the more heavily gilded senior officer was down to two hundred and twenty-eight meters, or two hundred and fifty yards; a difficult but not impossible shot. To use the Ferguson's rear sight effectively, it was important to judge the range exactly; it required a seasoned eye and an experienced intuition. He factored in wind-speed and direction, and allowed the canny part of his mind to take all needful measurements; his brain carefully logged the calculations and determined he could manage a successful shot. He wondered if Dale, with his Baker, was performing the same routine. Probably so; Dale was the best shot he had ever seen.

He found a boulder and used it as a firing platform. He made one last mental note that the wind was rising slightly. He extended the rear sight to its full height and allowed for the arc of the bullet. He elevated his piece to fifteen degrees, above the head of his target.

That angle would guarantee a hit in the chest. All distractions vanished and his whole world became the man on the prancing horse. He inhaled, held his breath, and then let it out slowly as he gently pressured the trigger with a baby's touch. There was the usual *clack, woosh, bang!* of a flintlock discharge, and a puff of smoke blossomed in front of his face. Nothing for a second, then he saw the result.

Colonel Dupleix clutched his chest as a red splotch bloomed on his sternum. He swayed back and forth in the saddle several times, like a broken weathervane, then fell slowly to the right and tumbled off the horse. A difficult shot requiring a good eye, a cool head, and a steady hand; one to be proud of. But truth be told, luck had played its part as well. First round to the British.

Pennywhistle reloaded.

As he did, the other officer on horse, investigating the fate of Dupleix, did not so much fall as was shoved backward out of his saddle; a large red aperture occupied the centre of his forehead. Dale! Round two to the British.

The French column lurched to a complete halt. It buzzed and sputtered with confusion and spastic activity. Pennywhistle heard cries of *"Merde!"* *"Putain!"* and *"Mon dieu!"* The British line stood boldly defiant, their presence a dare for the French to advance, a red flag waved in front of a bull.

The French focused their bewilderment into a surprisingly imaginative variety of imprecations shouted at the British. They were good at that, but it would have no effect on his men, Pennywhistle knew. If anything, it amused them, revealing their opponents as amateurs.

Chef de battalion Roland Lannes hurried forward on foot and assumed command. Considering the fates of his predecessors, he was naturally hesitant and less than completely decisive. He wondered what his cousin, the great Marshal Jean Lannes, would have done. Marshal Lannes had died a hero at Wagram, but his relative worried he was not cut from the same heroic cloth.

In defiance of their orders, a few soldiers loosed off some

desultory rounds in the direction of the English. A natural enough reaction, but Pennywhistle knew it indicative of poor discipline.

Maxwell watched the shambling column move steadily closer, but stayed rooted to the ground and merely tightened the pipe-clayed strap on his Brown Bess.

It was not quite two hundred yards now, but Pennywhistle thought the provocation had had the desired effect. The French were panicked, angry, and under uncertain control. "Marines, retire!" he shouted.

The marines unobtrusively broke ranks and retired to their prepared hides in the dunes and gorse. Blandon walked slowly backwards, contemptuously facing the French. His defiant posture was typical; the marines would show the enemy no fear. The hides were shallow and gave little actual protection, but they had the effect of making the marines vanish from the French view.

Private Jacques Valjean's thoughts were those of many in the column. He truly believed all of the patriotic notions his officers constantly preached. Who would break the rules of civilized war and deliberately assassinate officers? Did these English goddams have no honour? Why did the cowards fire, then hide? Why did they not dare show themselves and fight like men? Could it be that English pride and arrogance were no match for the spirit of a people in arms, a people with *libertié, egalité, fraternité?* They would rain thunder and confusion on the heads of the enemies of the Empereur! Nothing could stand before them!

Directly in the path of the oncoming French column, thirty-six British marines waited silently and patiently in their hides. They lay prone in the sand, muskets loaded, bayonets fixed, resolve steeled. Smooth bore muskets of .75 calibre were not accurate, save at very close range, but against densely packed bodies of men their large, malleable lead balls made very destructive projectiles. Low velocity, to be sure, but lead balls flattened, ballooned, and fragmented. They compressed internal organs, caused compound fractures, and their slow speed ensured that the projectile often remained in the body, along with infectious pieces of clothing it carried in with it.

Five hundred yards to the left, hidden behind a large sand dune, Moore's men lay in wait on their bellies. He crawled along the line and did a check of weapons. His men had plenty of pikes, pistols, swords, and tomahawks, but nothing that would serve in a fire fight with the French. He would leave the gunplay to Pennywhistle.

Moore was eager to attack; the thrill of battle was far superior to the County Kildare fox hunts he so loved but, for now, he had to wait. He had to catch the French in flank at the moment of their greatest discomfiture. His eyes glowed with grey fire as he thought of the beating he would give the French. Unlike Pennywhistle, he hated Monsieur Jonny Crapaud, and the more of them he sent to perdition, the better! It occurred to him that the marine captain was attempting one of the most difficult feats in warfare, a double envelopment. *He* preferred to go straight at the enemy and smash them up, but that was hardly possible with today's inferior numbers.

On the right, also sheltered by a large sand dune, Meers and his men were in position. Meers implored God not to let him muck things up in his first fight. He reviewed his instructions: "Don't move until the carronades have done their business. Attack only when the French seem about to collapse." He told himself to try not to over think it, to just follow orders.

The French tide rolled on. *"Vive la France! Vive la France! Vive la France!"* shouted the soldiers, more loudly than ever as their anxiety increased. The kettle drums continued their own chanting.

The English breakwater was silent, hidden, waiting.

Some French rankers yelled angry suggestions about what the English could do with their mothers. Their anger masked a rising sense of alarm. A nagging feeling was beginning to grow in them that when these English opened fire, the result would be very, very nasty.

Pennywhistle crawled along the line of men and whispered encouragement to each marine, as did Dale. Corporal Wainwright nodded brusquely to Dale. He needed no encouragement to kill the French. Private Addison looked worried, but smiled weakly when Dale told him to "wait and aim for their kneecaps."

Pennywhistle decided against more sniping. The Frenchmen's own fears of random death from nowhere would work quite as well as actual shooting. It was always good to conserve ammunition.

The advance was so clumsy! The difference between the seasoned veteran and the green recruit was the difference between lightning and a lightning bug. Lightning was powerful, sudden, hard to oppose; bugs could be squashed easily. Beyond heroic tales or fantasies spun by old veterans in taverns trying to cage drinks from gullible young yokels, Pennywhistle knew most of the French had no idea what was about to happen. They spoke a different tongue, but they were of the same classes and were no more brave or cowardly than the young men he had under his command. One group shouted *"Vive l'Empereur!"* The other, *"God save King George!"* The difference was his men were well led, disciplined, and experienced. They would react well. Virtue had nothing to do with who would die today. It was all about training.

The French were about to receive the cruelest training of all.

The 5th Regiment was one hundred yards out. Seventy-five to go.

Three

The French column halted again. The drums stopped, but peevish whispers floated back and forth. A lonely ranker yelled a defiant, *"Vive l'Empereur!"* Ranks and files were roughly dressed. There was an air of expectancy, edged by anxiety.

Chef de battalion Lannes extended his spyglass and surveyed the ground ahead. After the death of his superiors, he wore the mantle of command uneasily. He could see splashes of red amidst the nondescript rocks and gorse, but no actual line and no individual soldiers. The goddams were out there. Why did they not form up, retreat to the boats, and depart? That is what he would have done. Surely they knew they were hopelessly outnumbered. But they were a strange people, as famous for their arrogance as their startling profanity.

Lannes' hesitation transmitted itself to the ranks. Un-blooded soldiers murmured crude and fearful guesses as to what was about to happen.

Private Valjean screwed his face into a defiant expression that betrayed no fear, yet disquieting questions crowded into his mind and would not be banished. Who would live, who would die? Would Lady Luck be a friend or foe? Would new heroes be born, or would they be ignoble cowards? Would they return home to cheers and glory, or as amputees destined to beg for sustenance for the rest of their short, miserable lives? Would they see home again at all?

Private Maurice Leroux knew this was the ultimate test. He was ashamed of himself as his stomach fluttered and twisted, his mouth grew dry, and his face assumed a deathly pallor. He was a conscript,

27

too poor to hire a substitute, and had no dreams of martial glory. He just wanted to survive to see his village of Valette again. A few tears coursed down his dirty cheeks. He started to shake slightly, then violently retched as his stomach emptied. He hoped that was that. But a mere minute later, his bladder let go with a quiet hiss. Then, preceded by a spectacular cantata of flatulence, his bowels voided. The front flap of his breeches yellowed deeply, and chocolate blotches dribbled down his legs. He was boxed in: nowhere to run, no way to leave the column to obey the imperatives of nature. In the midst of so many closely-packed men, he had never felt so alone and exposed. He reached for his canteen; it did not contain water but the cheapest rotgut brandy. He drained its contents greedily, in the hope alcohol might steady him. He felt a momentary surge of courage.

Small knots of men left the rear of the column to do in private what Leroux had done in lonely agony. Officers ordered the men back into ranks, but they were ignored until nature had been honoured. Even then, a few refused to return, despite threats. Here and there soldiers fired their muskets in the direction of the English and others shot them skyward in hope the noise alone might unsettle their foes. Sergeants cursed their insubordination. Officers exhorted men to close up formation, to maintain proper distance between files.

*****

Pennywhistle observed their reactions with satisfaction, knowing he had read the mentality of the column correctly. The optimists among the soldiers cheered. A few fools shouted, *"La victoire ou la mort!"* Some silently mouthed curses against their own officers, while others damned the English loudly. The invisibility and complete silence of their opponents was eroding their reserves of courage.

Pennywhistle's muscles sang with tension. The parched mouth, acid stomach, and slight tingling in his fingers held no fear; they were old companions, signaling that danger had entered the lists. It was not altogether pleasant, for it made him feel fully alive. It was a good thing; it reminded the body that it was about a deadly business.

His thinking became magnificently lucid, focused, and powerfully incisive. Details of every object waxed crystal clear and extraordinarily vivid. People and things seemed suspended in space, to be viewed at any angle through his mental scope. His mind's eye rotated items to be analyzed and catalogued. His hearing grew more acute than usual and he dimly noted cries from Illyrian beach swallows in the distance. His olfactory senses heightened as well. He could quite literally smell not just garlic from the French, but the scent of fear. It was a sharp, unmistakable, musk-like aroma.

The design he was about to execute would be suicide against well-led, experienced troops, but green troops were similar to a flock of children on All Hallows Eve suddenly confronted by a menacing adult in a goblin mask. Fear and inexperience disposed them to give the fantastic credibility. They would see not with their eyes, but with their imaginations.

*****

Nervous French soldiers shifted their weight from one foot to the other, then back again. Lannes knew he needed to make a decision. They could not stay where they were. *Merde*! Why did he not have the inspiration of his late cousin? Retreat? Unthinkable. He would teach these arrogant *Roastbifs* a lesson. He had to advance! But should it be in column or in line?

To shift from column to line was a complicated parade ground evolution. It would enable far more men to bring their muskets into action, but a line was more difficult to control. The lack of tightly packed support behind reduced group cohesion. A line broke and ran far more easily than a column. Given what he saw around him, the most likely result of shifting to a line would be delay and chaos. He needed to move forward now. He had to keep it simple for these thinly trained men. It would have to be sheer weight of numbers and shock action.

Lannes raised his sword high above his head and faced the troops. "*Soldats, en avant!*"

The drums pounded the demanding, insistent beat of the advance,

29

muskets went to the support arms position, and the column lurched forward at a slow, walking pace. It was like watching a very long, very lethargic snake. The French, unlike the British, marched with sixty pounds of equipment on each man.

"Vive la France! Vive la France! Vive la France!" It sounded like low, very distant thunder.

*****

Fifty yards out, twenty five to go. Pennywhistle could see Gallic faces now. They looked fish-belly white, uncertain, and young; very, very young. For some, the first battle was preceding the first shave. Many wore a look of pure terror. Some grotesquely distorted their faces into demon-like visages, like threatened animals seeking to ward off a predator. A few grimaced in angry defiance. Others bit their tongues and made faces as they fought to hold back tears.

It puzzled him no one had ordered the column to fix bayonets. Slack, very slack; the officers were probably little better trained than the men. They were so mesmerized by keeping the column in order that they had apparently forgotten to issue a basic order. More musket shots rang out from the column, and the officers cursed the men who fired without orders.

These recruits appeared unused to commands. They had probably had little time to get to know their officers or their mates. They seemed more like a tribe than a modern regiment, wavering and tentative. Two important officers were already dead. A third casualty would show the men just how vulnerable their command leadership was.

Lannes reminded Pennywhistle of a bantam rooster, the way he strutted and waved his hands. He shouted slogans like a drum major, urging his troops forward with maestro-like gesticulations. Pennywhistle steadied the Ferguson on a boulder. He aligned the sights with Lannes' forehead, slowly let out his breath, and tickled the trigger.

"Soldats—" The *chef de battaillon*'s emphatic order was cut off in mid-shout as the .62 calibre ball neatly removed the entire top

half of his head, splattering several nearby officers with bits of hair, skull, and grey matter. A fine red mist arced in the morning light. The corpse remained upright for a moment, as if the muscles refused to believe death had touched them, then flopped to the ground.

The column halted, stunned. There was disbelief, murmuring, and confusion. Another officer dead? How did the English shoot so well? But Pennywhistle knew the paralysis would pass quickly. Thirty yards, close enough. Now or never.

He gave his best stentorian bellow. "Marines, up and at 'em!"

Thirty-six lobster backs rose out of the ground. Or, as it seemed to the French, from hell; red devils appearing out of thin air to form a solid line in an eye-blink.

The French froze. It was a natural reaction from men startled by the unexpected. He'd counted on that. "Marines, by the right wheel, march!" The line calmly swung round like a gate pivoting on its hinges. "Halt." The line now faced the head of the French column at a forty-five degree angle, perfect for enfilade fire. "Dress ranks!"

The French watched in utter bewilderment. All of the 5th Regiment's field grade officers were dead. The inexperienced junior officers were ill-trained, inexperienced, and unused to exercising initiative. The *sang froid* of the British in the face of overwhelming numbers stunned them. They simply froze and issued no orders, unprepared to assume command.

"Make ready." The marines brought their muskets to a perfectly vertical position. Thirty-six determined redcoats full cocked their pieces with a loud click. The precision was awe-inspiring, intimidating. The humid air hummed with the energy of rhythmic, lethal intent.

"Present." Marines leveled thirty-six pieces horizontally.

They took careful aim at the front and sides of the column. Heads bent close to musket stocks, eyes narrowed, and trigger fingers thrummed with anticipation.

"Shoot for the kneecaps!" shouted Dale in a voice that could probably be heard back on *Active* itself.

Time stopped. For a fraction of a second, the French and British

31

literally saw the whites of each other's eyes. Men noticed buttons, belts, regimental insignia, and a wealth of unimportant details. War had become very, very small and very, very personal. The Ultimate Question was about to be answered for many.

Leroux's attention riveted on the three wide, white chevrons on Dale's scarlet sleeve. *Odd*, he thought, *the man wore a crimson sash. Why were sergeants allowed to wear the sash of command?* The enemy was no longer an abstract idea. As he looked directly into the steady eyes of the redcoated sergeant, he realized the man must be about the same age as his father. Leroux's eyes were wide with fear; the marine's were hard, unforgiving sapphires. Leroux's last thought was that the British were actually just men, not monsters.

Pennywhistle's cutlass flashed down. "Fire!" A thunderclap erupted and a cloud of gritty, grey-white smoke obscured the column.

Thirty-six musket balls sped toward French flesh. Without pausing to gauge the effect of the first volley, the marines reloaded their firelocks in eighteen seconds. "Fire!" A second volley crashed out. The marines again reloaded, and Pennywhistle bellowed, "Fire!" a third time. One hundred and eight bullets slammed the column in under a minute.

A gust of wind whipped away the soaring, pungent thunderheads of smoke.

The volley savaged the first five ranks of the column. Bullets scythed men down in neat, serried rows in an awful parody of a human wheat harvest. Blood, mangled bodies, and half a head lay at peculiar angles to the column. The head had belonged to Leroux. Not all were dead. Some on the ground crawled slowly away in agony: a grotesque, writhing rug of not-quite-but-soon-to-be dead. Those still alive looked at the bodies with utter disbelief. It was their first time seeing the effect of a real volley fired in anger. The impulse to break and run flashed across the minds of many. The brimstone smell of burnt gunpowder made some retch.

Once they stood up, the British were exposed, naked. Their small number was painfully obvious, or would have been to more sane observers. But the French did as Pennywhistle expected: they refused to believe their eyes. They were in the grip of hysteria, slaves to fear-fueled imagination. So many men dead, so many wounded. They saw what their brains told them: that any group capable of causing so much damage could not possibly be just the few redcoats in front of them; others must have fired from hidden positions. The smart French move would have been an immediate charge. Even in their present state of disarray, sheer numbers were on their side. But they were incapable of grasping the truth. They were rattled, fatally so.

Pennywhistle had gambled on fear being his best ally and he had been proven correct. He was tempted to order a bayonet charge to decide the business, but with the force available it would be reckless. Prudence won out. It was illogical to risk it all on one throw of the dice, when he could ensure the same result if he exercised patience and cunning. The best plan was to wear the enemy down, chip away at their numbers and their rapidly eroding morale.

Above the confusion, his steady voice took absolute command. "Marines, take cover! Reload, quick time. Fire at will!"

The marines found their hides and began to direct a steady *pop, pop, pop* of musketry at the column that sounded like hailstones on a cobblestone street. At thirty yards and with a large, almost unmoving target they simply could not miss. They took careful aim nonetheless, determined to make every shot tell.

The French were exposed, the British hidden. The British had command, cohesion, and most of all, training. The French lacked all three. The British were deadly, trained soldiers; the French, merely confused animals.

A very spotty volley flashed haphazardly from the front three ranks of the French column. It was spontaneous and ragged, the result of fear rather than command. Understandable; this was the first time they had fired their muskets against a real enemy. Moreover, this was the first time they had even fired the weapon with a live ball instead of a blank. The nasty recoil caused most to flinch as their Charlevilles discharged, sending their bullets high.

They knew nothing of marksmanship, and there was no longer a solid wall of men to shoot at. The 120 musket balls were wasted in merely frightening seagulls. More soldiers tried to step forward to use their muskets, but it had the effect of creating a giant traffic jam. Soldiers jostled, shoved, and elbowed to get in firing position. With no officers in charge, the column was degrading into chaos.

More French soldiers went down. Not in whole ranks, more like random pieces dropping out of a jigsaw puzzle. Soldiers stumbled, staggered, fell. Once bright, white uniform facings were stained by blotches of red. Large, jagged gashes appeared on legs, arms, and chests. Private Valjean felt something pluck at his right hand; when he looked down it took his brain a second to register that he no longer had one. He was still staring at the stump of his wrist when he passed out a minute later.

The marine fire changed to a steady, rolling rattle that sounded like dense raindrops crashing on a tin roof. Each man fired three carefully aimed rounds. Private Blandon could see the Frogs had no training and thanked God for his own. He was certain he had accounted for at least three Crapauds. He reloaded quickly but carefully, making sure each bullet had a paper cartridge wrapping to ensure a tight fit and increased accuracy. Without the paper carapace, a ball bounced down the length of the barrel and could veer off in the most unpredictable directions.

Return fire from the French was ragged, uncoordinated, and not a single marine was struck. These green soldiers didn't even know how to aim. Confused, leaderless, demoralized, they simply had no idea what to do.

Pennywhistle calculated that the requisite shots had been fired. The British temporarily held an advantage, but it was unwise to push their luck. "Marines, to the launch!" Better to do the unexpected. Led by Dale and the dourly earnest Corporal Wainwright, the marines retired unhurriedly, still full of fight. Discipline and training told.

Pennywhistle's men beached themselves in front and on either side of the launch, flat on their stomachs.

Rowlinson and Private Martin had the launch's carronade ready. Rowlinson took the firing lanyard in hand and Martin adjusted the quoin, a wooden block below the barrel for determining elevation.

Gunner's Mate Williamson in Meers' cutter, twenty yards to starboard from the launch, readied his own carronade. Gunner's Mate McKidd in Moore's cutter, twenty yards to larboard from the launch, did the same. Rowlinson's fire would hit the column head on, while Williamson's and McKidd's smashed the flanks. More than one thousand musket balls lay in readiness for the French.

At this point, all firing stopped and a peculiar, unnatural quiet descended upon the battlefield. After the thundering din, the oppressive silence felt like a leaden straightjacket. For several minutes, absolutely nothing happened. A heavy foreboding permeated the sticky air. Pennywhistle had the sense of a massive, wounded, frightened animal gathering its will.

Finally, a low, inchoate buzz emanated from the French column: indistinct noises, as if a body with no brain were trying to decide how to proceed. Most of the surviving junior officers hesitated, but Lieutenant d'Auverge did not. He screamed, cursed, and finally shamed the men into moving forward.

The British waited.

The French column slowly shuffled and lurched toward the beach. At this point, it no longer resembled much of a column. It was more like a huddle of armed rabble than a disciplined body of soldiery. It was a mob with weapons. They were, after all, conscripts with no experience of battle and no proper combat intuition. They cautiously edged down the slope toward the beach. Most of the officers were not sure what to do, but Lieutenant d'Auverge waved his sword toward the British and shouted at his men, *"De l'audace, de l'audace, toujours de l'audace."*

Pennywhistle took up a position on the launch, just behind Rowlinson and Martin. The carronade was properly elevated and sited. He restrained his eagerness. The smasher was best at very close range. He breathed deeply and waited, as time slowed to a snail's pace. As the men and boys arrayed against him reluctantly advanced, he could see the pimples on their very young faces.

At twenty yards, he gave the command. "Fire!"

Rowlinson jerked the lanyard hard: the barrel blossomed flame, the launch shook, and the carronade shot back on its slide. Half a second later, the other two carronades spat forth their deadly contents. Twelve hundred musket balls flew through the air: a giant, lethal, expanding buzz-saw.

There was a staccato whine of lead and the centre of the French mob simply vanished. Arms, legs, heads, torsos, muskets, and shakos flew into the air, now permeated with red drizzle that mingled foully with the gritty, grey smoke. Those left alive clutched their stomachs and retched. There were now two smaller, separate mobs.

The mobs stopped dead.

Pennywhistle realized in amazement that he might be able to get in another shot. It would have to be fast. Meers and Moore were scheduled to attack after the first carronade discharge, but it was just too good of an opportunity to miss. "Reload!"

Rowlinson and Martin looked surprised, but discipline prevailed. The piece was swiftly swabbed, reloaded, and run out. Observing this, Williamson and McKidd did the same with their carronades. Pennywhistle himself adjusted the launch carriage to incline left. He was good at combat geometry and, for maximum destruction, the precise angle was important.

"Fire!"

Rowlinson yanked the lanyard. Williamson and McKidd did the same with theirs.

The second round was, if possible, more lethal than the first. A blinding hurricane of lead ripped through the French. There was the odd, distinctive *squish squelch* sound of iron tearing flesh, akin to the noise a bare foot makes when plunging into soft, deep mud. Bodies exploded. When spinal cords were blown out, there was nothing to hold a body together. Unidentifiable body parts littered the beach, and a red haze drifted over them, a wind-borne, nasty, crimson variant of the pea-soup fogs that regularly enveloped industrial London. Some French soldiers started to back slowly away, and others turned to run. The French now had no left, no centre, only a right.

Some dropped their weapons before running. Completely

illogical, but a sure sign of beaten troops. Animals always shed the extraneous before making a mad run to evade a predator.

The moment had come. Pennywhistle jumped from the launch and waved his cutlass. "Marines, make ready!"

The marines rose up on the word. Blandon checked his bayonet; he was eager to be at them! At this point, a few determined, disciplined men would be able to stampede a much larger mob. A heavy weight balanced on a tiny fulcrum needed only a feather-weight touch to push it into eternity.

"Marines! Now's your time! Charge bayonets! Cold steel only." Pennywhistle held his cutlass high and flourished it in three quick circles. "Charge!"

"Huzzaaaah!" Hours of pent-up tension burst forth as the marines cut loose with a mighty cheer from the bottom of their collective soul. Blandon felt his yell could be heard all the way to Paris. They sounded not like a section of marines, but a regiment of crazed banshees bent on the destruction of everything in their path. Sound was a hugely effective weapon in war, even better than bullets and bayonets at critical moments. The gale of ferocity from marine lungs magnified their numbers a hundredfold in the unbalanced minds of the fleeing French.

The marines launched into a flat-out run up the slight incline. The seventeen-inch bayonets transformed their muskets into five-foot-long lances. They expected to savage, mangle, and eviscerate the French.

Pennywhistle knew better. He had been in a dozen bayonet charges; as long as men had somewhere to run, they broke well before bayonets touched skin. It was only when men were cornered that bayonets had a chance to rend and tear flesh.

The French mob let loose a mass ululation of terror. The majority threw their weapons away and fled the beach as fast as their legs would carry them. Paris was apparently their next stop.

The stalking pursuit changed to a footrace, or, rather, a massive fox hunt. Dale led the hounds. The old poacher loved a good chase, but he also knew when to quit and rein in the lobster-backs.

Blandon was frustrated. He had his bayonet advanced, its sharp point lusting for action, but the French were just too damned fast.

One small, determined cluster of French remained on the beach. Resolute twenty-one-year-old Lieutenant d'Auverge exhorted the men to stand fast. But then, "Huzzah, huzzah, huzzah!" Meers' band of sailors came running over the dunes on the right flank, brandishing all manner of swords, pikes, and tomahawks and shouting mightily. Meers led from the front, hatless, his platinum blond hair brilliantly reflecting the sunlight.

On the left, slightly behind schedule, Moore's detachment approached, moving at the quick-step rather than running. Moore grinned and his men cheered with intimidating gusto.

The sight of these sailors was simply too much for the remaining French. They broke and ran. D'Auverge bellowed for them to halt but panic made them deaf to his pleas. He shook with rage and tears of despair flowed down his cheeks. Raised on tales of glory, duty, and honour, he could not comprehend how men, even in the worst extremity, could forsake all three. Others might run, but he, never!

Pennywhistle approached. "Surrender, monsieur." He said it calmly and with a certain admiration for this young officer's bravery. Courage was not an exclusively British trait.

"*Non, monsieur!*" The French officer's defiant voice matched the stubbornness in his face. "I fight for the honour of my country, my emperor, and my family."

Pennywhistle sighed in resignation. One of the "death or glory" types. He had a good idea of what was about to transpire; nonetheless, he hoped reason would prevail. He carefully composed his reply.

"Monsieur, the fortunes of war have gone against you, but your own conduct this day has been most admirable. Allow me to felicitate you on your bravery. If you will surrender and give me your parole as an officer and gentleman, you will be free to go. As long as you fight no more against the British until properly exchanged, we may conclude our business with honour. May I know your name, monsieur?"

The officer was surprised by the Englishman's French. It was devoid of foreign inflection and sounded Parisian. In his limited experience, he had found Englishmen disdainful of any tongue but their own. "Pierre Louis Etienne du Charmont, le Comte d'Auverge, your servant, monsieur." He doffed his hat and made a gallant, sweeping bow in Pennywhistle's direction. "Lieutenant of the 5th Regiment."

Pennywhistle touched his hat in a return salute.

"Might I know yours?" The Count had reverted to the bearing and manners of his privileged upbringing.

"Thomas Pennywhistle, Captain, Royal Marines, at your service," Pennywhistle replied in a studied, ornate manner that matched the Count's, and which came naturally to him.

"An honour, sir," replied d'Auverge with unfeigned courtesy. It struck the Count that, by his manner, poise, and correctness of address, this must be one of what the French called a *milord Anglais*, even though he bore no formal title.

"Now sir, to the matter at hand. Keep your sword, you have earned the right to retain it, but I must demand your surrender, sir. Have I your parole?"

"I cannot give it, monsieur, and live with the shame," replied the Count.

Pennywhistle's expression grew pained. *Un gentilhomme en reconnaît toujours un autre* was how his tutor, du Motier, would have summed up the situation.

"If you do not surrender, sir, then I must kill you. I ask you, Monsieur le Comte, what purpose would be served by the useless effusion of blood and the untimely end of a life I feel certain would otherwise be filled with honour? I am sure you have many loved ones who would weep inconsolably to hear your departure was occasioned by a quixotic devotion to a chimeral notion of honour. Monsieur, I assure you, from the depths of my heart, you have given much more than gallantry demands. I entreat you to listen to the admonitions of reason and family." His language was flowery and courtly, but the emotion behind it was iron, sad, and sincere. He hated waste, especially among those willing to stand up bravely for ideals in which they truly believed. The gallant recognize each other and causes matter less than conduct.

The Count sighed deeply and replied in a melancholy tone, as if acknowledging the power of forces beyond his control. "We are creatures of tradition and training, are we not, *mon capitaine*? I come from a military family, monsieur, whose line stretches back to Hugh Capet himself. My people died defending the Huguenots of La Rochelle against the apostate Richelieu. They held steadfast to their spiritual principles even when the siege was lost. They never yielded their honour when Richelieu offered them their lives if they would return to the Old Faith, the manacles of religion, the chains of which he held. Honour is the most sacred word in the French language, and my watchword. I am disgraced by the conduct of French soldiers today. I will not further sully French honour by ceding what remains of my own."

"Very well. I am saddened, but I understand." A creature of duty, willing to become cold meat rather than betray an ideal. He wondered for a split second how he would behave were the positions reversed. With regret, Pennywhistle slowly drew his cutlass from its black leather scabbard and waited. Cold logic told him to simply shoot the Frenchman, but a ghost of chivalry arose unbidden and firmly counseled that it would be deuced unsporting. A man like the Count would prefer to die fighting rather than be the victim of an execution. Even in the madness of war, there was something to be said for vouchsafing a gallant heart a death with dignity.

The Count drew his sword. It was expensive, with a gold, lion-headed pommel and very high quality blued steel. It was a meticulously balanced piece, perhaps thirty-five inches in length, five inches longer than Pennywhistle's weapon. His sword was short because it was designed for fighting in the cramped spaces of ships at sea.

The Count saluted with his sword. Pennywhistle returned the compliment.

"*En garde, monsieur!*" The Count's tone was fierce and combative. The Count's sword lashed out with blinding speed but

Pennywhistle's blade was a split second quicker. A cloud of blue fireflies danced as the blades slammed together. The Count darted back, crouched, then sprang up and lunged energetically for Pennywhistle's chest. The marine parried expertly. The angle of the thrust showed training but not experience. The Count had probably only fought in the training salon, never in actual combat.

Pennywhistle felt the heat of battle rising in his veins, transforming him; his eyes blazed with primitive fury and his heart thundered. His cool head calmly began compiling a mental ledger of the Count's moves, vulnerabilities, and level of skill. A part of his brain grimly calculated where he would administer the death stroke.

Like some stately minuet, the game of thrust, parry, riposte, feint, and counter-slash was underway. A sword fight comes down to a very simple idea: using accelerating mass to concentrate force at a particular point. The trick was in the aim, and the timing.

The Count's style was precise, scientific, designed to emphasize maneuverability. He retreated quickly when closely pressed and looked always for the ideal opening to administer a quick kill stroke from maximum distance. He slashed in wide half circles, using the shoulder muscles to maximize force. His footwork was elegant, graceful, by the form. He slashed hard and repeatedly at Pennywhistle's chest and belly. Pennywhistle parried with quick, economical, low guard blocks.

Pennywhistle favoured less footwork and a quick, flexible wrist for both attack and defense. It was much faster than a shoulder stroke, although it lacked power. He compensated with the strength of bent knees and calf muscles. It was a "stand your ground" technique suited to fighting on a crowded, pitching quarterdeck, with little room for maneuvers.

Pennywhistle would narrow the distance quickly, cramp and jam his opponent's stroke; the Count would expertly dance away and administer a riposte from distance. The Count drew first blood on Pennywhistle's arm. In turn, Pennywhistle inflicted a serious cut on the Count's leg. Cut, block, slash, deflect, lunge, retreat, attack; the advantage fluctuated. As the minutes wore on, fatigue slowed the responses of both combatants. They seemed well matched, and a crowd of sailors gathered to watch, some probably to wager on the outcome. In the end, Pennywhistle's greater experience won out.

He blocked a thrust to the head and instead of withdrawing to riposte, boldly rammed the hard brass clamshell guard of his cutlass into the Count's chin. The Count staggered, surprised and disoriented. Pennywhistle's rational self had offered honourable quarter. His battle self had no such compunctions. He drew back and ran his blade under the Count's sword. It entered the chest just below the left nipple and lanced the heart. A brief look of astonishment fluttered on the Count's face, then he dropped to the ground without a sound.

"Well done, old man!" It was the cultured voice of James Moore. "Damn fine piece of sword play!"

Pennywhistle looked up. He was crimson and his eyes blazed with madness.

"He did not need to die. He should have listened to me! Stupid! Stupid!" A gallant life ended to no purpose.

As the bloodlust faded, Pennywhistle surveyed the carnage on the beach: reddened sand; pulped and shredded muscle; arms, legs, and heads without owners. The Count's crumpled body was at least intact. The bloody mess to its left was almost unrecognizable as having once been human. Sand crabs popped from their holes and hungrily scuttled towards it. Clouds of flies already buzzed above the stinking corpses, the cloyingly sweet, slightly metallic scent of fresh blood mingled with the rotten egg smell of spent gunpowder in the heavy air. It was a gruesome tableau, seared into his mind, never to be forgotten. This was the glory of war? What rot! His stomach shot flares of bile.

He noticed a sign of life among the gory pile. A slight, blond boy, no more than thirteen, slowly crawled away from the mound of death, towing the remains of a kettle drum. The drum was in tatters, but the boy clutched it as if it were life itself. His face was deathly pale, but he appeared uninjured.

"Corporal Wainwright, see to the boy, get him some food. Bring him with us; we'll figure out what to do with him later." The idea that a mere stripling should be exposed to the horrors of battle troubled Pennywhistle, particularly since drummers were often singled out as targets because they kept the marching cadence. This one was very, very young. Legends to the contrary, most drummers were not boys, but young men.

"James, you and Steven assemble the men." He forced iron into his voice and pushed the post-battle weariness aside. "We need to get them sorted out and fed. Our task is just beginning. This French lot is done, but we need to move inland and link up with the main assault." He turned to Wainwright. "Pass the word for Sergeant Dale." His tone was clipped and preemptory.

The sun was now well up. The heat was already making distant objects shimmer. And it was only 6 a.m.

Four

Marines and sailors feasted together upon the food left in camp by the fleeing French. Blandon found French stew spicier than he liked, but the meat it contained was a pleasant surprise: the product of beasts slaughtered recently, not the rotting contents of a brine-filled barrel packed years before. The bread was reasonably fresh and, unlike the stale biscuit he ate at sea, contained no weevils.

Their stomachs full, marines and sailors tramped toward Groa, roughly two miles distant. But between them and Groa lay a series of low, sandy ridges, perfect for concealment, should the French turn the table and ambush them.

Alert to this possibility, Pennywhistle sent Dale and McCarthy three hundred yards ahead as scouts. Both had been poachers and had spent years detecting and evading constables. These same heightened instincts worked equally well in the military. MacLeod and Stratton acted as flank guards on the left, and Addison and Maxwell performed the same function on the right; all chosen because they possessed exceptionally fine eyesight and had consistently demonstrated great individual initiative.

One other protection loped gleefully along in front of Dale. It was Dale's dog, Mercury. The one hundred and eighty pound English Mastiff was well trained, quiet, and moved gracefully for such a large beast. His nose was extraordinarily sensitive, and he knew how to use cover better than any human. He was frequently able to approach the Crapauds entirely unseen. When he reported a find back to Dale, his bark was low and disciplined. Formidable looking, he nevertheless had a friendly disposition and had come to be a mascot to the marines, considered by many of them to be a good luck charm.

The red-coated marines marched in good soldierly formation. Blue-jacketed naval detachments followed closely, in more relaxed order, their rolling gait pronounced. Marching on land was very different from movement on a reeling deck. They proceeded in disciplined silence; no talking or murmuring. Even the company drummer stowed his sticks. With luck, they might still achieve some measure of surprise. The sand absorbed the dull *thud, thud, thud* of marching feet and the only sound was a distant *wook, wook, woo-oo*, the mating proclamation of a lonely turtledove.

Dale noticed a few French soldiers cowering behind dunes. They wore the dull, apathetic looks of beaten curs. These were merely frightened strays, wanting only to escape and survive, not part of any organized force. He smiled. Captain Pennywhistle had really put the scare into them!

In addition to the musket on his left shoulder, Wainwright carried over his right the exhausted French drummer boy. Pennywhistle had discovered the lad's name was Pierre Ducot and that he was from Paris before the boy had passed out from exhaustion and shock.

Napoleon would have approved of Pennywhistle's action: he marched toward the sound of guns, or at least in the direction where they had been sounding twenty minutes ago. Now it was unnaturally quiet: ominous, but plenty of acrid, grey-white smoke in the air was indicative of stiff fighting.

Pennywhistle was troubled by the French numbers: so many more than had been here two days previously! He and his men were lucky to be alive. But a part of his mind that disdained humility begged to differ, arguing that the outcome was not luck, but his doing. He thought of the faces of those who had died, and they troubled him for an instant; yet he had smashed a battalion, no small martial achievement. A cautious leader might have stopped to regroup and re-evaluate the mission in light of the increased French numbers. Pennywhistle thought a quick, decisive advance a better course. The men were flushed with success. It was wise to exploit their energy and keep them moving.

He needed to link up with the main landing force. Gun smoke said they were close, but where? Lieutenants William Slaughter and Donat O'Brien had most of the marines from the *Amphion* and *Cerberus* and a strong detachment of sailors: one hundred and forty men. Ten yards ahead was the rendezvous point, a crumbling Corinthian temple from Vespasian's time, but it was devoid of any human presence.

Meers and Moore trudged up to join Pennywhistle. Meers looked tired, dusty, and winded, but Moore appeared immaculately groomed and managed to convey the impression he had just stepped out from an elegant soirée at St. James Palace. Moore spoke.

"Tom, what is going on? Those French chaps were poor excuses for soldiers, but there were a damn sight more of them than we expected."

"We got it wrong, James. Those ships were carrying troops, not just naval stores. I think they were to have reinforced a number of garrisons down the coast with small detachments. Now that they are holed up in port, we are up against many more than we planned. We ran into a battalion earlier; my guess is that the rest of the regiment is close by. That probably accounts for why Slaughter and O'Brien have not made the rendezvous. Look at all the smoke. A lot of rounds have been fired."

Meers piped up, "Captain, I hope you are not considering a withdrawal. I know it might be advisable, given the numbers, but I shouldn't want to leave with my tail between my legs. And, confound it, the men want a chance to take a swipe at Boney! They are already deciding how to spend their prize money."

"Not my plan, Steven," replied Pennywhistle. "We need to find what has become of Slaughter and O'Brien. We have three advantages. We have the element of surprise; so far, they have not been expecting us. Second, if we made a mistake with their numbers, they clearly have no idea about ours. With sufficient theatrics and audacity, we can create the illusion of a very large landing force. Third, did you notice the way the French performed earlier? It wasn't just the lack of training and experience. Bonaparte is scraping the bottom of the manpower barrel now, and those soldiers might not have been all that healthy in the first place. Add in dehydration from sea-sickness, plus typhus and dysentery, and you have soldiers in need of many weeks to regain their health. Their lethargic movements make me certain they have not fully recovered."

Moore's face was thoughtful. "One thing troubles me, Tom. If those ships were carrying soldiers for the garrisons, they might be carrying field pieces and artillerists to man them as well."

"I think that's a very real possibility. Particularly if they have light horse artillery, flying batteries to move at the gallop and deploy quickly. Even small six-pounders would be a problem. What we did this morning to the French, they could do to us. And those artillery fellows are reckless and efficient, always spoiling for a fight—a very different kettle of fish from those sad, young fools we faced earlier. Artillery attracts the best, smartest, and most professional in any army. Bonaparte winkled us out of Toulon because he was a master artillerist. Anyone can shoot a musket; few have the mathematics to use a cannon efficiently. My tutor taught me that long ago." He paused and looked at the sky. "And the smoke over there, there is your proof. It's got dark grey in it. That's what you'd expected from the coarsely ground powder used in cannons."

At that moment, a low boom echoed across the beach. Seconds later, another followed. Pennywhistle had aural proof of his predictions. It was not the light tenor of musketry; it was the bass voice of cannon.

Pop, pop, pop! Musketry erupted, sounding like dozens of champagne corks being pulled simultaneously. More cannon fire followed, more musketry, then more and more of both. It sounded like a few raindrops spattering a tin roof, quickly progressing to a downpour laced with thunder.

Pennywhistle concentrated his attention on the dull thuds. It was not the full-throated roar of big ordinance, but the staccato purr of light pieces. Probably six-pounders, just what a flying battery of horse artillery would have. Statistics flashed through his mind.

Artillerie a Cheval, forty-eight horses, one hundred men. And close, maybe half a mile. No wonder Slaughter and O'Brien had not made the rendezvous.

Dale returned with his patrol and gave his report with restraint and his customary exactitude. "Horse artillery, sir. Up the road six hundred yards. Four guns, and they look to have five infantry companies in support. Ravines ahead, right down to the beach. From the direction they were shooting, Lieutenant Slaughter's party must be pinned down directly in front. They were only using canister, no ricochet from solid shot. They did not see us, and, sir, they have not posted any pickets on the road. They don't know you are here. They're not expecting any trouble from our quarter."

Pennywhistle made some swift computations. Five infantry companies, three hundred men, one battery of horse artillery, one hundred men. Factoring in Slaughter's force, they were only outnumbered a bit less than two to one. The odds were improving!

"Well, Tom, looks like we will have plenty of opportunity to add to our heroic reputations," drawled Moore. "This will be an amusing nut to crack." His tone was merry, his eyes hard.

Pennywhistle's face assumed a serious expression. Slaughter was a solid, reliable officer, but one with a limited imagination; Pennywhistle trusted that he would welcome tactical suggestions. Turning to Meers, Pennywhistle said, "Lieutenant, I need you to establish contact with Lieutenant Slaughter. My respects to him and convey our situation. We will get an attack underway, and we will signal our attack with rockets. Our force will be the hammer and his, the anvil. It's a perfect trap. We just have to spring it."

Meers burst into a big, buck-toothed grin. "Right, sir, it will be my distinct honour." He departed enthusiastically.

Pennywhistle turned to Moore, who had been listening intently. "James, we need to do something immediately to take the pressure off Slaughter's men. We brought a few of Mr. Congreve's little toys, did we not?"

"We did indeed. But those rockets are bloody unreliable, Tom. It's very hard to predict their flight. Sometimes they even turn back on the shooter. Still, for creating sheer terror among troops who have never encountered their hissing, sparking, evil ways, they provide plenty of loud diversion."

"How do you think horses would react?" Pennywhistle arched his eyebrows in conspiratorial inspiration.

Moore laughed loudly. "Too right, Tom. Horses would go wild, break their tethers, and stampede! Men might stampede too. Especially if the rockets dropped in from the rear."

"How many do we have?"

"Six."

"The gunner's mates know the drill, right?"

"They have practiced, Tom, but I doubt they ever expected to have to use them in action."

"There is a first time for everything. They could do some real good if even one hit the reserve artillery ammunition. Fire all of the rockets in rapid succession. I want the air filled with lots of unnatural, unexpected noise. Just before the first one fires, Dale and I will bring down the battery commanders. When the crescendo of confusion gets loud and frenzied enough, I will order a general assault of marines and sailors. Cold steel again. Slaughter is a conventional officer, but not without some intelligence and initiative. He will see what is happening and will order his men forward to support us. Panicked troops facing an unknown weapon and suddenly caught between two fires; how do you think that will play out, James?"

"I think the fight will be ours in short order!" Moore was pleased and his eyes lit with the excitement of impending action. The fox was cornered; time for the kill.

"James, let's get the people moving." Pennywhistle wondered why so many of the French troops were so green. If they were not battle ready, why had they been sent to the area? Perhaps they were a *régiment de marche* on their way for further training and something had upset their schedule. He put those speculations aside and focused on the essential fact: someone had miscalculated on the French side, had not expected these troops to see actual battle, at least not yet. He would exploit that miscalculation.

Five

Two hours later, Pennywhistle lay perfectly still behind a low mound of beach grass in which he had embedded a Y-shaped wooden support for his Ferguson Rifle. His marines had silently and stealthily crawled and slithered the last two hundred yards to their present positions. Prone, Maxwell and Blandon brushed the sand off their uniforms and checked to see no grains had penetrated their muskets. Spread out in a loose skirmish line formation, eighty yards ahead, the black and red shakos of the French artillerists were in easy sight of their muskets. Four deadly six-pounder field pieces were also in clear view. These kept up a steady barrage of grape and canister on the sailors and marines to their immediate front, but that din and the replying British musketry concealed from French ears the approach of another British force on their left flank.

Sailors under Moore, with pikes, pistols, tomahawks, and swords at the ready, lay spread-eagled to the right of the marines. At the extreme right, directly behind the French position, Rowlinson and McKidd trimmed and adjusted the fuses on six Congreve Rockets. They had four six-pound case-shell warheads and two twenty-four pound canister specimens. The rockets closely resembled fireworks on the end of a six-foot stick and were lit off in the same way. Rowlinson and Williamson, with the help of Dale, carefully braced the shafts against some boulders and endeavoured to sight the shafts methodically on the French ammunition chests in the rear; but with no fins to guide them, the final flight path would be mainly a result of wind, weather, and simple luck. Still, the mere appearance of these new-fangled bringers of death would be enough to disconcert and scatter even veteran troops. The British attack on Copenhagen had proven that. The rockets had set fire to a good portion of the city, unbalanced the defenders, and allowed the British to seize the Danish Fleet without much difficulty.

On the far left, a quarter mile away, Slaughter waited nervously. As senior officer, he was in overall command of all British personnel, but until Meers had arrived, he'd had no idea of the fate of Pennywhistle and his people.

Slaughter's men had been roughly handled this morning. The cutters and launches had grounded on some unexpected mudflats, then come under persistent and maddening fire from a line of voltigeurs, French light infantry skirmishers. Eventually they'd driven off the voltigeurs, but then a force of French line infantry had appeared from behind a gully. They too, had been driven back, until a flying battery of cannon deployed and gave new life to the retreating French. Their resistance had immediately stiffened. Slaughter had stripped out the carronades on his boats to pack in more men, and so had no way to respond to long range weapons. The British had taken refuge in the dunes and kept up a desultory fire on the French. Canister and grape kept British heads down. British musketry did the same to the French. Stalemate.

The French could be patient. Slaughter had a time-table. High tide was at eight that night; they had to be on the ships and underway before that time, if they wanted to clear the harbour bar and get out to sea.

Slaughter liked the plan Meers had explained to him. His troops kept up an unremitting fire as Pennywhistle maneuvered into position. Any minute now, the Congreves would fire and he would attack. The opportune appearance of Pennywhistle on the French flank and the use of a new British weapon meant that the morning's casualties had not been in vain. His men were eager to break forth from their confinement. The morning's fight had not dampened their spirits.

Dale brought word to Pennywhistle. "The rockets are ready, sir."

"Excellent. Tell the gunners' mates two minutes. I'll take down the battery commander, then you and I will go after the first cannon crew."

"Right, sir, be careful, sir." Dale dashed off, followed closely by Mercury.

*****

Captain Andre Foulard, commanding the French flying battery, was delighted by the behaviour of his men. He had seen battle before, but his men had not. A former school teacher, his training methods were paying handsome dividends. The men performed their duties with teamwork and clockwork precision. Their high rate of fire was hammering the British. Foulard found the British dull, unimaginative fellows, but they were certainly persistent. He wondered how many more rounds of canister they would absorb before they did the sensible thing and cleared off.

*****

Pennywhistle took some deep breaths. His breathing became slow, steady, and regular. He felt himself calmly descending a winding mind's eye staircase to an inner mental library of knowledge and measured repose; a sanctuary of intense yet relaxed focus. It was a deeply meditative state, one which would help design extremely violent action. The world seemed to stop, go silent, fade to a soft blur, then disappear entirely.

Except for his targets. Every detail about them shifted into extremely sharp focus, every movement thrust into bold relief like bleached rocks tossed on a beach of black volcanic sand. Every syllable they uttered grew as loud as the surging rush of a turbulent waterfall. Distance, elevation, wind, parabolas of bullets, and expected movements of men, flashed through his mind in the fraction of a second. Calculations were made and logged. He had a penchant for mathematics, although theoretical applications bored him. But this was no abstract exercise.

He had a minute before the Congreves fired. Six shots, six lives to end.

He'd almost instantly selected for his targets the French artillery captain and the crew of cannon number one, the potential impact of their deaths evaluated carefully and methodically. Pennywhistle was two men at this point. The humane representative of civilization retreated to a bombproof area of the heart and carefully bolted the door. The other self, the intellect of survival, logic, and amoral reason emerged from his bunker and came coldly forth to point and control the Ferguson. He saw the French not as men, but as killable puppets.

Captain Foulard and his men shouted in elation and derision of the British as they went about their noisy and bloody business. The cannon muzzle shot flame and the carriage rumbled back in recoil. Swab, worm, cartridge, ram, wad, ram, canister, ram, prick cartridge, insert vent quill, apply linstock. Grab the handspikes to reposition the piece for the next shot. The deadly cycle proceeded.

Pennywhistle felt detached, no fear, no animus, just a determination to do it right. He had a certain talent as an amateur artist, and those instincts to create beauty and perfection now manifested in a strange desire to do the same with his shots. This was his art now, the targets his canvas, the gun his brush. His product might be spoken of with respect, but rather than enriching the world, it would diminish it. Yet, it would diminish it in a way that would save lives and bring victory. War was nothing if not contradictory.

Foulard's hussar-style blue tunic featured three vertical rows of bright brass buttons. Pennywhistle aimed for the centre of the middle row. He squeezed the trigger gently. The captain shook briefly like a leaf in a rising wind and collapsed a half second later, a look of utter bewilderment on his face.

The men continued the reloading and noticed nothing.

Pennywhistle pulled the trigger-guard down and right, opened the breech, inserted a charge, and seated the greased patch and ball on top. He twisted the guard up and left and engaged the breechblock. He shoved in finer grained priming powder to the pan from a special flask for faster ignition. He closed the pan and quickly checked the flint. His nimble fingers completed the job in ten seconds.

He lined up the firer, the man who applied the linstock that ignited the weapon. He zeroed in on the intersection of the white shoulder belts holding the man's bayonet and cartridge box. The round slammed into the Frenchman's chest and he went down.

Pennywhistle reloaded, never moving from his prone position.

The sponge-man, the crewman who swabbed the breech to kill lingering sparks, died next. Pennywhistle's shot took him in the throat.

He reloaded. Thirty seconds, three down.

A caisson driver next to the ammunition box clutched his stomach, pitched forward, and lay unmoving. Dale's aim had been unerring; good, because a second shot would have taken time. The Baker was still a muzzle-loader and slow.

The vents-man, whose leather thumbstall prevented air through the touchhole causing an unwanted ignition, was next in Pennywhistle's sights. He turned toward Pennywhistle just as the trigger was pulled, so the shot caught him on the right side of his skull rather than the front. A jet of gore splattered the pricker with grey and red matter; he absent-mindedly wiped brains from his left eyelid so he could see.

The cannon crew stopped reloading. Blue-coated infantrymen approached cautiously. They moved in circles, a few men gesturing extravagantly and shouting curses. They had no idea what was happening. The captain was gone, no orders were forthcoming. Confusion assumed command.

Pennywhistle reloaded.

The pricker slowly started toward the other cannon crew. Some survival instinct caused him to duck at the last second, before Pennywhistle's shot told. It caught him in the shoulder. Not fatal, but he was not going anywhere now. He'd probably lose the arm.

Pennywhistle reloaded.

A second driver, standing next to the horses, hit the ground as if smashed down by a giant hand. Dale again!

The last member, the loader, gave way to full-bore panic and broke into a run to nowhere in particular. This gave Pennywhistle a difficult and challenging tracking shot. He was equal to the task. The loader slammed into the ground, bleeding from the abdomen.

Pennywhistle felt satisfaction, his inner artist propitiated. He took no joy in killing and wanted no more than was necessary, yet he could rejoice in the efficiency of a task well done. It was like finding the precise shades of colour to portray an elusive sunset on canvas. His well-aimed bullets had just brought sunsets to six French lives.

The preliminary pen and ink sketches were done. Time for the oil on canvas.

The first rocket arced high into the sky with a loud woosh, then headed out to sea, trailing plumes of red and yellow smoke and fire. It caught the attention of the French, but did no damage. The long shussing sound as it continued its path along the sky reminded French soldiers of the voice of an angry dragon: loud, feral, and frightening.

Woosh! Woosh! The second and third rockets were fired in rapid succession. They landed on the French left with loud *wham, wham* concussions, and canister showered the French infantry. A few men went down, the rest broke and ran.

The fourth rocket turned back upon the shooters and flew over the heads of the British in the direction they had come earlier that morning.

The fifth one detonated among the horses attached to the second limber, killing two of the eight and sending the others rearing in wild, unreasoning fear. It splintered the wooden yoke holding the team; their frenzied bucking finally caused it to break entirely. Whinnying loudly, the horses rent their tethers and dashed madly in whatever directions their fear took them. Some plunged directly into the French infantry and artillerymen. The terrified drivers' efforts to control their maddened charges were half-hearted and unsuccessful. They too wanted to run, they just did not know where.

It was the sixth and final rocket that shattered all remaining traces of equanimity, order, or reason. In what was the ideal outcome for Mr. Congreve's quirky, unpredictable invention, one rocket hissed loudly, and rose majestically into the air, a brilliant red-orange tail riveting the attention of both sides like the firework it vaguely resembled. It stalled briefly in mid-air, almost like a man deciding a course of action, then plunged earthward. It landed squarely in the middle of an open chest filled with ammunition. Pure luck, but British luck.

The resulting explosion sent a huge cloud of wagon, men, and horses skyward. The firing stopped; everyone watched, transfixed. Several horses at the edge of the explosion stumbled crazily away, missing legs and trailing yards of red-grey intestines. Their crazed whinnying was a sound of raw pain. A few seconds later, heads, arms, chests, and horseflesh obeyed the iron law of gravity and began the return to earth as human and equine detritus. It was a crimson hailstorm that bludgeoned many survivors to the ground and covered others with rags of animal and human flesh.

Pennywhistle's stomach lurched when he spied a black horse with its lower jaw blown away and one eye dangling precariously from its socket. It turned its head piteously toward him and its remaining eye begged him personally to relieve the pain. It just stood there, patiently trusting someone would help. He nearly retched when the beast uttered an awful cry that defied description. He had seen plenty of men die, but to see animals missing rumps, bellies, and limbs race round senselessly, driven mad by pain and fear, struck him as an obscene violation of the laws of the universe. Men understood; beasts did not. Not that there was much glory in war for a man, but there was certainly none in it for an animal.

But he had no time to stop for mercy, remorse, or random observations on the horrors of war. It was what it was, and he could change nothing. Duty reasserted itself. Time for brutal efficiency.

The plan had worked. This was the decisive moment. The French were on the edge. They needed one good push.

Pennywhistle rose to his full height, flourished his cutlass above his head, and loudly yelled, "Charge!"

The good push began.

Six

A long, rolling cheer rose up and rippled along the British lines. Sailors and marines jumped to their feet and bounded forward in a headlong rush. Like a pack of maddened bulls or a rogue wave at sea, their fierce momentum would have been frightening to steady troops. Against a milling, swirling, writhing whirlpool of running men, rearing horses, and smashed equipment, the British rush was the face of sheer terror. Running with a look of maddened glee, bayonet advanced, Private McCarthy outdistanced his fellows.

Pennywhistle's command covered the eighty yards to the French left in under a minute. Thirty seconds later, Slaughter's force launched a direct frontal assault. Caught in a rapidly closing steel vice, the bewildered French mounted no effective defense in either direction.

Pennywhistle wanted to drive the French, but his first objective was to secure the four six-pound field pieces. He toyed briefly with the notion of spiking them, disabling them with iron bolts through their vent-holes, then discarded the idea. With luck, they could turn the pieces against their former owners. Marines were schooled in performing all functions of serving ship's cannon, so four small field pieces would present no challenges.

The snarling, mustached face of a gigantic French *sergeant* appeared in front of Pennywhistle, his arms thrusting a bayonet. The marine neatly sidestepped, parried the cut away and down with his sword, then thrust quickly upward, his blade severing the Frenchman's carotid artery. Blood spurted skyward like magma from an angry volcano. The Frenchman collapsed with a horrible chuffing noise. Pennywhistle dashed impetuously toward the guns.

The battle became hand-to-hand. Pennywhistle saw Blandon block a gun butt to his head from a lanky French corporal, then riposte with a diagonal bayonet slash, which put an angry slit trench into the corporal's heavily scared face. The Frenchman collapsed like a punctured balloon, a mewling bundle of pain. Pennywhistle felt as if he were in the middle of a huge, demented court ball with partners wildly to-and-fro-ing, not with fans and fancy, but with cold steel and colder hearts.

The French did what he expected them to do. They clubbed with the butts of their weapons, rather than use the bayonet as trained. Their scant training forgotten, they bashed at the heads of sailors and marines with their five-foot wooden clubs like wild-eyed cavemen.

The British marines remembered their training. Pennywhistle had constantly drummed into his people that the blade always bested the butt—metal over wood. "Metal over wood," echoed in Private Stratton's head as he blocked a French musket and thrust his bayonet into the man's stomach.

Block, thrust, develop, gore, recover; Dale had made the men practice it until they could have done it in their sleep. It was a lethal dance and the marines did it supremely well. Block the opponent's piece, be it musket, pike, or sword. Thrust forward, preferably at the chest or stomach, but exploit any opening. Push the bayonet in vigorously. Twist violently, in several directions. Withdraw the blade smartly. Begin the cycle anew.

MacLeod, on Pennywhistle's left, gave his own refinement to the cold-steel quickstep. A chubby French fusilier swung at the burly Scotsman's head. MacLeod thrust forward and parried it, then reversed the motion and hit his opponent's groin with the butt of the musket. The Frenchman dropped his piece and doubled over in agony. MacLeod executed a neat parade ground step backwards, then plunged the blade through the fusilier's chest and out his backside. He put a foot on the chest for purchase and yanked the blade out. It was like skewering a potato and pulling the steel clear.

A second red-faced fusilier, crying out with anger and hate, rushed at MacLeod to avenge his comrade. His bayonet was held at waist level and he closed the distance with MacLeod quickly.

MacLeod stood immobile, giving nothing away, waiting until the last second to raise his bayonet and intercept the strike. Steel chips flew and blades locked into immobility as equal force challenged equal force. Eyes met, one set angry and scared, the other disciplined and determined. MacLeod, in the merest fragment of a second, withdrew his bayonet and made a sharp downward thrust. The tip buried itself in his opponent's thigh, puncturing the femoral artery. Blood spurted in quick, narrow jets: miniature, macabre geysers.

Wainwright confidently leveled his bayonet at a third on-rushing French fusilier. He wondered why the French were putting up such a fight instead of breaking, then realized that, sandwiched between two fires, they had nowhere to retreat. The man stopped abruptly five feet from Wainwright, looked deep into his cold dark eyes, blinked, then threw down his musket. He ran like a frightened deer in the direction from which he had come.

Pennywhistle dueled briefly with a French second lieutenant, the only remaining Frenchman with the presence of mind to try to protect the field-pieces. He looked about twenty and new in his rank, judging by the pristine epaulettes that looked hastily tacked on to a battered enlisted uniform. Pennywhistle was only ten feet from the breech of the first gun when the officer cut at him. He deftly blocked the slash at his chest with a quick side parry. The lieutenant followed with a clumsy cut at the Englishman's head. The marine dismissively redirected it up and away. He might as well have been fighting an inexperienced schoolboy. Two parries and ripostes later, he administered the coup de grace with a powerful strike at the neck that nearly severed his opponent's head.

How did one become an officer with no training in sword play? he wondered. Of course! Bonaparte promoted from the ranks, something uncommon in British forces. The chap must have had merit, but he clearly had not been born a gentleman.

"Marines, to me!" Pennywhistle's shout summoned a knot of marines. "Marines, five of you on each piece. Canister only. Let's give them a taste of what Slaughter's boys got this morning!"

The marines cheered and set about their business with skilled resolve. They loaded, wrestled handspikes, and carefully reversed the direction of two cannon. Two minutes later, the pieces stood ready, but Pennywhistle could not fire into the main mass of men with both sides jumbled together.

A band of French fugitives had broken loose from the main battle and had started a dog trot down the road. They seemed under no coherent leadership and were clearly bound for anyplace but more battle. Over half of them had discarded their weapons. It was flight, pure and simple. Fusilier Bontemps was typical of the fugitives. He been in the army just two months, had just seen his first battle, and decided it was quite enough for him. Extreme fear had abolished his notions of glory. He knew his leadership had failed, but he had done his part. He had no plans to remain and tempt fate any further.

Pennywhistle estimated the range at two hundred yards. Much too far for an aimed musket shot, but excellent for a load of canister. The container holding two hundred musket balls would disintegrate some distance from the muzzle, spraying the lead in a tidal wave of death. Even if the range was underestimated, the ricochet possibilities were still lethal. A case of canister hitting the ground and disintegrating would send the balls rocketing upward toward the portions of men's anatomies most closely guarded—their private parts.

Pennywhistle took one glowing linstock himself. Stratton held the other one over the vent-hole of the second field piece.

"Fire!" Pennywhistle touched the glowing linstock to the powder over the vent-hole. A second later, Stratton did the same.

Both pieces discharged almost simultaneously. Flashes, billowing smoke, and echoing booms sent clouds of birds, driven mad by the noise, screeching wildly into the air.

The ground was choked with smoke that obscured the carnage. Cries of agony, groans of pain, and loud wails of despair told Pennywhistle his aim had been true. Well, almost true. The canister had dropped a little short of the targets but had achieved what farmers would have called "a gelding harvest."

As the smoke cleared, the road was littered with reddish-grey human waste, drums, ripped uniforms, and military accoutrements. A tall teenaged French private lay on the ground, one of many feeling for genitalia that no longer existed. Mercifully, in the teen's case, the fragment had also severed the femoral artery, so he only had to endure the pain and humiliation for a little while before he bled to death. It was worse for the living. One middle-aged fusilier had a sucking chest wound that would extract hours of agony.

A thick, unwelcome smell pervaded the air: not the usual rotten-egg smell of spent powder, but the nauseous stink of excrement from hundreds of dying men voiding their bowels mixed sickeningly with the reek of urine. It was vile enough to cause two case-hardened marines to empty their stomachs.

Demoralization was infectious and spread quickly. The resolve of the mass of Frenchman ensnared by the two British assaults was close to collapse, but individuals fought on. One grizzled old *sergeant* continued to fire his Charleville and shout maledictions at the English, but he could not inspire his men to do the same. They looked toward the English with shocked apathy. Most of the French felt no ferocity, only a deep desire for it all to be over. If that involved surrender, so be it. Honour and glory had no place here; this was about surviving.

One private raised his hands in surrender; then another and another. The effect rippled through the formation. Larger and larger groups of men threw down their weapons.

Captain Emile Joubert saw what was inevitable, and knew it was important that an officer be in control. He tied a white handkerchief to the end of a long stick, waved it frantically, and shouted loudly in passable English, "We surrender!" He was experienced enough to know that he would get no more fighting out of these men. He could at least seek honourable terms to spare their lives.

Pennywhistle bellowed for his men to stand down. It took a while for men in the mad grip of blood lust to understand. The cannon crews were slowest to respond.

"Marines, to me! Attention!" he said with forced calm. He needed to cool the heated pulses of the men. The men formed up creditably.

"The French have surrendered. I am going with the other officers to work out the formal terms. I want no firing, no untoward actions. These people fought gallantly and deserve proper consideration as honourable opponents. They are men, soldiers like us. Understood?"

"Aye, aye, sir!" the marines chorused.

Five minutes later, Pennywhistle confronted Captain Joubert, who was now the ranking French officer. They exchanged pleasantries as if at an elegant court *levee*, even though they were both covered with a thick layer of powder grime, sweat, and dust. Lieutenant Slaughter arrived, tired and winded. As the senior British officer, Slaughter conducted the surrender formalities, which he did in clumsy, schoolboy French, but the message got through.

"Captain, your men have fought well and will be treated according to the conventions of war. The officers will give their paroles as soon as is expedient, and the men will be confined in the city. We will provide food and water, of course, but *Monsieur le Capitaine*, I need to know how many troops you now have the honour to command in order to carry out this obligation properly."

Captain Joubert looked pained. "Sadly, I have approximately only one hundred left, Lieutenant. Your men are, I regret to say, very proficient killers." It was an accurate, if ungallant characterization.

Slaughter noted the regret and resignation in Joubert's voice and endeavoured to be kind. "The officers will be separated from the men and billeted separately. NCOs will be allowed to stay with the troops. British marines will escort you, as, you may have surmised, the sailors and I have other, more pressing, business ahead. I would ask you, monsieur, how many other French troops are in the vicinity?"

Joubert gave an amused half-smile. "I am sure you understand, Lieutenant, that both my honour and my duty forbid me to answer that question. You will have to work out that puzzlement on your own. But I would say, your success may be... temporary."

Slaughter responded, "I expected no less from a man of honour. However, disabuse yourself of any idea that your numbers will remain hidden for long. Our scouts will discover that information soon."

Pennywhistle thought the Frenchman's cryptic statement sounded ominous. There had been too many surprises this morning, and he had the feeling more fighting lay ahead.

He didn't particularly like the idea of his men as prison guards, but the French troops needed wardens. He would use the minimum number necessary. He would form the rest of his men into patrols and set up a schedule. He needed to know what was out there. He wanted to discover any further surprises before they arrived.

The Blancpain read exactly noon. Damn! High tide was only eight hours away!

Seven

The entrance to Groa lay a quarter mile ahead, its steeples and soaring campaniles gradually becoming visible above red-tiled roofs. Pennywhistle's marines marched in good soldierly formation with smiles on their faces and springing steps, proud of their twin morning successes. Mercury preceded the column, as usual.

One very angry and slightly drunk French sergeant, completely disgusted with army life, had been more than happy to give Pennywhistle a thorough description of the city's layout and contents.

Groa squatted on a sandy isthmus, connected to the mainland by a single road. It had no fortifications to speak of and perhaps two thousand souls. It was a typical city of the area with narrow, meandering streets and high-backed, red-roofed houses of local stone in varied architectural styles. Most of the homes had some sort of business on the ground floor. There was an ornate *hotel de ville* for the local government, several gilded Renaissance churches, and two fine Palladian mansions belonging to successful merchants. The city was an *entrepot* port, specializing in trans-shipping goods to cities along the Illyrian and Dalmation coasts. It had plenty of what was to be expected in a port: taverns, brothels, pawnbrokers, flophouses, and ship's chandlers.

The harbour itself was shallow and shaped like an inverted C. It was not well suited to larger draft vessels. A small, rectangular-shaped island filled in the interior of the C, and its southwestern corner marked the entrance to the main channel. It was packed with shipping, mostly small coasting vessels. The twenty-five ships of the French convoy were much larger, and ranged from three to nine hundred tons' burden. They were spread out next to the town quay and most had gangplanks extended to allow quick access. They rode easily at anchor, in the gentle swells of early afternoon, their drooping and drowsing crews completely oblivious to the fate rapidly advancing upon them.

There were garrison pieces in a crudely built red brick ravelin, which stood sentinel at the point where the ship's channel merged with the Adriatic. It was toward this work that Pennywhistle directed the column. He halted the men, unshipped his glass, and made a careful survey of the wedge-shaped fortification and its garrison. The ravelin contained twelve-pounders, manned by crews who appeared bored and listless, eager only to finish their stint of duty and speed directly to the city's fleshpots. The soldiers faced the sea, focused only on a water-borne threat. They had not the wit to think danger might come from the land. No pickets, scouts, or patrols were visible.

The gate to the ravelin stood wide open while soldiers herded cows inside. The bullocks were likely intended for their evening meals for the next few days. Most of the men were lounging, talking, and smoking their pipes outside the gate, apparently determined to enjoy the fine weather rather than confine themselves to the dingy interior of a smelly old fort. Pennywhistle could see only two men on the parapets.

He furled his glass and decided bold theatricality was his best option. Screams, shouts, huzzahs, and a quick rush of howling marines would probably put its tiny garrison to flight or induce a quick surrender. Bloodshed might even be avoided. *Lord knows, I've seen plenty of that already*, he thought. He had sixty-five men remaining at his disposal, after the fifteen marines had been dispatched to guard the day's prisoners.

He formed the marines quickly into line and instructed them to make enough noise to shame an army of berserkers. He raised his cutlass, and for the third time that day, bellowed, "Charge!"

"Huzzahhhhhhhhhh!" The marines swept forward like an incoming tide, their yells making a tsunami of sound. Mercury ran ahead, barking fiercely.

The French outside the gate heard the thunder and spun round. Instead of mustering or fleeing, they stood transfixed. The cows, however, ran, increasing the confusion. One gap-toothed private expressed the general sentiment when he exclaimed, "*Merde, ce n'est pas possible.*"

The monster-sized dog coming straight at them was particularly terrifying. The men were like animals caught in a sudden, blinding blaze of bright light: muscles paralyzed, debilitated rather than energized by fear. No one thought to herd the men inside and simply bar the gate.

With the onrushing marines at only twenty yards distance, their behaviour became that of pack animals. First one soldier slammed down his musket and threw up his hands; then, like a line of dominos, all of his comrades followed suit, and in a moment all of the unarmed French were yelling, "Quarter, quarter!"—probably one the few English words they knew. They were terrified that these oncoming demons might not follow the laws of war, being bent on wholesale butchery.

Pennywhistle stopped the charge just short of bayonet range. He saw unadulterated panic in French eyes. It was not just from the noise and bayonets. A number murmured, "*C'est le chien du diable,*" convinced Mercury was Satan's personal pet. Mercury stood resolutely at Dale's side and growled menacingly at the French.

Pennywhistle approached a sergeant who had his hands up and looked to be their leader. Addressing the man, he put dread and fire into his best French.

"Your surrender is accepted, you have nothing to fear." He looked past the sergeant and spoke directly to the soldiers. "The marines will escort you to town. Do as you are told and you will be treated well. Disobedience or treachery will result in your instant death." His eyes shot daggers as he stared disdainfully down the line of frightened men. Miscellaneous gulps, gasps, and grimaces made it clear he had been understood on a primal level.

The Frenchmen quickly formed as ordered; broken men

harkening to a strong voice of command, even if it was an enemy's. Pennywhistle selected marines for guards; marines who, none too gently, pushed their new charges toward town.

He and Dale made a thorough inspection of the fortification. The twelve-pounders would now pose no hazard to the squadron when it stood in this evening. The obvious expedient was to spike the guns, but if the guns were reversed and pointed toward land, they might well create a formidable hazard if stray French troops in the area decided to make trouble. It would reduce his force to keep them manned, but the cannons were good insurance against the unforeseen. There had been a lot of "unforeseen" this day.

The first sailors and marines into the city had found it unoccupied by French troops, inhabited only by sullen townsmen, surly strumpets, and sailors in various stages of intoxication. Private Greyson's feet marched straight ahead, but his roving eyes noticed with great interest several of the town trollops casting amorous glances in his direction. Greyson had once worked as servant at a very discreet London bordello. Much as he loved the adventure of marine service, he missed the ladies. He hoped there'd be opportunity for adventures of a less militant nature.

*****

Pennywhistle set up headquarters on the ground floor of Il Tramanto, the best inn in the city. From the bay window, he could see the quayside bustling with activity. He was satisfied things were proceeding as expeditiously as possible, but it was still a race against time and the French. Ships were being unloaded and lightened, the better to clear the harbour bar at the earliest possible moment. Rigging was being repaired, sails mended, blocks replaced. Most of the French crews had been rounded up with ease and had either been pressed into service or confined below decks. Many were showing the after-effects of shore leave and were subdued, even docile. After all, they were merely merchant sailors; they had neither interest in nor training for scuffles with the British.

Still, Captain Joubert's taunt gnawed at him. It hinted that a large

French contingent was unaccounted for, which squared with his own guess that he was up against at least a full regiment. It was never the sure threat you could confront directly that posed the gravest danger. It was the menace that could not possibly materialize in the rational universe that got you. No one planned for it, protected by the blissful logic that said the impossible could never hurt you. He prepared for the impossible.

He had sent three five-man detachments to patrol the main road leading into town, spread out in a wide *cordon sanitere*, six miles from the city gate. He'd put Dale in charge and trusted Dale's poacher's instincts to give him early warning of any enemy movement. Mercury would contribute his well-schooled nose as usual. More French were out there, somewhere, but with luck, they would not put in an appearance until after the British had sailed away on the tide. Still, a man had no right to expect luck if he failed to exhibit any forethought. Lord Cochrane had taught him that complete and thorough preparation was the key to victory, as well as a way to keep the butcher's bill low.

Cochrane had also taught him the value of deception and misdirection in war. His own outspoken support of Cochrane during the Basque Roads controversy had almost ended Pennywhistle's career. It was only through the timely intervention of his cousin that he had secured his present command, which was ordinarily a lieutenant's billet. Still, he would not have done anything differently. He was more than willing to stick his neck out for men he respected. Cochrane might be undiplomatic, but he was unarguably brilliant, and he'd been right to insist that Gambier's lack of support had prevented a mere minor victory from becoming what should have been a second Trafalgar and a conclusive end to Napoleon's naval might.

*****

Ten miles to the northwest, a weary column of French soldiery wound its way back to Groa. The four hundred men of the 81st Regiment had had a bad time of it. Sent to chastise the village of

Tranazo, a notorious haven for local banditry, they had failed to nab a single brigand. The expedition had then degenerated into an orgy of looting and pillaging. The French were notorious throughout Europe as foragers, but this had been extreme, even for them. Little of value remained in the village.

Captain Rene LeMere's lively brown eyes flashed in disgust and the corners of his wide, sensual mouth were turned down in contempt. A member of the Imperial Guard, he was merely an observer and could only watch in exasperation. *Chef-de-battalion* Jean-Luc Gaspar was in actual command, and a worse martinet could hardly be imagined. His discipline both extreme and capricious, he had favourites and informers; the rest resented him. A strict disciplinarian who was harsh to all but even-handed in meting out punishments would be respected, if never loved—provided, of course, he won battles. Men forgive much in a leader who thrashes the enemy in every encounter. But Gaspar had fumbled an ambush set to capture the bandits and allowed them to escape. He'd then blamed the men and selected three privates for a thorough flogging. That in itself was outrageous: flogging had been banished from the French army with the coming of *La Revolution.* The men had grumbled, murmured curses, and taken their frustrations out on the town.

Captain LeMere had been selected by Napoleon himself to assist Commodore Bernard Dubordieu, the French naval commander in the area. Overtly, he was to serve as an aide-de-camp and military advisor. Covertly, he was to send Napoleon occasional private and frank reports of the military situation. LeMere was a keen observer and a fine soldier. More than that, he was a driven man and exceptionally ambitious. The Emperor had recognized those qualities, since he possessed them all himself in outsize proportions. He considered LeMere an exceptionally useful man with a bright future. Patience, however, was never LeMere's strong suit, and right now he was thoroughly out of it. LeMere had debated relieving this dolt on the spot; his Guardsman's rank was considered more than a grade higher than a similar one in the regular army, but Gaspar would certainly dispute it vehemently. Disunity of command was a recipe for disaster and would only confuse men already very uncertain. No, the best course was to cajole and persuade.

"Gaspar, I know I vex you, but really, a two hour halt? This is not dinner at Versailles. I believe we are needed urgently in Groa. Our column has already encountered and absorbed sixty fugitives from the 5th, so the men know something very bad happened this morning. They grow uneasy. No doubt the stories of British fighting prowess that are being bandied about are exaggerated, but they surely suggest a need for haste. Where else would the British be headed but Groa? What other target can they have but the convoy? Twenty minutes is more than sufficient for food and refreshment. We must press on!"

"LeMere, my men are tired and need rest." Gaspar's eyebrows met over his lowering gaze. "This is the Mediterranean; the afternoon siesta is traditional and my men expect it to be honoured. You do not know—have not served here. These fugitives think to disguise their cowardice and poor showing by turning a simple British scouting sortie into a huge pitched battle. I would not put much stock in the fables they tell. The British lack the manpower to attempt anything important. We need not concern ourselves with speed. We will get to Groa, but it will be when we are properly fed and rested. I take care of my men, LeMere. Perhaps that was not an important concern in the Guard. You should be more of a student, LeMere, and benefit from my greater experience in this theatre."

Hidden in a streambed, not ten yards away, Dale overheard this conversation. Mercury's nose had proved unerring; the huge mastiff had sniffed out the men whose existence Pennywhistle had deduced, and lead his master to a place where he could observe them undetected. Dale did not understand French, but he grasped the emotional purport of the exchange: bad blood, divided command, lax discipline, long rest. He needed to get this information to Pennywhistle forthwith. After making his stealthy way back to his men, he dispatched Addison, his fastest runner. Dale and his men would continue to shadow the column. Pennywhistle was being given a valuable gift: time.

Eight

"And that's the way it is, Captain. Those lazy froggies look to be takin' a leisurely bivouac and ain't goin' nowheres for a while. Sergeant Dale says them Frenchie commanders looks to want to kill each other and can't agree on nothing." Private Jonas Addison concluded his report with pride. The runaway shoemaker's apprentice had only been in the marines a year, but found he had a knack for soldiering and was considering it as a career. So far, it had been a vast improvement over dyes, leather, the condescension of customers, and the reek of their unwashed feet.

Pennywhistle acknowledged, "Thank you, Private, your report has been most useful. Now go get yourself some victuals; you've earned them. Dismissed!"

Addison touched his hat in salute and let the blissful smell of hot food guide him down the alley toward Il Tramanto. Pennywhistle pondered the situation. He had been right, but the numbers were even larger than he'd expected. Four hundred coming, but not for a while.

There were no fortifications of importance in Groa, but there was an old town gate. It lay at the end of the isthmus that connected the town to the mainland. The barbican was of solid brick construction, thirty feet high, and the main road passed through it. It could be barricaded and turned into a solid blocking point. Many officers disdained the idea of improvised field fortifications, feeling it made men "shy." Their philosophy was "always take the offensive, never dig in." That struck Pennywhistle as utter nonsense. Small numbers in the open could be easily brushed aside; small numbers behind

71

barricades were much thornier obstacles. Fortifications boosted the morale of the defenders, as well as inducing caution in attackers. Most importantly, fortifications would buy time.

A search of the vessels in harbour revealed that one was carrying a shipment of older Potsdam muskets. Second-rate pieces to be sure, intended for auxiliaries, not regulars, but the aged Prussian weapons would take a Brown Bess ball, unlike French Charlevilles. The extra muskets might come in handy.

Then he had an inspiration. The ships in harbour were carrying naval stores. Pitch, tar, sulphur, antimony and a few other choice ingredients could be mixed and inserted into old wine jugs. Lit, they made very effective smoke and stinkpots. They could come in handy in the confined streets and alleys, if the marines had to make a fighting retreat to the quay. The hundred French prisoners posed a serious problem, but there was a way to turn that liability into an asset. He could make the French prisoners unwitting enemies of their former comrades. He summoned runners and began to issue orders.

*****

Gaspar launched into another of his seemingly endless verbal jousts with Captain LeMere. Their acerbic sparring provided plenty of diversion for the troops. As usual, LeMere urged speed, dispatch, and security. And, as usual, Gaspar came down firmly on the side of prevarication, sloth, and braggadocio. The rankers, those who did not flat out hate their commander for the random brutalities he directed at them, felt amused contempt for Gaspar, whereas they instinctively knew that LeMere was a solid soldier.

From his hide, Sergeant Dale smiled every bit as much as his French counterparts. This lot would not hang together well when the bullets started flying. It wouldn't take much to push them over the edge.

*****

Pennywhistle was well satisfied with the sum of his marines' exertions. The three-story barbican was all that remained of a much earlier town wall. It had embrasures on the third floor for observation and, presumably, archers. It had been repaired many times and now

72

seemed more a monument to past achievements than a modern fortification. Still, the brick work was several feet thick and would be useful protection against musketry. It stood alone, a hundred yards in front of a fifteen-foot wide stone bridge over a marshy tidal creek. Any French force headed into the city would have to march over that bridge. The actual gates had long since vanished, and only beach grass and sand abutted its decaying sides.

His men spent the early afternoon with coats off and sleeves rolled up, shouldering wooden spars and cordage from the convoy. A crude line of stakes provided an effective skeleton for dozens of mast spars laid sideways. The palisade was thirty feet wide, double the width of the road through the gate. The increased width would enable the defenders to overlap the flanks of any attackers debouching from the bridge. Enfilade fire was always more effective than direct frontal volleys. He envisioned the marines in two lines, one marine per foot.

Master's Mate Hudson had managed to whistle up a small supply of shovels from the convoy ship *Hercule*; using those and beach sand, the marines constructed an earthen fire-step. Men would step up to fire in safety and step down to reload.

Since Pennywhistle's right was protected by the sea, the French would certainly try to flank the left. He had the marines manhandle two of the twelve-pounders from the harbour ravelin into flanking positions, one hundred yards west of the gate. Five men crewed each piece, enough to operate them, but not enough to move them. They would provide a nasty surprise to the French, and probably cause a good deal of disruption in their ranks. How much disruption depended on the quality of French leadership and ability to recover quickly from a *coup de main*.

Pennywhistle decided to mine the bridge. It was a single-arched, barrel-vaulted structure built sometime in the early Middle Ages. It was stoutly fashioned of local stone and roughly sixty yards long. He made a thorough survey of it from underneath. He took his time, calculated blast radii, and personally supervised the placement of each ninety pound barrel of powder. Since the arch was low, most of the explosive force would be tightly confined, increasing its destructive power. Still, it was a heavy structure and it would take quite a few barrels of powder to blast it apart. Powder was one quantity not in short supply, because two of the prize ships were filled with hundreds of barrels of the finely corned, fast burning variety.

Ideally, he would be able to detonate the charges when it was packed with French troops. Lighting the fuses would be dangerous, possibly fatal to the man who volunteered for the task, yet he knew there would be no shortage of volunteers; survival guaranteed promotion.

Green troops were easily demoralized and a surprise explosion that decimated their ranks might fatally unman the survivors. At the very least, he could sever the link between the French front and rear. Divide, isolate, and chop up piecemeal. It was a formula as old as Caesar.

Nine

"Gentlemen, our luck appears to be turning. The wind is freshening from the south. I know you will want to be off, but let us review our plans one last time." Commodore William Hoste spoke with a confidence tinged with relief that their timetable could be maintained.

A bell striking six times was clearly audible in the great cabin of HMS *Amphion*, 36 guns. Since it was the afternoon watch, the time was just 3 p.m. The three captains of the squadron had just finished a fine dinner of fresh turbot, roast chicken, and steak and kidney pie. The servants discreetly removed the remains of dinner and bottles of claret, then laid out a fine dessert of oranges, pears, assorted nuts, Stilton cheese, and coffee. The captains attacked the dessert with gusto.

The great cabin occupied the entire stern of the main deck, just below the quarterdeck. Six large windows opened onto the sea, all framed with curtains of calico chintz. Two undistinguished oil paintings adorned the bulkheads, pleasant scenes of English country life reminiscent of Constable. Four small elm book cases stood below these, crowded with reference books on the Adriatic. Canvas-covered deal partitions sectioned the cabin into dining area, day cabin, and sleeping compartment.

The Sheraton mahogany table, urn-backed chairs, Sheffield silver, Wedgewood china plate, and Waterford crystal completed the impression of something elegant and civilized: a sea-going version of White's or Boodle's back in London. But this was not a gentlemen's gaming club; this was a fighting ship. All one had to do was look at the four blunt, ugly eighteen-pounders with their attendant gun ports and the racks of swords on the bulkheads above the paintings to know the elegance was but a mask.

The mask could be put aside quickly. All of the partitions in the cabin were thin, collapsible, and removable to create a single open gun deck running the entire length of the ship. The eyebolts holding the furniture to the deck could be loosened and all of the contents of the cabin stowed swiftly. Captain's cabin it might be, but the captain's first allegiance was to Bellona, Goddess of War.

Commodore William Hoste, protégé of Admiral Nelson, favoured Nelson's method of discussing his battle plans informally over dinner. It was a relaxed, collegial way to make absolutely certain his ideas were understood as well as encourage subordinates to make their own suggestions. It strongly resembled tutorials at Cambridge, and the very act of discussion informed his captains that he reposed trust in their initiative, should the original battle plan come apart.

The three captains at the table could not have been more different in appearance, background, or personality, yet they all shared an eagerness to beat the French, and beat them decisively.

Hoste enjoyed the temporary rank of commodore, signifying he was the senior captain in command of a squadron. He was short, in his early thirties, with bee-stung lips and a delicately sculpted, almost feminine face. His head was crowned with thick, curly auburn hair and his general appearance spoke more of an artist than a warrior. He was an intense man who spoke directly and forcefully. It sometimes unnerved officers more used to courtly circumlocution. For all of that, he was an essentially kind man, and he treated his sailors well. An excellent seaman, he subscribed to Nelson's policy of total victory and thought a battle in which even one enemy ship escaped no victory at all. His dogged pursuit of the French convoy into Groa was proof of that. The classic Admiralty orders of "sink, burn, destroy, or take as prize" perfectly represented his plan for the entire Groa convoy. As the son of a prestigious but poor country parson, any resulting prize money would also be most welcome.

Captain Henry Whitby of *Cerberus*, 32, was of medium height and had coal black hair cropped short and an olive complexion. His large, pumpkin-shaped face featured a pug nose, a slit of a mouth, and a perpetually saturnine expression. The son of London merchant, he was a bookish man who was quiet-spoken and inclined to weigh matters carefully.

Captain Gordon of *Active*, 38, was a powerful oak of a man, more than three inches above six feet. He had the face of a Homeric hero: determined chin, sensitive, deep-set blue eyes, slightly aquiline nose, high, intelligent forehead, and dark blond hair. A sprig of minor Scots aristocracy, he had once been a rebellious, vexatious midshipman who had surprisingly blossomed into a fine officer. He was charming, funny, easy-going, and voluble; the sort of hale fellow to whom strangers naturally flocked. It was easy to miss the steel core underneath. An intelligent sailor, he was neither a great reader nor intellectual, but he knew everything there was to know about his ship. He made sure every officer knew the names, backgrounds, and skills of the seamen in their divisions. The men loved him for this, and floggings on *Active* were practically unknown. Like Hoste, he valued initiative and encouraged it, not just in the officers, but in the men as well.

Hoste continued, "Captain Whitby, your ship is the smallest and draws the least amount of water: fourteen feet, I believe. You will take the place of honour as first, since your ship can stand closest into shore. Have a leadsman sound the depths constantly, but push it right to the edge. Beware, there are sandbanks and shoals; our charts are incomplete and only marginally reliable. And remember, as Nelson said, the safest course is not always the best. We will need to provide covering fire for Slaughter and the prizes. You shall be at the extreme range of your eighteen-pounders. I'd prefer to spare the city and only target French soldiers, but since we can only usefully employ solid shot at that range, rumbling down a few buildings would be an effective way to delay any French advance. Use your judgment."

"Aye, aye, sir," replied Captain Whitby. "You do me a great honour."

"Captain Gordon," Hoste faced him directly, "I will follow Whitby in *Amphion* in line ahead formation. You will be third because your ship has the greatest draft. You and I will provide what fire support we can, but the truth may be that only Captain Whitby will get close enough to be effective. Nevertheless, use your initiative and do what you can."

Captain Gordon wondered how Pennywhistle was faring. Now there, he thought, was one man who knew how to use initiative.

*****

Pennywhistle, at that moment, was in earnest remonstration with Corporal Wainwright, in charge of guarding the French prisoners. The little drummer boy, Pierre Ducot, slept placidly at Wainwright's feet like a dog staying close to his master.

"Sir, you want me to get the Frenchies drunk, sir, and let 'em go? That don't make no sense, sir, if you pardon me speakin' plain." Wainwright was earnest, reliable, but not terribly perceptive.

Pennywhistle laughed out loud. "Yes, I want them foolish with liquor, but I am not asking you to betray your country, honour, or duty. I most certainly do not want it done right now! We may have to beat a fighting retreat to the docks if things go wrong. The French will be directly on our heels, and we will need to buy some time. My idea is to get the prisoners stinking drunk and, as soon as we pass this place, turn them loose. Leaderless, weaponless, witless, they will impede their own comrades. To add to the fun, our men will toss a few stinkpots into the mixture. The smoke of the stinkpots, not to mention the aroma, should give us a cloak to make good our escape."

Corporal Wainwright's dirt-brown eyes gradually grew wide, as Pennywhistle's objective slowly percolated through layers of poorly-developed grey matter. "That's a real smart plan, sir, real smart. I think that would work right well, sir. But I have two questions, sir. Where do I get the spirits, and when do you want me to start?"

"Send two men and a cart to the docks," Pennywhistle replied. "There is plenty of alcohol from the ships on the quay. I recall there are leagers of Calvados, a French brandy, which will do the trick very nicely. Make sure you choose two reliable men, Corporal Wainwright. I don't want them sampling the spirits on the way back. Tell the men they need to keep their wits about them. I know they will be tempted, seeing the French indulge, but their survival and the success of this expedition depend on their utter sobriety. You can promise them, on my authority, an extra ration of grog when we get back on *Active* as an incentive and reward for abstinence. I want you to dispatch men for the quay immediately, but don't let the prisoners start tippling for another three hours. We want them drunk enough to walk, or at least stumble; we don't want them asleep."

"Aye, aye, sir! Wainwright turned and shouted, "Stairns and Bracewaite, front and centre! I have a task for you."

After listening to make sure the men understood their orders and the singular importance of their mission, Pennywhistle departed.

His next port of call was the rear of Il Tramanto to see how the stinkpot factory progressed. Pennywhistle referred to the fumes as "noxious vapors"; his marines called them "shitgas." By any name, they caused eyes to tear up and abruptly close. In narrow alleys, they would have a significant disabling effect on any pursuers.

*****

The French command continued to argue.

"Gaspar, I know you would loudly praise the angels you so foolishly believe watch over us if I were suddenly struck mute, but since the power of speech does not elude me, I will continue to make representations most forcefully. Have you not noticed that since we left Groa on our punitive expedition, we have heard absolutely nothing? No scouts, no foraging parties, not even a solitary horseman with a dispatch. Does that not arouse your suspicions that something untoward is afoot? We only left a scratch garrison of fifty in the city. I counseled vehemently against such a tiny contingent, if you recall, and we have had no communication whatsoever with them for more than a day. I am afraid, very afraid, that something very bad has happened to them. That is why we must increase our pace. Every second we delay increases the danger!" The energy in LeMere's voice matched the intense, earnest expression on his face.

"I don't need some headquarters poppinjay to tell me my business, LeMere," replied Gaspar haughtily.

"We must move faster! The convoy and the men in the city are our responsibility," said LeMere with urgency. "I fought at Austerlitz and Jena; my instincts are based on experience and well-developed. Right now, they tell me a fight lies ahead, and soon. Very, very soon!"

Sergeant Dale, who had been shadowing the French unit, observed this in silent concealment. Time to pull back all of his scouts toward the city. The French were marching faster now, and there was no doubt where they were headed. There was nothing more to discover. Dale would have agreed with LeMere if he could have understood his words. A fight was ahead, and soon.

*****

Pennywhistle was, at that moment, in animated conversation with several marine privates at Il Tramanto. The privates had set up a workshop of sorts, something which later Victorian England would call an assembly line. Their product, the stinkpots.

"It looks like you are making commendable progress. I just want to make sure you used the proper ingredients in the right proportions. Don't stint on the sulphur and antimony."

Maxwell looked at Pennywhistle with a gleeful earnestness. "We done just like you says, sir. Got all of the ingredients from down at the quay. Lots and lots of sulphur, sir. Mixed it all just right. It's got a proper horrid odor, sir, and we ain't even lit 'em. We been cuttin' little fuses, then using the sail-maker's needles to punch holes in the cork stoppers to insert them. The stoneware jugs won't blow, but the cork will dissolve in a trice, and they will simply spew smoke and stench. Don't do to imagine how it will be in the streets when our boys is tossin' 'em about. Makes my eyes water fierce, sir, when I even gets close to the pot where we gots Barneswell stirrin' it, sir. Don't know how 'e stands it. It's like being dropped into ship's bilge filled with all the usual shi...uh, stuff, sir, but with loads of rotten eggs and onions added."

"Excellent, Maxwell, if it has that effect even in its inert condition, I am sure the fully active final product will do the job most handsomely. I want a hundred of these contrivances. I want fifty brought up front to the gatehouse, twenty-five at the piazza, and twenty-five to be stored at the quay, hard by the sail-maker's loft. I think a fighting retreat may well prove necessary and the pots will serve as our rally points. Have you got all that?"

"I do indeed, sir. I will have a marine standing by each cache with a tub full of glowing linstocks so they can be easily lit. Underhanded works best, sir," Maxwell said confidently.

Pennywhistle looked puzzled.

Maxwell explained, "I means for throwin 'em, sir. Grip 'em by the holders and toss 'em underhand."

"Useful insight, Maxwell. I need to be off the quay. I had one other idea for our preparations, and I need to see if we can strip a few things from the ships to do it. Might have to borrow a few shellbacks to carry it out. Not as good as marines, mind you, but we all have to make sacrifices, don't we?" Pennywhistle flashed a droll smile and was gone.

On *HMS Active*, a contrite Marine Second Lieutenant Peter Spottswood faced a stern Captain Gordon.

"Lieutenant, I am sure I do not have to tell you I am most displeased by your indisposition last night when Captain Pennywhistle set out. You would certainly not be the first officer to overindulge, but really, sir, before a major operation, it is absolutely unconscionable. What have you to say for yourself?"

Spottswood's eyes were bloodshot and of a piece with the colour of his hair. He fidgeted with his gorget, a small crescent-shaped piece of gold finery emblazoned with the arms of King George. It hung from a black ribbon tied around his neck and its presence on his chest proclaimed he was a King's Officer, enjoying all of the honour and obligations thereof. It was twisted askew, and he straightened it in an effort to bring some sort of dignity to this formal summons. He tightened the crimson sash around his waist as well. He was in the last gasp of a major hangover, but he drew himself erect and came to parade ground perfect attention. At five foot nine, he was above average height, but seemed short before Captain Gordon's lofty frame.

Spottswood spoke without hesitation, the chagrin plain in his voice. "Captain, I offer no excuse for my behaviour. It was reprehensible. I let you down, sir, and for that I am truly sorry. I know Captain Pennywhistle was disappointed, and I will never forget the look of disgust on his face when he realized I was too befuddled to go. He could have dragged me, but he said my presence would actually endanger the expedition. Endanger it! That hurt, sir, but he was right. Captain, I came to fight, and I beg leave to have a chance to prove it."

Spottswood's honesty impressed Gordon and he replied in a voice of calm encouragement. "Lieutenant, you come from a proud family and I am sure that anything you have done to blot your family's escutcheon causes you the most exquisite pain. Captain Pennywhistle speaks highly of you. You are as smart as an Oxford don and a thoroughly ingenious fellow. Your alert presence this evening is mandatory. As soon as we have established the proper fall of shot, I want you to assume command of Lieutenant Meers' Division, as he is ashore with Captain Pennywhistle. I know you are familiar with the cannon drill and the men like you. At the very least, you will have a chance to see how you stand fire. This will be your first action, sir, will it not?"

"It will indeed, sir. And I signed up to fight, not be some bandbox marine on the Plymouth parade ground. I know I am sometimes over-fond of drink, sir, but I promise you, last night has greatly stiffened my resolve to be more abstemious. I want to earn the reputation of which, at least until last night, Captain Pennywhistle thought me capable."

"We all stumble sometimes, Lieutenant," said Gordon. "Lord knows, when I started as a midshipman, I caused the officers plenty of hair pulling and consternation. But we learn from our mistakes and we become better gentlemen and better officers. A man who makes no mistakes is a man who takes no chances, and who never advances in life. He is like a horse perpetually confined to the starting gate.

I feel confident you have learned from your transgression and will demonstrate that this evening. At any rate, I suggest you repair to the wardroom and snatch some supper. Battle is hard on the body. You will need all the vigor you can summon, and you need a full stomach for that. You never know, this could be your last supper!"

Spottswood looked queasy and Captain Gordon laughed. "Come, come, young sir, I meant it as a jest! I have a feeling about you! I think many honours and glories lie ahead in a long future."

Spottswood managed a wan smile. "I hope so, sir. I am here to do my duty and am eager for battle, not a pleasure cruise."

Captain Gordon nodded. "I believe your wish is about to be granted."

Ten

Three miles distant from the city gates, Sergeant Dale's scouts convened by a small copse of olive trees. The men sat informally, but the air around them was charged with the electricity of incipient battle. With Mercury by his side, Dale addressed them.

"If I understand your reports, the only body of French troops with which we have to contend is the one directly to our front, on the Tranazo Road."

Private Larkin responded, "Just so, Sergeant. They don't look to have put out a proper line of piquets. I heerd all this stuff about them voltigeurs bein' so tough and fierce, but I ain't seen no evidence that any of them is. The Frenchies look like lazy field hands, like they was goin' on some kind of Sunday apple-pickin' or May Day party."

Hawk-nosed Private Parker, the best at drill of all of Active's marines, chimed in, "They don't march very well, Sergeant. They don't seem to be able to maintain a proper cadence, and I noticed men are dropping out of the ranks all the time, to drink or just rest. I saw what looked like a whole squad leave the line to loot a pear tree."

Whelen, a pleasantly cynical Irishman, added his view. "I noticed a big gap has opened in the column between the main body and its rear. There's lots of straggling."

Dale said, "I agree with all of you. Captain Pennywhistle is using all of his cunning to shore up the city defenses and we need to give him time to do that. We can't stop the French, but we certainly can annoy and bedevil them. We can be a persistent swarm of bees, buzzing about the column, stinging, retreating, and vanishing. Each time they have to stop to swat at us, it deranges their discipline and buys the Captain more time."

Parker spoke again. "Sergeant, this might be a good occasion to use some of the Shorncliffe procedures that the Captain has spent so much time in drilling into us."

The world's most advanced light infantry tactics had been developed at Shorncliffe Camp. Marksmanship, use of cover, and attention to minute detail were stressed. Unit and personal pride, self-discipline, and individual initiative were emphasized to develop already good characters, with the result that flogging was virtully unnecessary.

Pennywhistle had gone through the training under the eagle eye of Lieutenant Colonel Kenneth MacKenzie, who pioneered the program with Colonel Coote Manningham. MacKenzie, like Captain Gordon, was a shirt-tail relative of Pennywhistle on his mother's side. Pennywhistle was an Englishman, but his mother had been a Scot, the former Patience Murray.

This was an era where family connections counted for much. This was especially true for Scots, who were a distinct, conspicuous, and illustrious minority in the British military service. Many English found Scottish speech, manners, and customs strange, particularly Highlanders, who seemed little better than recently civilized barbarians. But no one doubted their valour.

The Scots also had long memories where family was concerned. The head of one particular family, John Campbell, fifth Duke of Argyll, had not forgotten that his dissolute grandson and heir had died in a duel with Pennywhistle; the Duke had determined that if his seed was to be swept from the Earth, the man responsible should forfeit his own life. Of a vindictive nature, the Duke had the power, money, and reach to exert his will.

Pennywhistle had fled Edinburgh University one step ahead of an angry band of Argyll's retainers, hell bent on his demise. His brother had hastily secured him a marine commission, rather than purchasing one in the army, for the simple reason that while Argyll wielded plenty of influence at Horse Guards, he had virtually none in the Sea Service. Once commissioned, Pennywhistle had been immediately packed off to Shornecliffe Camp because Kenneth MacKenzie was a family friend and could watch over him. All of the men participating had been thoroughly vetted, and it was unlikely Argyll could plant an assassin.

All of the marines perceived that Pennywhistle was a vigilant officer; they never guessed it was partly because of two attempts on his life, courtesy of Argyll's hirelings.

Dale alone knew the truth. His timely intervention had once saved Pennywhistle's life. Pennywhistle had been attacked one evening in Portsmouth by some of Argyll's men disguised as a press gang. Dale was returning from leave, saw something terribly wrong, and pitched in for no other reason than he "could not resist a good scrape." It formed a bond between the two men that the other marines knew existed but could never quite puzzle out. Dale always kept a weathered eye on the captain lest any more attempts on his life materialize.

"Good point, Private Parker," said Dale. "These French have no initiative; we need to use ours. I admit I have sometimes thought the captain a bit obsessed with Shorncliffe, but I allow the procedures have paid handsome benefits. I will use the Baker on the officers; distance will be my advantage. You marines will have to get close in. Fight in pairs, operate as a team, cover each other. Discharge and dash, discharge and dash! You remember how Captain Pennywhistle made us repeat that over and over. Today, that will be our motto.

"I know you tire of hearing it, but there is no such thing as too much preparation. Fire from cover. Don't get pinned down. Keep shifting constantly. Don't let them get a read on your position. Bees are hard to swat because they are small and move fast. Let's work not on the head of the column, but on the rear. The stragglers already want to leave the column; let's make it easier for them. Nothing unnerves soldiers more than to see men drop, not in front of them or beside them, but behind them."

Several of the marines nodded their heads in agreement with this statement.

"We open fire in twenty minutes. Seven pair on the left, seven on the right. Keep low. Watch the column, and when you hear the crack of my Baker and see an officer fall, it will be the signal to commence fire. Try to fire at least five rounds, but be safe. If it gets too hot, make for the city as fast as you can. Above all, stay alive!"

The marines rose, paired up, touched their hats in salute to Dale, and headed off in two directions. Parker and Larkin were both superstituous and regarded Mercury as a good luck talisman. They gave his head a quick pat before moving off.

Dale carefully cleared his rifle's touch-hole, swept out the pan, and inserted a new flint. He methodically wormed and cleaned the piece of fouling and applied a fine sheen of gun oil to the barrel and the lock-plate. Dale believed the way an NCO cared for his weapon was exactly similar to the way he cared for the men under his command. Both required constant maintenance and supervision, but the reward was exceptional performance in battle. His Baker was ready, and so were his men.

The slack French column of the disspirited marched listlessly, heedless of the storm that was gathering.

*****

The *Hermes*, shallowest draft of the French merchant vessels in harbour, taken as prize, began her journey towards the harbour's mouth. The diligent Lieutenant Donat O'Brien conned her carefully and conversed with a harbour pilot who spoke pidgin English. *Hermes* had every ounce of canvas set, as the wind was light and variable. She was making barely two knots, but was moving steadily out of the harbour into the main ship channel. Two other ships, the *Bon Amis* and the *Celeste* followed in close succession, the *Hermes* serving as pathfinder.

"Lieutenant, you need to alter course three points to starboard. This part is very tricky; the current shifts the sand daily." The hired pilot spoke with an authority he did not quite feel.

"Very well, Senor Beltrami. Quartermaster, starboard three points." O'Brien mistrusted the pilot, but had little choice and so followed his instructions.

"Aye, aye, sir. Making it so!" said the quartermaster.

The bow of the ship tacked sluggishly toward the northern shore of the channel.

Hermes was on her new course, a fourth of the way down the mile-long channel, when a large, leisurely hand reached up from the bottom and wrapped its sandy fingers around her hull. There was a sudden lurch, and a soft shuddering of timber. The sails flapped impotently and a large crack wound its way up the foremast. The ship was utterly frozen, as if by the breath of Boreas himself. All forward motion was arrested. She was well and truly aground.

Close astern, the *Bon Amis* and *Celeste* desperately tried to avert a collision. Both scrambled frantically to back sails in an attempt to heave-to, but only the *Celeste* was fast enough. In spite of her best efforts, the *Bon Amis* continued a slow and wobbly course toward the *Hermes*. The jib-boom of the *Bon Amis* glided across the stern quarter of the *Hermes*, slamming into her with the nasty sound of splintering wood. The two ships became locked fast in an embrace that completely blocked the channel.

Slaughter saw the whole thing with horror through his spyglass. He wondered how badly grounded the *Hermes* was. He would have to warp her off using kedge anchors. He would also dump overboard anything not absolutely essential and hope the lightened hull would float free. It would take time, a commodity that was in very short supply.

There was even a possibility too horrible to contemplate. He might not be able to float the *Hermes* free. She might block the channel for days. They would have to burn the whole lot and withdraw to the squadron in their boats. All the expedition's prize money would literally go up in smoke.

"Damn and blast!" muttered Slaughter under his breath.

Seaman Carstairs heard. "Sir?"

Slaughter came back to himself with a start. "Damn it, we don't have much time. Don't spend it loitering about. We need to get some boats organized! Now!"

*****

In twenty minutes, Dale's marines were in position, concealed in an arc around the rear of the slowly moving column. Despite the shouts of the officers, straggling had increased and the column had slowed from the normal march pace of two miles an hour to something closer to one.

Dale squatted behind a low boulder and braced his piece against it. Mercury lay patiently next to him, his ears back and alert. His canine expression indicated he sensed the melancholy mood of the column on a fundamental level.

Dale estimated the range to the shambling column at one hundred and fifty yards. There was very little wind. He adjusted the rear sight. His poacher's training served him well. He'd found a dispirited animal begging to be culled from the herd: a lonely officer, a captain; probably not more than twenty-five, with long sideburns. His uniform looked snappy and spotless, yet he trailed his sword carelessly, dejectedly shuffling along. He made no efforts to hector the badly straggling men back into line.

Dale lined up his shot, led the officer, and fired. There was a puff of smoke and a second later the well-dressed captain stopped in midstride, a puzzled expression on his face, and then collapsed like a cheap accordion. The men continued forward for several paces, the realization not yet having reached their stagnant minds that death had made an intrusion into their ranks. Then there were murmurs, heads turned and looked at the corpse, and the dull collective consciousness of the group started to appreciate that perhaps the captain had not collapsed out of fatigue or inebriation, the two primary causes of problems that day thus far.

Corporal Leroy trudged over to investigate. He looked down at the handsome face of the captain, the brown eyes now devoid of sensibility. "Horreur, cet homme est mort!" he exclaimed. The corporal saw the ragged hole just above the officer's gorget. He shouted to a bearded sergeant of sappers hurrying toward him, the only one who seemed energized with concern.

"*Qui diable a fait cela? Serait-ce des brigands?*" the sergeant demanded.

Corporal Leroy was a broken-down old sot, but he had seen duty in plenty of theatres and knew that such a wound did not come from brigands. They tended to be like pack animals, courageous only in numbers, fleeing when any large organized body of soldiery was in the area. They were just brutish peasants after all, with no real training. Their weapons were crude, their aim abysmal. Whoever fired this shot was good; really good. The corporal looked closer. The bullet hole was smaller than a musket. *Quelle surprise!* A Baker Rifle! The British!

As if to confirm Leroy's mental calculations, a group of shots rang out. They could not really be called a volley, as they were not simultaneous. Soldiers fell here and there in the column, and adrenaline finally started to flow through wine-rich veins. Even the dullest saw men die and realized the unimaginable was happening. They were under fire! One recruit but twenty days in the army looked in vain for the source of the bullets. Finding none, he threw down his weapon, hurled himself to the ground, and curled up in a fetal position. He shook and sobbed like an infant.

Another group of shots peppered the column. A tall private toppled, pierced through the heart; a short private clutched his stomach and doubled over; and a porcine private collapsed as a ball penetrated his femur.

Callow second lieutenant Garnier shouted desperately to restore order. This was his first assignment, and the twenty-two-year-old from Tours desperately wanted to do the right thing. He issued commands for the column to halt and endeavoured to form a line. *"Arrêtez immédiatement! Préparez-vous à former la ligne et livrez une volée."*

The poorly trained men shuffled clumsily; changing from a column into a line was something they had only done a few times on the parade ground, and even then they'd done it badly. Under fire and stress, men bumped, tripped, jostled, and moved in ways that were at complete cross-purposes with good military evolutions. Another ad hoc volley killed a few more soldiers.

Whelen and Stratton, operating as a team on the right, nodded to each other in satisfaction. Both were combative Irishmen who loved a good fight nearly as much as a good drink. Frenchmen who had not seen battle before were finding that death, when it called, was not neat and picturesque as politicians and artists would have men believe. It was bloody, repulsive, ragged, and sometimes agonizingly, excruciatingly slow. The *"dulce et decorum est pro patria mori"* stuff was absolute claptrap.

One young soldier, a painfully thin lad of not more than seventeen, rolled and shrieked on the ground in agony, bathed in black blood and begging for someone to shoot him. His messmate next to him shook his head in sadness. He had heard from his father, an old soldier, that black blood signified the liver had been fatally damaged. It was just a matter of time for his friend.

MacLeod's musket ball ripped away a fusilier's lower jaw. He was still upright and his mates started at him in absolute horror. Not surprising, since the hanging shards of gore in place of his lower mandible made him look like a ghoul on a dark All Hallow's Eve. He had been a perfectly proportioned physical specimen with a classic square-jawed face. The ladies in his village back in Normandy had once proclaimed him the handsomest male resident.

MacLeod saw with repulsion the results of his shot, but his pity did not prevent him from reloading quickly and lining up his next victim.

Second lieutenant Garnier continued to shout frantically. The men's fear was palpable now and it spread like wildfire. Even he, an officer of the Emperor, was not immune from its siren call. He hit soldiers with the flat of his sword and shouted. *"Mes hommes, ne courrez plus. Ralliez-vous derrière moi! Formez une ligne, Formez une ligne. N'oubliez pas honneur et regiment."*

The young lieutenant impressed Dale. A brave man and a fire-eater. Rather a pity, but of course he would have to go. Dale sighted his piece on the man's chest.

"Regroupez-vous autour de moi! Nous pouvons encore gagner ce combat!" Garnier's words died in his throat as the bullet smashed through his chest.

Lieutenant Garnier's death was a tipping point for the troops. The end of the column did not break into a run; it melted away, as small groups of men simply exited the road: one group, then another and another. Each group was larger than the last. They did not see themselves as deserters, merely sensible men doing the sensible thing in a nonsensical situation. They'd had enough.

"Je me fous de ça! Je ne vais pas rester ici pour être massacré!" Exclaimed one panicked corporal as he and his three mates fled the road and lay down behind a small pear tree. They had no plan and no direction, they only knew they did not want to remain on the road, naked to gunfire coming from God knew where.

LeMere led from the front, and so was late realizing what had happened behind him. Even at the run, he was too late to arrest the confusion and dissolution of the column. The column's rear and middle had disintegrated, like grains of sand blown away by a strong wind. He grabbed a bewildered old sergeant by the lapels and tried to shake some consciousness of duty into him. "Get those men back into line. Immediately! That damn fool, Gaspar! I told him we needed a line of piquets!"

Gaspar shook his head. He couldn't believe it. The British really were out there!

*****

Pennywhistle mounted the platform atop the city gate and plainly heard gunfire, as did his men. They had worked feverishly to get the nettings and fortifications ready, and their preparations were nearly complete. He heard desultory rifle reports, followed in quick succession by musket fire, and knew exactly what it signified. He smiled.

Good. It would take a while to reform broken troops. Dale had handed him a little more time. The rest of the day's work depended on it.

Eleven

Slaughter watched with mounting tension as sailors, swinging axes, severed the jib-boom of *Bon Amis* and floated her free. It would take a while to jury-rig a new jib-boom, but carpenter's mates were hard at work at the task. The ship she had been accidentally mated to, *Hermes*, was another matter entirely.

O'Brien had backed all sail the moment *Hermes* hit the sand bank, in a frantic effort to stop her driving deeply into it, but she was still stuck fast. Everything that could be jettisoned to lighten her had been tossed overboard or removed, but it was unavailing. Kedging was the only way to float her free. O'Brien knew the consequences of failing to do so, and they drove him to push his men hard.

Four boats stood by, roped together in pairs. The first pair would tow the second, which carried the kedge anchor between them, an unwieldy piece of iron weighing well over a thousand pounds. The kedge anchor was attached to a messenger cable rove through a hawse hole and connected to the *Hermes'* capstan. The ship's drum-shaped capstan would be turned by men pushing its protruding pawls in a twisting, circular fashion. As the ship was pulled toward the anchor, it would be lifted off the sandbank. The capstan certainly multiplied manpower, but it was grueling hard work. Everyone on board knew the urgency of the situation, however, so there was no shortage of volunteers. It was not only about survival, but blessed prize money.

A few French sailors were not too gently persuaded to assist as well. This was a task that called for brute force and no seamanship whatsoever.

Boatswain's Mate John Cameron, leadsman in one of the boats, sounded the depth as one and three quarter fathoms, about ten feet. He had long ago worked salvage jobs off the Godwin Sands and this reminded him a bit of that. *Hermes* drew nine, so if she could be refloated, she should clear the harbour. Maximum depth of the channel at high tide was thirteen feet, but that was several hours away. The largest two ships of nine hundred tons would require all of that.

O'Brien leaned forward in the larboard boat of the second pair. He judged the distance as three hundred yards from the *Hermes'* bow. The sailors looked at him expectantly. He nodded quickly. "Let go and pay out."

The sailors on both boats gave a mighty heave and the anchor dropped heavily into the water. The men in the first pair of boats pulled on the sweeps, or oars, in order to cause the flukes of the anchor to bite horizontally into the bottom of the channel, so as to afford maximum purchase. Less than a minute later, the cable pulled taut. The anchor was secure.

O'Brien barked through his speaking trumpet to the men at the capstan. "Fleet the messenger! Heave!"

With grimaces, grunts, and expostulations, the men began to push, and, almost imperceptibly, the capstan began to turn. *Clank, clank, clank;* the noise was like chains being drawn across an iron grate. The messenger cable drew round the capstan, ever so slowly.

Nothing happened. The minutes dragged slowly by; *clank, clank, clank,* the only monotonous sound. The men in the boats grew anxious and perspiration beaded on the backs of the thirty sailors pushing the ten bars. Slaughter watched the process through his spyglass with a rising sense of alarm. They had to clear the channel!

"Come on, you lubbers, put your backs into it!" Boatswain's Mate Steven Cameron jeered. He was John's identical twin brother. Unlike his gentle-spirited sibling, he was a pusher and a driver. He believed that what you didn't get by challenging men, you would not get by mercy. The men on the capstan shot him baleful looks.

Clank, clank, clank echoed off into the torrid afternoon sky, but this time, the individual sounds were closer together: the capstan was turning faster. Less resistance; something was happening.

Then there was a noise. Not much, just hint of a grumble. *EEEEEEERRRRRRRRRRRR!* Ears twitched and strained on the boats and the ship.

Then it grew louder, a definite creaking noise that shifted to something like a low moan. *CROOOOOOOOHHHH!*

There was absolute silence among the sailors. Then they heard a very loud groaning noise, like timbers in pain. AHHHHHHHHHHHHHH! It was not much, but the bow of *Hermes* started to move. Half a foot, three quarters of a foot, an entire foot.

"Huzzah, Huzzah, Huzzah!" The men in the boats cheered to chase the tension away.

Now the *Hermes* was making slow, but noticeable, progress.

"Come on, come on, she is almost there, just a few more heaves," Cameron exhorted.

There was a loud crack, then a startling *Boom*! *Hermes* burst free of the bar and slid into the channel.

"Surge the messenger!" shouted Cameron. Seamen stopped pushing on the capstan bars.

O'Brien burst into a spontaneous grin, matching those of his men. He pounded a fist into the flat of his hand in triumph. He had been a prisoner-of-war in Verdun for three years, and after two failed escapes had finally succeeded on the third try. He was eager to make up for lost time, both in glory and prize money, and was delighted Commodore Hoste had sent him on this expedition. The prospect of losing his first command would have been a horrid trick of fate.

Frowning, he directed the men to weigh the kedge anchor and return to the *Hermes* directly. Her hull might have taken damage in the grounding. The question was, how bad? If she sank, that was worse than grounding. She had pumps, of course. If the pumps could stay ahead of any leaks, she would make it. Minor damage might be handled with frothering, stretching a tarred, greased sail externally over the ruptured planking. The flow of the water against her hull would force the heavy canvas taut over any gaps and serve as temporary plugs. If they could get her out to sea, the combined efforts of the squadron's carpenters could probably have her ready to sail for a prize port in a matter of days.

The inspection would have to be quick and cursory, O'Brien's assessment swift and accurate. *Hermes* was still athwart the main channel and that had to change. Fast.

*****

Dale was delivering his usual authoritative and detailed report. Mercury managed to cage a few well-deserved pets from Pennywhistle, as well as a treat, during the narrative. The rest of the marines took up positions along the new fortifications.

Pennywhistle was pleased at the way his improvised fortifications were shaping up. The marines had discovered some crutch-shaped iron stanchions in a nearby storehouse, which looked to be horse-holds—posts around which to wrap a bridle. They were about four feet high and had solid iron points on the bottom, to be driven securely into almost any kind of soil. They were the perfect complement for the netting Pennywhistle had brought.

The cannon embrasures were already complete and the cannon muzzles completely hidden from view. Marines then used bits of brush and vine to overlay the nettings. At a distance, the cannon looked like two unimportant humps, probably just some orphan boulders. The two "humps" could be unmasked in seconds to reveal two very lethal pieces of ordinance.

The marines started to do with the main line what they had done for the cannons. Twin lines of netting were unfurled and bound to the twin lines of stanchions. The line stretched from the end of the palisade to the edge of the cannon embrasure. Pennywhistle had required every marine to learn the basic sailor's knots. It had occasioned much grumbling, but now it came in very handy.

Once they got all of the netting in place, spare hammocks cannibalized from the convoy ships filled in the gaps between the two lines of netting. They would provide good protection against musketry. Along with the bits of loose stone and brick, they would also provide anchors for the lines of boarding pikes that would be inserted at ninety degrees, just below the top of the fortifications.

A stockpile of stinkpots stood ready at the rear of the fire step. In a traditional, open field fight, they might be of marginal value, but in a confused clash in narrow streets, their shock and surprise value would be considerable.

The Potsdam muskets from the merchant ships had been uncrated and distributed. Each marine would have two of them, in addition to his regulation Sea Service Brown Bess. The extra muskets would give them a welcome boost in fire power and might serve to keep the enemy in the dark about their true numbers. As long as they saw little flashes of red, they'd attribute greater numbers to their unseen foes.

Pennywhistle had come up with an added refinement. He had each marine fashion a stick to hold up his plumed round hat just above the level of the palisade. If they had to pull back fast, a line of hats might convince the enemy his marines were still in place. It was not much, but it might buy some time.

He had read most of the recognized authorities on war, from Caesar to De Saxe to Frederick the Great, but it all distilled down to a simple idea in his mind. Trick the enemy into believing the illusions you broadcast and let his plans proceed from a host of false assumptions. War was not about what really existed, it was about what one side or the other thought existed. Objective reality mattered little; perceived reality was everything.

He had a great regard for keeping some measure of honour in warfare, but he considered a so-called fair fight—simple brute force against simple brute force—as stupid and wasteful. It was much better to use the mind to create some *ruse de guerre* and secure advantage before the battle was even joined. Superiority of force at point of contract had long been recognized as a key to victory, but Pennywhistle believed superiority of mind at point of contact was a much better guarantor of success.

Convince your opponent that you were much stronger, or more dangerous, or had the moral ascendancy and had seized the key moment in a decisive way, and the day was yours. Concealment behind fortifications, hidden firepower, hats on sticks, and arcane chemical confectionary were today's manifestations of centuries of strategic insight; deception used to alter perception.

He permitted himself a momentary mental smile at the expense of his mother's memory. She had constantly berated him as too much the dreamer, too much the impractical visionary. "You obsess over the silliest things!" she would often say. She never understood the compelling curiosity that drove him to read everything he could find about a subject that excited his imagination. She could not understand that imagination was a gift, not a curse, and the first quality necessary for an accomplished mind. Imagination demanded constant feeding, but it came in very handy in battle.

*****

"*Putain!*" Captain LeMere rarely swore, but he was livid with anger. An hour and a half had been squandered in rounding up the French fugitives after Dale's smartly executed spoiling attack. It had taken threats, shaming, patriotic appeals, beatings with the flats of officer's swords, and swinging halberds from the sergeants to whip the men back into something vaguely resembling order. The men were surly and disputatious, but at least they were back in line.

They marched faster than before, angry and eager to come to grips with the foe that had hurt them. They were now only a mile and a half from the city.

"I warned you, Gaspar, to put out scouts and flank guards. I told you the British would not stand idly by as we advanced. This was designed to slow us down and give them more time to perfect their own defenses in the city. I have been observing the city gate for the last quarter hour with my glass, and there is a hotbed of activity. They mean to mount a determined and spirited defense. I expected no less. I do not know the name of the British commander, but it would be a capital mistake to underestimate him, as we have both done thus far." LeMere spoke with the vehemence of an unheeded prophet.

"LeMere, much as it pains me to concede that a headquarters' *élève's* speculations have any merit, your guess that the British aim to hold the city long enough to seize the convoy looks to be correct. We shall have to be more vigilant. I think we must hold a council of war to determine further action." Gaspar, faced with a legitimate command decision, wanted to spread the blame if something should go wrong.

LeMere almost allowed a look of disgust to seize control of his face, but his sense of tact asserted itself and his countenance turned blandly reasonable. "Let us put past differences aside, Gaspar, in the interests of redeeming what has become a bad situation. We may not agree on methods, but surely we both want to do honour to French arms. The British attack should never have had the effect it did, but it says much about our morale and training methods. That so many could be stampeded by so few is disgraceful. That it took so little to shatter the men's spirits is truly alarming, yet those spirits may yet be restored. They have seen their comrades perish and their friends grievously wounded; they hunger, no, they lust, for revenge. They were assailed by shadows, by invisible harpies at whom they could not strike back. I know they long for a fight where they can see their opponents and deal out the sort of battlefield retribution which has made French arms renowned throughout Europe. These are not bad men, merely bewildered men, who, properly led, will strive to fight as heroes.

"I would suggest, however, we dispense with a council of war. It would consume too much time. Each passing minute gifts the British with more time to perfect their defenses. The more we delay, the tougher will be our task. I would suggest a full-scale assault at the earliest possible instant. I would urge a flanking movement of some sort. Pin the enemy in front, then take him from the rear. Might I advise that the two of us move forward with our glasses and make a personal reconnoiter? With our combined experience, I feel certain we can quickly devise a condign and successful plan of attack."

"I confess amazement, LeMere, at how quickly you can switch from honey-tongued salon habitué to a plain-spoken infantry officer.

But perhaps that is how you charmed your way among the Paris military cognoscenti to early promotion. Again, it pains me to admit it, but that is a very sensible idea. Although I trust you will defer both to my rank and to my longer experience." Gaspar hated the idea of giving any credit to LeMere, but felt he had to yield to the inevitable.

"Of course, Gaspar. As always, I am not about my personal glory, but only the glory of France."

Gaspar winced inwardly when LeMere spoke. He simply could not get beyond his own cynicism and believe that a man might fight—actually fight—for unadorned patriotism rather than personal gain.

*****

On the archer's platform atop the city gate, Pennywhistle surveyed the French lines with his spyglass and began to assemble a mental précis of the French situation and intentions. He reckoned they had at least four hundred effectives. Then he recalculated, as he realized they'd probably picked up strays who'd escaped the morning debacle. So, make it five hundred, give or take. They would probably deploy voltigeurs in skirmish order to screen the main advance. Because of the marshy nature of the terrain and the narrow tidal creek, the main assault would have to come directly over the stone bridge, which lay one hundred yards in front of the main gate. At fifteen feet wide, it would limit the size of the column's front.

The gate would have to be held at all costs. As long as the French behaved with the gallant ineptitude he had observed thus far, he was confident his Fabian tactics would succeed.

Pennywhistle shifted the glass and scanned his own defenses. He had stripped all of the landing forces of every marine for this battle. He had sixty marines stationed at the main gate barricade and fire step. He had five on the archer's platform above. Ten crewed the cannons and ten more crouched behind the nettings to give them covering fire. Counting himself and Dale, he had eighty-five men against five hundred. Bad odds, but not dissimilar to the ones he had faced at the start of the day. He'd prevailed then and he felt he would do so now.

Pennywhistle decided his best command position would be on the archer's platform above the gate, armed with spyglass and speaking trumpet. Dale wanted to be at his side, but he needed Dale to be in direct command of the troops at the barricade so he could maintain a more expanded view as the battle developed. When the battle was well underway, he would employ his Ferguson against the officers.

He remembered that Bonaparte had once said that the best laid battle plans were as evanescent as rainbows and dissolved utterly under the first salvos of gunfire. That had been his experience as well and he knew that, in the ear-shattering din of battle, his speaking trumpet would be difficult to hear. He trusted his men to use their initiative.

Private Barnes bounded up the stairs. His face was flustered, his manner breathless. A good fighter, he was prone to exaggeration, and now he started to babble. Pennywhistle told him to take a deep breath and start over again, slowly this time.

"Captain, Private Maxwell sends his respects, and," he hesitated briefly, "well, sir, we've got trouble. A load of Frenchies in one of the houses started taking shots at the men making the stinkpots. Killed one of them, and shut down our little factory. Maxwell isn't sure how many there are and wants to clean out the hornet's nest, but he doesn't have much experience in house-to-house fighting and knows you do."

Damn and blast! Who the blazes were those people? It came to him. Probably some stray troopers trapped in the city who had decided to cause trouble when easy targets presented themselves. He could hardly fault soldiers for doing their duty, but it was one more vexing problem with which to be dealt. He could not suffer an armed castle along his line of retreat.

Barnes watched him closely, but Pennywhistle kept his face impassive. He had only cleared a house of armed men once in his career, and it had been a very bad business. Fighting almost blind in smoky, narrow, confined spaces brought out the worst in men.

With nowhere to retreat, soldiers typically offered and expected no quarter. He could leave it to Maxwell, but quickly decided against it. Maxwell was brave enough, but not over-gifted with finesse, and the situation definitely required finesse.

Not long ago, Pennywhistle had acquired a rather strange weapon in a boarding action, and it occurred to him now that it could prove useful. From his kit he drew out a stout leather bag containing the piece and slung it over his shoulder.

"I'll come." He picked up his speaking trumpet. "Sergeant Dale, get up here on the double."

Dale complied and came to attention. He knew Pennywhistle well enough to see through the mask of composure. Something was up.

"Sarn't, a spot of bother has developed in our rear. I'm afraid I shall have to attend to it directly, so you will be in temporary command here."

Spot of bother; it must be serious. "Not a problem, sir, I know your instructions, and I will keep things ship-shape here."

"Good," said Pennywhistle tersely. "C'mon Barnes, let's move. We haven't much time before the French reach the gate. Lead the way. Walk, don't run. Calm down, Barnes. No point in alarming the men."

A few minutes later, he was in animated conversation with Maxwell, crouched low behind a row of barrels. Bullets ricocheted off the staves from time to time, serving notice that the French across the street were feeling playful.

"Started half an hour ago, Captain. I heard a couple of pops, and I saw Periwinkle fall. No warning, then I heard more bullets hitting the cobblestones and I told the men to scatter and take cover. Shots are coming from that third floor window yonder." Maxwell pointed and Pennywhistle unfurled his spyglass for a closer look.

The window was shuttered, but four holes had been smashed through the shutters. Every minute or so, muskets would flash through the holes, fire quickly, and withdraw inside. There was no way to tell how many were inside, but probably not more than eight; one group loading, one group firing. Maxwell had sensibly spread the marines out, told them to hold fire and keep down; no point in advertising their position, or wasting ammunition.

Pennywhistle was running out of time. He was Horatius holding the bridge and the Crapauds would soon be upon it. The damned bloody snipers would have to be eliminated quickly. Hit them fast and hard. Most of the homes in town were built on similar plans; probably a winding staircase to the third floor. His men would be painfully exposed and the third floor room would probably be barricaded. He would need cover, something to mask the approach. The stinkpots! Perfect. He sat back in deep thought.

Maxwell watched as the captain's eyes seemed to change to a darker green.

Finally Pennywhistle spoke. "Maxwell, I'll need you and your best man to set things up. I will clear the house with a half squad; bayonets and one grenade each. Take some of the pitch you have here and coat each grenade with it thickly so it will stick to anything." He explained the rest of his plan quickly. "Got that, Maxwell?"

"It's crystal clear, sir," said Maxwell, smiling at the ingenuity of it. His look changed to puzzlement as Pennywhistle produced an odd contrivance from a red baize bag emblazoned with a fleur-de-lis. "What the devil is that, sir?" he asked without thinking.

Pennywhistle held up a heavy, ugly pistol with one hammer and eight barrels. The barrels were splayed out like a fan, designed to cover a sixty-degree arc of fire. The butt was festooned with fifteen short iron spikes, useful for clubbing. "Ducksfoot; designed for stopping mutinies. One pull of the trigger gives a nice, smart volley. No good at distance, but marvelous at close range in cramped spaces. Might be just the thing today. Let's get things moving. We'll launch in five minutes."

It actually took six minutes to get everything ready. The Frenchmen continued their potshots, but more slowly once Scorsby and Lemon, sturdy and experienced former farmhands, opened a covering fire. Grayson and Maxwell made their dash with the stinkpots. They were prepared to kick in the ground floor door, but Grayson was a thoughtful man and had the presence of mind to check first. He smiled as the latch yielded to his touch and rose easily; the Frenchmen had neglected to bolt the door. It opened easily. The two marines carefully placed the stinkpots beneath the winding iron stair, ignited them, and ran back across the street, smug smiles on their faces.

Pennywhistle watched the minutes tick by on the Blancpain. The four marines behind him methodically sharpened their bayonets on a whetstone, oiled them carefully, and inserted fuses in their grenades. The shots from across the street ceased. Pennywhistle stowed the watch, grabbed his spyglass, and aimed it at the third floor window. Nothing; no movement, no Charlevilles either. He listened carefully. Complete silence, then the faint sound of coughing.

Excellent! He drew his sword and held the ducksfoot in his left hand. He nodded at the four marines, then pointed across the street. The five rose to their full height, double-quicked across the narrow avenue, and stopped just short of the building's threshold. Smoke poured from the entrance. They each took a deep breath, held it, and dashed in. They could hardly see a thing, but found the wrought iron staircase. They lit their grenades; slow-burning, twenty-second fuses.

Pennywhistle raced up the circular, twisting stairs, seeing little but the steps above. He held his sword ahead of him, almost willing it to slice through the cloud cover. Up and up, round and round he went, followed closely by his marines. When they reached a landing at the top, they saw a non-descript oak door. "Now!" yelled Pennywhistle. The marines dashed up to the door and solidly fixed their sticky grenades to the hinges. They darted back and quickly ducked below the last few steps. They covered their heads and held their breath.

Pennywhistle crouched, full cocked the ducksfoot, and brought it to a point.

BOOM! The sound of the grenades was deafening in the confined space, which amplified the sound. The door blew off its hinges and flew sideways, leaving the entrance wide open. Two French tirailleurs lay dead, but three others stood bunched together in the doorway, stunned and covered in soot and dust. They fired their muskets through the smoky entrance, certain the attackers would come through immediately.

Pennywhistle had banked on that. Once the muskets were discharged, he rose up slowly, coughed a bit—the stinkpots really were foul—and methodically walked toward the bewildered Frenchmen, whose tearing eyes looked as if they were seeing a ghost. At five yards, he raised the pistol and fired at the centre tirailleur's broad torso. Eight barrels flared into life with an ear-splitting bang and four rounds gutted the man's chest cavity. The Frenchmen on the right and left absorbed two rounds each and became fragments of bloody rags blown against the back wall. Two other tirailleurs grabbed for their backup weapons, but before they could point them, they were bayoneted by Greyson, and a new man with only a month's service, Adams. Everyone still alive started to cough, slowly at first, then more violently.

"C'mon!" gasped Pennywhistle, "let's get out of here." The job was done, the Frenchmen were dead, there was nothing more to see. The factory could restart.

Back on the street, Pennywhistle sucked in huge draughts of fresh air, as did the other four marines. He checked his watch. Twenty minutes gone. He had to get back to the gate.

"Maxwell, take over. Marines, well done!" He smiled confidently, turned on his heel, and began a brisk walk toward the gate and another fight.

Dust clouds swirled skyward from the French lines as Garpar's men moved ever closer to Groa. Along the British lines, a gleaming horitzontal line of steel-headed pikes smiled brightly from the British fortifications and awaited the opportunity to give the French a properly charming reception.

*****

At that moment, cheers erupted along the quay. Lieutenant Slaughter cheered loudest. *Hermes*, after all of her tribulations, finally cleared the harbour and proudly stood out to sea. *Bon Amis* and *Celeste* moved purposefully toward the harbour bar and prepared to follow. Three more prizes, *Ville de Paris, Ville de Tours*, and *Belle Marie* entered the main channel. The object of the expedition was about to be accomplished. It was a sublime and satisfying moment for William Slaughter.

The moment evaporated as a huge gust of wind first relieved Slaughter's head of his black *chapeau de bras* and then, a fraction of a second later, slammed him ignominiously into the sea. Snarling thunderheads of smoke morphed into a sickly, yellow-orange pall as a rotating maelstrom of spars, canvas, guns, and men erupted over the harbour. A lifetime later, a huge thunderclap of noise boomed, temporarily deafening everyone on the quay. *Josephine*, the ship carrying a hold filled with gunpowder, was no more. Something had gone terribly, terribly wrong.

Bits and pieces of flaming wood and canvas fell everywhere around the harbour. The thing sailors in wooden ships feared most, fire, made multiple unwanted appearances on numerous decks. Roofs along the quay smoldered as they were showered with sparks. The explosion instantly snuffed out the lives of the ten on board *Josephine*, while the force of the blast wave stunned and dazed most of the occupants of the other ships in the harbour. The evacuation of prize ships ground to a complete standstill.

*****

The French spotted the fiery geyser above the harbour, but it was the sheer noise of the blast, oppressive even at this distance, that compelled their complete attention.

Gaspar exclaimed, with baffled awe, *"Putain! Merde!* What was that infernal noise?"

LeMere clapped the sides of his head gently several times, to make sure his ears still functioned, then replied, "Explosion, and a very, very big one. I would say one of the ships carrying powder has just died a violent death. Gaspar, this is a stroke of luck, perhaps even an omen! I cannot believe that it was anything but an accident caused by carelessness, one that indicates the British are rushing things and are anything but invincible. They will be disorganized, they will be fighting harbour fires; they will not be able to give their entire attention to us. We must attack, immediately!"

Gaspar actually laughed. "For once, LeMere, I am in complete agreement!"

*****

The noise of the blast shook Pennywhistle's men as well, but as they were somewhat removed from the source, his men recovered more quickly than the sailors on the quay.

Dale vigorously massaged his ears with his hands. "What the bleedin' hell was that, sir? Pardon my French!"

"Trouble; our situation just got a damned sight worse. Sergeant, have the men stand-to immediately. The French will be on us very, very soon." One blasted thing after another today! He was worried.

Twelve

Captain Gordon on *Active* saw the explosion and alarm tightened his face.

"Captain, might I give the word to beat to quarters?" Dashwood's question was logical for a first officer.

"You may indeed, sir, most prudent. Mr. Dashwood, beat to quarters!"

"Very good, sir," Dashwood replied with carefully measured calmness. He was a generally phlegmatic man not given to strong emotions, but even he felt a rising sense of excitement. Still, it would be bad form to let it show.

The marine drummers began their throbbing, insistent rattling and everything changed. It was a magnificent and terrible transformation. Hundreds of feet pounded the decks in a frenzied yet ordered movement to battle positions. Eight short minutes later, ship and men fused into a living lethal entity with but one purpose: the utter destruction of the enemy. HMS *Active* was no longer a beautiful greyhound of the sea; she was a sleek and swift predator, a ship of war on the prowl.

Six miles away on shore, a similar transformation took place as French officers summoned up and stiffened their resolve to turn hundreds of individuals into a collective engine of moving destruction. LeMere was in his element and loved it. He pushed and prodded. Drummers savagely thundered the assembly.

Four hundred soldiers of the 81st Regiment formed into a column. Another hundred arrayed themselves in loose skirmish order, two hundred yards in front of the column. Officers with swords drawn moved slowly and deliberately up and down the front and at sides of the column. Sergeants walked behind the officers and used the heads of their long-necked halberds to check the column's alignment. Men put their hands on the shoulders of rankers in front of them to see if files were properly spaced. Regimental and national flags proudly sought the breeze, but it was uncertain, sporadic, and they fluttered only occasionally. The excitement was palpable as French soldiers prepared to revenge themselves upon the British for their earlier humiliation. The men stood at attention, utterly unmoving, yet the electricity of impending action raced through the formations.

The bass, steady, pounding beat of French kettle drums made the heavy, moist air ripple in waves across the coastal plain. It quickly reached the tensed ears of Pennywhistle at the city gate. From his position on the archer's platform, he closely observed the French through his spyglass and began making calculations about the forthcoming attack.

The French were roughly a mile and a half away. At their usual battle marching speed, it would take them twenty-four minutes to cover the distance to the gate. Their skirmishers, or *voltigeurs*, deployed in front of the main force, would reach the British works in eighteen minutes. Their task would be to keep up a steady nuisance fire, disrupt British morale and alignment, and divert the defenders' focus away from the main force. The barricade at the gate and lines of netting, earth, and pikes would afford the defenders plenty of protection, but there would be the temptation to fire back at their tormentors, squandering ammunition and reducing the impact of the first volley.

Individual firefights seldom produced any worthwhile result. The ability to wait patiently under orders while bullets whizzed about, to control the primal urge to immediately strike back and instead let the enemy close to lethal distance, was the truest test of military discipline. The confidence soldiers reposed in their officers to know the precise moment to strike was what differentiated an army from a mob. His men trusted him completely. They would be silent and withhold fire until the French closed to point blank range. Not many troops in the world had the nerve to do that, but the British were legendary for it. The shock of that first thunder of gunfire, after complete silence, could be paralyzing. The French had already been badly disrupted earlier and would be cautious and wary attacking the British a third time. They might be bent on revenge, but they would not have forgotten what happened earlier.

Pennywhistle wanted a triple opening volley. The Potsdam muskets were of uncertain quality, but each only needed to be fired once. Instead of reloading his Brown Bess, each man would snatch up an already loaded Potsdam, fire a shot, then grab the second and discharge another round. He wanted a relentless barrage of lead that would give the French no time to think or regroup.

The sun drooped very low on the horizon. It would be dark in an hour. Daytime attacks were difficult enough, but night attacks were pure confusion, where control was sporadic, doubtful, and friend was almost as likely to be shot as foe. As an added refinement, Pennywhistle had ordered his men to tie a white rag around their left sleeves so that they might distinguish each other from the enemy in a night contest.

The red glow in the sky from the harbour signaled an ominous wild card in play. Pennywhistle had no idea how bad the fires were, or if they would compromise the British evacuation. He had dispatched Private Addison to the quay, but Addison had not yet returned. All he could do was wait and prepare.

He dreaded the idea of a fighting retreat through narrow streets, but that remained a possibility, if the French breeched the defenses. At least the stinkpots were manned and ready. His French prisoners were, at this moment, drinking themselves silly. It was a matter of timing their release correctly so as to cause maximum consternation to the French.

Where was that damned runner he had dispatched to Slaughter? He needed to know if boats were ready and standing by to take his men off once their job was done. He had made careful, thorough preparations for evacuation, but with the harbour explosion he had no idea if those preparations were still viable. He needed information, always a critical and elusive thing. "Fog of war" was not an idle phrase.

*****

At that moment, his runner, Private Addison, was talking animatedly with a somewhat muddle-headed Lieutenant Slaughter, who was clearly suffering the after effects of the explosion.

"Yes, Private, you have conveyed to me very well Mr. Pennywhistle's concerns," Slaughter said. "Tell him nineteen ships have cleared the harbour so far, six left to go. The fires are being brought under control, but frankly, we don't have the manpower to do a thorough job. Every sailor we have is needed to man the prizes, and our French sailors don't seem to care at all if the whole harbour burns down. Three of the cutters were wrecked in the explosion and fire, so it will be a tight fit to pack the marines in the ones that remain. I have a petty officer standing by with the boats. Tell him that directly when we evacuate the harbour with the final prize, the remaining powder ship, the *Basque Rades,* will have to be detonated. We don't want to leave the French any store of gunpowder. Knowing Mr. Pennywhistle's proclivities, I assume that he will want to perform that task himself."

Addison responded, "I think I have it all, sir. I'd like to ask, sir, respectfully: how much time will you be needin', to gets all of the prizes out to sea? The cap'n will be asking me that straight away, sir."

Slaughter rubbed the forehead that was still causing him pain. "Hard to say, Private. One, maybe two hours to get this lot clear. The more time he can furnish us, the better. And, Private, when you give my compliments to Captain Pennywhistle, tell him a squadron is standing inshore, ready to provide covering fire. They will wait for his signal."

Addison, grubby and scruffy from earlier fighting, touched his hat brim quickly, in a smart salute to Slaughter. "Thankee, sir. I best be gettin' on my way. The cap'n will be wantin this information right quick."

*****

Miles away from the chaos in the harbour, twenty-year-old

Sergeant Etienne Foy of the French 81st felt proud, grandly heroic, and stood to ramrod-straight attention. He was the best soldier in his company and had recently earned a great honour. He held the pole bearing the sacred regimental eagle high and straight. He fully believed the propaganda of Napoleon about the splendour and mystical appeal of the eagle. The previous eagle-bearer had died ignominiously earlier in the afternoon when the regiment broke and ran after the baleful attention of Dale and his marines.

Foy was determined to redeem the regiment's lost honour. It was his intent to seal the forthcoming victory by planting the eagle firmly upon the enemy's works. It would be the capstone of glory to a day the regiment would never forget.

The drums began their seductive pounding and the column began an advance. He focused on the throbbing, alluring melody and put one foot after the other in the disciplined battle step that would bring the French to a smashing triumph. How strange! Death might lie just ahead, but he had never felt so alive!

Foy swelled with pride as he looked over the nine rank marching column of blue and white. Each French regiment was composed of three battalions, but the attack force Gaspar and LeMere mustered today was slightly short of a full battalion of five hundred and fifty men. The formation was a variation of the French manual of arms *colonne d'attaque par division,* a column with a front of two companies, a formation easy to maneuver and control. It occupied a front of one hundred and twenty feet, or forty-five metres, as the Metric system calculated things. Foy idly wondered why the British were unwilling to adopt a logical system of measurement that was one of the great achievements of *La Revolution.* Perhaps it was the same stubborn blindness that prevented them from seeing the greatness of the Empereur.

Perhaps it was LeMere's appealing oratory, or the provost guards he sent out, or desire for revenge or honour, but numerous stragglers had materialized from nowhere and augmented the French ranks. Foy knew that French soldiers would always rally, given the right leadership. Even though he could feel skepticism emanating from some of the strays, he was certain they would all quickly become imbued with the fine fellowship that surged through the column.

*****

As the column moved closer, Pennywhistle got a better view with his spyglass and noted the increase in French soldiery. He shook his head slowly. Not good, not good at all. French morale had not been as completely wrecked as he had hoped. Still, his plan was good, his dispositions sound, his men resolute.

He carefully surveyed his marines. They were tense, but alert and vigilant. They were also very busy. Purposeful action was the best way to deal with fear. They cleaned and oiled every weapon before loading. They loaded the Potsdam muskets with extra care, since they did not quite trust them. They inserted new flints, just to be sure; flints had a life expectancy of fifteen to thirty shots and changing them in the heat of battle was difficult. They carefully chipped the edges to make them sharp, with uniform striking surfaces. Even with new, well-shaped flints, misfires occurred an average of once out of every ten shots. They loaded cartridge boxes, filled canteens, and prepared buckets of urine.

Pennywhistle laughed to himself at the sight of the little blue buckets of urine, but these were experienced marines. In battle, muskets heated quickly and unburned powder formed a residue that constricted the effective diameter of the barrel. Standard balls became too big to fit in a fouled barrel. The best way to cool a barrel, as well as remove residue, was to piss into it. There was no time to perform a formal cleaning, and this was the time-honoured expedient. Besides, it was just as well to relive your bladder before battle.

He decided an inspection of his men was in order. It would be a useful way to burn off the nervous energy building up inside him. Not an inspection really, so much as the exchange of a few words of encouragement and confidence. A word or two of praise shared quietly and individually gave each man the idea that the outcome of the battle depended on his personal efforts. It was as simple as saying, "I know I can rely on your marksmanship, Blandon," or "You fought very well this morning, Stratton." He always addressed a man by name during such moments, rather than his rank or the impersonal "marine." It surprised him how few officers used a man's name, save when administering a reprimand. A name was a powerful thing, commanding instant attention; so much better to use it for constructive, rather than condemnatory, purposes. You got much more out of a man by recognizing his basic humanity, rather than dismissing it.

He had his men divided into sections called firings, small groups which could fire independently and in sequence so that the French would not receive even a second's respite from bullets. He began his inspection with A Firing. He knew most of the men well, but three of them, Leicester, Sheffield, and Clearwater, were recent arrivals and he made it a point to talk with each for a few minutes. It was a matter of letting the men understand that it would simply never occur to their officer not to trust them. He asked them the same question he asked every new man: Where are you from and why did you become a marine?

In many ways, the three men were typical new marines. They were all about the same height, roughly five-seven, and the oldest, Clearwater, was but twenty years of age. All came from the industrializing Midlands, two from small towns and one from a more rural area. Leicester had been a cordwainer, Sheffield a wheelwright, and Clearwater a printer's devil. Not a one was a jailbird. It annoyed Pennywhistle when civilians referred derisively to marines as Jollies, assuming that condemned men from the assizes were the primary source of recruitment.

The men's motives for joining were representative. Leicester joined for the bounty, Sheffield because of a failed romance, and Clearwater out of boredom and a thirst for adventure. All seemed eager and willing to have a good bash at the French, and that was all he really needed to know.

Once he finished talking to the men at the gate he headed out toward Private George on the left. George was the best marine artilleryman he had ever seen and the perfect fellow to be in charge of the twelve-pounders.

As he walked, a surge of pride welled up in him. Victory was never just about sheer numbers, but very much about the quality of those numbers. One trained and experienced soldier was certainly worth five green ones. He had good, solid men who would fight hard and long. He was badly outnumbered quantitatively, but in reality, the odds were even.

*****

The French continued their steady advance. Men tramped purposefully forward in a carefully measured cadence as sergeants hovered about the flanks yelling words of encouragement and correction. "Close up, close up, close up those ranks," an old, scar-faced, beetle-browed sergeant major intoned relentlessly to no one in particular. The column surged toward its bloody rendezvous with the British.

"You there, pick up the pace!" The old sergeant major bellowed at a lackluster private. "Support arms position, soldier, support arms! Don't ever let me see you drag a musket, soldier. The musket is your friend. The musket is your mistress, your lover. Treat her as such and she will always take care of you!" The private smartened his posture and and the old veteran smiled.

There was a great deal of talking as the ranks marched. A murmur of conversation hovered over the column like a storm cloud. Part wonder, part malediction, part gasconade, the noise of hundreds of voices gave the sense of a collective identity greater than the sum of its individual parts.

The dying beams of sunlight glinted brightly off of Foy's eagle and he had never felt so alive. Looking ahead at the grandly marching mass of French soldiers in bright blue and white uniforms, the voltigeurs with their distinctive green and yellow epaulettes and splendid similarly coloured helmet plumes, and harkening to the primal thunder of the drums, he felt he was finally living the purpose for which his Creator had designed him. The spectacle was exactly like what he had seen in picture books as a child. Destiny had tapped him on the shoulder and he was ready.

"Column halt!" The stentorian shout of *chef-de-bataillon* Gaspar echoed down the French formation. In a well-trained, battle-tested formation that stop would have been on the instant, but with this untried lot it took a bit longer.

Foy tensed with bubbling excitement. He knew exactly what this halt meant. The narrow bridge lay five hundred yards ahead; the city gate, six hundred. As soon as the officers made the final dispositions, they would attack.

Thirteen

Pennywhistle was observing the French forces. So, they were going to try to turn his flank. Not unanticipated; still, he had expected they would bet all on a powerful frontal assault. Enterprise and originality from the French? Unusual. Who was the inspired thinker? Early in the Wars of Revolution, their fighting methods had indeed been revolutionary, but over the years they had become *researche*. As the wars killed off the best and smartest of their soldiers, French armies increasingly relied on brute force and shock, less and less on cleverness and finesse.

The flanking movement was a problem. He was spread wafer-thin on the left. Other than the cannon crew and a few marines, his left was held with swagger and bluff. If the French got across the stream, his flank would collapse in short order and the strength of the main position would be compromised.

Pennywhistle summoned his considerable powers of concentration and ignored the ominous *ba bum, ba bum, ba bum bum bum* of the French drums, the steady *thud, thud, thud* of hundreds of feet, the bellowing of their sergeants and the ringing exhortations of the officers. Something had to be done, and fast. He motioned for a runner—it was Private Addison again. He was proving to be a zealous, reliable chap.

"Addison, get over to the left on the double. Tell them they are about to be attacked by voltigeurs. Tell them to forget firing toward the esplanade, but direct their fire to their immediate front. It will make our task at the gate more difficult, but we can still do it. If they support us instead of looking to their own safety, they will be overrun. Three shots before they go, spike the guns and retire to our position here. Got that?" His green eyes narrowed in stern inquiry.

"Aye, aye, sir. I'll get that to them right away."

Down at the harbour, *Chalmette,* under prize captain Meers, entered the main ship channel. The moon-faced lieutenant thought his first command a real beauty. *Belle Fleur,* under prize captain James Moore, followed one hundred yards astern. Moore found his first command a wallowing, leewardly sow. Both noted with delight that a good steady breeze had finally sprung up. Their passage to sea would be steady and swift. Twenty-three ships at sea now, only two left to go.

The breeze also fanned the many fires burning in the harbour. The flames danced higher and higher, hotter and hotter. The fire threatened to engulf the entire waterfront. Most of the inhabitants had fled and most of the sailors had taken ship. There was no one left to stifle the flames. A lone petty officer remained guarding the cutters. He constantly mopped his brow with a wet cloth, trying to ward off the oppressive heat. His red face looked anxious.

At sea, a cutter pulled alongside HMS *Active* and a boathook from the deck hauled it in close. Sailors scrambled up the steep entry port steps and used the manropes to steady themselves. Captain Gordon stood at the entry port, desperate for information. Master's Mate Hudson obliged him.

"Beggin' yer pardon, Captain, I gots news from Lieutenant Slaughter about the prizes. All out but two, sir; bad fire in the town. Captain Pennywhistle is holding the edge o' town, sir, but he is about to be attacked by a big French force."

Gordon looked grim. "Our lookouts saw the dust clouds and knew something was up. We have been reluctant to open fire lest we get in Captain Pennywhistle's way." His voice sounded grave, devoid of its normal buoyant optimism.

Hudson said, "Captain Pennywhistle still has one of them blue signal rockets. He says he will send it aloft if things gets real dicey. He'd be much obliged if you could drop a few balls in the direction of the rocket when he does." He was worried for Pennywhistle, as was everyone on board *Active*.

"Where is Lieutenant Slaughter now, Mr. Hudson? Is he not staying behind until everyone is clear?"

"Lieutenant Slaughter was on board one of the prizes, gettin the ship ready for sea. The last ship, is near to bein' ready, Captain."

"But surely Lieutenant Slaughter at least left a detachment to guard the boats, to make sure they were held safely to evacuate the marines? They could fall prey to either fire or the French!" Captain Gordon spoke with suspicion and a hint of anger.

"No, Captain, it was gettin' too hot on the quay, and the Lieutenant did not want to risk any extra lives. He said the men were safer aboard ship. With so many ships, he could only afford a skeleton crew on each. He is so short-handed he has even pressed some of the French sailors into service. He left one petty officer ashore to guard the boats."

"That bloody, god-damned rascal!" the captain exploded. Nobody on board could ever recollect hearing him using intemperate language, let alone cursing. They became absolutely silent.

"If he were on my quarterdeck...." Gordon left the sentence ominously unfinished.

With iron discipline, he regained his composure and spoke to his first officer in short, clipped tones. "Mr. Dashwood, my compliments to Mr. Spottswood, and get him here immediately."

Dashwood carried out the order with alacrity and more than a little alarm. This was a side of the captain he had never seen. The captain disliked stupidity, but usually corrected it with gentle admonitions. Such was his prestige on *Active,* he seldom even raised his voice.

"Lieutenant Spottswood, reporting as ordered, Captain." Spottswood was eager, champing at the bit. His slightly bloodshot eyes actually sparkled.

"Mr. Spottswood, a King's Officer has done a damn stupid thing! Maybe not cowardly, but certainly not consonant with his duty. I need for you to set things right. I told you earlier, Mr. Pennywhistle might need your help."

"Of course, Captain, I well remember and I am at your immediate service to provide it." Spottswood sensed what was coming.

"A fire is burning out of control and the boats necessary to take the marines off are in danger. Your orders are to proceed to the harbour with all possible speed, secure those boats, find Pennywhistle and his marines, and get them out of there. Sway the cutter down from the port davit and take any people you need. We will be standing by on the guns, waiting for his signal to open fire. Any way you look at it, Lieutenant, you will be in for a very hot time!" Captain Gordon fixed Spottswood with a stern look he hoped the callow lieutenant would never forget. "Don't let me down, Mr. Spottswood, the entire ship is counting on you!"

"I already let you and the ship down once, Captain. Never again. On my life and family's honour, I swear to you, I will bring him back!" He had never been more sincere in his life. After all of the times his father had called him an undependable rascal, he finally had a chance to prove he was something more. He banished any thought of failure from his mind and focused on selecting a steadfast crew.

*****

LeMere, fording the stream with his men, congratulated himself on his *coup d'oeil*, the gift of being able to survey and correctly size up the tactical significance of a piece of ground in the twinkling of an eye. The Emperor had the same talent; Gaspar certainly did not. He wondered briefly why the British commander had not done more to shore up this flank, but he reasoned it came down to harsh necessity. The British lacked numbers, the French did not. The pikes were meant to compensate for the lack of troops. They were menacing, yes, but they would merely slow the advance. Still, something nagged at him. The British commander had shown himself to be a resourceful antagonist; would he not anticipate LeMere's advance? Did he have a surprise prepared? LeMere fretted, then thrust those thoughts aside. It was morbid to worry and right now his troops needed his inspirational leadership.

"Forward, soldiers of France!" He forced a fierce smile on his face and his voice throbbed with confidence. "The day will soon be ours! We will make our fellow soldiers envious and our Emperor proud." LeMere's words were not spoken loudly, but were heard by enough soldiers to garner low murmurs of approval. Sometimes the most ridiculous and flagrantly sentimental words delivered with conviction and sincerity had amazing effects on soldiers moving into battle.

Under the bridge, the aptly named Private Chance fidgeted and reviewed the instructions Pennywhistle had made him repeat before setting out. The previous volunteer, Hawkins, had had a change of heart. Hawkins was an older man with a wife back in Portsmouth, and he'd told Pennywhistle she had no one to provide for her if he fell. Pennywhistle attached no censure to Hawkins' decision. It was not called the forlorn hope for nothing.

John Chance had no wife to worry about. He was a young, cheerfully ambitious, sturdily built former tinsmith from Cumberland who figured all of the marines were taking big risks anyway, why not take one extra and wind up with a promotion? He examined the fuses and decided they were still viable. Once lit, he would only have seconds to run. He wedged his back against the main support of the arch and took comfort in the fact that he was impossible to see unless someone investigated under the bridge. He also felt satisfaction that he would make a real difference in slowing the assault and protecting his mates.

Two hundred yards from the far end of the bridge, Gaspar made his final dispositions. He narrowed the column enough to cross the bridge. Much as he did not particularly relish leading from the front— he had long since outgrown any antiquated notions of glory—it was the only position that afforded real control. The courage in the bank of his soul ran low, but he had enough left for one grand gesture. Besides, he wanted to show that conceited upstart LeMere a thing or two about experienced leadership. He would give the command to charge at exactly the right moment. He did not trust anyone else to recognize that special second of supreme opportunity.

An older sergeant with a long scar on his left cheek, one of a handful of veterans, waited with cynical anticipation. Just another battle, just another thing to survive.

A new recruit of seventeen, with a face as fresh and hairless as a Languedoc peach, wondered what real battle would feel like.

Sergeant Foy grinned brightly and held the eagle pole with confident firmness. The troops would look to him and his standard for inspiration.

*****

Pennywhistle finished loading the Ferguson. He wondered about the enemy commander. If he led from the front, he had a very short time to live. He checked the one blue rocket he had saved. It seemed in working order. He was going to need it.

*****

Captain Joubert released himself and his two companions from their agreeably comfortable confinement at precisely the agreed upon time. Pennywhistle had provided them with a good meal and left them unguarded because he knew Joubert to be a thoroughly decent fellow who would rather suffer death than betray another gentleman's trust given in honour and mercy.

Joubert wished all of the opponents of France behaved with the honour of Englishmen. The flames from the quay alarmed him. He and his companions needed to exit the city as quickly as possible. The city gate was the logical choice. It was probably fortified, but he was sure Pennywhistle would let him and his officers pass.

On a parallel street two blocks away, Wainwright herded his contingent of French prisoners forward. Some were merry, some were sullen; others felt nothing at all. A few were steady, many stumbled, and some tried valiantly to convince others they were not drunk by a carefully measured gait. None had any idea at all where they were bound. One happily grinning Frenchman, rendered grandiloquent by drink, put his unsteady hand on Wainwright's shoulder and launched into a cavalcade of animated language of which Wainwright understood not a word, but correctly identified the sense. The Frenchman was clearly executing the Gallic version of the "let me tell you a little story…" routine, common to drunks convinced God had vouchsafed them a particularly amazing insight into the human condition.

*****

Alongside the looming *Active*, Spottswood put the mast up and hoisted a lateen sail on the cutter. The wind had picked up nicely, so oars were unnecessary. The wind came over the port quarter, the sail billowed, and the boat dashed through the waves like swift dolphin. Spottswood saw the flames in the harbour and felt the heat from them on his face. *Dear God!* The situation was worse than he'd imagined. Still, he would carry out his orders, no matter what. He owed the ship and Captain Gordon, but most of all he owed Mr. Pennywhistle. The captain had always believed in him and he desperately wanted to prove this night that his trust was not misplaced. The coxswain moved the tiller slightly to starboard and the cutter entered the ship channel into Groa.

Slaughter, on board the penultimate prize, could not wholly focus his thoughts. His head throbbed and things shifted irregularly between clarity and blur. He did not know it, but the force of the earlier explosion had left him with what physicians would have diagnosed as a moderate concussion with a subdural hematoma. He could not recall the name of the ship he was on, but he knew he had to get it to sea quickly. He recalled the necessary commands with great effort, but God, he was so sleepy! He just wanted to rest. Pennywhistle, Pennywhistle, what of Pennywhistle? Damn it, the man had boats and he was resourceful, he would figure a way out. What else did he have to do? Thoughts very slowly bubbled to the surface of his disordered mind. Oh, right, the powder ship, something needed to be done about that. Pennywhistle could handle that too.

He slowly realized a sailor was trying to talk to him. "What's that?" Slaughter responded with anger and confusion. "Yes, yes, I know, damn it!" He spoke with blunt frustration. "I will make it exceptionally simple for you, sailor. We don't have time to weigh anchor. Cut the anchor cables, shake out the courses, brace them round, and let me con this cursed ship out of here!"

*****

Active moved to final firing position, and lay hove-to. Captain Gordon communicated a rough idea of the situation to the two other ships via Popham's System of signal flags. Hoste and Whitby already had their men at action stations and awaited Gordon's signal. Gordon posted lookouts with spyglasses at every possible vantage point; they swept the shore for the appearance of the blue rocket.

*****

The first of LeMere's men emerged from the creek bed and gazed up at the fortifications in front of them. They were going to advance, but Sergeant Lefebvre, who was more cautious than enterprising, told his men, "Wait until we get direct orders from Captain LeMere."

Gaspar's troops continued the *thump, thump, thump,* of a measured advance to the bridge, twenty eight inches to the pace, three hundred feet per minute. The drums beat their insistent cadence, *ba bum, ba bum, ba bum bum bum.*

"*Vive la France! Vive la France! Viva la France!*" The shouts grew louder and deeper with each step. The first Frenchmen were just yards from the bridge. Now Foy felt the stomach flutters and dry mouth common before a first battle.

The concussive waves of hundreds of massed feet carried well in the humid air and assaulted Chance. *Ba bum, ba bum, ba bum bum bum* sounded like a malevolent dirge and echoed off the stones of the bridge. Fear suddenly gripped him and he retched violently. He cleaned himself off and, strangely, felt better. He was ready and wanted that promotion.

Dale mounted the fire step alongside Private Whelen. Mercury accompanied Dale, nostrils wide, eyes bright, and ears cocked back. Whelen was a pleasant cynic, yet he had a definite sentimental streak; he gave Mercury a quick pat on the head. The dog calmly padded down the length of the firestep, garnering strokes and smiles with every pace. Mercury might not wield a firelock, but as far as the men were concerned, he was worth more than a platoon of muskets because his nose brought them warning and his presence brought them luck. There was no talking, no murmuring, and no need to give any further commands, save the one to fire.

Pennywhistle balanced his Ferguson on the lintel. As soon as he finished the lead officer, he would put down the rifle, pick up the speaking trumpet, and give the command to fire. He mentally reviewed the hand-drawn map Slaughter had sent him. He plotted the fastest course from gate to boats with the rally places as steer points, but knew the route might have to be more circuitous if protracted fighting in the street developed.

His nerves were steady, despite the paper mouth, metallic taste on the tongue, itchy skin, and acid stomach. You never really got used to battle, never got comfortable with it. Indeed getting too acclimated, too confident, was inclined to make you slack and careless, often with fatal results. A good, stiff, bracing surge of fear kept you alert and gave you just the right edge. Fear pushed your senses into a preternatural sensitivity. It might not feel good, yet it was an extraordinary sensation.

Some felt the need to work themselves into an inner frenzy before a fight and mentally characterize opponents as subhuman devils. That made no sense. The French were neither devils nor evil, merely men who supported a political system opposed to his own. Killing the enemy was best done with a cold, measured logic. Hot-heatedness was the enemy of efficiency.

The noise swelled to a crescendo that pained his ears. *Ba bum, ba bum, ba bum, bum, bum.* "*Vive la France! Vive la France! Vive la France!*" Almost time. Steady!

Fourteen

"What are you men waiting for?" LeMere demanded imperiously. "Advance!"

"What about these pikes, sir?" asked scarecrow-thin Sergeant Lefebevre. Fifteen yellow and green plumed voltigeurs had clawed out a foothold on the embankment. A line of pikes blocked their path; they stuck out eight feet and pointed downward toward the ford. The rope and earth fortification in which they were embedded was at the top of a very slight rise of ground. The works appeared unmanned. LeMere slogged out of the creek, his once resplendent attire now rather the worse for water. Others rapidly approached on the right.

"Damn it, use your axes!" he bellowed. "Clear a path for the others! Now! Hurry! Hurry!" LeMere knew all voltigeurs carried axes as standard equipment because the regiment had no sappers. It amazed him the men had not simply used them forthwith, but had waited to be told. That's what came of poor training: initiative died!

Fifteen voltigeurs industriously hacked away the pikes and rope impediments. *Chop, chop, chop*; the pikes had almost disappeared and a path for themselves and the others was nearly clear. Their concentration and the thud of their axes masked a rustling noise a few yards away.

A small section of the fortification abruptly vanished and was replaced with the black, vicious snouts of two twelve-pounders. Some hidden instinct caused one Frenchman to glance up. His eyes widened in stark terror and he yelled, "Can—"

His cry was cut off by a loud British voice. "Fire!"

126

A huge roar and a wide jet of red flame erupted. Hundreds of musket balls sliced through the heavy air on their lethal paths. The voltigeurs closest to the cannons were the safest, since the cannon could not be depressed sufficiently to hit them, but the blasts savaged the ones behind them and killed twenty not yet out of the ford. A baleful chorus of shrieks, groans, and agonized cries erupted. One Frenchman had his face completely blown off, another lost an arm, still another, a hand. The chest-high water made things worse. Wounded men who might have crawled to safety on land succumbed to the weight of their packs and drowned. One private, at five feet two, the shortest man in his unit, was wounded in the leg, lost his balance, and dropped beneath the water. He briefly struggled for breath, then drifted slowly down to the muddy bottom.

The marines frantically reloaded the cannon.

LeMere recovered quickly from the shock and sized up the situation. The volitgeurs had to get out of the stream. It was a race between his men and the cannon. "Come on, come on. Move! Your lives depend on it!" He madly waved the troopers toward his position on the bank.

The British marines were now visible, hardly a stone's throw away. Stone's throw! An idea hit him just as British muskets opened up. *Pop, pop, pop!*

"Voltigeurs, grenades!" LeMere shouted with mad abandon. Grenades were seldom used, because they needed proximity for effective employment. Well, they certainly had proximity now. He knew most soldiers carried a few in their packs. They were small, hollow-cased iron shells filled with powder and a protruding fuse. They could use the sparks from their flintlocks to ignite the fuses. That is what LeMere hollered at his troops to do, and exactly what they did.

Jets of red-orange flame belched forth again and ten Frenchmen in the stream died a variety of horrid deaths. Canister shredded flesh the way a cheese grater flayed cheddar. The marines started to reload for a third round, but they never finished the job.

A phalanx of hissing, steaming grenades landed in the heart of the marine position. They detonated with terrific noise; iron fragments blossomed in every direction. In seconds, five marines were dead and the cannons were utterly useless. LeMere waited ten seconds and ordered a headlong charge. His soldiers responded with cheers, yells, and animal cries of victory.

The two marines covering the cannon crew fired shots at the oncoming Frenchmen, then prudently remembered orders and dashed for the main force at the gate.

Private George, the most experienced artilleryman, lingered and cursed that he had no time to spike the cannon. The full ammunition chest was another matter. Cannons were ignited by flintlocks, but a burning slowmatch was kept as a back-up firing mechanism. Before he ran, George gleefully tossed the slowmatch into the ammunition chest.

LeMere and the others dashed past the cannon, just as the chest exploded with an ear-splitting *boom!* By a providential twist of fate, LeMere was thrown clear, to rise with only a sore shoulder and a few bruises, but many of his men were not so lucky. Two were blown in half; two reduced to bloody shreds. Many others had wounds ranging from minor to lethal

Each cannon had had a wheel blown off and LeMere cursed that he could not use them against their former owners. George's impetuosity had halted the French, but only temporarily.

*****

Gaspar's assault force reached the near edge of the bridge. "Column, halt!" he thundered. He looked at the other side of the bridge. Only a few yards, but it might as well have been a world away. He turned, faced the head of the column, and dramatically drew his sword. The drums and chanting stopped. It suddenly turned deathly quiet. Every eye in the column focused on him.

He addressed the troops and put as much resonance into his voice as he could manage. "Follow me across the bridge. I will order the charge as soon as I reach the other side. If I should fall, remember, charge anyway!"

He turned back toward the hidden British, raised his sword above his head, and shouted, *"Column en avant!"*

The drums started up again. French soldiers gulped in fear and resolution and marched slowly forward. Foy squared his shoulders, thrust out his chest, and hoisted the eagle as high as it would go.

Just over one hundred yards away, Pennywhistle locked the Ferguson's sights onto Gaspar. He recognized the accoutrements of rank; it must be that used up older officer one tavern habitué had derisively mentioned. But neither his name nor reputation was of any moment. He was simply the leader. He was not a man, he was the solution to a problem of physics. Decapitate the head, eliminate the brain, and killing the enemy immediately became much easier.

The French drums thudded the advance as Gaspar led them majestically across the bridge. The *tramp, tramp, tramp,* of hundreds of feet echoed off the stones. *"Vive la France! Vive la France! Vive la France!"* Chance felt the vibrations under the bridge. The French were directly overhead. Not long now. The fuses were good and the linstock match glowed with health.

Dale adjusted the sights on his Baker. Shooting men was so much easier than poaching. Animals had to be stalked and outwitted, while men marched calmly into your sights. You just had to be patient! Since the Captain wanted the commanding officer, he searched the column to find another suitable target. He spotted the Eagle and its banner, bobbing gently up and down at the column's rear.

He knew the French put great stock in their eagles. It seemed just a cheap metal cuckoo bird to him, but he allowed that sentimental Frenchman regarded it differently. It would be a real triumph if he could capture one, but that was unlikely. If he could not capture the eagle and its standard, he certainly could kill the bearer.

*****

Spottswood's boat entered the main harbour. The town was ablaze. Two ships passed his swift moving cutter; the last two prizes. As far as the Admiralty was concerned, the mission was now a complete success. Spottswood, at this moment, didn't give a fig for what the Lords of the Admiralty thought. His sense of ethics told him it would be a complete moral disaster if he failed in his mission of rescue, and his men would have agreed had he spoken those thoughts. He raised his glass and spotted the five boats for the evacuation. They appeared in good repair; however, a quayside fire was moving closer. He and his men would have to douse that. Save for the petty officer near the boats, no living soul was present along the quay. *Where is Pennywhistle?* Spottswood's mind shouted. His actual voice calmly said, "Furl sail."

*****

Wainwright dashed up the stairs to the archer's platform, which caused Pennywhistle to glance up from the Ferguson and lose his shot at Gaspar. He responded with unusual and uncharacteristic testiness. "Damn it, Wainwright, speak up and be quick! You can see we are almost out of time. The French are upon us!"

"Sorry, Captain, but I have the prisoners a block away and I wanted to know what you want me to do with them. They aren't causing any trouble and are as docile as lambs right now. Doubt they'll be that way when their hangovers hit."

"Line them up in front of that shed over there." Pennywhistle pointed to a crumbling blacksmithy twenty yards away. "Keep them there until you hear the French coming. They have pierced our left and it won't be long before they head straight at you. When they do, release the prisoners, or, rather, stampede them. Push them, kick them, punch them if you have to, just get them to move directly at their brethren. Have them shout, *Ne tirez pas. Nous sommes des soldats Français. Nous sommes vos frères!*

Wainwright was bewildered. He was reliable, but not terribly bright and certainly no linguist. He tried to repeat the phrase. *"Nez tear-ay pass sum..."*

"No, damn it." Pennywhistle produced a pencil and wrote it on the back of his mess bill. "I wrote it the way it should sound, Wainwright. Even if you don't say it right, your prisoners will understand."

"What does it say?" Wainwright inquired.

"Don't shoot! We are French soldiers. We are your brothers," Pennywhistle replied irritably. "Have them repeat it endlessly. It should work. Now be off with you!"

He resumed his position and placed the Ferguson back on the lintel. His concentration returned. He adjusted the sights once more and drew a bead on the officer just stepping off the bridge. His officer's gorget was an excellent target.

*****

LeMere shook his head slowly to clear his vision, brushed scraps of other men's bloody flesh off his uniform, and came back to himself. The British depredations had reduced his force from one hundred to fifty, but those fifty men could discern no opposition between themselves and the British force at the barricade. It was time for a stealth attack.

Gaspar's troops tramped slowly forward and soon were three quarters of the way across the bridge. He was surprised there was no shooting. Prussians or Austrians would have fired long ago. He raised his sword higher in preparation to give the command to charge. He thought briefly of his mistress, Marie. He waited a second too long.

Pennywhistle squeezed the trigger and the figure of Gaspar abruptly stopped, as if hitting a brick wall, then silently toppled to the ground.

Dale fired a second later and the eagle of the 81st tumbled precipitously to the ground.

The column halted in stunned silence, seeing their leader fall. They waited for an order that never came.

Pennywhistle seized the speaking trumpet and yelled, "Fire!"

Fifteen

Three score and seven weapons roared as one. Five seconds later, a second deadly volley crashed out. Seemingly without a pause, a third volley thundered forth. The bloody harvest was momentarily cloaked by roiling clouds of grey-white smoke, but everyone knew it was there. At sixty yards, against thick rows of men, few shots did not find a mark. Over two hundred rounds slammed into the narrow column in under twelve seconds. Not a round went high; everyone followed Dale's advice and aimed for the kneecaps.

The French advance was now blocked by their own dead and dying. Pennywhistle yelled, "Reload, give 'em two more volleys, my lads! Smartly now!" Twenty seconds later, they fired, reloaded, fired again, and one hundred and thirty-four more balls rocketed toward the falling, bleeding, dying French. This was the kind of volley fire that ground the enemy into human rubble: fast, relentless, and point-blank.

"Reload, quick time, by the firings!" Pennywhistle yelled through his speaking trumpet. Men now fired in small groups called *firings* to maintain steady, rippling discharges. The firing began on the right flank, shifted to the left, and then to the right centre and left centre. By the time the last group had fired, the first was reloaded and ready again. As one group stepped up to the fire step to discharge their pieces, another stepped down to reload them. The sound resembled hundreds of wooden sticks being scraped across iron gratings.

The British fire devastated everything in its path. The first three volleys swept the head of the column away, as if with a giant ploughman's scythe. The second two cut down any staggering wounded survivors. In the immediate rear ranks, soldiers tried to crawl away. Wounded men who were still upright stumbled about in confusion. Officers struggled to frame a response, to move the column off the bridge into something resembling a line to return fire. The effect was to break the integrity of the column into little clumps of frightened and confused men.

The British marines maintained their rolling fire. "Pour it into 'em, boys!" Pennywhistle yelled as the fury of battle took hold. Frenchmen fell like stray pins struck down in a game of invisible skittles. Little groups of them returned a ragged and spotty fire. Most of it was aimed high and only tore the air. The British presented poor targets behind their barricade.

A few new recruits who had made it off the bridge and onto the esplanade followed the lead of an old sergeant. They fired their weapons, then flopped down on their bellies in a vain effort at concealment. They struggled to reload but had a rough time of it, having no experience reloading a five-foot musket lying prone while being shot at.

The British were protected; the French, exposed and immobile. French morale plummeted as the rippling winds of lead destroyed more and more of their number.

The rear of the French column started to back away from the bridge, uncertain and hesitant, but so slowly that the men directly on the bridge were still trapped, unable to move either backward or forward.

Private Chance made his decision. Now was the time. He lit the fuses and, for a fraction of a second, was transfixed as the hissing, undulating snakes of black sped toward the powder kegs. With eight seconds to spare, he broke into a run that would have outpaced the thoroughbreds at Epsom. Marines later said he'd run as if he were pursued by demons and, to Chance's way of thinking, they were not far wrong.

Aware of his mission, the marines spotted the running figure in the brick-red jacket and halted fire. The French continued theirs, but it was desultory, their aim thrown off by their own movements, and slowed by the need to reload.

Chance jumped onto the barricade directly upon reaching it, and his grinning mates hoisted him over the top to safety.

At that moment, the fuses reached their destinations.

Sixteen large barrels of finely corned, fast-burning gunpowder had an impressive explosive potential in a tightly confined space. Fourteen hundred and forty pounds of powder gave a low rumbling sound and the stones of the bridge commenced to vibrate, then separate. It was really very quick, but to those witnessing it, it was all in macabre slow-motion. The front of the bridge disappeared and the middle shot skyward, carrying with it a large part of the French column. Troops not borne aloft fell into the creek. Many were dead; others, alive but dazed, were unable to regain their footing and drowned. Those who had crossed the bridge looked back in bewilderment; those of the column behind the collapse made their next decision with their feet. They threw down their arms and ran.

Cries for help, water, and death rose from the French side. An older fusilier's intestines trailed out, and he begged his mates to shoot him. One now faceless young man wandered about mindlessly repeating, "*Poutain! poutain! poutain! Mon Dieu, mon Dieu, mon Dieu!*" There was no effective leadership, and French shooting now dropped to a few random shots.

Three loud *Huzzah!*s rose from the British side. Pennywhistle yelled, "We have 'em boys! Hammer 'em! Hammer 'em! Volley fire, smartly, two more rounds!" The marines did just that, shredding the remains of the column. After that, there was no French response.

Pennywhistle, however, knew it was no time to relax and savour the triumph. He trained his glass on the left and saw a French line of voltigeurs advancing quickly out of the west, the fast waning sun behind them.

He motioned for a runner. "Marine, tell Corporal Wainwright to release the prisoners. Go!" Unlike the troops who had just been crushed, the voltigeurs' purposeful advance looked to be under the control of an officer who knew his business. Pennywhistle needed it stopped, or at least held up. He turned back to assess the damage to the column. What was left was not going to be fighting any time soon, yet there was the possibility that an enterprising survivor, such as the officer with the voltigeurs, might rally troops and pursue once the gate defenses had been discovered to be vacant. He decided to be prudent. A little extra help was called for.

He put down his glass and moved the blue signal rocket into firing position. Unlike the Congreves, it was not important what flight path it followed, as it was not designed to hit anything. It would merely soar aloft, and as it was almost dark, it should be clearly visible.

Pennywhistle ignited the fuse, then raced down the stairs to the expectant marines at the barricade.

"Marines, time to go!" He spoke in classic command voice, yet was careful to keep the volume low. "Put your hats on your sticks and position them so they show above the palisade. Let them think we dare them to come at us again! Sling your weapons, then pick up two stinkpots each. Don't forget a piece of slow match. Column of fours and march for the first rally point. If we have to separate, make for the quay and the boats. With luck, it will be awhile before they know we are gone. You have done well today. Let's move!"

In a few minutes, the barricade was deserted. When LeMere's men cautiously rounded the flank, muskets at the ready, they found nothing to shoot at.

*****

On board *Active*, the blue rocket was seen by everyone.

Captain Gordon's exclamation of relief expressed the sentiments of the entire crew. "By God, Pennywhistle is alive after all!"

Gordon, in his anxiety, had absent-mindedly laid his sword upon the capstan. He picked it up and bellowed. "Mr. Dashwood!" The First Lieutenant discreetly appeared at the Captain's side.

"Aye, sir," Dashwood acknowledged.

"I would be obliged if you would instruct the signals midshipman to hoist the signal, *Engaging enemy*. No need to wait for an acknowledgement. Their cannon will do for that!" A hint of excitement insinuated itself into Gordon's calm voice. He looked down the line of ship's cannon and men ready to fire at his word. The signal flags fluttered to the masthead.

"Very good, Mr. Dashwood. And now, Mr. Dashwood, if you please," the Captain paused for dramatic emphasis, "open fire!" Gordon's sword flashed down.

The entire broadside of *Active* roared out. Flames lit up the night sky. Cannons leapt back on their breeching ropes and were swiftly reloaded. A year of drill paid dividends.

The guns of *Amphion* and *Cerberus* followed suit. The night blazed with lightning, thunder, and fury. Scores of solid iron balls hurtled their way toward Groa. The vibrations of their passing shook homes in the city.

Spottswood had landed on the quay. He put guards on the boats and killed the fires that threatened them. He sent a marine toward the city gate to find Pennywhistle. He would have preferred to go himself, but he remembered Pennywhistle saying his first responsibility was to take care of the men. Haring off on his own to satisfy a need for redemption would elicit nothing but a look of sad, detached contempt from Captain Pennywhistle. The captain's stern counsel echoed into his mind. "Above all, the men need leadership. They don't want friendship, fellowship, or love. They want command; give it to them!"

*****

Darkness had fallen before the clouds of malevolent, stinking, blinding smoke finally dissipated, and LeMere's men advanced cautiously in the blackness, uncertain of what lay ahead. The British commander was clearly a man of skill and resource; LeMere determined to press his attack anyway.

As he led his men in the advance, two completely different sounds struck his ears. One was a low whizzing, whining noise that sounded like canvas ripping. He instantly recognized it. Cannon balls in flight. Damn! Their fleet had begun firing, just what he did not need! The second was much more puzzling: a rising crescendo of voices. It sounded like French voices, and a lot of them. The speech sounded slurred and confused. He thought he heard singing as well, the sort of well-lubricated chorus heard in waterfront taverns.

A mob of stumbling, weaving solders wandered into the formation of his voltigeurs, interrupting their advance. These bobbing, shambling vagabonds surely were not soldiers, yet they wore French uniforms and spoke the language. It came to LeMere, these must be prisoners taken earlier by the British. But how could they be so drunk? Soldiers were always resourceful, ingenious even, when it came to ferreting out hidden stocks of alcohol. You could hide it in the darkest, deepest cellars, yet somehow they always found it. But how could *prisoners* obtain it?

Revelation dawned on LeMere and he mentally kicked himself for being so dim. This was no misstep or accident! This was another stratagem on the part of the British commander! A clever way to obfuscate and delay. It vexed him, yet it elicited in him both admiration and a curiousity about his British opponent. It was the sort of clever ploy the Emperor himself would have appreciated.

He realized he had no choice but to stop and sort the matter out. He would still pursue the British; it would take extra time, but he would not let them get away!

*****

Pennywhistle halted his column and listened to the cacophony of French voices on the left. Overhead, cannon balls whined on their way to wreak havoc. It was dark in the streets, but the fires from the quay provided illumination and a kind of beacon. The retreat was proceeding in an orderly, disciplined manner and he was pleased with his marines. On the other hand, it never hurt to have some extra insurance. Those stinkpots were a pity to waste.

He ordered six marines front and centre, keeping his voice low, speaking in serious, intimate tones, yet with a hint of humour in his voice. "Marines, let's not make it any easier for the French to organize their long-lost comrades. I want you to approach them from the rear, each throw two stinkpots, and get back here on the double. The more confusion, the safer we are."

The marines smiled broadly. This was not just a duty. This was a pleasure.

Sixteen

The stinkpots gleefully tossed by the British had a profound, debilitating effect on the inebriated French soldiers. Their stomachs were fluttery anyway, so the stinking clouds induced violent retching. Just short of a hundred sick, confused, and disoriented drunks blundered heavily into the voltigeurs. Sober men confronted drunks mewling, groaning, vomiting, and demanding help. One surly drunk turned combative and lashed out with his fists. It took three voltigeurs to batter him into submission. Pleas, shouts, and curses flooded the air. Darkness, leftover gun smoke, and swirling stinkpot mists made it hard to distinguish much of anything in the narrow streets. Sick, blinded men negotiated winding alleys; people used touch, hearing, and intuition to sort out who was who. The advance ground to a complete halt.

Laughing unrestrainedly, the six Marines raced back to tell the tale to Pennywhistle, who promptly formed the marines into a column and set out for the quay.

Far behind them, LeMere shouted, thundered, and cursed. He was blind with rage at this fresh delay. He thought he could get his men through the city quickly, but it took twenty critical minutes.

Pennywhistle's column marched in an orderly, confident way that would have won full approval of staff officers back in Plymouth. They marched through the streets swiftly, yet gave the air of unhurried nonchalance. The flames at the quay soared higher, there was the resounding thunder of off shore cannon, and they sometimes had to dodge falling hunks of stone and masonry, but that disturbed their equanimity not at all. If anything, it increased their satisfaction. They

138

were a marching bulwark of discipline navigating a sea of chaos.

Pennywhistle himself was approaching exhaustion. Battle used up a soldier very quickly, and he had been fighting since dawn. The sword cut in his arm was throbbing. He summoned up his last reserves of strength, knowing he could not rest until his men were safely aboard the boats and the job was done.

One last duty made an unexpected appearance. Captain Joubert and the other officer parolees hailed him.

"Ah, Captain Pennywhistle, we meet again!" said Joubert jovially, seemingly unaware, or perhaps unconcerned by the danger from cannon shot and fire that threatened them all.

"It is most agreeable to see you, again, captain," said Pennywhistle with a courtliness he did not feel but which surfaced anyway from long years of habit. "I regret I do not have time for pleasant discourse with you upon either matters trivial or profound, but you will understand the strictures of duty command me away. Your paroles will, of course, be honoured by us. I think you may find some distressed countrymen ahead. I know you will not assist them in any way to pursue us, but there are wounded to be attended to. Even in war, the dictates of humanity should always be honoured. I would add, I have a personal charge for you. Corporal Wainwright, bring young master Ducot forward."

Wainwright brought the drummer boy up to Pennywhistle. Ducot favoured him with a grateful half smile. The boy looked tired, but much better than the pale, terrified waif they had found that morning. Mercury gently sidled up to him and gave him a doggy grin that seemed to calm him. He petted the dog with one hand, but kept his other firmly on his battered drum with something approaching pride. The marines had thought to keep the drum as a souvenir, but the boy seemed so attached to it that they decided it was wrong to separate a matched pair.

"Captain Joubert, Britons do not make war on children. I would take it as a great favour if you would take the lad under your personal protection. He has shown great pluck and fortitude. I wish him a long life."

"I will be delighted to honour your request, Captain. I shall not soon forget the humanity you have shown to all of us." Joubert bowed. "My officers are grateful and regret we will not have the opportunity to return the favour. And yet, one never knows! One cannot foresee the future after all, and the vicissitudes of war can turn captor to prisoner in an hour."

Pennywhistle smiled, an expression of amusement and fatigue. This was getting too gallant! "Perhaps someday and in happier circumstances we shall meet at the *Academie Françoise* to discuss moral philosophy. Until then, gentlemen, I bid you good evening and *bon chance!*" He touched his hat in salute and returned to his marines. The French officers proceeded on their way, first dodging a large piece of falling red-tiled roof.

LeMere finally succeeded in sorting out the chaos of the drunken solders. He sequestered them in a spot where they would do no harm and could sleep off their intoxication. He detailed only one man to watch them, he could spare no more. His opponent had cost him valuable time, but not enough to ensure his enemies' escape. He would have the English in short order. Wounded everywhere demanded help, and he would have liked to provide succor but he could not, would not, diminish his small force by even one more man. His first duty was to pursue the retreating British, and his was the only organized French force left. It was regrettable, but ruthlessness was often necessary in war. It was the job of an officer to compel sacrifices; to push soldiers beyond their limits. This was one of those times. He walked among dazed survivors, talking quietly but forcefully, and persuaded fifty weary soldiers to join his voltigeurs. Once they were all formed up, he addressed them all.

"Soldiers of the Emperor! Listen! You have beaten the British! I am proud of you! Your fellow soldiers have been unlucky. Those who have done this to your brothers in arms are escaping as we speak. This cannot be allowed to happen. Double-quick to the docks; we must destroy them before they gain their boats!"

The men responded to LeMere's rallying words with a cheer. They could still pluck some degree of triumph from the evening's bloodshed. The British were retreating; their enemies were fleeing! All they had to do was catch up and visit retribution upon their tormentors.

*****

Spottswood greeted Pennywhistle with unalloyed joy when his men reached the quay, his broad smile of relief threatening to outshine even the leaping flames. "It is so good to see you, Captain, I was almost beginning to give up hope, but then again, you always contrive to escape unscathed no matter what the danger. I hope I shall be so lucky!"

Pennywhistle clapped him on the shoulders and laughed. "By God, you and the boats are a sight for sore eyes! You look decidedly better than this morning! Now to business. The French will be on us in minutes. We need to get the men back to the ships. Immediately! As soon as a boat is fully manned, send it on its way. Stop for nothing. I am guessing that no one has attended to the powder ship *Basque Rades*?"

Spottswood frowned. "No, sir. I knew that it would be the last act of this play and I was not willing to do it until I was sure you were safe."

"Don't worry about it, Lieutenant," Pennywhistle said kindly. "You have more than done your duty. I can see that I was right about you. I will attend to the ship. I have more experience with fuses than you, anyway. One thing; take my Ferguson and sword. Keep them safe, but if anything happens to me, they are both yours. Treat them well and they will never fail you."

"Don't talk that way, sir! You will be naked without weapons! I can't just leave you! I promised Captain Gordon I'd bring you back!"

"I can look after myself, Lieutenant. There is no sense in having you or any of the men risk their lives unnecessarily. Our job here is done. Only one task remains, and it can best be carried out by one man acting alone. Enough of our people have died today. Let's not add to the butcher's bill. Mr. Bentham's Utilitarians have it right: the good of the many outweighs the good of the one."

Spottswood's voice quivered as obediance fought with sentiment. "I still don't like it, sir. It just doesn't seem right."

Pennywhistle replied with sympathy, "It's called duty, Mr. Spottswood. Your heart does you credit and flatters me, but part of being a King's Officer is making decisions that, while correct, feel bad. The hardest part of our Service is developing an ability to ruthlessly hazard the lives of those we hold most dear, if the mission demands it. It took me years to grasp that. I don't expect you to absorb it all in a day. Now, carry out your orders, Lieutenant!"

"I will carry out your orders to the best of my ability. For what it's worth, I will follow my mother's childhood advice and say a prayer for you, sir." There was a slight moistening at the corners of Spottswood's eyes.

"Thank you, Mr. Spottswood, I am genuinely touched! Frankly, I am grateful for any help, divine or otherwise. But now it's up to us! God helps those who help themselves, right?" Pennywhistle gave an avuncular smile. "Really, Mr. Spotswood, just do your duty and things will work out."

The lieutenant returned a wan smile, snapped to parade ground attention, and touched his hat in both salute and homage. Pennywhistle returned the smile, then bounded swiftly down the quay toward the *Basque Rades*.

It took him twenty minutes to find fuses, cut them, and lay trails from the quarterdeck to the powder in the hold. It was a painstakingly slow business, making certain the fuses would not be in any way interrupted by deck obstacles. There was no way to rush things. Multiple fuses were necessary in case some sputtered out. He was determined to leave nothing behind for the French, and he was painfully aware he had but one chance to get this right. God, he was tired, and eager for the blissful of oblivion of his hanging cot back on *Active*.

Ten minutes after Pennywhistle headed for the powder ship, the first of LeMere's voltigeurs appeared at the edge of the harbour. They moved forward slowly and warily. The heat of the rioting flames in the harbour was unpleasant and unsettling, but by their light they could distinguish the outlines of men boarding vessels. The *pop, pop, pop* of their muskets served notice of their arrival. Their shots missed, but Spottswood ordered Maxwell, Blandon, Larkin, MacLeod, and Stratton to spread themselves out in front of the boats and act as both a rear guard and skirmish line. They opened a brisk and accurate fire on the Voltigeurs that caused them to seek cover before returning fire.

It bought Spottswood enough time to bundle the marines into boats. Despite the flying lead from the voltigeurs, the men remained calm and the evacuation was orderly. Dale and Mercury were the last ones onto the fourth boat.

Once the four boats had hoisted sail and headed out of the harbour, Spottswood gave the order, "Marines retire!" and the five marines of the rearguard jumped in the boat. He ran the sails up the halyards himself as they settled themselves. As he did so, a bullet clipped the top off his hat's plume. He used his cutlass to sever the rope holding the cutter to the quay. The boat shot out into the harbour like a greyhound that had slipped its lead. The wind was with them and the cutter quickly gathered speed.

The first four boats cleared the Groa channel and entered the open sea. Spottswood's cutter was far behind, just entering the channel. Unlike the other boats, which were crammed to the gunwales with men, Spottswood's was almost empty. It held himself, five marines, and a coxswain who conned the craft.

He should have felt relieved and proud, but he tasted bile and a wave of self-loathing washed over him. He glanced at the men. They looked downcast and sullen, when they should have been happy and congratulating themselves at their escape.

Spottswood's heart knew it was all wrong. His intellect said he was doing the right thing: following orders, saving lives, focusing on the mission. It would all look so impeccably proper in the report to the Admiralty. But sometimes a debt of honour to a good man rendered all of those concerns secondary.

He had a grave choice to make. If he made the wrong one, his body would survive but his soul would be in jeopardy. This was about his personal redemption: doing something better than he would ever have believed himself capable. It was not a military choice, it was a moral one. It was not just about what it meant to be an officer; it was what it meant to be a human being. At that moment, Pennywhistle's voice rang clear in his head. "Officers should use their initiative at all times."

"Damn it, that's it!" His voice was a thunderclap. "Helm! Full about! We're going back!"

Armstrong burst into a broad grin and responded with a hearty, "Aye, aye, *sir*!" The marines in the boat smiled and let their breath out in satisfied unison. MacLeod simply forgot there was an officer present and burst out, "Bloody damn right!"

Spottswood braced the sails round and the cutter tore back through the water toward Pennywhistle.

*****

As Pennywhistle made one last check of the fuses before lighting them, he heard a familiar and unpleasant buzzing noise. Something rocketed past his ear. Damn it! He was under fire. The French had arrived. He crouched on deck and looked over the side. The ship's dinghy was still there, but there were volitigeurs on the quay nearby, and as soon as he boarded it he would be naked to their fire. With so many muskets, even the worst marksman might score a hit. He desperately reconsidered his options.

Pennywhistle kept low to the deck as bullets whizzed overhead. He was running out of time. More volitigeurs appeared on the quay and the fire became as hot as the burning linstock he held in his hand. The longer he waited, the worse things would get. After a few minutes of supine suspense, he decided to make his move. He would light the fuses, then just jump. There was no hope of gaining the dinghy. He would have to swim for it, but to where? It did not really matter; he just needed to be off the ship and in the water. Once the ship blew, he'd figure something out.

A loud, hissing sound assaulted his ears. It came not from the deck, but from above. He looked skyward and saw a bold blue arc racing across the inky heavens. What the..! A British signal rocket! It was the loveliest sight he had ever seen.

He saw Spottswood standing in the bow of a cutter bearing toward his position, waving his arms and hallooing madly. That damn fool! But against will and reason, the corners of his mouth curved up into a grin.

He found a discarded speaking trumpet, then summoned up every ounce of his failing energy to make his bellow heard. "Spottswood, get down! I'll swim to you!"

Spottswood waved in acknowledgment. The cutter ploughed steadily on. Bullets smacked into its bow. He told the men to stay low; only he and the coxswain were visible above the gunwales.

The air buzzed with the sound of angry bees, but Pennywhistle was too tired to care. He heard a whine just below his ear and his left epaulette flew off. A jolt of nervous energy shot through him at that. He tore off his coat, shirt, and boots, hastily lit the fuses, and executed a fast, graceless dive over the side.

The fuses ignited. They had thirty seconds to burn.

He was a strong swimmer, but he was injured and nearly spent, and it was an effort to maintain his crawl stroke. The cut in his arm pained him greatly. He kicked as strongly as he could, but his legs felt as if they were made of old bread dough.

*****

LeMere saw the dark shape of a man diving from the deck and guessed it must be the British commander. He had saved the last and toughest job for himself. Commendable—that is what he would have done. He admired the man whose name he did not know. Part of him thought it unsporting to shoot at such a brave fellow and was of a mind to do nothing.

"Come on, Captain Pennywhistle, you can make it!" shouted a frightened Spottswood, his voice carrying over the water.

Pennywhistle! So that was the man's name! *What an odd appellation for such a heroic officer*, thought LeMere. His ruthlessness reasserted itself. To let this brave officer live would be an affront to his sworn duty to the Emperor, whatever his personal feelings in the matter. He called for a musket. Pennywhistle's head was silhouetted against the glow of flames and only sixty yards away.

LeMere leveled the musket and aimed.

"Oh, no you don't!" shouted an enraged Spottswood. The Ferguson defiantly spoke a single word.

LeMere was about to pull the trigger when something punched him hard in the shoulder and the impact pitched him ingloriously on his backside. "*Merde!*" he sputtered angrily. The British commander would escape, but LeMere felt in his heart this would not be their final meeting. The last word in his mind before he slipped into unconsciousness was "Pennywhistle."

Spottswood was proud of his shot. The Ferguson was indeed a superior weapon! After all he had been through, he was damned if he was going to let some blasted Frog officer snatch away his captain's life at the last second. The cutter raced toward Pennywhistle. Bullets pounded the hull, but the stout wood protected the men.

The fuse burned: ten seconds to go. The flames in the harbour soared higher and few buildings remained untouched. It was a scene out of Dante's Inferno and the cutter was headed into the middle of it.

LeMere's angry men cut loose with a volley. Bullets kicked up small spouts of water in front and behind Pennywhistle. His stroke faltered and he could hardly raise an arm out of the water. But then the cutter sped alongside and friendly arms were extending a boathook. With his last strength, Pennywhistle grasped it. Spottswood, MacLeod, and Larkin pulled him aboard, and all the men breathed huge sighs of relief.

The breeze was no longer a breeze, but had grown to a strong wind. It whipped and swirled the flames into a magnificent, terrible frenzy and blew fresh life into the host of fires attacking the harbour. The place would be a blackened ruin by tomorrow morning. Spottswood felt the hot breath of the wind on his reddened cheeks, but it caused him to smile. Wind was exactly what they needed. He quickly braced round the cutter's driver and jib.

"Keep her straight and steady, helmsman," ordered Spottswood with a decisive calmness that surprised him. They ran before the wind. He guessed the wind was a solid twenty knots. The cutter positively raced toward the channel.

Five, four, three, two, one. The fuses reached their destinations.

A tremendous explosion rocked the harbour and a column of wood and smoke roared upwards into the obsidian sky. The fearsome noise speared everyone's eardrums. Large, flaming pieces of wood barely missed the cutter. The heat and buffet of the explosion startled everyone on the boat; everyone except Pennywhistle, who smiled as the blast wave sped the cutter's departure. He then fell asleep, quite content.

Spottswood took one last look back at the blazing hell they were leaving, then set his face confidently toward the open sea. He knew he had made the right choice. He had only been in the marines three months, but now he knew *Active* was his real home, just as it was Pennywhistle's.

Seventeen

The rhythmic swaying of the hanging cot soothed, comforted, and reassured. Combined with the darkness of the tiny cabin, the rocking suffused the sole occupant with a womb-like sense of well-being. The familiar, comforting sounds of order and routine were present: the clang of the ship's bell, the patter of hundreds of feet, the shrill ruffles of boatswain's whistles. The sea gently passed under the keel with a steady *swoosh, swoosh, swoosh* that seemed almost a heartbeat. The rank scent of unwashed bodies, damp clothing, old gun oil, and decks impregnated with brimstone residue would have repelled a newcomer, but had the opposite effect on Pennywhistle. He was in the pleasant twilight land between dreams and wakefulness.

He came full awake with a start. A lance of pain shot through his arm and assured him he was still amongst the living. He was disoriented for a moment, then the familiar, musty smell made him realize he was back on *Active*, in his own cabin. He could not recall how he'd got there. He glanced down and noticed he was in his long cotton nightshirt. His battered, heavily patched old uniform hung from a beam. It was neatly brushed and looked as good as a threadbare garment could. It was a pity Gieve's of Saville Row was a thousand miles away. He really needed to find a good local tailor very soon.

He remembered a boat hook and the extended arms of Spottswood and the men on the cutter. They had looked so worried. He thought perhaps he had heard the sound of a massive explosion, but it was all a bit uncertain and jumbled. The throb in his arm demanded attention. The sword cut from d'Auverge was deeper than he'd realized, but it had been neatly stitched. He tried to reconstruct the events of the previous day, but found that the effort was too great. For now, he lay back and luxuriated in the satisfaction of being alive. He had survived one more fight. He permitted himself a few seconds of self-congratulation, which segued into wondering how much his survival came down to one simple thing: luck. Or perhaps Fate. Yesterday had not been his time. One day it would come.

He tried not to think thoughts of death, an ever-present reality for the fighting man. Many in his profession superstitiously believed that any deep consideration of it might hasten its appearance. A number of "blue lighters," led by Admiral James Gambier, sought answers in the Bible. He found "Dismal Jemmy" and his evangelical associates dour, canting hypocrites and judged their alleged insights worthless. Others simply ignored The Ultimate Question as too deep, too far beyond their ken; but he could not.

He had a driving curiousity about what lay on the other side of The Grand Divide, the Great Mystery. His instincts and his intellect both told him that something marvelous and beyond imagining beckoned. He had read some of the early Christian mystics at university, such as St. John of the Cross and Meister Eckhardt, and felt that while their observations were inconclusive, they were worthwhile and pointed in the proper direction of an answer. Plato's story of Er, the soldier who came back to life on his funeral pyre and related a remarkable tale of the Great Beyond, fascinated him. Er spoke of a tunnel, an intense light, and a beauty inexpressible in earthly words. It seemed an observant, factual accounting of someone who had done what Shakespeare had said was impossible. He had been to "the undiscovered country," and had actually returned.

He realized he was sailing headlong into morbid speculation. It was often thus after a hard fight. All well and good to think deeply about things, but done too often, that could lead to depression. It was one thing to reflect at length, quite another to become obsessed. Things needed to be kept in balance. He did not want to succumb to "the black dog": a dark, pernicious mental affliction which had destroyed his father. Pennywhistle noted that whatever "the black dog" did to the mind, it appeared to have an affinity for the reflective, moral, and intellectually gifted members of humanity.

His thoughts drifted to the recent battle at Groa and he involuntarily shuddered. He knew the warning signs. Officers never even hinted at the malady in official correspondence, and he doubted many mentioned it even in the sanctity of private diaries. It was only spoken of in hushed tones, very late at night, when officers were well into their cups. Even then, it went by the innocuous term "soldier's loneliness." He preferred his own term: "combat hangover."

The symptoms varied in type and severity, manifesting after the real danger had passed. Battle itself was less damaging than the persistent weariness, anxiety, and general distress of mind and soul which followed after. He had once seen a brave officer lapse into a five day state of catatonia after Trafalgar, his sanity in serious question.

It came down to paying a debt, greater for some than others. When huge demands of courage, exertion, and resourcefulness were made on the mind and body, hundreds of critical, split-second decisions called for, and when great cascades of adrenaline surged through the veins, the body wrote large drafts on its physical and psychological banking accounts, often going into the red.

The body exacted a price for these withdrawals; mysterious body aches, lethargy of movement, and occasional, unprovoked shivers. Tremors, twitches, and tics were common as well; all undergirded by a general lassitude and melancholia of mind. There was often a heightened sensitivity to sounds in the days after a battle; men jumped at unexpected noises. The contemporary word was "jittery."

Some men could not sleep at all, others slept far too much. Bad dreams sometimes forestalled sleep from knitting up the raveled sleeve of care. Like an alcohol hangover, it gradually passed. One just had to give it time. He sighed; he would have to relive Groa again in exquisitely painful detail when he composed his formal report.

It was at least a predictable foe. His ability to handle it had improved greatly. He accepted it as a warrior's portion in life. He was a sensitive man by nature, but also one who believed that an intellectual understanding of a problem would go far in helping the body master it. The mind could guide emotions to serve reason.

No one had ever told him of the after-effects of battle. After his first fight at Trafalgar, he'd had to discover it on his own. It seemed to him that no man escaped damage, but some concealed it better than others. It reminded him of something his disagreeable mother had once said about pregnancy; "If the truth were fully told, no one would undertake it."

Melancholia of the spirit and its attendant behaviours were never found in the glorious accounts of battle, written long after by men of letters who had never been there. Old generals and admirals knew all about it, but carefully expunged any mention of it from their memoirs. The myth that the nation loved demanded that all British officers be brave, zealous, and untroubled by overactive psyches.

While most did their duty and suffered in silence for it afterward, every battle had officers who were conspicuously absent when bullets flew. Some did not run, but simply froze. Others acted confidently but shouted insane commands that got innocent men killed. He had heard ugly rumours that Lord Northesk, Nelson's third in command at Trafalgar, had been less than zealous in the performance of his duties. All of this was deleted from official accounts. Warriors could never be allowed to show flesh and blood frailty, lest the public's appetite for war be dampened by brutal, unwelcome reality.

Directly after Trafalgar, he had gotten a bad case of the shakes. He'd had trouble bringing a cup of steaming coffee to his mouth without spilling most of the contents. He had not been alone in this. He'd also had no conscious idea of how he performed his duties, but Lieutenant Cumby later said he did a fine job.

A huge storm had engulfed the badly damaged fleets the day after the battle, matching the mood of naval men distraught by the loss of their hero, Lord Admiral Nelson. He'd slept very little over the following three days. Often stupid with sheer fatigue, he'd stolen little catnaps on deck between tasks. He drank barrels of coffee. He directed and supervised men in a numbing variety of tasks.

Once, he even put his own shoulders into the mix. This was normally unthinkable for an officer, but casualties had left *Bellerophon* desperately short-handed, and she had been badly holed below the waterline. When one of the crewmen manning the constantly working pumps dropped to the deck from sheer exhaustion, Pennywhistle took his place for the next four hours. During the height of the storm, it became a race against time and the sea, as *Bellerophon* was in real danger of sinking.

When the battered ship was finally on its way to Gibraltar, Pennywhistle had fallen into a deep and exhausted sleep that lasted a full day.

Things were better today. No odd sweats or split-second bloody flashbacks. He looked at his hand. Firm and steady; no tremors. He wondered how long he had been out. He idly ran his fingers through his sandy red hair, then felt the disagreeable stubble on his cheeks. Judging from the whiskers' length, he must have slept quite a while. The interior of a frigate was very dark, illuminated mainly by the uncertain light of lanterns. Sunlight flooded the stern and side gallery windows of the captain's cabin, but little reached the berth deck, one deck below, where Pennywhistle's cabin was situated.

He lit a candle and looked over the tiny cabin, just under six feet square and barely big enough to house his mother's old grand piano. It contained a sea chest for his personal items, a folding chair, and an old Chippendale bureau of Honduran mahogany, the top a retractable desk for correspondence, the bottom three drawers for clothing. The cot itself was stowable and hooked to the deck beams. There were two small storage lockers built into the forward bulkhead. A thin partition of deal pine with a door formed the side bulkhead of the cabin. All of it could quickly be cleared away for battle.

He picked up a small looking glass and beheld a disagreeably gaunt, haunted face staring back at him. His eyes looked sunken, dull, and weary. Crow's feet had begun to form at their corners. Battle always stamped its imprimatur on the face.

His eye caught sight of the Ferguson. He noticed it had been thoroughly cleaned. Even in the dim, flickering light, the tiger-striped maple stock radiated a lustrous brown, and the barrel glistened with gun oil. He had a brief thought of his father, a scholarly man who had had the Ferguson restocked to increase its precision; maple absorbed recoil better than the original walnut. His father would have approved of the care it had been given. It had to have been Mr. Spottswood. He had gripped the Ferguson like he was being handed the Holy Grail. It had pleased Pennywhistle, as he considered the rifle his most valued possession.

There was a discreet rapping at the bulkhead door. Glancing through the window of carved pilasters, he noted with pleasure the arrival of Manton, his servant. Every officer was permitted a "fart catcher." Manton was six feet of gangly, almost-seventeen-year-old youth, just learning his trade. He had been a main-topman, but a foot injury prevented him going aloft. Pennywhistle liked the boy's intelligence and eagerness. His previous servant, Manners, had been an older man in the later stages of consumption, who had finally gone to Fiddler's Green the previous month. He had been a disagreeable misanthrope who performed his duties with profound indifference. Pennywhistle hoped for better luck with Manton and, so far, he was not displeased.

"Are you awake, sir?" inquired Manton. "Didn't want to disturb, seein' as how you had a very active day yesterday!" Manton chuckled at the pun he made on the ship's name. "But I heard some movement in the cabin and I thought you might be up. Figured you'd probably be powerful hungry!"

Pennywhistle heard a growl and realized it was his own stomach. He had eaten little yesterday and he was indeed famished.

"What time is it anyway, Manton?" Pennywhistle stretched, but did not stand to his full height. The deck beams could not accommodate his six-foot, two-inch frame.

"Just struck seven bells on the mornin' watch, sir."

Just about seven thirty then. He had been asleep nine hours. Breakfast was served at eight for the officers of wardroom rank.

Manton said brightly, "I took the liberty of doing what I could with your old coat. Shined all of your buttons. I talked the captain into lending you a spare pair of his boots. I took a whetstone to your cutlass. I was going to clean and oil your rifle, but Mr. Spottswood wouldn't hear of it. He treated that weapon like it were his own child, sir!"

"Thank you, Manton. You have thought of everything. I don't suppose you'd have some hot water there for a shave? I detest the idea of appearing scruffy on deck. I do not feel fully awake until I have banished the night's growth of whiskers."

"Not a problem, sir, I know you like close shaves." Manton grinned again, having made yet another pun. "I have real hot water here, just the way you like it, right from the Brodie." The Brodie was the ship's stove, used for cooking and heating water.

"Thank you, Manton. Please give my respects to Mr. Dashwood and inform him I will be joining him for breakfast. I assume Mr. Haye is officer of the deck?" Haye was a silent, unsmiling, enigmatic officer whom Pennywhistle could never quite figure out, but who was sedulous about his duty.

"Correct, Captain," replied Manton. "Everyone at the mess will be wantin' to hear your tale of what happened last night. I know I do!" Manton was young and impressionable enough to believe all of the tall tales about the glories of battle.

"Did Mr. Moore and Mr. Meers make it back aboard, Manton?"

"No, sir. There is still a heap of work to be done on the prizes. I heard Mr. Dashwood say he doesn't expect them back on board until tomorrow."

"What's the mess got planned for breakfast, Manton? I am truly ravenous!"

Manton beamed with real pleasure. "Oh, you won't go away hungry, sir! We have fresh eggs from the chickens. One of the hogs was butchered yesterday, so there will be lots of gammon steak. Some fresh tripe sausage, too, and cold tongue. Plenty of fresh bread, toast, and biscuit. Tea and coffee. The coffee is strong like you like it. Strong enough to stand a spoon upright!"

"That does sound like a fine feast. Now if you will excuse me,

Manton, the razor and my beard have a pressing engagement. I will be along shortly."

"Very good, sir," replied Manton. I will have your chair ready." At meals, a personal servant performed as a footman to his officer. "I really want to hear what happened last night, sir, we all saw the big explosion!"

"I can only tell you what I saw, and I promise you, it was nothing so dramatic or romantic as you seem to imagine. I caution you, I am a marine officer, not a spinner of rattling sea yarns!"

Eighteen

Gordon's last-second high block barely deflected the cutlass aimed expertly at his head. Silver-blue sparks jumped from the blade with a discordant klaaanng. He had not recovered when another thrust rocketed toward his ribs. He slammed his own cutlass forward, executed a poor vertical parry, and quickly stepped back. His breath came in fast, laboured gasps; his foe's was steady, disciplined. Cutlasses collided, withdrew, collided again. High cut, low cut, block, retire, advance, thrust. His opponent attacked relentlessly, pressed him hard and closely, cutting at his head, stomach, and thigh in skilled, rapid succession. His opponent's thrusts seemed to have a strategic rhythm, but Gordon, more fatigued with each passing second, could not puzzle it out. He had no time to initiate, could merely defend. He batted each blow aside, but each block was slower than the last. It was power versus speed. Gordon was a big man of great strength, but his opponent moved with a lithe, quick, whippet-like grace that dodged or parried every blow.

His opponent's blade feinted at his ribs, then shot toward his sternum. Gordon jumped back, partly missed his block, and the cutlass flashed by, an inch in front of his coat. His grip slipped as sweat slicked his palm. His opponent sped up his attack and forced Gordon steadily back. The deck rolled slightly, disturbing his already uncertain footwork. He was just recovering his balance when his foe made the decisive move. The tip of his blade sliced under Gordon's block and connected solidly with the guard on Gordon's sword. A quick flick of his foe's wrist and a circular up-thrust of his blade caused Gordon's sword to fly skyward; it would have continued into space if it had not been attached to his wrist by a sword knot. His throat was exposed. He waited for the death stroke.

"AAAAAAAHHHH," Tom Pennywhistle exhaled a long sigh of exasperation. "Captain, I have told you, power comes from the calves and maneuver from the wrist. Bend your knees deeply and loosen your wrist. Your grip is stiff and inflexible and you do everything with your feet instead of trusting your wrist. Be easy, fluid in your movements, and don't let your opponent near enough to use anything but his blade as a weapon." He paused and gently smiled. "But then, how many times I have I told you that in the past month? Three times, or is it four?"

"Blast it, Tom, my mind knows that, but my muscles are still ignorant. I just need more practice. But I lasted a lot longer this time than the last. You have to give me that." Gordon smiled ruefully. His weekly two hour sessions with Pennywhistle embarrassed him, but his chief marine officer was an excellent and supremely patient teacher. He himself had improved markedly since the start of the cruise and had an iron determination to improve even more. "Same time next week, Tom?"

"My pleasure and honour, sir," Pennywhistle replied with a merry half-smile. He sheathed his blade with a purposefully showy flourish, then bowed deeply.

Gordon laughed at this memory of last week's lesson, and decided to walk the quarterdeck, enjoy his command, and simply revel in the splendid day.

Active's bowspirit pitched higher as she majestically crested a sky-blue wave. As she plunged gracefully downward, she rolled slightly to larboard, then corkscrewed in the opposite direction. The sea surged along the length of her keel, lifting her, and passed forcefully under her stern. Ship and sea throbbed with a natural, symbiotic rhythm. A friendly sun and fleecy clouds were a pleasing compliment to the strong, quartering wind out of the southeast. The white-capped waves whipped by with an energetic, soothing beauty.

James Alexander Gordon was a captain in the new tradition of Nelson. He was approachable, affable, and welcomed suggestions.

He was twenty-eight years old, but had the nautical wisdom of someone much older. He had gone to sea at eleven. His naturally buoyant optimism led him to expect the best from his men. His genuine concern made him a popular figure. He was forward looking and had instituted the three-watch system. With two watches, men never got more than four hours of uninterrupted rest, whereas the new schedule allowed them a real night's sleep. Fatigue driven accidents had vanished almost immediately.

He had a rich, commanding voice, yet seldom raised it above pleasant conversational tones. A slight hint of disapproval on his face was enough to move the most hardened shellback to mend his errant ways. His drills were demanding and difficult, but he taught with praise and suggestion rather than with imprecations and the lash. *Active* was a happy ship, and yet, as she had proven yesterday, an eminently sound fighting platform.

This morning, however, old customs were in force. The windward side of the quarterdeck was the traditional, sacrosanct preserve of the captain where he might ruminate, walk, or just enjoy watching the seagulls, undisturbed by petty distractions. The men assumed he had great and mighty considerations on his mind. They assumed something clever that involved harming the French. They made every effort to treat him with the utmost consideration. Complete silence was enjoined within the captain's earshot.

They were wrong. He was actually in a fine mood and would have been delighted to talk to his officers or even banter with his men. James Gordon was neither a deep nor a complex man, but he was a good one. For a few minutes, he simply wanted to stroll the quarterdeck as a relief from the twenty-three forms, requisitions, watch bills, muster books, shot, and powder expenditure reports, the punishment book and other paper minutiae that awaited his attention. He had completed his log entries, but he needed Pennywhistle's verbal and written report before he could compose the after action summation that would go to Hoste and eventually the Admiralty. Pennywhistle deserved a long rest and hearty breakfast first. He was due at nine, after the officer of the watch made his report.

Gordon loved *Active*. She was the finest ship on which he had ever served and he considered himself privileged to captain her. She was the sort of command reserved for what were colloquially coming to be known as "star captains." These were young captains of daring, decisive resourcefullness, and enterprise, clearly intended for high rank and greater commands.

Active was one hundred and fifty feet long on the gun deck, forty in beam, and one hundred and eighty in total length. She had a burthen of one thousand and fifty-two tons and her sleek lines had been copied and improved from a very fast captured French ship, the *Hebe*. Launched in 1799, she was part of a popular series designed by Sir John Henslow that came to be known as the *Leda* Class. She was not only swift, she was maneuverable. Sailors called her stiff and weatherly, which meant she was a stable ship that held her course and did not drift leeward. She officially carried thirty-eight guns and was designated as a fifth-rate frigate; rating having nothing to do with quality, but rather the number of guns carried. Her carronades, or smashers, were not counted as part of the official tally, so she actually carried forty-six. She was the perfect instrument for scouting, raiding, screening, or convoying—the type of ship always in short supply. Nelson once said in frustration, "If I died at this instant, want of frigates would be emblazoned on my heart." Anything *Active* could not outfight, which was nothing save a ship-of-line, she could deftly outrun.

She was crewed by three hundred and fifteen souls, more than the usual frigate compliment. Because of the massive size and requirements of the Fleet in 1810, with over seven hundred ships and one hundred and forty thousand men on the books, British ships were chronically undermanned. *Active* was an exception because her captain was popular and there was no shortage of men eager to serve with him. Her crew gloried in being all volunteers with not a single consignee of the press gang. A captain like Gordon ensured adventure, honour, and glory, and most important of all, prize money.

Gordon thought of the prize money to come and it added to the cheeriness of his mood. He came from a well-connected Aberdeen family, but that family was land poor: plenty of real estate, not much ready cash. A captain's salary was substantial, but so were expenses. Setting a good table, entertaining his own officers as well as visiting dignitaries and superior officers, were all extra expenses that came out of the captain's personal funds. Extra paint for the hull, gilt for the filigree work on the stern, supplying a better carved and coloured ship's figurehead; all were charged to the captain.

Uniforms for ordinary seamen had not yet been standardized, so before Gordon left Portsmouth he'd invested most of his extra cash in bolts of navy blue cloth. Hawkes, the sail maker, and his mates transformed these into jackets for the crew. They were short, cinched at the waist, with seven brass buttons, and contrasted nicely with the traditional bell-bottomed, white duck trousers. Crimson neck scarves and rose red checked shirts added additional colour. The sail makers had also crafted tarred leather round hats with "ACTIVE" in black letters on a wide gold band. The crew took great pride in their smart, distinctive appearance; it added greatly to the ship's *espirit de corps*.

Prize money from the sale of captured ships was the traditional way to cover these costs. Last night's efforts had substantially added to his coffers.

But prize money was not, in the main, about either greed or expenses for James Gordon, it was about love. He was quite smitten with Miss Lydia Ward of Marlborough, and she with him. Her parents approved of him in principle, but he was hardly a suitable match until his financial prospects improved. He thought of her dark, slim figure, her close-curled brown hair, her impetuous chin and rich, full lips and it made him inwardly shiver. That shiver was not just romantic passion. He was a sailor, after all! Every prize he took brought the day of his marriage one step closer. The idea that something might go wrong and he might lose her drove him mad. He sometimes envied his cousin, Pennywhistle.

In Gordon's view, Pennywhistle had a rather relaxed attitude toward women. Gordon realized he was speculating about his relative, but his observations confirmed his intuition. Pennywhistle had never tasted the promise of real love and the pain of its imminent loss, he decided. He did all things in moderation, and, Gordon realized from his love for Lydia, true love was anything but moderate. Love was an intoxicant, like alcohol. A glass of claret at dinner sipped slowly was fine, pleasant, and beneficial, but downing a whole bottle at a single sitting promised dangerous, possibly addictive, consequences. Pennywhistle liked women and they liked him, but he also liked life neat and orderly, and love was the opposite of that.

He treated women with grace and courtliness, but always spoke plainly in quiet, genteel, tones. He avoided the silly banter and boastful self-promotion that was common among Regency bucks. He dressed smartly, revealed little, and encouraged women to speak freely about themselves. He observed carefully and complimented honestly. He gave every woman the subtle impression she was God's most gorgeous and beguiling creation by the simple expedient of paying attention. When talking to a woman he allowed no distractions; he made her the centre of his immediate universe. He listened closely, spoke sparingly, and asked perceptive questions based on what she had said. Above all, he knew when to keep silent and merely nod sagely. He was always pleasant and conveyed the impression that he was discretion itself about all matters confidential. He was available, but elusive; handsome, but an enigma; forthright, but not forthcoming. Gordon knew him as well as anyone, yet he was still something of a mystery; there was always something held in a deep personal reserve.

There was something of the chameleon about him, and his personality tended to blend artfully with local surroundings: pleasing in manners and discourse, then allowing the friendlier parts of people's imaginations to fill in the rest as they chose. People came away feeling they knew Pennywhistle well, yet they really knew little.

His cousin was abstemious in all things. He ate sparingly, and while he appreciated good food, it mattered little to him whether he ate it on a regular basis. He preferred coffee to wine and found one glass of wine a day with dinner quite sufficient in an era when such behaviour was considered hopelessly déclassé. William Pitt, Prime Minister when Pennywhistle had fought at Trafalgar, was known at formal dinners as a "three bottle man."

Save for a meticulous attention to the quality of his attire, his tastes were Spartan. He was obsessed with cleanliness and bathed often when ashore. Gordon imagined he would be just as happy sleeping in a monk's cell as a squire's mansion. Indeed, his self-discipline had a bit of the monk about it. Gordon imagined him momentarily as an early Benedictine happily creating an illuminated manuscript. Pennywhistle's only pressing need seemed to be for an unending supply of books.

He had the sleek, whipcord physique of a human greyhound and a fitness regimen that was demanding and unrelenting. He frequently walked the deck and enjoyed racing seamen up the ratlines. But his main form of exercise was the refinement of his cutlass technique. He energetically sought partners to improve his skills. Indeed, his interest in swordsmanship had become part of the culture on *Active*.

Gordon knew if he could ever beat Pennywhistle, he'd be reckoned the best swordsman in the Navy! He felt Pennywhistle practiced with him out of kindness; more to help his Captain increase his skill than provide himself with a real challenge.

Class and rank had little relevance to his cousin when it came to perfecting his military skills. He valued sincerity and earnestness. He had had an excellent French trainer in the blade and he was more than willing to share his cutlass technique, whether it was with officer or humble seaman. He was an artist, a perfectionist, and knew at a certain point that even the best swordsman only improved his technique when he was willing to teach it to others. He welcomed all aspirants, and promised a guinea to any man who could best him. Friday afternoons at three became known as "Pennywhistle's Challenge." He was always friendly and hearty when he made the challenge. All knew he merely wanted a fair test of his skills. No one felt chagrin at being beaten by him; it was expected. Indeed, it became a point of pride on the ship to say, "I once took on Mr. Pennywhistle!"

His most frequent challenger, and one who sometimes came close to beating him, was Master's Mate Neville, a twenty-year-old organist who had once worked in Durham Cathedral. Neville was at first awed by Pennywhistle, but quickly accepted his earnest request to forget rank and observe, learn, practice, and hold nothing back. When Pennywhistle and Neville fought, a quiet descended on deck. Sailors invariably rooted for Neville, hoping against all odds, that maybe, just maybe, he might prevail this day. It became a very pleasant sporting event, and Gordon suspected more than a few wagered on the outcome. Men looked forward to it all week. It crossed divides of class, rank, and outlook, bonding the ship together as a family. The men admired Pennywhistle, but they always wanted to see if Neville might penetrate his defenses. Everyone loves a dark horse. Meanwhile, Pennywhistle's message got through: practice makes perfect.

Neville would sometimes come close to administering the coup de grace, but at the last second, Pennywhistle would inevitably slip away and reverse the positions. The contest generally ended with Pennywhistle's blade to Neville's throat and a merry, "I have you, sir!" The crowd would groan. He would then burst into laughter, drop his sword, and congratulate his opponent with a ringing, "Well done! That was very close!"

Even those humble souls who never dared duel with him learned from his technique. It was instruction disguised as a sporting event. More than a few of his moves were copied by his audience and successfully employed against the French. Gordon felt many seamen owed their lives to Pennywhistle's obsession with the blade, and he was grateful.

Spottswood was the most earnest of all of his challengers. He was constantly beaten but refused to quit. He was improving, but only very slowly. Gordon had noted that while Spottswood's skill with the blade was rudimentary, and would probably remain so, he was turning out to be a very fine marksman with almost any long arm. He truly had the eyes of a hawk.

Whatever else Pennywhistle was, he was a priceless asset to

the ship and her prospects for success. His military achievements were direct, impressive, and indisputable. He was easy to talk to, intelligent and well informed; amenable to reason and logic, slow to anger or fancy a slight. If he held some things back, well, everyone had secrets. Gordon knew some dark event had caused him to leave university and propelled him into the marine service, but did not know the details.

The wind grew stronger. Gordon sadly decided it was time for him to quit the quarterdeck and repair to the confines of his cabin to begin the mundane business of the day. He paused to savour the sheer majesty of the ship with a good wind at her back, then briskly walked past the wheel, looking forward to hearing Pennywhistle's report.

Nineteen

Favourite, the 44-gun heavy frigate that served as Commodore Dubordieu's flagship, arrived off Groa at half-past two, just as, eighteen miles to the east, Hoste's squadron was getting underway. Wisps of smoke curled into the night sky. Small fires still burned, but most of the big ones had played themselves out. The waterfront resembled a blackened cesspool and reeked of burnt rope, wood, and flesh. Townspeople wandered about in confusion, trying to sort out the wreckage and make sense of what had happened.

Captain La Meilliere was shocked, but not surprised. When Hoste made war, he did not do it gently or by half measures. Still, the destruction was excessive, even by British standards. He wondered why the French troops had not defended the town. Something had gone badly wrong. He wanted answers, and he knew his Commodore felt the same. Nothing remained of Boudreau's convoy. Not only was its destruction a serious setback from a military standpoint, it might prove far worse in terms of damage to French morale.

La Meilliere showed none of his concern on the surface. He was something outside the British experience: a dignified, quiet Gallic warrior. To the average Briton, the Frenchman was always a boastful, talkative creature, notable mostly for extravagant emotions. To his men, La Meilliere appeared imperturbable, even at the end of a long day. They had no idea how hard he worked to project that impression. His uniform was part of that image. He was clad in the dress uniform of a *capitaine de vaisseu*; what the British called a post captain. It was a tight-fitting, single-breasted, dark blue tailcoat cinched at the waist, with scarlet collar and cuffs. Nine gold buttons with an anchor design, surrounded by lace, also of gold, fastened the jacket. Prussian-blue breeches and high-topped black boots completed the outfit. The rig was immaculate; a sharp contrast to the dismal shape the city was in.

He had not yet had time to lower boats and send a shore party. Through his glass, La Meilliere spotted what looked to be an old scow being rowed inexpertly by soldiers. An officer harangued them as they pulled slowly toward *Favourite*. The soldiers appeared seasick and dazed.

La Meilliere had his sailors standing by with boathooks when the craft pulled alongside. A rope ladder was lowered from the entry port and the boat's officer was helped up the steep tumblehome of the frigate. His shoulder was bandaged. The wound was recent.

Once aboard, the newcomer recovered his dignity and imperiously rose to his full height. He stood an inch over six feet, his body well proportioned and athletic. His enormous bearskin shako with its distinctive red-tipped green plume added a good six inches to his height. He acknowledged La Meilliere's superior rank and saluted crisply.

La Meilliere recognized the double-breasted blue uniform as that of a *capitaine of the chasseurs a pied of La Garde Imperiale*. The Malteste cross of the *Legion d' Honneur* hung from an apple red ribbon on the man's left breast. The coat was amputated at the waist, save for an interruption in the shape of an inverted "v" that reached to the diaphragm and revealed an ivory waistcoat beneath. The cuffs were crimson and the coat's long swallow tails were lined in a brilliant shade of ruby red. The bone white breeches were so tightly fitted that they appeared painted on. The newcomer also sported the personal hallmarks of that elite unit: coal black hair ending in queue, handlebar mustache, and a single gold earring. The ornate uniform was damaged, but not the impressiveness of its owner. He looked imposing, fit, and hard; a man to be reckoned with and exactly what you would expect from a soldier with a combat record distinguished enough to secure a coveted appointment to the Guard.

La Meilliere returned the salute and awaited the man's address.

Officers of the Guard were notorious for arrogance.

"Captain, whom have I the honour of addressing? I presume you command this vessel?" the officer inquired brusquely, without ceremony.

"I do, Captain. I am *capitaine de vaisseu* Etienne La Meilliere at your service and have the honour to command the Emperor's frigate, *Favourite*. And whom do I have the pleasure of addressing?" La Meilliere was scrupulously courteous.

"I am Captain Rene LeMere, of the Emperor's Imperial Guard, at your service, sir. I have been seconded by the Emperor himself to serve as the Commodore's military aide-de-camp." LeMere looked closely at La Meilliere to see if the invocation of the Emperor had an effect.

"Honoured, sir," replied La Meilliere. His demeanor remained unchanged. His mouth widened gently into a non-committal smile.

LeMere spoke now with a breathless urgency. "Much as I would like to continue this very pleasant conversation, I need to see your Commodore urgently. I have very pressing news!"

La Meilliere nodded. "I presumed you were on an errand of great urgency. Naturally, we are all anxious to find out why the convoy is gone and the city a burnt out cinder. If you will accompany Lieutenant Reneaux, he will conduct you to Commodore Dubordieu immediately. If you like, I can have our surgeon examine that wound of yours. He is an excellent doctor."

"Thank you, but wholly unnecessary. My wound is trifling. My duty is to give my report and start to sort some of this..." LeMere looked toward the smoldering city with distaste, "debacle out. I was witness and participant, yet portions are obscure to me. I just know if I had been heeded, this would not have happened."

A few minutes later, LeMere stood at attention in the great cabin of *Favourite*. Dubordieu looked tired, older than his thirty-seven years. His face was haggard with worry and deeply lined by fissures of overwork.

"Captain LeMere of the Imperial Guard reporting, Commodore!" He snapped his heels together smartly and saluted briskly. His expression was haughty, but he looked slightly green from the onset of seasickness. He forced energetic conviction into his voice and continued. "I deeply regret the British have delayed my arrival. Allow me to give you a full report on recent events here. Captain Boudreau is dead, as are the regimental colonels. Sadly, I am now the ranking officer."

Dubordieu regarded the newcomer. So this was the man from the Guard via the *Tuileries*! He was familiar with his battle honours but guessed he came with a much wider directive than any written orders would indicate. He presumed the captain had the eyes and ears of the Emperor and would send confidential reports. He would have to watch this one and tread carefully; he had a plan to keep the man busy.

Dubordieu, like his Flag Captain, La Meilliere, was nothing if not well-mannered and considerate. "I am very pleased to meet you and eager to hear your news, but please, you are wounded and it has been a long day. Let us not stand on ceremony; please be at ease and sit. Have a little of this excellent Brugerolle Cognac; spirits to revive your spirits. I have some fine bread and Rochfort cheese as well. Even in wartime, the responsibilities of a good host are not suspended. Think of it as an easy talk between gentlemen. Now forgive the indelicacy of my next question, but what in God's name went wrong? Tell me everything you know!"

It took more than an hour for LeMere to tell his story. It was highly opinionated, charged with invective, flattering to himself, but for all of that, quite accurate. Dubordieu listened in rapt attention. He said little, other than an occasional *"Oui,"* and nodded his head from time to time. He took copious notes.

The very smooth cognac had a marked effect on LeMere, who took healthy swigs from the bottle every few minutes. Under its liberating influence, his narrative swelled to heights of prolixity he seldom attained. Part of him was inwardly embarrassed at his grandiose rhetoric, but part of him did not care. It was vitally important that Dubordieu understand. The Emperor's mission must be carried out! The shame to French honour must be expunged!

"Please, Captain, have no worries about us doing the right thing." Dubordieu spoke in quiet tones of patience mixed with weariness.

Dubordieu continued. "Captain, I am as eager to serve the Emperor as you are. We may be in different services and uniforms, but we are of the same mind. You are among friends here. I embrace your frankness and your observations. However, if you will postpone sleep a bit longer, I have some questions I should like to pose."

"Of course, Commodore, duty is the most sublime word in the French language," replied LeMere gallantly.

"Very good!" replied Dubordieu. He realized LeMere was a true acolyte of the Emperor. "How large were the British forces? I need to know if Hoste has been reinforced. Has Whitehall dispatched regular army troops to increase Hoste's striking power?"

"I do not believe so, Commodore. I believe we confronted only sailors and marines, perhaps four hundred men in all." He had no way of knowing he had been opposed by only half that number. "I saw no evidence of army troops, only the round hats of the marines. They way they moved, the way they used concealment, the initiative they showed, they could not have been army troops. Most of the British army is tied up overseas, or in Spain under Wellington. I doubt they could spare any for this area."

LeMere paused, lost in thought, then continued. "The thing that struck me was how expertly commanded they were. Every failing we had was detected, exploited, and used against us. Their troops were well trained, but I swear they were led by a sorcerer. He seemed to not only anticipate our every move, but to impose some strange compulsion upon us to make it. I remind you, of course, I was not in command and had to defer to *chef de battalion* Gaspar. He died with honour, but it was his incompetence that cost his own life and the lives of so many of our men. He ripped the victory we should have had from our grasp."

"This British commander, this sorcerer you spoke about, did you find out anything about him? Was he a naval or marine officer?" Dubordieu was curious. Whoever this man was, he was a thorn in the side of the French navy and would undoubtedly reappear.

John M. Danielski

"I saw him, Commodore. He wore the scarlet jacket and strange round hat of an officer of the Royal Marines. I had him in my sights, literally. I was about to fire when one of his compatriots inflicted this wound," he touched his shoulder, "the wound you see here. I heard them call out 'Pennywhistle.' I believe that to be his name. I hope to meet him again, and when I do, the results of our confrontation will be quite different. If he were French, I would welcome him into the Guard as a brother. The exigencies of war however, will compel me to kill him at our next encounter."

Dubordieu smiled inwardly. Here indeed was the arrogance of an Imperial Guard. However, he could see sterling qualities in this man, exactly as Napoleon had. This LeMere might be a very useful man to have in his squadron. Dubordieu had a plan originally intended to merely keep the Emperor's emissary busy; but it was just possible this LeMere might be able to make it work. It was time to pitch it.

"Captain LeMere, I know it is late and you are tired, nonetheless I beg you to listen to a proposal I have to make. As you know, we carry no specialized marines as such. They were abolished during the reforms of the early Revolution. We have sailors trained to perform the functions of marines, but I am sad to say they are inferior to their British counterparts. You have seen the marines in action, you have a clear eye for observation, and you thirst for revenge. I propose we take some of your land soldiers and train them as a special *corps de marine* for this squadron. I would want you in charge of all soldiers on every ship in the squadron. You would be free to train them in any way you saw fit; I would give you a free hand. Combining the training of Guardsmen with those of marines would make a formidable hybrid. I feel certain we are heading for an inexorable rendezvous with Hoste, and if you join us, you will surely have a chance to achieve the victory you so earnestly desire."

LeMere smiled broadly. This was more than he could have hoped for. No more having to defer to fools like Gaspar. He could train soldiers to have the skills and pride of Guardsman. As for copying the tactics of the British marines, that would be a challenge. He would have to write a new manual based upon his own experience and others who had fought the British. Had the French captured any marines? Had any deserters come over to the French side? Did the British use a special manual French intelligence operatives might procure? French Intelligence was first rate and almost no piece of useful information lay beyond their reach. His mind raced with possibilities and courses of action.

"Commodore, it would give me the greatest pleasure and honour to accept your gracious invitation. It will take much work, but be assured, I am more than equal to it. If it is acceptable to you, I should like to begin tomorrow."

Dubordieu smiled with satisfaction. LeMere had not just taken the bait, he had taken it with alacrity. "I had no doubt a man of honour and trusty courage such as yourself would accept. We will discuss the formal arrangements tomorrow, but for the present let me suggest you retire and get some well-earned rest. My steward will conduct you to your quarters. Let me just say, welcome to the Navy, Captain!"

"One thing, Commodore: what about the original mission of placing small garrisons in cities along the coast?" LeMere looked concerned.

"Have no fear, we will be able to do both. I know we were savaged badly at Groa, but we will still have enough men to provide garrisons and a battalion left over to become a *corps de marine*." The Commodore gave LeMere a look of reassurance. "The Emperor's orders will be executed fully and completely."

"That was my only concern; thank you for assuaging it. Again, thank you for the honour, sir. I bid you good night and look forward to the bold enterprise we begin on the morrow."

After LeMere left, Dubordieu considered his decision. LeMere might be pompous, but for all of his arrogance, he was probably as good as his word. The man clearly wanted distinction, and Dubordieu's plan might give it to him. Dubordieu inwardly congratulated himself. He would not only co-opt this spy, he would greatly improve his chances of beating the British.

Twenty

A week after the departure of the prize fleet, Hoste arrived off the French base at Ancona. The base was mostly empty, no sea-ready French ships anywhere in evidence, and no visible defensive earthworks or fortifications. *Active* deployed seven miles off the harbour mouth, *Amphon* twelve miles out, and *Cerberus* fourteen miles beyond that. It enabled the ships to watch a lot of sea for prizes. They were able to relay signals from their mastheads; to any French in harbour, only one ship would be visible, yet they would be able to reassemble quickly should Dubordieu's fleet make a sudden reappearance.

The harbour contained two ships in the first stages of preparation for sea. To Hoste, the arrangements looked slapdash and dilatory. A commander's will was important; the absence of Dubordieu's personal energy and drive had apparently left the dockyard in a state of enervation.

A harbour that was a major enemy base, rich in supplies, yet poorly defended, was far too good an opportunity to pass up, but with limited resources, Hoste had to choose his targets precisely. True, a strike at the enemy base would be a mere pinprick in the side of of the French body politic; still, it would let them know the British had the audacity to go after them in the place where they should have felt most safe. The British would have the moral ascendency, that ineffable sense of superiority that they could go anywhere, strike anywhere, and emerge victorious, no matter what efforts the French made to the contrary. It was a reinvention of the old adage, "Man proposes, but God disposes." The French stood in for man, the British for God.

Hoste ordered a night reconnaissance. Pennywhistle was the obvious choice to lead it. He was good at destruction, but Hoste surmised that an officer of his resourcefulness and perspicacity would be adept at intelligence gathering. He needed good and detailed intelligence beyond that which could be seen from the sea. He needed maps and a thorough accounting of the supply situation.

*****

After a briefing from the commodore, Pennywhistle met with Spottswood to make plans. Hoste's intentions were clear, but the details were left to Pennywhistle.

"Mr. Spottswood," Pennywhistle said, "before we hazard any marines, a personal call on Ancona is in order, and we are the only two French speakers on the ship. My accent passes for Parisian, so if any talking is necessary, leave it to me. Sadly, your patois smacks of a few lessons in the schoolroom. I mean no insult, Mr. Spottswood, but one has to be realistic when planning a mission. Absolute honesty, a passion for exactitude, and complete attention to even the most minor detail are the secrets of success. Moreover, they are the keys to bringing yourself and your men back alive."

"No offense taken, Captain. My French is not very good. I understand it well and write it perfectly, but sadly, I learned it at a local dame school and the mistress was not a native speaker; my French has inflections of Country Cork." Spottswood laughed. Since Groa, his confidence had grown. He spoke more in the wardroom, and occasionally even made jests, rather witty ones, too. Underneath what had been a sullen exterior, there lurked an observant mind and ebullient sense of humour.

"Then we shall go in tomorrow evening at high tide, around nine. The sail maker can whip up two uniform coats. I think the 21st Chasseurs best, but frankly, whatever the sail maker can manage will suit. Of course, if we are captured, we are liable to be shot as spies, but the uniforms only have to pass muster in darkness. Our ranks will be as they are in our service. We will be an officer and his newly minted subordinate out for a good time.

"Mainly, it will be how we wear our uniforms. We want to appear aloof, imperious, about important business and brooking no interruptions. It is a posture, a facial expression, a walk; all must project a collective sneer." Pennywhistle grinned. "Of course, neither one of us is anything like that!"

"It will be less difficult then you think for me, Mr. Pennywhistle. I will merely recall the painful times I spent with my father. He was surely the most arrogant, cold, untouchable being I have ever encountered. I have but to be him." Spottswood frowned.

"I am truly sorry for your misfortune. But consider, Mr. Spottswood, your father has given you an example of that which you have no wish to become. Every action you take that differs from his, every step you take away from the path he chose, moves you far from his shadow and into the light. You have nothing to live up to, perhaps, but every action you perform of a superior moral nature moves you to truly becoming your own man. I sensed you did not want to be your father, but had no idea who exactly you did want to be. I think the recent events at Groa have changed all that." Pennywhistle felt awkward dispensing advice, as he had no family of his own, but Spottswood clearly admired him and needed a father figure.

"Mr. Pennywhistle, I was truly lost for the longest time. Some mornings I dreaded even waking up. I thought I would never live to see my 21st birthday. When our family solicitor first proposed the idea of a marine commission, I found it peculiar, to say the least. I thought it was just another meddling blue lighter trying to do an odd form of missionary work. Now it seems that God has a quirky sense of humour and has decided to give me another chance at life. When I was first shot at and did not run, it was like blinkers had been removed. In an instant, I saw myself having a future and a career as a good man and a good officer. I compared the knave I had been with the man I was capable of being. At that moment, all of the slurs and belittling insults my father threw at me lost their power." He spoke rapidly, as if his words needed to be said before he lost the resolve to say them.

"I commend you upon your progress, and I am glad to have you on *Active*. You saved my life. I will always owe you a debt. Let us agree then, we are both fine fellows." Pennywhistle laughed again and Spottswood smiled. "But let us now return to the planning."

He unfurled a map. "There is a creek a mile or so from town, near the ruins of the Castle del Vecchio. There is no moon tomorrow night, so we should be able to land undetected. Our primary mission is to scout the dockyard and pinpoint suitable targets for a raid. We may have to do so at distance, using our glasses. Above all, we need to locate their supply of powder. Wellington once said that the amateur soldier frets over strategy while the wise one focuses on logistics. The French are brave adversaries, but without powder they can do nothing."

Spottswood smiled. This might be rather entertaining.

*****

LeMere hunched over a small kneehole desk built into the bulkhead of his cabin on *Favourite*. He was revising the drill and manual of arms he had composed for his *corps de marine*. The idea was taking splendid form: his training squad was eager and progressing rapidly. He pondered adding new skills to their already impressive repertoire.

Thank God, his seasickness had finally departed. He laughed inwardly at his reflexive use of a deity's name, since he knew God was a myth invented to keep the masses in line. He looked at the gentle swaying motion of the single lantern that illuminated his small cabin. Not long before, seeing its movement had induced the violent emptying of his stomach.

He reviewed his position with Dubordieu. While he had control of what he had begun to call marines, he had none over the sailors in the fleet, and no jurisdiction over how the ships were sailed and fought—that belonged to Dubordieu. He had come to respect the Commodore but harboured his master the Emperor's deep-seated suspicion of sea officers. He'd sent back his first optimistic report to Paris, describing his project. Napoleon liked innovation and would approve of his comprehensive training program. He would do with his men what the Emperor had done with the *Grande Armee*. He would give them pride, dignity, and an unshakeable faith in themselves. He smiled with conviction as he thought of the phrase, "his men." It had a good ring to it.

LeMere had been born to privilege. His father was a marquis, but he regarded aristocrats with contempt. Their pampered conceits had driven France into bankruptcy and undermined her martial prowess. Perhaps *La Terreur* had been extreme, but a good many worthless friends of his father had deserved the attentions of *Mademoiselle Guillotine*. Napoleon had ruthlessly swept away unworthy officers, whatever their experience or pedigree, and replaced them with men who truly knew how to lead. Real privilege was commanding good men in a good cause, a privilege earned by hard work. LeMere believed firmly in his Destiny, but he also believed that a good man created his own luck.

The question that obsessed him was how he could he make his forces the decisive element in the next encounter with the British. Perhaps the Commodore would succeed in his Herculean efforts to bring seamanship and gunnery up to something approaching British standards. If he did so, well and good; but the one person in whom LeMere had complete and unbounded faith was Rene LeMere.

LeMere calculated that the British would always have better gunnery. He disliked admitting it, but ruthless honesty in appraising oneself and the enemy was important. In a traditional sea battle, the British fired faster and more accurately. They could keep their distance and pound the French fleet into wooden rubble. At close range, the destructive power of their carronades, of which the French had few and inferior copies, invariably proved decisive.

What the French had was manpower. Their sailors were poorly trained, but they had many more of them. The fleet also had a much larger supply of soldiers. His mind's eye brightened: marines! Why not use their superior numbers? Close quickly with the enemy and board. If they could not silence the British guns, use small arms fire and grenades to kill the men who manned them. Big gun to big gun was a losing proposition for the French, but well-managed small arms fire in numbers against big guns might well be a winning equation. Captain Lucas in the *able* at Trafalgar had come close to taking *Victory*, a much bigger ship, with just such a strategy. What might he have accomplished with superbly trained men? The British excelled in seamanship, but quickly closing and locking two ships together in a death embrace would remove their ability to maneuver. It would become a contest not of skill but of numbers; the French would be able to overwhelm the British.

It was also a matter of heart and philosophy. He had been trained in the spirit of the Emperor. Attack, attack, attack! Seize the initiative and never let it go! Take the fight to the enemy! Dubordieu and the French navy repeatedly defended. The navy mentality had always been to preserve the fleet, not destroy the enemy. Live to fight another day. LeMere knew that was fundamentally wrong. It sapped a fighting man's spirit and destroyed audacity.

He would change that. Frenchmen would not be defending French ships. They would make the British defend theirs. It would be a new spirit, a new order of things. It was high time! Napoleon had shown that all things were possible. There was no reason the spirit and outlook of the Imperial Guard could not be transplanted to the French fleet. This was a small beginning, but LeMere felt a surging confidence that it was the start of something much greater: a whole new tradition of victory.

Better marksmanship was essential. It still rankled in his memory, how ineffective the French armsmen had been at Groa compared to British snipers and sharpshooters. Fixed, unmoving targets were convenient, but unrealistic. Then he had a flash of insight, pure brilliance. Why not have his men fire at unused floating barrels dropped over the sides? He chuckled to himself. It was surely something the British would never think of. There were advantages to being a Guardsman! Studying at the foot of the greatest soldier in history taught lessons impossible to duplicate elsewhere.

A niggle of doubt disturbed his reverie. There was someone on the British side who might have thought of it—Pennywhistle. That Englishman would have appreciated studying under Napoleon.

He forced his mind away from his nemesis and back to the matter at hand. They would need a copious supply of grenades in various sizes for the men to practice hurling them properly. Sailors would have to improve their use of boarding pikes and swords. He would importune the Commodore to see to that. They might not be under his command, but if he could spread his ideas, his spirit, his force of will, even the naval officers would see the inescapable logic of his methods. A knock at his cabin door interrupted his dreams of glory. It was Dubordieu.

"May I come in, Captain?" inquired Dubordieu.

"But of course, Commodore, you are always most welcome. How may I be of assistance?"

"I wanted to ask if your program might be extended to our Venetian allies? I am most pleased with your progress. It would be good if all ships in the fleet were up to French standards." Dubordieu spoke as if that prospect were doubtful. Well, given the performance of Venetian troops in the past, that was not unfounded.

"I think that will eventually be possible, Commodore, but may I humbly suggest that we wait several weeks? I want our own men to be proficient, up to Guard standards, before I export my designs. And the Italians... some of it may need to be re-worked for them." His expression suggested those re-workings would need to be extensive.

Dubordieu nodded. "I expected you might say something like that, and I will bow to your opinion. I ask because I dispatched Captain Pasqualigo in *Corona* to Ancona for supplies yesterday. I prefer to keep our French ships here for now. He is the most steadfast and reliable of our allied captains, and I thought his ship would be the best on which to begin your program. I thought perhaps when he returns...." Dubordieu left the sentence unfinished.

"I met him briefly and I share your opinion, Commodore. A stalwart man. His ship will be an excellent place to begin the spread of the program. I thank you for consulting me on this matter." *Oh yes, we will spread this to the entire fleet, but it will be on my terms, my schedule.*

"Then I will not trouble you further, Captain. I have duties which beckon, and I can see you have as well. I trust you will be joining me and my officers for dinner?" Dubordieu set a fine table.

"Of course, Commodore, it is always a pleasure. I do not know which is more delightful, the food or the conversation." LeMere was being honest to a point. He liked Dubordieu. His real agenda at the dinners was to promulgate his ideas in a relaxed setting. As the wine flowed, tongues loosened, ears opened, and his considerable eloquence stealthily assumed centre stage. His incessant talk of victory was like a drug that insinuated itself into the blood of everyone at Dubordieu's table. He was an evangelist for a new mode of war, and he found willing disciples. Even the worldly Dubordieu was not immune. LeMere, a combat soldier first and foremost, was also a practiced and polished court intriguer of the first rank.

"You flatter me too much, Captain. I will see you at two. We have a very fine rack of lamb for today's feast. I trust you will be hungry from your exertions. I bid you *au revoir* until then."

Dubordieu departed. As he climbed the companionway, he thought with satisfaction: *My plan is working. LeMere will work with his heart and soul on this, little realizing he is gradually becoming my man.*

LeMere returned to his earlier thoughts. Much remained to be done, a million details; but it was as the Emperor said, the key to victory was in the details. *I am well on my way to subourning Dubordieu to my ends.* But he could not help wondering, *Where is Pennywhistle?*

*****

Thomas Pennywhistle fidgeted as the cuffs of his new coat were lengthened. Peter Spottswood was alongside. Hawkes, the sail maker, had protested that the uniforms of the 1st Light Infantry were easier to copy than the 21st chausseurs. Deferring to Hawkes' judgment, they were now dressed as officers of the voltigeur company of that regiment. Hawkes was a self-taught tailor, and while his work was not up to Parisian standards, the uniforms were convincing enough as products of provincial tailoring.

The two marine officers were caparisoned in double-breasted jackets of cobalt blue with silver buttons and white piping, complimented with green and gold epaulettes. Their trousers were a matching shade of blue, their boots black. The blue and gold shakos, souvenirs of a raid, had been crudely altered to conform to the rest. They were the least convincing part of the attire, but on a moonless night, they should pass muster.

"This stupid shako is deuced uncomfortable!" Spottswood protested. The marine coachman's hat was so much more practical.

Pennywhistle laughed, "Yes, but it makes you look taller and more imposing. A cruel necessity, Mr. Spottswood—it is the capstone of our disguise. Remember, it is designed to impress, not for the wearer's comfort. Wear it with pride!"

Spottswood gave a rueful grimace. "Very well, Captain, but I will not put it on until absolutely the last minute!"

"Understood, Lieutenant. And now we will need to attend to our *accoutrements*. We cannot wear cutlasses nor possess English arms. I don't think anyone will be terribly perceptive this evening, but it is as well to be prudent. The armourer canvassed the ship high and low and produced these poor specimens." He reached down to the deck and picked up two swords, handing one to Spottswood. "These are hardly Wilkinson steel, but they are French. I know they are not in good repair, but the armourer's mate put a decent edge on them. The most important things are the pommels. They are of a clear French design." He reached down again and produced two small calibre pistols. "The pistols are somewhat better. They are not sea service pistols, but well made St. Etienne gentleman's side-arms. We have Captain Gordon to thank for their loan." Pennywhistle smiled. "He told me he would like them back in pristine condition," he paused, then add with sincerity, "along with their borrowers."

Spottswood smiled back. "I would never think for a moment of disobeying the Captain's orders."

*****

Captain Pasqualigo of the *Corona*, 40, was eighty miles out from

Ragusa Harbour, bound for Ancona. A brisk wind and gently rolling swells propelled *Corona*—a beautiful day for sailing. He was happy and relaxed; this was a routine voyage with an entertaining shore leave at its end. Eager as he was to meet the British in battle, he knew that was about as likely as a Protestant becoming Pope.

Twenty-One

Pennywhistle and Spottswood splashed ashore at the mouth of a small tidal creek a hundred yards in front of *Castle del Vecchio*. Master's Mate Hudson was already standing out to sea with the cutter; the two marines would trouble the French for transportation home. A wide beach stretched from the picturesque old gothic ruins to the French dockyard at Ancona a mile away. The night was wonderfully crisp and favoured with an invigorating light breeze that gently ruffled the surface of the waves. The sky sparkled with a glorious carpet of stars although there was no moon. It was a fine evening for a pleasant stroll.

Pennywhistle was enjoying the walk and idly star-gazing constellations when they passed close to the castle's crumbling gatehouse. He heard a rustle of movement behind one of the walls and instantly shifted his vision.

A flying body slammed into Pennywhistle's shoulders from behind. The impact flung him violently forward, but he instinctively arched his back, extended his arms, and used the energy to roll into a ball away from his attacker. He unfurled himself, sprang to his feet, and pivoted to face his unknown opponent. His muscles sang with the energy of danger, his will became icy clear, and his eyes flashed fire. He drew his sword with blinding speed.

There were five bandits in all, the oldest not more than twenty. All were dressed theatrically in colourful, long cloaks and plumed floppy hats that seemed an homage to MacHeath of the Beggar's Opera. None of them an impressive physical specimen, but there was strength in numbers. They had convinced themselves they were warriors for a greater *Italia* but in truth, they were a cowardly pack of delinquent scavengers out for easy prey. They had the outsize confidence of practiced footpads used to robbing and executing unwary soldiers too surprised to offer resistance. The two volitgeur officers walking along the beach appeared easy marks, probably loaded with valuable trinkets. They hesitated briefly, since there were two soldiers instead of one, but greed and a few shots of rot-gut brandy erased what little good sense they had.

A split second mental flash told Pennywhistle that the gatehouse had probably been used as an ambush site many times before. Spottswood was dazed, but Pennywhistle sized the situation up quickly. The stench of cheap liquor pervaded the air; Dutch courage. From their weapons, postures, and positions, he knew these were no soldiers. Their expressions were fierce, but it was only the facial camouflage of amateurs with no stomach for a real fight.

Damn and blast these bastards, they would pay! He fought real soldiers, not brutish criminals. He was a King's Officer, not a constable. He had better things to do tonight than play rubbish collector!

He flourished his long saber in a swift, mesmerizing half circle to distract his opponent, then raised the blade vertically above his head, the guard even with his face. Grey Cloak clumsily brought his blade up horizontally to block. Pennywhistle feinted a cut to the head, jerked rapidly downward, and slammed the saber's heavy iron pommel into the man's groin. The man screamed in agony and started to double over.

Pennywhistle fueled the kinetic energy of the jab with his anger and continued upwards. He rammed the pommel into Grey Cloak's nose then raked his eyes. He crashed his elbow into his Adam's apple, crushing the bandit's windpipe. Grey Cloak collapsed, making inchoate mewling sounds. Pennywhistle's heavy boot slammed into his temple. The mewling stopped. He forced the corpse aside with his left boot and saw a second attacker running forward with his sword extended.

Brown Cloak waved his blade wildly, stupidly, his face a mask of brutish hatred. Pennywhistle's battle senses let him see the attacker as if in slow motion. He executed a brisk sidestep in the manner of a toreador and crouched slightly. He cocked his arm, unfurled his fist, and readied the palm heel of his left hand. His hips corkscrewed violently upward as his arm telescoped out and one hundred and eighty pounds of fury drove the cartilage directly into the man's uneducated brain. The force of the blow lifted the bandit three inches off the ground. He gave a short *AAARRRGGH* sound and swiftly crumpled to the ground like a blacksmith's worn out bellows.

Blue Cloak, directly behind Brown Cloak, stumbled over his fallen comrade. Pennywhistle grabbed him by his collar, guided his energy, and then tripped him with his boot. He hurtled through the night air and landed with a heavy *thunk*, face down, stunned. He tried to catch his breath, twist his head round and rise, but succeeded only in positioning his neck at an odd and inviting angle. Pennywhistle raised his left boot as high as he could manage. A dissected corpse from the Edinburgh anatomy theatre flashed into his mind. He smashed his heavy heel down with cold precision on the third cervical vertebra. *Snap!* The spinal cord parted and understanding left the eyes.

Spottswood rolled over and over, with Green Cloak on top, his powerful hands fastened securely on Spottswood's neck. The marine began to see stars. His neck burned with fire. Suffocation was damn painful! He fought for breath, smelled the alcohol-soaked sweat of his attacker. He strayed close to a fatal blackout, but a deep, howling anger sent a jolt of primal energy spiraling up through his torso. He wrenched a hand free and purely on instinct drove four of his fingers, spatula fashion, into Green Cloak's right eye. The bandit let go, fell backwards and rolled aside, clutching his face, and shrieking with pain. Spottswood kicked out wildly and his boots connected solidly with the man's pectorals. The brigand uttered a faint wheezing sound as the breath departed his lungs.

The pain in Spottswood's neck helped him retain consciousness. He slowly struggled to his feet, shook his head quickly to clear it, and drew his saber. He sucked in deep, gasping breaths. He towered over the bandit. For a split second, his eyes and the bandit's locked. Spottswood saw pure, naked fear; an ugly thing. He felt sorry for Green Cloak for fragment of a second, but mercy departed like a hummingbird chased by hawks and he raised the blade above his head. Holding it two-handed, to increase power, he plunged it violently earthward, directly through the man's right occipital ridge. The bandit's eyes widened, shouted fear, disbelief, then rolled harmlessly upward. The light of life vanished, like someone snuffing a candle. Green Cloak let out a low rattle. The transition from man to corpse took only a second. This was far different from killing a man at a distance.

Black Cloak, their leader, turned tail and ran. His violent bluster masked an apparently timid soul. Pennywhistle took no chances he would raise the alarm and dashed after him. In truth, the marine was actuated far less by logic and far more by anger and the eagerness of a predator to chase down a weakened quarry. He felt a deep ire against undisciplined, wanton violence in the service of mere greed .Tonight's attack was a clear case of mistaken identity. He wondered how many men of honour had died at the hands of these brigands. Whatever the number was, there would be no more after tonight.

The marine's lean, muscled legs closed the distance quickly. His target was not only shorter of leg and stride, but simply a slower runner. He could hear Black Cloak's painfully laboured breathing and smell the sharp stink of fear. He was on his target's heels, his sword advanced. He kicked at the back of Black Cloak's right calf, while he simultaneously grabbed the left side of his cloak and yanked violently backwards. The bandit lost his balance.

As he fell, his head flashed into a perfect position for dissection, as if locked in a vice. Pennywhistle brought his heavy saber down in a swift and deadly arc. The force of the blow sliced through bone as if it were merely fog. It cleft the bandit's misshapen skull in two, like a chef bisecting a ripe pumpkin. The blade easily powered on through the *corpus callosum*. The left half of Black Cloak's gnarled, grey brain plopped down on the beach, just in front of Pennywhistle's feet. Blood gushed, but missed his uniform entirely.

A mad, black shot of jocularity squirted into Pennywhistle's excited brain. "The man's lost his mind," he exclaimed aloud with surprise. He stopped dead in his tracks and laughed. Not very rational, he realized. It worried him. That was the way "the black dog" had started with his father.

He breathed in and out, slowly and deeply, for a full minute, calming himself. His hot passions cooled. His rational mind took control. He methodically scanned the night to make sure no more bandits lurked in the shadows. He walked past all of the corpses and prodded them to make absolutely certain no life remained. He thought he saw a twitch from Grey Cloak. He thrust his sword through the brigand's temple, to be sure. He had never enjoyed killing, but he could not deny he felt satisfaction at this moment. He had expunged human vermin as a public executioner. The citizens of Ancona would sleep a little more safely tonight.

Spottswood walked slowly up to him, his deliberate, measured steps like a drunk trying to convince someone he was perfectly sober.

Pennywhistle recognized the walk. It was the heavy tread of a young man who had just inflicted his first battle death at close quarters. Killing in hand to hand combat was the most physically intimate act in the world short of lovemaking. Struggling victor and victim saw into each other's souls for a few brief seconds and forged a strange, deep bond. That bond was never forgotten by the survivor and he would forever carry with him some portion of the loser's essence. The victor would always be cursed with flashbacks, and could later recall with exquisite clarity the terror in his adversary's eyes, the garlic on his breath, the large size of his hands, or any of a hundred other unimportant details.

He remembered the feeling. It was never pleasant, unless you were seriously unbalanced, but it was always powerful. It was an awesome event in the completely Biblical sense of the term. It was similar to losing your virginity; you would never be the same after. Only here, you were overwhelmed not with pleasure, but with feelings of surprise and uncertainty, often tinged with a hint of remorse. Your motives mattered, but much less than the central fact you had relieved another human being of his life. Whether that life had been one of glorious triumph or weary burden, it was over.

It was a true rite of passage but there was no real preparatory ritual as with Holy Communion or knightly investiture, only a swift choice that propelled you across a threshold most men never crossed or even approached. Every warrior dealt with it in his own special way. You might long for the innocence you had before at some point, wish the event could be extirpated from memory, but you were permanently and irrevocably branded and altered. You would meet your first kill again in dreams. Guaranteed.

Sir Atholl's death in the duel never troubled Pennywhistle because it had been in the service of saving an innocent woman and done in hot blood. It had forced him to leave university, but he had done right and relieved the world of a very bad man. His second kill, at Trafalgar troubled him greatly because it was so impersonal, so cold-blooded. He had watched in macabre slow motion as his pistol ball exploded the man's right eye. The Boatswain had done him no harm, had merely been doing his duty. He remembered the swarthy face exactly and wondered what kind of man the French sailor had been.

Eyes were where a reaction manifested. As Spottswood came closer, Pennywhistle saw that his blue eyes were as wide and bright as full moons and radiated a strange, detached luminescence. Spottswood had probably seen the light leave one man's eyes. It was as if that light had been absorbed by Spottswood's and increased their intensity.

"Are you all right?" Pennywhistle asked with real kindness.

"Yes, thank you, sir, I believe I am." Spottswood stopped and seemed to conduct a mental self examination of his physical parts to verify the truth of his own statement. "I confess, I am a bit... unsettled, sir. It all happened so fast." His eyes looked skyward hoping for some kind of divine guidance and understanding. "I just killed a man, sir, put a sword through his head." He spoke with an emotionless monotone as if his mind were just discovering the fact.

"Yes, yes you did, Mr. Spottswood," said Pennywhistle in a calm understanding voice. "I am glad of it, too, else we should not be standing here having this conversation. You did what was necessary, don't ever forget that. Battle is cruel, and separates men into two kinds; those who act and live, and those who hesitate and die. You may be feeling... well, feelings that you don't understand, but I have been down the same path, and I assure you that you performed admirably. The people we killed tonight were parasites, blackguards preying on the weak. I have a feeling they were as much a problem to their fellow countrymen as to the French. You did your duty. It may seem strange to say, but taking a life in the fashion you did is part of the process of your redemption, your transformation to a better self; a warrior. Moreover, that fellow you slew might have attacked me, so you might just have saved my life a second time. Now much as it pains me to say, I must recall you to your duty. We have a vital task to perform tonight and we cannot let these contemptible poltroons divert us. Breathe deeply for a few minutes, Mr. Spottswood, calm down, then let's be about our business. Are you with me, Mr. Spottswood?" The best medicine was activity and focusing on the mission.

Spottswood's mind took a few seconds to absorb Pennywhistle's words. But the confidence the captain had in him and the conviction and sincerity in Pennywhistle's voice overcame his own mental shock at what he had just done. It made him realize he was a King's Officer with a duty, and deuced proud of the honour! "I am with you, sir! Let's make trouble for the French!"

For the next fifteen minutes, they walked together toward the town in complete silence. During the interval, tension gradually faded, although enough remained to give their faces a troubled cast. Pennywhistle decided they had had one piece of luck. During the fight, neither had had his uniform damaged and, almost miraculously, they had no blood on them. Their cover story could still work.

Twenty-Two

Drunkenly hunched over a table in the dark rear of the tavern *Il Casso del Tessoro*, Major Pierre du Grandchamp brooded on his misfortunes. He could not believe it! It could not be happening! He would not let it happen! God damn them all! A plague on the *commandant* and the pox on all his children! Send him home? Relieve him of duty? Impossible! He came from one of the oldest families in France. He had connections. He would write letters. He had two cousins at the *Tuileries*. This would come to the attention of the Emperor himself! This would not stand! He poured another draft of ale into his leather tankard and took a deep draft. Bah! What was this local horse piss anyway? When he got back to Arles, nothing but the finest brandy.

He had made one mistake, one. He was a good officer, a brilliant officer, the best adjutant for which a commander could ask. He handled all of the details of the post and yard flawlessly. It was he who worked long watches into the night sifting through an endless torrent of reports, lists, books, and forms. It was he who consulted with the officers, listened to the complaints of dockworkers, filled out the reports for Paris. It was he who made the written and verbal reports to Commodore Dubordieu.

He poured himself another shot. He liked the deadening effects, but this ale was atrocious. The host had recommended it. Really, these Italians had no taste for the finer things. He had ordered ale because it seemed the least offensive. Italians simply had no conception of a good wine. Horse piss? He had been too generous! Donkey piss!

His career was in tatters and it was because of one mistake. It had nothing to do with his efficiency. His abilities were widely admired and most officers admitted privately that he ran the base.

The *commandant*, Colonel Chartres, was a figurehead, a cipher. He was old, lethargic, and weak. He had been badly wounded and wore a peg leg. Napoleon had given him this post as a reward for past services. It was a virtual sinecure and the actual work had devolved to du Grandchamp. It still rankled when he thought of the *thud, thud, thud* of the wooden leg as he walked, free of care, on the floor above while du Grandchamp patiently slaved away.

Colonel Chartres had a beautiful Italian mistress, a black-tressed, voluptuous beauty of soaring bosom and long legs, but twenty years of age. He doted on her, ravished her at every opportunity. He'd installed her in a fine mansion and showered her with gifts.

She was of a good family and accepted him, not out of passion, but practicality. Her parents were dead, killed in the wars, and she was, above all, a survivor. She was accustomed to the finer things in life, and Chartres provided them.

It was inevitable that she and du Grandchamp would meet. He handled all of the paperwork for everything, including her expenses and her monthly stipend. Sabrina had been but a name and a leger entry until the afternoon she came into his office with some minor problem about payments to her couturier. Their reaction to each other was instantaneous, startling, and powerful: love, or rather lust, at first sight, a grand, mad passion beyond all reason and discipline. Du Grandchamp was as young, handsome, and virile as the colonel was not. The hormones of two attractive people simply seized control.

As they gathered the leftover shreds of the clothing they had torn off each other, they both knew this had to happen again, and soon. The colonel must never know, for both of their sakes.

Du Grandchamp poured another large shot. Damn it, why had he let it happen? He was a precise man of regular ordered habits, the consummate staff officer. The whole thing had been madness. He smiled to himself. Yes, but glorious, unforgettable, all-consuming madness! Strangely, its forbidden nature had added to the spice.

Of course, passion made them careless and their secret was discovered. Colonel Chartres banished her and relieved him of duty, preparatory to sending him home with a career-ruining report. Du Grandchamp wondered where she was.

"Good evening, Major, you look like you could use a friend. We are both new to this city and are eager to make new friends. May we join you?" The voice was sonorous, resonant, and the accent suggested someone from Napoleon's court.

Du Grandchamp looked up and saw two officers dressed in the uniforms of the lst Volitgeurs. One was tall, well built, with deep-set eyes that suggested an active brain. The other was shorter, but wore a similarly thoughtful expression.

Du Grandchamp searched his alcohol-fogged brain. He did not recall any new officers scheduled to arrive. He should have been informed. But perhaps he had been. Everything had collapsed when Sabrina fled. What the hell! They seemed pleasant and agreeable chaps. And damn it, he was angry! He needed to talk!

"Certainly, Captain," du Grandchamp slurred. "I could use a friend. Have you ever lost a woman who drove you utterly mad?"

The Voltigeur captain responded with a sincere tone. "I have indeed! My dear wife Louise died in childbirth. I know well the pain I see in your eyes. Let me get you a drink. I will be happy to listen." He and his companion settled in for a long tale.

Thirty minutes passed in a flash for du Grandchamp; it felt longer for his new companions.

"And so you see, my friends, life has proved a cruel mistress! I am undone! I am reduced from a good officer to the wretch you see before you!" Du Grandchamp quietly started to sob. "And my Sabrina is gone."

After forty more minutes and two more ales, Pennywhistle and Spottswood were now the friends of his bosom. They had gained his trust and confidence.

"You have my deepest sympathies, Major," responded Pennywhistle with sympathy that was not entirely feigned. This man had hit a bad patch, but now it was down to business. Pennywhistle and Spottswood had only pretended to drink their ales, while du Grandchamp had drunk liberally at their expense. Pennywhistle had learned much about the state of affairs at the dockyard, and even more about the hated Colonel Chartres. Time now to seek specifics about security and ways to gain entry to the dockyard. Pennywhistle had a mental image of sailors manning the twin-levered Bentinck pumps on *Active*, to bring up water from the stinking bilges. What he and Spottswood were about to do seemed eerily similar.

"I understand men like Colonel Chartres, men who are past their prime, puffed with bile and pomposity, worse than useless. They usurp positions that properly belong to young, vigorous men like ourselves. They avoid the work, yet reap the honours and emoluments. They steal our women and our chance at glory. And yet, their arrogance and carelessness can also make them vulnerable."

"Vulnerable? How so?" The idea of Chartres open to harm pierced du Grandchamp's alcoholic haze.

"You have been burdened with paperwork. You fill up the forms, the reports, attend to the details. But that drudgery also allows access to his secrets. Surely there is some detail, some peccadillo, some indiscretion that can be used against him?" Pennywhistle prodded gently.

"Sadly, nothing suggests itself. He maintained a mistress," du Grandchamp spat angrily, "but that is common enough among high ranking officers stationed abroad. The Emperor regards such things as spoils of war. As long as the expenditures from the public coffers are not excessive, it is officially winked at. Chartres is a bad man, but appears guilty of no financial peculation or black market activity."

"You collate and summarize the reports Chartres forwards to you, Major; is it possible matters could have been deliberately misreported? For example, powder and shot stocks and expenditures. Perhaps he has sold some on the black market; the most basic supplies of war are always in demand. If he bribed subordinates to make false reports, you would have no way of knowing the real situation. You are an honest man, I am sure, Major. Yet your reports are only as good as the information you receive."

Du Grandchamp looked shocked. "I have never considered it. As adjutant, I fill out the forms, but I am not the inspector general. And if the inspector general were in on it..." His voice trailed off in surprise, as if contemplating a vast conspiracy just revealed. But then he turned angry. "Damn! It is possible, yet I have no way to find out. The colonel placed me under arrest and it is only because of the kindness of Sergeant Dugard, my jailer, I am permitted this one last night of freedom. He, too, knows what it is like to find true love and have it snatched away!"

Pennywhistle tried to keep a sly smile off his face. "Tell me, other than Dugard, does anyone know you are relieved of duty and under arrest?"

Du Grandchamp pondered slowly. "No, I think not. This terrible business just took place this afternoon. It probably will not be public knowledge until tomorrow."

Pennywhistle replied, "So as far as everyone in Ancona knows, you are still the adjutant and your orders are still valid?"

"Correct. The colonel is lazy. I am sure he has done nothing about appointing a replacement for me. If I know him, at this moment he is probably pursuing some common town doxy. That man cannot live without the joys of Venus!" He spat the words with derision.

"Then permit me to help. I have known you only briefly, but I feel I have formed a special bond with you, rooted in our common loss. And I, too, have suffered under an incompetent ingrate of a superior. You are under arrest, but I am not. Let me make my own inspection of the dockyard this evening, particularly the powder and shot. Give me the password and countersign. I will say I am acting under your orders and am on urgent business. When I find evidence of the Colonel's peculations, I will find a way to convey the information to Commodore Dubordieu himself; he is, after all, in charge, and you will be exonerated. And I am sure a few tokens of esteem to Sergeant Dugard will result in his having a relaxed attitude to your confinement." Pennywhistle smiled and waved the purse full of coins. "I have a feeling, no, I am certain, I will discover evidence which will completely exonerate you at your court-marital. I regret I can do nothing about your beloved Sabrina. But if the one thing can be resolved in your favour, there is always hope the other may be as well."

Du Grandchamp's eyes filled with tears of gratitude. "You would do this for me? But why?"

"We are kindred spirits, both men of honour, and must assist each other when the situation and spirit occasion it. It is part of our code. You would do the same for me, if our positions were reversed."

"Indeed, I would, monsieur, indeed I would. I will be forever in your debt. Now tell me what your need." The alcohol had increased Du Grandchamp's earnestness quotient considerably.

"If you would sketch the layout of the dockyard, that would be most helpful." Pennywhistle pulled a piece of folded paper from his pocket and spread it on the table. He added a small graphite stylus. "Powder and shot magazines, sail lofts, rope yards, pitch, and tar storage... everything specific you can remember. We must be thorough in our inspections, if we are to bring this duplicitous dog, Chartres, to justice!"

Du Grandchamp begin to draw. His hand was unsteady, but he sketched and labeled everything with great care. Pennywhistle inwardly frowned at the artistic quality, but smiled outwardly at the wealth of information being given. Du Granchamp added little notes to the sketches of each building, extra details about contents. The man was meticulous, truly the ideal staff officer.

"Thank you so much, Major, your zeal and diligence will undoubtedly go far to exonerate you!"

Spottswood moved closer and whispered in Pennywhistle's ear, "His zeal and diligence will get him the firing squad!"

Twenty-Three

Captain Luigi Pasqualigo sailed *Corona* comfortably toward Ancona harbour, fourteen miles distant. The voyage had been routine. Better than routine, quite pleasant actually. It was a warm, almost sensual, night with a six-knot breeze. The hint of the *Bora* allowed them to sail one point off the quarter. There was no moon, but stars sparkled in the sky. Truly, a *bella noche*. His French allies had their gifts, to be sure, but the ability to appreciate the delicate beauty of a wonderful night at sea was not one of them. They simply had no sense of romance, unlike Venetians.

A cry from the masthead lookout pierced the night. "Deck there! Sail ho, off the port beam!"

Pasqualigo yelled up, "What do you make of her?"

"Hard to tell, sir." People who have not spent time at sea often fail to realize how hard it is to identify another ship in the blackness of night if that ship has no wish to be seen. Ships without lights could pass close and miss each other entirely. The lookout shouted down, "Can't make out much, sir, but she is not small. Ship-rigged she is, three masts, sir. Lying hove-to, maybe half a mile."

Pasqualigo pondered. Most of the local trading crafts were brigs, two-masted. More curiously, why was she lying hove-to, essentially stationary, on a night like this? This was an ideal evening for sailing, unless.... This was the edge of a nautical piquet line. She must be a warship! Hoste? It had to be! He wasn't supposed to be here! As if in confirmation of Pasquaglio's wild surmise, there was a long whistling sound, followed by the unpleasant noise of ripping canvas. A long tear appeared in the fore course. His ship was under attack!

Pasquaglio was stunned. This was an emergency of the first order. But he did not panic. He quickly and coldly reviewed his options. None were promising.

*****

Cerberus was ready for anything. Captain Whitby had ordered the two twelve-pound bow chasers to open fire, and one had scored a hit. The *rat-tat-tat* of the marine drummers rang out "beat to quarters." The ship came alive.

"Brace the main yards round!" yelled Whitby. The sails had been backed, or reversed, to keep the ship in a stationary position. As masses of sailors hauled with all their might on the braces, the sails angled round to catch the wind. Like the hellhound for whom she was named, *Cerberus* leapt forward.

*****

"All hands aloft! Shake out the topgallants and the royals!" shouted a shocked Captain Pasquaglio. He needed every ounce of canvas he could muster. He knew a night chase at sea was a risky and bewildering exercise, one that actually favoured the pursued. Of course, the first thing a good officer would do if he wished to escape would be to douse the lanterns. Pasqualigo did just that. *Corona* went totally dark.

Too late. Shattering glass and splintering timbers announced the destruction of the windows of *Corona*'s great cabin. Pasquaglio turned toward the report and saw a looming black shape coming at them, bows on, from almost directly astern, less than half a mile distant, perfectly positioned to pivot at the last second and bring a full broadside to rake his stern, the weakest and most vulnerable part of a ship. Shots from a broadside would travel almost the entire length of the ship, causing enormous damage and human destruction.

It had happened so quickly, Pasquaglio had not even had time to beat to quarters. His crew was slow and inexperienced in gun drill. And that was in the daytime. To fight a night battle against the British was to enter a suicide pact. But *Corona* had a reputation as a fast ship, and her men were well schooled in sail drill. These were slight advantages; he prayed they would be enough.

Pasquaglio gave the command to tack, to bring the bow of the ship through the wind and change direction. The order was executed promptly and smartly. No one had to tell the men how desperate their situation was. The wind being strong, *Corona* swung quickly away from her pursuer.

"Fire!" Whitby brought his sword down and sixteen guns crashed out, the full broadside of *Cerberus*. Thunder crashed through the silence of the night, giant tongues of flame darted out, and cannons jumped back on their tackles.

Timbers shattered and massive gashes appeared along *Corona*. It was as if a giant fist had punched a huge hole in the stern. Men screamed and rolled in agony, their blood making the gun deck treacherously slick. Most were felled not by the shot itself, but by the hundreds of lance-like splinters the shot sent flying.

Pasquaglio had one piece of luck. The ship was already turning when the broadside hit. The ship lurched and shuddered, but had actually swung clear of the full force of the broadside. The damage was severe, but nowhere near fatal. They might yet escape.

Pasquaglio looked into the night sky. Could it be? Was it possible? A squall line, and not far distant! He checked the glass. Barometric pressure was plunging. A quirky Mediterranean mini-storm, spawned by the *Bora,* was approaching. These appeared at odd intervals and were short lived, but the winds could reach over 100 knots. If he could gain the shelter of the storm, in the thunder and confusion, he might be able to shake his pursuer. It was risky, very risky. Storms were a sailor's nightmare. Far more ships died as a result of storms than enemy action. *Corona* would no doubt sustain damage, but the British would, too. What he knew for certain was that in his present position he had no chance. The squall gave him a slim one.

"Fire!" Captain Whitby's sword flashed, and again the broadside of *Cerberus* thundered, but it was hard to aim. The intermittent flashes of lightning played havoc with eyesight. The gun crews had only an indistinct mass for a target, one that was turning out of their line of fire. Screams on *Corona* served notice some shots had told, and her mizzen top sail went by the board. Most of the second broadside, however, went wide; not surprising in a situation similar to playing darts at the bottom of a Welsh coal mine.

It crossed Whitby's mind that whoever his opponent was, he was a fine ship handler. He tacked smartly, always more efficient than wearing, but riskier. He wondered why he had not fired back. No experience in night actions, he guessed. Probably making a virtue out of necessity. Running was the logical move. He noted the enemy was pulling away fast. *Cerberus* was a stout ship, but a slow sailer.

Pasquaglio decided to literally throw caution to the winds. He ordered the stay and studding sails set. All of those sails were designed for light airs, to take advantage of even the slightest puff of wind. They would be dangerous in the present rising wind, but they would give the ship her maximum turn of speed. He would have to reef the rest of his sails very soon, then furl everything just before reaching the squall. The timing would have to be careful and exact, or there was a very real possibility the masts would be ripped from the deck. The ship would become a bobbing cork in a turbulent sea. Such corks had limited life spans.

"Fire!" A third broadside lit the night sky. This time only a few shots hit. *Corona* was drawing out of effective night range. *How the deuce was he managing that?* Whitby wondered. Then it hit him. The captain must be clapping on every ounce of sail he had, very dangerous in this fast, growling wind. It was a bold move. "No!" he spoke aloud. His first officer turned to him in surprise. "Not bold, foolhardy!"

Corona was making ten knots. The squall, sanctuary, lay only a few miles distant. The British were still in pursuit, but had fallen behind. Pasquaglio listened to ominous creaks and groans as the masts protested under the terrific strain. He ordered a single reef taken in on the tops and courses. A warning voice told him it was time to dispense with stay and studding sails, but he ignored it. His plan was succeeding, but only if he pushed it right to the edge.

On *Cerberus*, Whitby reached a decision. He was a good captain.

He knew the difference between a flamboyant risk and a calculated one. His opponent was taking a rash course. Perhaps it was because he had no choice. Whitby had a choice. He would take the calculated one. He turned to his first officer. "Mr. Johnstone, give the order to cease fire."

"Aye, aye, sir! Do you wish to continue the pursuit?" Johnstone inquired.

"Most emphatically, yes. But there is little point in continuing to expend powder and shot in this murk. You see that line of squalls, Mr. Johnstone?" Whitby pointed skyward.

"I do indeed, Captain. Looks like the *Bora* is having a tantrum! Do you think he is actually heading for them?" Johnstone asked with surprise.

"Yes, I believe he is. He means to give us the slip."

"Do you purpose to follow him in, Captain?" Johnstone looked troubled.

"Mr. Johnstone," said Whitby with exasperation, "I am not a fool, so please do not treat me as one. By no means will I follow him inside. But I do mean to follow him as close to the storm as we can, to drive him inside. If we take away his chance to furl sail and he goes in with almost everything set, I would not answer for his chances of survival beyond five minutes. We must push him, and push him hard, give him no chance to think. Our timing and seamanship must be impeccable. Once we sheer away, we will have to furl everything but the driver and the flying jib."

"That's a risky plan, if you will pardon my saying so, Captain. Now would be a good time to sheer off." Johnstone blanched, realizing his remark might appear impudent. "Not that it won't work, Captain. In fact, I am sure it will."

Whitby smiled. "Your concern is well warranted. I take no offense; quite the contrary, I am glad you are sensible enough to recognize the risk. I have not taken leave of my wits, but this is the sort of situation we have worked for, trained for, set our minds and spirits for. We may not take her a prize this night, but I am damned if she is going to escape!"

Mr. Johnstone opened his night glass. It was a telescope with special lenses that gave a curious upside down image of the target, but it was a functional enlargement, useful to those accustomed to making the requisite mental adjustment. "He is definitely drawing away, sir."

"I'd be obliged if you'd get the men aloft and furl the royals, Mr. Johnstone. Two reefs on the topgallants and topsails as well. It will slow us some, but we still have enough speed to maintain the appearance of pursuit. We can concede a little sea distance. As long as our pursuit continues in any form, he will have little choice but to continue on his present course. For ourselves, we need to slow a bit before sheering off. Let's not cut it too fine."

Pasquaglio noted the fast rising wind with alarm. The storm was dead ahead, its precursors already making their presence felt. All of the sails were tightly sheeted home and filled to capacity. The ship was making thirteen knots, flying across the waves. She had never gone faster. This was the kind of speed sailors fantasized about, but rarely achieved. The warning voice now shouted in Pasquaglio's ear that the amount of sail he was carrying was dangerous, insane, possibly fatal. Yet the British were still in pursuit.

Riiiiiiiiiiiiiiiiiiiiiiiiip! A huge extended tearing noise erupted as the port studding sail was reduced to canvas strips in the twinkling of an eye. Pasquaglio watched in horror as the shreds billowed and flapped like fleets of angry frigate birds.

Craaaaacccccccckkk! The boom holding the sail developed fissures, just as a pane of glass does before it shatters. Pasquaglio had waited too long.

"Take in the courses, Mr. Johnstone." Whitby's command was one of experienced prudence. *Cerberus* ploughed ahead. Whitby kept an eagle eye on the topsails. He would have to furl them in next. They would soon be under driver and jib only.

They were five miles from the storm now, three miles directly astern of *Corona*. He could make out *Corona* and see she was still under full sail. Her captain was either a raving madman or a desperate gambler; maybe both. He should have been under bare poles minutes ago and let the momentum of the sea carry him in. Part of Whitby felt satisfaction in knowing an enemy was about to die. Part of him felt pity for the loss of so graceful a vessel. The sea was a beautiful mistress, but she could be a harsh, judgmental, and unforgiving one as well.

"Mr. Johnstone, get the topsails furled, if you please." Whitby's timing was superb.

Pasquaglio knew he had waited too long. He ordered everything furled, save driver and jib for control. The men hurried aloft as the wind threatened to blow them off the ratlines. It took a full fifteen minutes, ten minutes the ship simply could not afford. The ship's bow was but a mile from the storm front.

"Mr. Johnstone, sheer away! Full about, make course sou' by southeast!"

Mr. Johnstone emphatically relayed the captain's command to the four quartermasters manning the ship's wheel. *Cerberus* answered the helm only slowly. She pivoted with churlish reluctance, but she did answer. She turned her face toward safety. *Thank God*, Whitby thought; *the gale must be Force 12 on the Beaufort.*

The sea rose majestically, in mountainous, grey-green swells, then fell viciously, creating dark abysses. Torrents of water battered *Corona*, foam frothed over her bulwarks, and cascades surged across her violently pitching deck. Five seamen washed overboard. The last view Whitby had through his glass was of *Corona* entering the tempest. He knew she would never emerge.

Twenty-Four

Pennywhistle and Spottswood encountered four guards at the dockyard gate. Pennywhistle gave the password confidently to the alert NCO who was in charge. The corporal returned the countersign, snapped to attention, and shot him a smart salute. The other three guards followed suit.

Pennywhistle complimented the non-commissioned officer on his posture and vigilance. He asked him his name. The fastest way to command a man's attention was to use his name repeatedly, then let him in on a secret.

"It's Corporal Gide, sir," the corporal said proudly, pleased that anyone would ask.

"Corporal Gide, you seem a capable, likely fellow. I am going to trust you with an important confidence. Colonel Chartes has scheduled a surprise inspection for tomorrow morning, Corporal Gide. There is a rumour about that the *Empereur* himself is coming to Italy on a tour of French military installations. The lieutenant and I have come on behalf of Major du Grandchamp to ensure there will be no unpleasant surprises. We will be conducting a thorough and exacting inspection of the yard for the next two hours. Corporal Gide, I have an important task for you and the guards. Complete it successfully and there will be a promotion in it for you. Can I count on your complete cooperation, Corporal Gide?"

"Absolutely, sir!" Gide said loudly with an enthusiastic smile. It awed him that he might get to meet the *Empereur*.

"Excellent!" said Pennywhistle. A vision of the dead brigands on the beach popped into his head. "You have probably heard of a gang of bandits that have been plaguing the area."

"Yes, sir, every French soldier here has. Their leader calls himself *Fra diavalo*."

Pennywhistle laughed inwardly at the bold nickname. The man had been merely a bully and a coward.

"I have it on good authority that they are planning a raid tonight. They mean to attack the ship *Marie*. Do not repeat this to anyone, but her hold contains several chests of gold intended by *l'Empereur* for payment to his allies in Italy. I believe, however, the bandits would abandon their plans if the ship was closely guarded by stalwart soldiers such as yourself and your men. You are not needed here, but you are badly needed at the *Marie*. My lieutenant and I are perfectly capable of handling things in the yard. Do I have your understanding and cooperation, Corporal Gide?"

Pennywhistle saw shock, then a look of pleasure flash across the corporal's face; a little man given big responsibility. The story had everything to tempt a would-be hero: bandits, gold, and the *Empereur*. He was glad du Grandchamp had thoughtfully labeled the ships at anchor in his sketches.

"Yes, sir! Of course, sir! Where is the *Marie* docked?"

"She is alongside the main quay half a mile from here. Her gangplank is down but she has not yet begun unloading her cargo. I wish you to report to her captain and tell him a raid on his ship is contemplated this evening and you are there to prevent it from even starting. You may say you act with the full authority of Major du Grandchamp. Now be off with you and your men, Corporal Gide. You must lose not a minute in countering this grave threat." Pennywhistle smiled. "Do not be surprised if tomorrow morning you find yourself called Sergeant Gide."

"Yes, sir! Right away, sir! We won't let you down." Gide barked orders and he and his men marched off at the double-quick. Pennywhistle and Spottswood now had the dockyard to themselves.

Spottswood laughed. "That was an impressive bit of nonsense, Mr. Pennywhistle. I almost believed it myself. You would have made a fine actor."

Pennywhistle frowned. He had done spy work in the past and realized he was distilling his undercover conduct into a method. Act haughty and disdainful. Strut a bit. Speak importantly of a secret mission, one of vital interest to the Emperor, then graciously condescend to ask the cipher of a guard his name, rank, and unit. Let him understand he was a nonentity, but perhaps this night, through the intervention of Providence and a man of vision and magnanimity, he might become much more. In return for help, he might be advanced in rank, win riches and honour. Demur or cause the slightest delay, and have all avenues of advancement permanently blocked. Add in a few words of praise when he agreed to cooperate, season with a hearty "Well done!" when he provided useful information, and top off with a confident, "your zeal and intelligence cannot fail to win promotion; I will personally see to it," and the formula was complete. It was exactly how Napoleon bound men to himself.

It dismayed Pennywhistle that he could manipulate people with the ease of a carnival trickster or confidence man. He told himself it was all in a noble cause, for king and country, but he hated to believe most men were venal and easily led specimens of low humanity who craved recognition and prominence above all things. The Enlightenment academic who lurked deep inside wanted to believe men acted out of honesty, decency, and principle. At Edinburgh, and in the grand spirit of the Scottish Enlightenment, he had been schooled to believe that appealing to the best instincts of man would produce a corresponding burst of good deeds in both the moral and intellectual spheres. It was a philosophy that beckoned seductively to the child-like part of his personality, the part of him so like his father. Sadly, that was exactly the part of him that excited the greatest contempt of his capricious, coldly cynical mother.

The enterprising and practical soldier who lived closer to the surface of his consciousness whispered in his ear that the reality of life indicated the reverse was true. Men acted out of everything but honesty, decency, and principle. They could be trusted to live down to their lowest instincts. It was not that goodness and honour did not exist. They were simply much more difficult to find than he had been taught at university. Perhaps, Diogenes had been right.

At any rate, tonight was a night to go with the tried and true, not engage in highly theoretical postulations about ideal archetypes. The scholar in him let him see possibilities and ideas, but the soldier gave him the resolve to carry them out in the most efficient way possible.

The professors who had trained him at university were good men, learned men, men of vision. They taught him to observe, to see the interconnectedness of things, to discern the subtle manifesting in the overt. They schooled him to believe the anomaly was always much more revealing than the expected and to recognize that the exception to a rule sometimes provided insight into the rule itself.

Yet they had acted outside of the law, when expediency demanded. The corpses used in anatomy class had been obtained through payment to grave robbers, unsavoury individuals politely known as Resurrectionists. The professors had wisely disdained any interest in their sources and methods. A tunnel had even been built at the university to allow corpses to be conveyed covertly to the dissecting theatre. Was it possible the real lesson they taught was do what needed to be done and fret about the cost later?

He wished he resided in the realm of pure, honest intellect. It was far easier to live in the safe bubble of an art or university than take your chances with life. Primitive, wild, ungoverned passion had resulted in the foolish duel that brought him to his present situation. It had beaten reason in a straight, if unfair, fight. He had killed for honour, he told himself. But mostly he killed Sir Atholl Campbell because a bad man deserved to die. He had become good at killing and it became just a little bit easier each time. It worried him.

He pulled himself up hard. This was not a time for musings that could easily slide into distraction or confusion. The amoral part of his mind sternly warned, *You have a job to do! Do it efficiently and get out.*

Spottswood spoke, "I say, that was damned easy, Mr. Pennywhistle! It would be splendid if the rest of the evening goes the same way! But sir, one thing I don't get is how you happened to fasten on Major du Grandchamp. I know he fit the bill as a loner and he was certainly well into his cups, but how did you know he would be such a font of information? We could have found somebody who knew a little, but the odds on finding someone who... well." His voice trailed off.

"Actually, Mr. Spottswood, it was not luck at all. It was observation. He wore yellow *aguilettes* below his epaulettes. You may not be aware, but those signify he is a staff officer. The rank insignia on his epaulettes were of a major. That is field grade rank, but a title appropriate for one who does not actually serve in the line of battle; a field grade officer who does would be styled a *chef de bataillon*. So we have a field grade staff officer, with the commanding officer a colonel. Clearly, he must be the adjutant, the chief shuffler of paper, the man who knows the details. We were indeed lucky, but we were lucky because we were prepared." He gave Spottswood an avuncular smile. "I assure you, Mr. Spottswood, if you had been more experienced, you would have reached the same conclusion.

"Our first order of business is to scout the yard for a means of egress. We need to have a craft properly loaded and ready for sea, as I believe our departure this evening will be hasty and not under ideal conditions. I also see there is one corvette at anchor in the harbour. She looks nearly ready for sea. Perhaps it is too much to hope for, but I would love to send her to the bottom before this night is done."

"I noticed her too, Mr. Pennywhistle. Maybe someone is on board, but there are no boats rowing guard. Commodore Hoste would never allow that! The French seem rather careless, sir."

"Almost as if they had no thought in the world of an attack!" Pennywhistle replied, then descended into deep thought. He began walking briskly.

Spottswood walked in silence beside Pennywhistle. Something weighty was on the Captain's mind. Probably improving on the evening's design of destruction, making it even more ingenious and wide-ranging. The Captain was like that. Always thinking, sorting, analyzing, sifting, re-ordering the variables of a plan with a view to discovering the optimum configuration. It was almost like he was a chemist mixing arcane ingredients to produce a new product. But his product was destruction and his laboratory was the battlefield.

They soon reached their destination, the main powder magazine.

Pennywhistle studied it in absolute silence for a full minute, then frowned.

Spottswood noticed. "What's wrong, captain?"

"It is as I feared, Mr. Spottswood. This is a purpose-built powder magazine. It's not just a building pressed into service. Look at those walls: stout construction, must be five feet thick, solid limestone. Notice the roof: ordinary timber. The building is designed to contain an explosion, to funnel the force of the explosion upwards rather than outwards. Force will pursue the path of least resistance and blow the roof. We may destroy the stock of powder, indeed we shall, but we will not be able to spread much of the destruction to the rest of the dockyard. I had hoped for more."

"Damn!" muttered Spottswood to no one in particular. Pennywhistle lapsed into silence; his brow furrowed and his mind shifted into intense activity. Only minutes passed, but it seemed several lifetimes to Spottswood, observing his captain.

Pennywhistle's face lightened; he had made his decision. "Here is the plan. We are going to blow this magazine, but first, we are going to relieve it of two large barrels of powder. We can load them on the cutter we discovered earlier. It is not only going to be our means of escape but," he pointed to the corvette in the harbour, "the engine of the destruction for yonder vessel. I think the flaming particles from the magazine will probably take care of the brig close in. Pitch, pine, and tarred ropes absolutely love showers of sparks. If we can float the barrels alongside, with properly fashioned waterproof fuses, and attach them near the corvette's rudder, we may be able to blow a large enough hole to send her to the bottom. Oh, she won't go instantly, but by the time they get men to her pumps and carpenter's mates to try to plug the hole, she will have passed the point of no return. I trust you are a strong swimmer, Mr. Spottswood?"

"I am, sir," Spottswood replied confidently.

"Good, it's a fine night for a swim," Pennywhistle said with a half smile.

An hour of meticulous labour later, the preparations were complete. Pennywhistle and Spottswood had removed their boots and donned the requisite slippers from the magazines stores. Since there was always the danger of a stray spark igniting a conflagration, slippers rather than boots and shoes were worn inside. They had gleefully swung large axes to stove in a dozen barrels. They were soaked in sweat, but powder now littered the floor. It was a hundred yards from the fuse heads to the cutter. Fuses were tricky and unpredictable things and the longer one was, the greater the chance something could go wrong.

Pennywhistle fashioned two fuses each of two minutes duration. One was the primary, one the backup. When Spottswood lit them, he would have to make a mad dash for the cutter. In the first modern Olympics at the end of the century, the hundred yard dash would be one of the first competitions, yet merely something of sport. Tonight, it was a life or death event.

There was a secondary powder depot, twenty yards from the cutter. There were perhaps fifty barrels of coarse grained, slow-burning powder that had been off-loaded, but not yet transferred to the magazine. They had been carelessly stored in a nondescript building. When they blew, there would be little to stop the waves of concussion. The trouble was, it was only fifty barrels. But fifty barrels unrestrained by limestone walls would do significant damage to the wooden harbour-side structures.

Pennywhistle and Spottswood used spare planks and boards to create makeshift inclined planes on which to roll three barrels from the magazine to the harbour. Pennywhistle found two barrels of finely grained powder, powder that would burn fast and hot. Perfect for the corvette. The fifty barrels more conveniently located, he rejected as simply too slow burning. The third barrel was not powder at all, but a very curious discovery he had made in the magazine. It was secreted in a corner, but both its remoteness and the fact that it stood alone commanded attention.

He examined the barrel closely. Whatever it was, it was clearly prize cargo, held in the highest security area, and reserved for someone of importance. Then he detected a faint odor. He put his nose to the barrel and sucked the odor deeply up his nostrils. And for no reason whatsoever, he began to smile, then chuckle, then laugh. He drew back in surprise. It couldn't be! He was willing to wager a lifetime's prize money it was for the colonel and his lady! The colonel did not just shower his lady with gifts, he gave her frolics!

A frolic was the *au courant* designation of a party which featured the use of a gas Joseph Priestly had discovered some years before, nitrous oxide. It induced euphoric intoxication and much merriment. It had quite naturally been dubbed, "laughing gas." He had never attended a frolic, had been far too staid in his adolescence for that, but he learned that Spottswood had been to several. He gave Pennywhistle a quick, yet thorough, summary of its effects. But more than that, he gave him an idea.

He guessed only a skeleton crew slept aboard the corvette. They probably would be sound asleep, with only one, possibly two guards keeping a watch. But the two massive explosions would wake everyone. The crew would be bewildered, but there was always the possibility they might spot Pennywhistle and Spottswood and act. The wind was strong tonight and the laughing gas could remove the crew as a source of danger. Properly placed, the fumes from the floating barrel would waft upwards and envelop the ship. The fumes would flow away from himself and Spottswood, so they would be unaffected.

It was an insurance policy; it would buy time. A pleasantly stupefied crew and violent explosions would go a long way to diverting attention from the obvious anomaly of two infantry officers manning a boat in harbour after midnight. They would merely be part of a confusing landscape.

"Cutter's loaded, sir! I don't think there is any more to do, or have I forgotten something?" Spottswood was at his most earnest.

Pennywhistle ran down his mental checklist. "No, you have not, Mr. Spottswood. I believe we are ready. And now if you are ready for a good run, it's time to light the fuses and set things rolling."

"Aye, aye, sir!" said Spottswood with real joy. Spottswood was young enough to be able to say to himself that blowing up stuff was... well...fun! He quick-marched to position, husbanding his resources for the run of his life.

*****

The storm fifteen miles away from Spottswood was a living being. Water smashed into *Corona's* sides with an almost human wrath. The gale howled its fury like a chorus of devils. The hills and troughs of roiled water came fast and hard now, like a series of compressed sine waves. The rigging shook with a high-pitched keening that was an almost human lamentation for mercy, as if the ship felt herself dying and protested to the heavens.

Crack! It sounded like a gunshot. The fore topgallant mast split, lurched sideways, and fell into the sea. *Boom!* Thirty seconds later, the main topgallant cracked, swayed, and embraced salt water.

The two collapsed masts acted as giant deadweights since they were still attached to the ship by masses of rope. Suction pulled them away from the hull, then compression slammed them back, like giant cricket bats hitting a fence. *Corona's* scantlings dented and started to buckle. She had been bow-on to the waves, much the safest course. Slowly, the unwanted anchors started to turn her port side toward a parallel course with the waves. There was every danger now she would broach, be swamped by waves smashing into her side, causing her to heel over on her beam ends. Fully sideways, her keel exposed, she would swamp and disappear.

"All hands aloft!" Pasquaglio ordered his men to cut away the ropes that held the masts fast. It was a race between men and the sea. Four heavily muscled quartermasters fought the wheel with strength and gallantry; they tried to keep *Corona* into the wave, but knew it was a losing contest. They could slow the result, not stop it.

It depended on men more than one hundred feet above a violently pitching and rolling deck, chopping grimly away with their axes, while sheets of wind and rain gleefully tried to fling them into space. They held on with one hand, chopped with the other. The listing to starboard grew more acute each minute.

The seams leaked badly. "Four feet of water in the hold, sir," came the cry from a boatswain's mate, one of many manning the pumps. Beyond six feet, the ship was in real trouble. If the pumps fell behind for any length of time, *Corona* was doomed. Gangs of men pushed the handles in the fashion of a schoolyard teeter-totter. Like the men aloft, they knew what was at stake.

The howling wind made even standing difficult. Men could barely see two feet in front of them as writhing sheets of rain snapped across the deck. The sea laughed at the arrogant impudence of mere men who thought they could be her master for even a moment. The ship was now nearly parallel with the waves.

Crack! The main top mast split and fell overboard, carrying with it masses of screaming men. Topman Ferrari watched in horror as he plunged toward the sea. He could not swim and his last thought before his head vanished beneath the waves was of his small pet terrier, Giorgio.

Masts were made in three parts; mast, top mast, and top gallant mast, all spliced together at mastcaps. The main top gallant mast already dragged heavily and when its lower companion went over, the anchor grew longer, more powerful, and increased drag to nearly lethal proportions. More men were ordered aloft to replace their brothers batted into the sea. They chopped frantically, now much lower down.

Men on the main deck struggled valiantly to rig life lines as waves surged to waist level, then quickly ebbed way. Successive walls of water fought them with an almost human vigor.

The winds battered the masts like a mad pile driver. A yard long splinter, the result of earlier cannon fire, tenuously attached to the main mast by small sliver of oak, gave way under the immense pressure. It shot through the air and struck one quartermaster in the head, decapitating him instantly. For a moment, pressure on the wheel eased. Before another quartermaster could be summoned, the ship came fully sideways to the waves. A giant wave hit her like a huge fist batting a small fly. She reeled from the blow and canted over at forty five degrees, on a knife's edge between recoverability and the angle of no return.

Captain Pasquaglio ordered all of the men on deck to the larboard side in a desperate attempt to achieve a counterbalance and right the ship. He looked at the sky. It was starting to lighten. One thing about these squalls, they were short lived. If she could just survive a few more minutes, she might make it. It was vital she survive. He had to get the information about Hoste's location to the Commodore. The Commodore would know what to do.

"Five feet of water in the hold, and rising, Captain!" A seamen shouted from below.

*****

In contrast to the chaos on *Corona*, a strong, if unspectacular, breeze graced the harbour of Ancona. Pennywhistle hoisted the sail on the cutter and it drew nicely. He had lashed the boat to the dock, a racehorse in check awaiting the starter's pistol. One hand held the tiller, the other his cutlass to sever the rope.

SSSSSSSSSSSSSSSSSSSSSSSSSSSSSSSS! The maliciously evil sound of sparks was the starter's pistol for this race. Two minutes! Spottswood was normally a fast runner, but tonight, in a manner of speaking, he was on fire. He covered the hundred yards from the magazine to the secondary charge opposite the cutter in just ten seconds, lit the secondary fuses, and executed an ungainly leap into the cutter. Pennywhistle sliced the rope. The cutter sped off into the night.

Pennywhistle looked at his watch. Less than eighty seconds. Seawater creamed past the cutwater as the boat gathered speed. Every second put more distance between them and the coming explosions.

The stern of the unfinished corvette loomed out of the darkness. He lowered the sail and the mast to reduce the cutter's silhouette. No lights showed on deck and no guard shouted a hail or challenge. Luck was running their way. The two of them hefted the nitrous oxide barrel over the gunwale, then punctured it with a carpenter's awl. The cutter moved quickly away and fumes began to spiral upward to the main deck.

Ten seconds left. Pennywhistle brought the boat behind the corvette's rudder. The bulk of the ship now stood between them and the explosion. Any protection was welcome.

Nine. Pennywhistle and Spottswood pushed the first barrel toward the gunwale.

Eight. The barrel went into the water and floated easily.

Seven. They shoved second barrel toward the gunwale.

Six. The second barrel went over the side.

Five. Spottswood began stripping off his clothing.

Four. Pennywhistle tossed the grappling hook onto the rudder pintles.

Three. He jerked hard on the hook.

Two. The grappling hook stretched taut and held firm.

One. Spottswood went over the side.

Rather than being a giant *boom*, it started as a low rumble as if the earth were having a monstrous attack of indigestion. The ground shook for a fraction of a second that seemed a lifetime, then huge plumes of orange-red flame rocketed into the night sky. A giant spiral cloud of smoke rose slowly. Large and small pieces of wood flew in every direction. Sound being slower than light, the noise and concussion waves reached Pennywhistle a few seconds later. The cutter rocked hard for a few seconds, but then righted herself.

The secondary explosion on the dock blossomed a minute later. It demolished two buildings and sent shards of wood and wadding skyward. Some of the burning bits touched the rigging of the second ship in the harbour. Pennywhistle noticed with a gleam of satisfaction that there was a small orange glow on several spots of the ship's rigging. Tarred rope and flame had a tendency to want to develop firm friendships quickly.

Spottswood swam with an efficient and easy crawl stroke. He thought the explosions quite rousing and was pleased with himself. The barrels bobbed heavily when the shock wave hit but did not travel far. He calmly and methodically coaxed them back toward the hull of the ship. It occurred to him that he was some sort of aquatic sheepherder, herding wayward beasts back into the fold.

"Mon Dieu, c'était une explosion. Que se passe-t-il?"

"Pennywhistle held his breath and listened closely as he heard voices above him on deck. They sounded baffled and disoriented. But there were only three of them. He was right: skeleton crew.

Spottswood pushed one of the barrels next to the pintles and attached it firmly. One fluke of the grapnel locked into place.

Then Pennywhistle heard it. Laughter. Loud, merry, and hearty.

Spottswood noted it as well.

"N'est-ce pas la chose la plus drôle déjà vu? Je ne peux pas m'arrêter de rire." More rounds of raucous, rolling laughter. Pennywhistle breathed a sigh of relief. Whoever these Frenchmen were, they were not going to be causing any trouble this evening. They were in for a jolly good time, if of short duration.

Spottswood anchored the remaining flukes of the grapnel. The first barrel was lashed firmly in place. He swam toward the second barrel and eased it in toward the first.

Pennywhistle looked toward the docks and saw the first signs of activity. Parties of bewildered men were making the first, casual assessments of damage and trying to puzzle out what had happened. It was all very haphazard and disorganized. It would take a while for the air of denial to disperse and organized parties under official control to begin their grisly inspections. Pennywhistle wondered if Colonel Chartres had been roused from his slumbers. He could hardly have failed to notice the explosions, but Pennywhistle guessed his attentions were deeply focused elsewhere. He had undoubtedly acquired a *femme de la soiree* to replace the fabled Sabrina. He did not seem the sort of man to mourn much of anything for long. He felt a pang of sadness that Chartres would find a way to blame it on du Grandchamp. Chartres was a survivor; for all of his gallantry and patriotism, du Grandchamp was not.

Spottswood continued his swim. The water felt warm and soothing. It quieted his mind and allowed him to focus on the task at hand. He gentled the second barrel into place alongside the first, then bound the two together using another grapnel.

Pennywhistle raised his small night glass for a better view. It could not be! But it was! A lurching, swaying du Grandchamp earnestly barked orders at soldiers. He must have come directly from the tavern after the explosion. He could not hear any words, but he guessed the general meaning. One last gallant effort to do his duty and set things right. Napoleon talked about marching to the sound of the guns. Du Grandchamp at least lurched to the sound of explosions.

Spottswood checked the heavily tarred, waterproof sack he towed with him. It had done its job; the fuses were intact. They had found standard issue two-minute fuses in the magazine and spliced two together for each barrel. He took care water did not penetrate the thin carapace that protected the powder from the water.

The fuses attached firmly to the barrels as the sticky goo on their bottoms took hold. He produced a piece of glowing slowmatch from a small metal tube within the sack. Slow matches needed no air, since it was a chemical reaction that supplied the burn. He touched it to each fuse and was rewarded with a satisfying hiss. The powder started its deadly journey. He swam.

Pennywhistle hoisted Spottswood into the boat and tossed him a stout wool blanket. He raised the mast and sail, then cut the grapnel with his cutlass. The wind held, the stars blazed bright, and a slight current conducted them toward the open sea. He set a course for the harbour mouth. In a strange variation of the Groa expedition, Spottswood fell into a deep and soundless sleep. Pennywhistle trusted it would be dreamless, but perhaps the face of the green-cloaked brigand would make an appearance. He hoped not; Spottswood deserved a comforting rest.

He noted with satisfaction that the smoldering rigging of the second ship had burst into a full blown conflagration. She was doomed.

The cutter had just cleared the harbour entrance when he heard the explosion. Not terribly loud, compared to the other two. He wished he could linger to see the results, but he knew in his heart the ship would soon be on the harbour bottom. They would try to salvage her, but he doubted they would have much luck.

The noise roused Spottswood briefly. "What was that?" he asked groggily.

"Success!" said Pennywhistle. "Go back to sleep, you earned it. I'll have us home by morning." He was as good as his word.

Twenty-Five

Active lay 15 miles off Ancona. The past few days had been profitable: she had snapped up two fat, unwary merchantmen. *Amphion* lay a similar distance out, but fourteen miles to the north. *Cerberus* had been dispatched to Malta as escort for a column of prizes, and to undergo routine maintenance in the large dockyard. She was badly missed.

Amphion had enjoyed extraordinary luck, capturing a prize loaded entirely with luxury goods, mostly silken sundries, clearly meant for the wives of officers. The two ships' spacing enabled them to patrol a larger area, but it also meant they were barely within supporting distance. It was a bold risk on Hoste's part, betting two ships could do the job that properly belonged to three.

Pennywhistle strolled the forecastle, enjoying the sunny weather. He looked upward at the billowing sails: brilliant white clouds of canvas. It was noon: the official start of the nautical day, but more importantly, dinner time for the crew. Time for the thing that made their hard life bearable—the first half of their daily ration of grog. Even diluted with three parts water, a quarter pint of Navy rum had a kick like an angry mule. The rum was seventy-five percent alcohol and, undiluted, would actually ignite. Sailors repaired to their messes on the berth deck. A minimum watch was maintained, just enough men to work the ship.

Pennywhistle deployed his easel and artist's board, inventoried his box of watercolours, then looked up to see foretopmen moving along the horses, or footropes, preparatory to taking in a reef on the fore t'gallant sail. It was a nautical ballet, framed against the striking azure of the early afternoon sky. A common enough occurrence, but remarkable nonetheless. He wanted to capture it with his brush.

At first the men had regarded his painting as an amusing eccentricity. But when they saw the results, they were flattered and impressed. His efforts seemed to invest the most mundane duties with grandeur, beauty, and importance. It made non-entities into somebodies. To the sailors, it was as if their efforts were being recognized, commemorated for generations of landlubbers to enjoy and puzzle over. They smiled like children when they recognized the face of one of their mates in his works.

Pennywhistle found painting relaxing, an anodyne for the exertions of war. He was a good officer and an ingenious, skilled killer. He took pride in being successful at his work, yet it troubled him that he would be remembered as a destroyer rather than as a builder or creator.

In his chosen profession, rewards were lavished upon those who destroyed: promotion, honours, financial emoluments. Their deeds would be commemorated in history books, heroic statues, and tales told by poets. The myth-makers, newspaper correspondents, and professional polemicists constantly romanticized warriors' grisly acts into something loved by the public, but barely recognizable to the originators. The blood, gore, dirt, and pure, naked fear were carefully filtered out. What remained were bright banners, smart uniforms, grand acts of derring-do and columns of fit men marching home. It played well with the easily gulled public. It was the bread and butter of glib-tongued recruiting sergeants in small villages, but it was not reality.

He knew he would never be a great artist like Benjamin West but, unlike West, he was determined to make his humble works depict some degree of realism. He focused on commemorating everyday actions, rather than the extraordinary ones West and his ilk romanticized. West's epic paintings, "The Death of Wolfe" and "The Death of Nelson," were classic representatives of the heroic genre. They convinced people that death in battle was somehow glorious, gallant, and tidy.

He hated the sentimentalism of those paintings. The uniforms of those inhabiting such paintings were always pristine, un-rumpled, not marred by patches, bullet holes, or dirt. The expressions of the men were always suitably grave, reflective, and dignified; not a face was to be found contorted in fear, confusion, or grief. The dead were beautifully intact; crushed, shredded, pulped bodies trailing gory viscera were absolutely never shown.

What bothered him most was the studied dignity. All the dead lay carefully posed, as if they had fallen asleep. The newly dead were usually in grotesque, unimaginable postures that gave the lie to dignity. No wonder people back home had misplaced notions about the "glories" of war.

He pondered whether having a speculative intellect was a gift or a curse. He wondered how it would feel to enjoy the deep, mindless calm that seemed the lot of the average bland, incurious country gentleman, worried most about his horses and hounds. But he could no more stop analyzing life than a dog could forswear barking or a fish refrain from swimming. He kept his deepest thoughts to himself, realizing he would make a great many enemies if he ever spoke honestly about how slow, creaky, and ponderous he found the cogitations of the average man. His arrogant intellect demanded constant stimulation and revolted against inactivity.

When not gainfully employed in duties or reading, his brain identified roiling currents in situations where others saw only a flat, placid sea. He grasped easily what others missed, particularly the interconnectedness of disparate events, whether in politics, war, or medical convention. It puzzled him how few people questioned assumptions labeled "common sense." He thought most "common sense" was merely an excuse to avoid real consideration. His quick, nimble intellect enabled him to discern multiple possibilities in an instant, where others saw only the obvious one.

More than three hours passed, and the watercolour progressed well.

"Deck there! Sail ho! Fine on the port quarter!" The cry from the masthead lookout penetrated Pennywhistle's pleasant reveries. A ship sighted at sea was always an event. It could be news from home and friends, intelligence of the enemy from passing neutrals, or of course, the enemy himself.

Dashwood picked up his speaking trumpet and shouted, "What do you make of her?"

"Hard to tell, sir. Too far off! But more than one ship for certain!" came the reply.

Multiple ships: ominous. Dashwood decided go aloft for a better look. He checked his small pocket spyglass, headed toward the ratlines, and started his climb.

Pennywhistle put away his brushes and paints, and with them the artist of the atelier. As he shut the box, the other artist inside came on full duty, the military one. His focus turned from immortalizing the beauty of the sea to preserving the ship and the lives of those aboard her.

Dashwood completed his climb to the top. He braced himself against the mastcap and unfurled his glass. The day was clear; from this height, with a telescope, he had a clear view out to nearly fourteen miles. He saw five ships, not one, all in reasonably disciplined sailing order—definitely not merchantmen. Five warships, all frigates, two of them very large; it had to be Dubordieu.

He scanned the opposite horizon. *Amphion* had moved out of range. No way to signal her the information. For now, it was one ship against five. Very bad odds. No time now for a slow, cautious descent; he donned the expensive kid dress gloves he always kept in his pocket, grabbed a rope and slid down it to the deck, in the manner of a man sliding down a pole. He reached the deck swiftly, but the friction completely shredded his once beautiful gloves. Once down on the deck, he ran to the capstan, Captain Gordon's usual command position on the deck.

"Slow down, Mr. Dashwood, slow down. You are a positive dervish of energy." Gordon was his usual pleasant, unflappable self. "I presume you have something of note to report."

"Aye, sir. Bad news. Five ships on an interception course with us. French, look to be frigates, two of them big ones. Has to be

Dubordieu, Captain." Dashwood gradually regained his breath.

"Is *Amphion* in signaling distance?" asked the Captain. "We could use her assistance."

"Regrettably, no, sir. Even with my glass, I could not spot her hull down over the horizon. We have no way to let her know of the danger."

"One ship against five," the captain said thoughtfully. "Not odds I like. The wind is good and steady; we can use that. I regret to say discretion is the better part of valour. We shall have to run for it and show them a clean pair of heels. Well, *Active* has a fair turn of speed, and this afternoon we shall have to use it. We will head toward the northeast and try to regain contact with Hoste. Mr. Dashwood, get the men aloft, and shake out every piece of canvas we have!"

*****

Commodore Dubordieu on *Favourite* delighted at the news from the masthead. One British frigate with no apparent support. It was almost too good to be true. That worried him. And yet, it was a glorious opportunity. He was one of the few French who had captured a British frigate in single ship combat; that glorious triumph had brought him his present command. Now he had five ships, and he would make them all count. If he could just close the distance before she could escape, he would have her.

Twenty-Six

Hoste in *Amphion* fruitlessly chased a good sized barque. Much as it galled him to admit it, the merchantman was faster. She was slowly and steadily drawing ahead and soon would be lost over the horizon. It had been a close thing at one point, but the contest was no longer in doubt. He gave the order to stand down from action stations. He had continued the pursuit longer than was prudent, letting the thrill of the chase lure him out of supporting distance of *Active*. It was time to remember duty and set things right. He gave the order, and the ship began to slowly swing round to her new course. The adrenaline of the chase drained away, and the ship returned to normal.

*****

For two hours, Gordon watched the French squadron narrow the gap between his ship and theirs. *Active* set every ounce of canvas she could carry; royals, topgallants, stay sails, for a steady nine knots, but it wasn't enough. French seamanship might be poor, but their naval architects were scientific and the most advanced in the world. French ships had well-deserved reputations for speed, their designers having sacrificed sturdiness and durability to achieve it. They were more thinly constructed, less able to keep at sea in bad weather than their British counterparts, but in good weather were invariably faster.

With Captain La Meilliere's approval, Dubordieu had set the two fastest ships, the flagship *Favourite*, and the smaller frigate, *Bellona*, to lead the chase. His strategy was that of the foxhunt. Use

Favourite, the fastest, to actually range ahead of *Active* and block her path, while the *Bellona* harried, hurt, and slowed her down. The three other, slower ships would then have the chance to close with her and finish the job. As long as the wind held, it was likely the strategy would work.

Gordon quickly fathomed Dubordieu's intentions. It was what he himself would do, if he commanded the French squadron. Over the past few hours, the French had closed the distance from fourteen to four miles. Gordon wondered briefly where Hoste was and racked his mind for ways to increase speed.

"Mr. Dashwood, let's get the fire engines working and get some water pumped onto the deck. Get the men organized into bucket brigades and have them douse the sails with water," Gordon ordered. Sails soaked with water drew more efficiently than dry ones. It would not increase their speed by much, but today, every knot counted.

"Aye, aye, sir," replied Dashwood. "I'll attend to it immediately."

Miles away, Hoste saw that the wind was dropping. It had been an hour since he altered course. The wind direction also shifted to the southwest. He gave the appropriate order and the ship was soon sailing close-hauled on the port tack, sails braced at an angle to coax maximum power out of the wind. He had lookouts armed with spyglasses posted on the masthead, but still no sign of *Active*. Was it possible she had left her station? Pursuit of a prize? Or, a more alarming possibility, had the French put in an appearance? He drove *Amphion* for all she was worth.

Forty minutes later, the wind began to fall off dramatically. The pursued and pursuers slowed, and went even slower. The wind seemed headed for extinction.

Pennywhistle approached the Captain. He was Gordon's friend and relative, but he did not wish to embarrass the Captain or upset discipline by making it seem as if nepotism guaranteed special privilege. But this was an emergency, and Gordon, like Nelson, knew good ideas did not always flow from the top down.

"Captain, forgive me for troubling you at such a time, but I wonder if I might have a brief word? I have a suggestion on how we might increase our speed." Pennywhistle was at his most diplomatic.

Gordon's anxious expression brightened ever so briefly with the hint of a smile. "Ah, Captain, let it never be said that you lack for ideas. Speak up; those French fellows are definitely gaining on us."

"Captain, we are definitely losing the wind. We have every sail we can manage hoisted, yet the French continue to close the distance. I think we can improve on simple towing. My idea is to use the kedge anchor roped to the capstan to haul us forward. We are just above the coastal shelf, the water is shallow enough here for its use. The boats will row ahead of the ship, drop the kedge anchor, then we will use the capstan to pull us towards it. My marines want to be useful, and will, of course, want to do their shifts manning the capstan." Pennywhistle waited for the Captain's reaction.

"Hmmm, kedge anchor, that's quite an original notion. And yet... well, damn me, it might actually work! And you are right, the wind is definitely dropping. Where is *the Bora* when you need her? It won't be long before the French are within cannon range."

"Captain, I know this is an extraordinary request, and I mean no disrespect to the lieutenants, but allow me to command the lead boat. This is all about geometry and physics, and I am somewhat better educated and more proficient. The lieutenants certainly have the advantage over me in seamanship, but I think I can do a better job in determining exactly when and where to drop the anchor." Pennywhistle liked and respected the other lieutenants, but he also had no sense of false humility. He simply was the best man for the job.

"Very well, Captain. I doubt any officer on the ship would begrudge you the responsibility. You proposed the idea, you should carry it out. I trust you will do it with your usual dispatch."

Gordon thought for a moment, then summoned the First Lieutenant and explained the plan. "We'll need at least a mile of cable to link the boats to the ship. We need to start splicing cable, and quickly. Get the men on it!"

"Aye, aye, sir." Dashwood acknowledged crisply. He was about to depart when Gordon said, "Wait. There is one other thing to be done. I am reluctant, but we need every advantage. Make a liberal assessment of how much water we will need for the upcoming day, remembering that towing is hot and thirsty work. Set plenty of barrels aside to keep the deck scuttlebutts full and lay extra hogsheads into the cutters, then dump the remainder of the drinking water overboard. That will lighten us by many tons."

Dashwood looked shocked and doubtful, but dutifully replied, "Aye, aye, sir!" This order made him realize how desperate their circumstances were.

*****

Dubordieu stared skyward and cursed. The wind had dropped to a lackluster breeze. They were still gaining on the enemy, but his ship had not been able to dash ahead. He could just make out the white lettering on the stern to read the name: *Active*. One Captain James Gordon, Intelligence said. Very little was known about him, save that he was a good seamen. He was certainly proving it this day; he was coaxing every bit of speed out of his ship. Nevertheless, *Active* would soon be in range. It was but two miles ahead. The bow chasers of five ships would soon be brought to bear on the *Active*, a total of ten guns. *Active* could only reply with two.

Then, with a suddenness that was just one of the oddities of the sea, the wind died. Sails hung limp from the yards, like old rags forgotten on a clothesline. All six ships were entirely becalmed. As Dubordieu watched, the *Active's* boats, each with several men aboard, swayed out from the davits and dropped to the sea. They were resorting to towing! The French quickly followed suit, but no one among them had thought of using kedge anchors.

It puzzled Dubordieu that the distance between the ships seemed to be… increasing. He frowned. That simply would not do. He estimated the distance between the forwardmost *Favourite* and its prey, and decided he was close enough to try a ranging shot.

*****

Pennywhistle sat calmly in the bow of the rear cutter while the rowers sweated, strained, and pulled on the oars with all of their might. Curses rent the air from time to time, but the work was mostly done in silence. The cutter plowed on, now a mile in front of *Active*. The anchor was carried in tandem with the cutter's twin, five yards to starboard. Two more cutters, fifty yards in front, were roped to those carrying the anchor, their rowers helping to pull the heavily weighted cutter forward through the water. Three burly seamen stood ready to heft the thousand pounds of iron over the side. The loss of wind made the day sultry. Many seamen cooled themselves by stripping to the waist.

It was time. Pennywhistle gave the order to drop the anchor.

Dashwood saw the splash from the deck with his glass. He made a motion and the men on the capstan began to slowly push on the pawls. *Clank, clank, clank.* Men strained, the drumhead slowly rotated, the rope tightened, and *Active* slogged painfully forward.

Twenty-Seven

"Fire!" Two cannon balls arced through the air, bound for the stern of the *Active*.

There was a long, tearing sound as two 12-pound solid iron balls journeyed to their final destination, which turned out not to be the oak of a ship's hull, but an unremarkable patch of sea. Two splashes, half a mile short of the *Active*'s stern, marked their graves. *Favourite*'s gunners had been over-eager. *Active* was not quite in range. On *Favourite*, there were cheers. They felt the next shots would be the ones to strike home.

On *Active*, there were jeers of derision for poor French gunnery.

Gordon watched anxiously from his post near the capstan. He was able to make out the French captain near the wheel, using his own glass to observe the British ship. Both saw each other at the same instant. Gordon smiled, doffed his hat, and flourished it in quick salute. Captain La Meilliere, never one to be outdone in gallantry, did the same. In a few minutes, these two men would be earnestly trying to kill each other, but for now, there was still time to show that manners, courtesy, and mutual respect among gentlemen had not entirely vanished from the earth. Command of a ship made them brothers, of a sort.

Pennywhistle saw that *Active* was now fifty yards from the kedge anchor. Time to weigh anchor and pull hard for the next dropping point. Hoisting an anchor aboard was backbreaking work, far harder than dropping it overboard. One tough old seaman loudly cursed the French, but stiffened his resolve and pulled harder.

His rowing mate, Able Seaman Harding, feared their efforts

might be in vain. Harding's muscles throbbed with pain, but it was steadfastly ignored. The crew was not just pulling the cutter to drop the anchor; since the cable was attached to *Active*, they were giving her a tow as well. *Active* weighed one thousand and fifty-two tons. The other three boats pulled in unison.

The whole thing was an aquatic minuet: slow, precise, stately. The rhythmic movements of the rowers, the lifting and dipping of oars, the curved knife of the bow slowly slicing through the silken sea with a gentle *swish, swoosh*, made the performance a thing of beauty, even if it was being done in deadly earnest. Pennywhistle found it hypnotic. It would make a fine subject for a painting. Someday, perhaps. For now, he just hoped he finish the day a free man.

Undeterred by the failure of *Favourite's* gunners, enthusiasm trumped sense and the four other ships of Dubordieu's squadron fired their own bow chasers. Eight shots arced high, then plummeted, splashed, and sank to the bottom of the sea, three quarters of a mile behind *Active*. She had pulled slightly ahead of her pack of pursuers.

On the poop deck of *Active*, sailors pounded ringbolts into the deck. A party of men armed with axes chopped away two sections of the stern taffrail. Sweating, heaving sailors manhandled two twelve-pounders into position facing directly astern. Breeching ropes were hustled forward and tackles rigged. It was a masterpiece of disciplined routine, and in twenty short minutes, *Active* had two twelve-pound stern chasers, cannons they could fire directly at their pursuers.

Gordon was not sure how much effect they would have, but they would serve three purposes. They might well give the French some pause, letting them know *Active* had vigor and bite. Firing them would give heart to the crew, give them the feeling they were doing something, not merely running. Finally, it came down to the morale of Gordon himself. He was a fighter, not a runner, even though running was the logical course right now. He felt he had to hit back, to show the French that even outnumbered, a British man-of-war was something to be reckoned with. He might not be able to stop the pack of hounds, but a few noses could certainly be bloodied.

Gordon thought a little music might put even more heart into the men, both at the stern chasers and the capstan. Being a Scot, he allowed himself a fine bagpiper to remind him of his native land. He found the pipes beautiful and inspiring, but more than that, their high-pitched skirl could be heard above gunfire. "Mr. Dashwood," he said calmly, "have Piper McLaren report to me on the quarterdeck. I think a few Highland Airs will be an inspiration to us all." He smiled broadly. Gordon assumed anyone hearing pipes immediately became their great and unreserved admirer.

"Aye, aye, sir," replied the unmusical Dashwood. To his ears, bagpipes did not skirl, they squealed.

On *Favourite*, La Meilliere turned to Dubordieu. "I fear we are falling behind in the chase. I am not sure why; we have all of our boats out towing, just like the British, yet they begin to pull ahead. Perhaps it is some technical refinement we have not yet discovered, but I think it is training. The enemy crew have been together much longer than ours; the bonds of time and discipline have infused them with the spirit of comradeship. In time, our crews will enjoy the same benefits. For now, Commodore, I have ordered more boats into the water to assist in towing, and ordered the officers in the boats to demand the men redouble their efforts."

Dubordieu responded, "Have patience and do not expect the impossible, Captain. We are doing well. We may lack their training, but we have numbers. Let us use that. I want the crews of the boats relieved frequently. Let us husband our strength, keep our rowers fresh. The British have no such reserves. Even determined, disciplined men must eventually wear themselves out. A hound must be patient; the fox will eventually tire and slow. When that happens, we will have them!"

"Fire!" Gordon gave the order, and two gunner's mates gave their lanyards a smart jerk. With a thunderous boom and a cloud of grey-white smoke, the two stern chasers sent iron flying across the water. One ball dropped harmlessly into the ocean, well short of target; the second ball struck the water at an odd angle that caused it to skip across the waves. It was a short skip, but enough for it to slam into the bow of *Favourite*, just above the waterline.

"Huzzah!" A cheer went up on the poop of *Active*. It was a hit; probably of no great moment, but a hit nonetheless. *Active* had teeth.

There was a dull thud, and the deck of *Favourite* vibrated briefly. "Commodore, I believe we have been hit," said La Meilliere with surprise.

"A lucky shot, surely," responded Dubordieu.

"Indeed, Commodore," said La Meilliere, "it cannot be anything else. But the attempt tells us something about this Gordon. He is a fighter; he is letting us know that. So much the better! The more able the antagonist, the greater the triumph!"

"Just so, Captain, just so. But let us send the same message, that we too are fighters. Keep the bow chasers firing. I will order the same for the rest of the squadron. It is not important if we miss. It is important we keep up the pressure, give them no respite."

Shots from the French squadron peppered the wake behind *Active's* stern. Plenty of spray, plenty of water spouts, plenty of noise, but no damage. It was like the words of the Bard: "full of sound and fury, signifying nothing." Not quite nothing. No hits were scored, but the barrage proved the French were demonstrating the tenacity usually attributed to British bulldogs.

*****

The men on the capstan pushed, heaved, and sweated. Seaman Beamis was one of the strongest men on the ship but he felt pressed to his limit as he pushed a pawl. The ship had never been threatened by five—count them, *five!*—French frigates before and extraordinary efforts suddenly needed to become commonplace. His lungs screamed and his arms seemed touched by fire, but he kept determinedly to his task.

Piper McLaren was tired. Bagpipes took a lot of lung power, and he had been playing for several hours now. Highlanders were noted for their stamina, but he was nearly spent, and reaching the end of his considerable repertoire of tunes. He was about to start repeating himself. He decided the men would not mind hearing "Garryowen" once again. Then he remembered he had forgotten to play "Over the Hills and Far Away." That would suit. He was proud his efforts were being well received. The men coming off the capstan favoured him with smiles, proof that his music had given them some diversion from their back-breaking efforts. Captain Gordon had said he was doing "a bonny job."

New men relieved the old on the capstan bars. This time, most of them were marines. Spottswood encouraged them. "Come on, marines! Let's show them how it's done!" His youthful enthusiasm sparkled through. The men erupted in a brief cheer. There was a rivalry, friendly for the most part, between marines and sailors. Spottswood would use that; anything to coax the last extra measure of effort out of the crew. The French had more men. Spottswood believed the British had better spirit.

"Fire!" *Active's* stern chasers roared out. The gunners had settled into a steady cadence of firing. "Fire!" The bow chasers of *Favourite* crashed out, nearly in unison with *Active's*. The shots of the opposing vessels passed each other in midflight and all dropped uselessly into the sea. It had little physical effect, but great moral effect. This was a war of wills, a test of nerves, and a contest in the steadiness of spirit.

The fiery sun torpidly crawled across the sky, but brought with it no sign of a breeze. Even the unflappable Gordon had to admit this was the hottest day he had met in a long while. He felt great sympathy for his crew. Blandon, just off capstan duty, snored loudly almost at the Captain's feet. Normally unthinkable, but Gordon didn't care. The man had given his all. It was all a test of brute manpower. Gordon looked up at the sails hoping for a miracle: nothing but acres of dead canvas.

Hour after hour, Pennywhistle and his men toiled, their routine seemingly eternal. Row, drop, row, weigh, recover, row some more and drop anchor. Harding actually fell asleep at his oar and had to be revived with an extra dose of water. The men drank copiously from the hogshead of water on the cutter, Pennywhistle filling and passing the ladle constantly. The barrel began to empty. No signs of heatstroke so far, good! His senses became more acute as his conscious mind quieted; a deep part of his subconscious took over. He got better and better at dropping the anchor in the best spot; no mental calculation needed, he just *knew*.

The cannonade thundered on, hour after hour, the British firing two shots for every one of the French. No hits were scored on either side, but the effort served to keep morale high on both sides. Gunners, stripped to the waist, their skin covered with a grey layer of grime and soot, settled into a routine. The ambient clouds of smoke and sulphur made their mouths as dry as the wastes of the Sahara. Open butts of drinking water on the decks emptied quickly. Men looked to the blazing sky for the relief of even a breath of air. There was none. The sails dozed.

One gunner's mate on *Active* became stupid with fatigue and accidentally ignited a priming quill which burned his hand beyond recognition. Surgeon Swayne would have a customer.

The chase ground on, everything in slow motion, like a tortoise trying to close with a snail and give battle.

In boiling, muggy air at sea, peculiar things happen with sound. Sometimes loud noises could be entirely muffled, even from nearby hearers, but the opposite could obtain. Noises that had no right to be heard beyond the immediate locality of their origin sometimes carried a great distance. And so it was this day. Hoste paced the deck of *Amphion*. An instinct caused him to stop suddenly, then survey the horizon with his glass. He cocked his ear, and listened intently. There was nothing to see, but he heard something: a low, rumbling noise like muted thunder and a dull, concussive thudding from some distance away.

His First Officer, the rakish Mr. Dunn, approached and spoke, "Do you hear that, Commodore? Is that what I think it is?"

Hoste spoke with alacrity. "It is indeed. Gunfire!"

Gordon was to be very lucky that hot, windless, muggy day. The strange carriage of sound waves provided Hoste a straight line direction for pursuit.

Twenty-Eight

The distance between *Active* and her pursuers had widened to two miles. It required tremendous exertions on the part of the crews to keep going, yet an outsider might have deemed their progress lazy and meandering.

Hoste on *Amphion*, some miles away, reasoned *Active* must be under attack. The lookouts could not yet see her, but she must be just over the horizon. Like the captains' ships this day, Hoste ordered the boats into the water to tow. He was determined to render aid. He cursed himself inwardly for allowing the merchantman to lure him off station. He had been entirely too confident! Gordon must be in the fight of his life; he would need help, and fast. If only he had some wind!

Supper on *Active* was served at its usual time of four o' clock and hungrily consumed by exhausted men. Men coming off the capstan, like MacLeod, sometimes just shuffled to the side and sank down along the bulwarks in a stupor of fatigue. Gordon allowed the men beer, but delayed the grog ration for later and promised a double ration to every man if they survived this day. That announcement was met with cheers.

Pennywhistle had no supper, but he had wisely stowed bread and cheese aboard the cutter. The men stopped their strokes for very short periods only. It was killing work, but they bore it without complaint. As the shadows of the afternoon lengthened, Pennywhistle hoped for relief from nightfall, which might generate a breeze as the land cooled. He felt like a naval version of Richard III after Bosworth: *A breeze, a breeze, my kingdom for a breeze!* The kedge went over the gunwale again.

The French ships suffered more in the extended pursuit than the British. Less inured to the rigors of sea-keeping than the British, the men began to sag and complain as the chase continued with a widening gap between. They performed their duties, but the initial excitement at the prospect of bagging a British frigate changed to anger and frustration as the enemy ship could be seen gradually pulling ahead in the race.

Four of the boats towing *Favourite* had not been supplied with sufficient water. Four seamen passed out from heat exhaustion. One man had passed to the next stage, heat stroke, and was near death. It was another example of inexperience at sea telling against the French.

The cannonade ceased once the distance between ships had widened beyond two miles. Gordon appreciated the morale and nuisance value of it all, but at that distance, being profligate with powder and shot was simply foolish.

Dubordieu was dismayed, but he was determined. Like everyone else, he searched the heavens for even the merest whisper of a breeze, but the limp sails frowned at him. He thought of LeMere and his marines. Galling as the situation was to him, it must be worse for LeMere. It was looking less and less likely that his marines would get to exercise their new-found skills this day. Dubordieu heard a thud behind him. A sailor had fallen asleep on his feet and collapsed on the deck. The crew was wearing out.

Dubordieu had supper served. The men needed energy, and it would boost morale, especially the French brandy, equivalent of the British grog ration.

The food was consumed hungrily and the brandy drunk eagerly. Under ordinary situations, watered down brandy would be savoured, in a relaxed fashion, and absorbed slowly. Drinking it rapidly under conditions of great stress and extreme fatigue had the effect of temporary jollification, but that passed quickly into something less pleasant. It made men already stupid with fatigue even stupider. Men began to stumble and reel, and they became very, very sloppy carrying out their duties. Two sailors got into a dispute over lyrics in a song and came to blows. Two of their mates fell asleep on deck. A few men began to grumble and curse. A carpenter's mate shouted a particularly outrageous vulgarity at an officer. An Ordinary Seaman threatened an experienced lieutenant, who ordered him back to duty. La Meilliere had to have boatswain's mates bully wayward crewmen with starters—sticks with whipcords at the end used for hitting, or starting, a man back toward the ways of discipline. Weariness and resentment were obvious in the sour expressions of most of the crew.

Active extended her lead to three miles. On both sides, men walked the decks like zombies, but here was where the superior British discipline and training began to tell. On *Active*, drills were executed a bit more slowly than usual, but still smartly and crisply. There was little talking and no grumbling. The only sounds were the occasional trills of the boatswain's whistle and the seemingly indefatigable playing of McLaren's bagpipes. "The Girl I Left Behind Me" drifted confidently across the water, reaching Pennywhistle's boat.

On *Favourite*, there was much extraneous talking and singing. The ship hummed with a low buzz of human voices. The tunes were ribald, or laced with complaint and lamentation. An older sailor sang a rousing chorus of "Aloute," which celebrated plucking the feathers, not from birds, but from the officers. The song spoke the language of the drained, the dispirited, and the uncertain. The French had courage and would fight, but right now their officers wished they had had more training and experience.

"Deck there! Sail ho! Two points off the larboard bow!" The *Amphion's* masthead lookout shouted boldly, the relief in his voice obvious. He carefully focused his glass. "It's *Active*! I'd know her rig anywhere. She has company. One, two, three...five ships, sir!"

Hoste took his speaking trumpet and yelled up at the masthead. "How far?"

"I make it five miles, sir, give or take."

The sun, a swollen, glowing red ball, was beginning its drop below the horizon. As the day lost heat, what everyone had been waiting for finally happened. Hoste noticed a slight flapping on the main topsail. Very slight, but there. The swells increased in size and strength, white caps and shadows appeared on the sea: telltale signs of an incipient wind. The land was cooling and let out the gentle whisper of an evening breeze, a breeze they could use. The sails bulged ever so slightly. If only it would hold, Hoste could order the boats in.

Gordon on *Active* noted the breeze as well. The sails showed a hint of life. Not much wind, but steady. Time to order the boats in. They and the kedge anchors had done their jobs. The wind was blowing against them, but by sailing close-hauled they could make good use of it.

"Deck there! Sail ho! Two points off the starboard quarter!" shouted the masthead lookout on *Active*.

Captain Gordon bellowed upwards, "What do you make of her?"

The joy was evident in the lookout's voice. "It's *Amphion*, sir. Five miles Northwest!"

Gordon's smile betrayed no mirth, only relief. About time! Two to five odds were infinitely better than one to five!

Pennywhistle smiled, albeit wanly, when he saw the signal to return to ship. He saw the ropes to the ship slacken as *Active* surged forward under the power of wind, rather than human muscle. His men were exhausted, but their efforts had staved off disaster. Nevertheless, the French were still after them.

*****

La Meilliere was so consumed with concerns of discipline that he was slow in noticing the return of the breeze. Getting the ship's boats back on *Favourite* consumed more time than it should have, and he cursed the men under his breath. He ordered every sail set, but his dilatoriness had just bought *Active* another mile of distance. She now had a lead of four miles.

The wind continued to build. *Amphion* sailed an altered course, gently running at three knots. It was now completely dark. Hoste thought of using blue flares to signal Gordon, but decided against it; his ship might not have been spotted by the enemy squadron. There was no sense losing the advantage of surprise. Night engagements were tricky things, very hard to control. There was the danger of collision, of damage from friendly fire, the difficulty of pinpointing exactly where your enemy was. Hoste well knew this, but he also appreciated the shock value of a ship with no lights suddenly appearing out of the night and opening fire. Surprise would be tremendous advantage and go a long way to canceling the French superiority in numbers. Flashes of light in pitch blackness played havoc with eyesight, which would work to British advantage. Captain Keats at Algeciras had once caused two Spanish ships he was pursuing to fire into each other, each convinced they were targeting the British.

Even so, Hoste was badly outgunned, and he knew he could not make a lengthy fight of it, but Gordon was a smart captain and would follow his lead once he opened fire. Hunted suddenly becoming the hunter appealed greatly to him, and would to Gordon as well. If they could deal the French a smart jab to the teeth, then immediately disengage and run like wraiths on an unexpected course, they stood a chance of escape.

*****

Pennywhistle sat alone in the wardroom. His servant, Manton, fussed over him and relieved him of his coat and equipment. Seemingly from nowhere, he produced a sizzling beefsteak, a sea pie, and a bottle of something red from the officer's stores. He continued to amaze when he disappeared and quickly returned with something very rare at sea: a pitcher of lemonade. Not terribly cold, but suitably tart. Pennywhistle was so thirsty he drained the pitcher immediately.

He was tired, and at present not possessed of the most discriminating palette, but he thought he had never had any meal quite so tasty. The beefsteak was less stringy and rangy than the usual fare and disappeared off his plate quickly. The sea pie was mediocre, but right now seemed fit for a king. The bottle of chardonnay was almost an afterthought. He poured himself a glass and reflected on the day. He thought himself fortunate he was dining alone and not in the company of French officers praising his gallantry and commiserating with him over the loss of his ship. Yet *Active* was far from out of danger, and such a meal remained an unpleasant possibility.

Spottswood entered the wardroom and touched his hat in salute. Pennywhistle wearily looked up. "Glad to see you survived the day in one piece, Lieutenant! I understand the marines under your command did a splendid job. Congratulations!"

Spottswood smiled. "Thank you, sir. I hate to interrupt your meal, but Captain Gordon wants you on deck. Something's up."

Twenty-Nine

The coming of night provoked an animated discussion on *Favourite* of how best to continue the pursuit of *Active*. La Meilliere urged caution; Dubordieu advocated vigor. La Meilliere argued it was impossible to guess *Active's* intentions, while Dubordieu riposted that he had a clear idea of them.

Dubordieu pondered the Captain's words and spoke with resignation. "I want *Active* badly, but much as it pains me to admit, your words have merit. Our little fleet lacks experience in night sailing. Spreading them out makes sense. But it will mean posting signal lanterns in the masts to get their attention, then dispatching boats to convey the message. We are fortunate that we are not moving with great speed and the swells are mild this night. I worry that the lanterns will give away our position, but it is hardly likely *Active* will turn on us. In fact, the lanterns may serve notice on her that we are relentless and will not abandon the pursuit until she strikes her colours. But you are wrong about one thing. She will not change her present course; she, like us, is ruled by the wind. It is very light and she must sail close to it to maintain much headway. No, she is out there, Captain, and I think in the same relative position as before. Morning will see her exposed to our guns."

Dubordieu peered into the night and could barely discern the bulk of French ships on the port and starboard beams. "Captain, post the lanterns and dispatch the boats. We will spread them out."

*****

Five miles away, a solemn colloquy of *Active's* officers peered into the stygian darkness. Most had their night glasses out, but the view astern from the poop deck was unrevealing. The French were out there, but where? Gordon had summoned not just the naval officers, but the two marine officers as well. Everyone spoke in hushed tones.

Gordon began in a calm voice, but there was an undercurrent of joyful excitement in it.

"Gentlemen! The French are out there, five, maybe six miles astern. They cannot see us, nor we them. I do not think the French commander is a fool; he will guess our heading and intentions. We need to find a way to join up with Hoste, break the pursuit, and affect our escape. Captain Pennywhistle has a remedy which will at least solve part of the problem." He explained Pennywhistle's plan, and the other officers smiled at its ingenunity.

Pennywhistle looked at his watch. It was time. He lit the fuse of the Congreve. It hissed threateningly, seemed frozen between heaven and earth for the longest second, then sped off into the night sky. It burst with a short, but very impressive, red glare that for five seconds gave the light of day to objects below. It made *Active* herself more visible than Pennywhistle planned, but that gave him the germ of an idea of how that could be employed later as an extra advantage against the French.

Ten seconds later, Spottswood let fly with his Congreve, and ten seconds after that, Gunner's Mate Jordan with his. They fired theirs from hastily built rafts towed astern of *Active*. The three serial flashes of light created the impression of a giant illuminated finger. It was an extremely short-lived fireworks display, but Spottswood thought the colourful illumination would have done credit to one he had seen done in London on the King's Birthday. He just hoped Hoste saw it.

Hoste did indeed see it. Everyone on board *Amphion* saw it. A brilliant blaze of unexpected light in a sable sky could not fail to compel attention. "Gordon, by God! He's pointing the way!" Hoste exclaimed with satisfaction. "Much closer than we thought, too, can't be more than three miles," Hoste said to his First Officer. "In this blackness, we might have sailed right past. Quartermaster, come starboard four points. Steer for the fireworks!"

Dubordieu in *Favourite* saw the three flashes as well. He turned to La Meilliere.

"What was that? I have never seen anything like that. Can they be signals of some kind? But the British use blue flares for signals." Or, he wondered, had something gone wrong on *Active*? Was it possible those were actually explosions? Had her powder magazine detonated? But, no noise. Maybe the moisture-saturated air masked it; very strange! The lights were so bright, yet so brief. "Well, Captain, we are all fatigued from the chase today. Perhaps someone on *Active* was tired, careless, and touched off a spark in the magazine. I cannot think what else it could signify."

Active's lookouts were, well, active. They were enjoined personally by the captain to be especially vigilant. They needed to both look and listen for a bulky form speeding out of the night. After two hours, their vigilance was rewarded as one materialized. The main masthead lookout raced down the ratlines with the speed and nimbleness of an orangutan and gave the message to a delighted and relieved Captain Gordon.

The dark form of a frigate slowly edged even with *Active* at perhaps two hundred yards distance. A minute later, Gordon stood at the entry port, speaking trumpet in hand. "Ahoy, *Amphion*!" Gordon shouted. The shout was returned joyfully by Hoste. "Ahoy, *Active*! Glad to see you. Give Dashwood the con and lower a boat." He had a lot to discuss with Gordon and not much time to do it.

A quarter of an hour later, Gordon entered the great cabin of the *Amphion*. "Captain, please sit, and pray have a glass of this modestly talented Madeira. I am guessing you have had a rough day. Tell me about it, and spare no detail. I wish I could tell you our night will be one of repose and relaxed discussion, but I fear we will be in harm's way before long." Hoste spoke with his usual directness.

Gordon furnished Hoste a summary of the day's events. When he concluded, Hoste leaned backward in his chair, steepled his fingers, and was lost in thought for several minutes.

John M. Danielski

When he finally spoke, it was with a determined expression, like a bulldog who had made up his mind to savage a fox raiding a henhouse. "You have had a trying day, one that was a great challenge to your seamanship, Captain. Your conduct is greatly to your credit as a sea officer. You have deftly escaped five ships, and that shall be duly noted in my dispatches. I was careless today. I let you down, and for that I am sorry. But now I think it is time for a little retribution against our French friends for the trouble they gave you. Does that sound congenial to you, Captain?"

Gordon smiled. He knew Hoste well enough to sense what was coming.

Hoste spoke. "We are outnumbered, outgunned, and outmanned. The night is pitch black, the breeze is light, and the odds against us are long. The French will be expecting us to run like smoke and oakum. It is the reasonable assumption that a reasonable seaman would make." He paused and permitted himself a small smile of satisfaction. "Therefore, we will attack!"

Thirty

Gordon's announcement in *Active's* great cabin won stunned looks all around, with the exception of Pennywhistle. The officers turned and looked at each other with expressions of disbelief. Their mouths were motionless, but their eyes shouted, "Did I just hear what I think I did?"

"Do not be so surprised, gentleman, your ears do not deceive you," said Gordon jovially. "It is really the only way. If we let them keep the initiative, their numbers will tell. We have little on our side, save one priceless asset: surprise. The last thing the French will expect is an attack. The other important point is, we will have the wind on our side. They will have had the wind nearly in their faces. When we come one hundred and eighty degrees about, it will put the wind at our backs. It should greatly speed our escape as well."

The elegant, worldly James Moore spoke up, his grey eyes aglow with eagerness. "Captain, forgive me for being taken aback by your first pronouncement; it took some time to digest. I think it will be a capital show! But, Captain, I have to inquire, how much time will we have to prepare our parts and our men?"

"An excellent question, Mr. Moore. I have spoken to the Master and his best guess is, if the wind holds and the French continue on their last known course, two big 'ifs' I grant you, we should make contact in nearly two hours. Say 2 a.m. We will clear for action, but not beat to quarters. I need hardly tell you the value of keeping noise to a minimum. Verbal commands and hand gestures will be the order of the night. We will forego drums and boatswain's whistles.

I would say this to all of you: make sure your men are well fed.

Explain to them exactly what is expected and what lies ahead. Serve small beer only. Tell them the grog I promised must be delayed until we are well clear of this. They will need their wits about them and will understand. If there is anything they like better than grog it's giving Johnny Crapaud a smart punch in the mouth. I want this to be a colossal surprise to the French, but nothing of the kind for our own men. They have been hard pressed today and have responded well. Persuade them one more effort is asked, and beyond that lies safety. The men have already gained more prize money than most crews. Tell them still more lies ahead. They will do their duty with stout and cheerful hearts; I know them. Gentlemen, we will not only survive this night, but will make it one to remember! And now, I will detain you no further from your duties. You are dismissed."

Favourite and her four consorts sailed on into the night. They had lost track of *Active*, but continued their present course in the expectation that she had done the same. Dubordieu knew sea chases were often drawn out affairs that lasted for days. Dogged persistence was needed most. Accurate guesswork helped. Knowledge of ports, winds, and currents could make that guesswork more informed.

Hoste checked his night glass. He could see a dark mass that he knew must be the French line. They were closing; he guessed the distance was down to less than half a league. He surveyed the deck. His men were in position. Everything was ready.

Gordon repeated a similar ritual on his ship. He and Hoste were of a mind about their cannon's ammunition. Gordon ordered them double-shotted, not with ball, grape, or canister, but with chain and bar shot. Once fired, this shot separated into halves connected by either a chain or a bar. It was used to rip, slash, and tear rigging. It would hamper a French captain's ability to control his vessel. The resulting unruliness would also increase the risk of collision with other ships of Dubordieu's squadron. Of course, what chain and bar shot did to rigging would be greatly amplified on any human flesh that got in the way.

Active carried eight thirty-two-pound smashers; *Amphion* ten twenty-four-pound ones. Not officially counted as part of the armaments, they would play a specific role. Gordon and Hoste ordered them double-shotted as well, but with canister. They would admirably fulfill their design function as giant short-range shotguns, splendidly lethal for clearing decks. Cannons would aim for the rigging, carronades for the men.

Pennywhistle carefully oiled his Ferguson. The repetitive circular motion of the oiled rag on steel induced a calm, measured focus. It brought his mind to a tranquil, dreamy place where he could contemplate the motions of himself and his command in the forthcoming battle.

He watched Spottswood going through the final preparations with the marines. He was no longer a novice. He knew the drill well and he was blooded in personal combat. Pennywhistle normally would have positioned and prepared the marines himself, but Spottswood had begged him for that honour. Pennywhistle kept a weathered eye on the dispositions and allowed it was exactly what he would have done himself.

The marines were positioned in three ranks to provide volley fire, since they would be firing from the windward side. It was not one continuous line, but more a small series of lines, broken up by the shape of the deck and objects upon it. Less protection than firing from the leeward side, but they would be able to bring more firepower to bear. Spottswood was engaged in a deep discussion with Dale. Mercury wagged his tail and cocked his head slowly from side to side as his master spoke, apparently trying to learn his part.

Pennywhistle was glad to see that Spottswood was perceptive enough to defer to the older man when he offered "advice." Some young officers disdained such counsel because it was not proferred by a gentleman. They usually did not live long.

He finished oiling the Ferguson. It gleamed with a deadly beauty that demanded employment. That demand would not have long to wait.

Thirty-One

Active glided through the dark waters with the silken grace and menace of the oaken shark she was. Her teeth were bared: her cannons had been run out and were cleared for action. Gordon, her brain, scented blood. Her prey, the French ship, *Favourite*, lay unaware, dead ahead. The sails *Active* hoisted were those for attack and would have been instantly recognized as such by other nautical predators. Her driver was furled and she was under jib, topsails, and t'gallants. The courses, the sails closest to the deck, were taken in to reduce the risk of fire from stray pieces of smoldering wadding. Men of the gun crews on the gun deck, quarterdeck, and forecastle were stripped to the waist both for comfort—battle was a very hot affair—and to reduce the risk of infection from wounds. It was well known that the worst infections developed from pieces of clothing carried into a wound. Sailors tied bandanas around their ears to deaden the terrible thunder of their guns.

Surgeon Swayne in the orlop laid out his kit. He had bandaged the gunner's mate's hand and was ready for more customers. The loblolly boys, his orderlies, waited expectantly.

The marines were posted in three major groups and three smaller ones. The largest group, under Spottswood, stood on the poop deck. The second group, under Dale, sheltered under the bulwarks of the quarterdeck. The third group, under Corporal Wainwright, was in position behind the wooden bollards of the forecastle. Marine sharpshooters, chosen by Pennywhistle himself, occupied the fighting tops, semi-circular platforms on the fore, main, and mizzen masts. Three were posted in each top, the main top also having a swivel gun loaded with canister. Pennywhistle took a position in the main top, which, one hundred feet above the deck, gave him an excellent vantage point. Normally, he would have commanded from the quarterdeck, but this would not be an extended engagement, merely a hit and run affair. Spottswood and Dale were perfectly capable of handling matters on deck. Pennywhistle felt he would be most useful picking off deck officers with his Ferguson.

He had reviewed his three G's of marksmanship with the marines: gold, gilt, and gorgets. The more gold lace an officer had on his uniform, the higher the grade. Quality gilt finish on his sword and epaulettes similarly signified rank and prestige. The gorget made an excellent aiming point, as it lay close to the heart. He had also instructed his men to close their eyes just before the Congreves fired to spare them the visual disorientation the flash would inflict on the French.

*****

Dubordieu had gone below to get some well-earned rest. La Meilliere was wide awake, tending to a mountain of paperwork. The eager, but woefully new, Lieutenant Augustain was officer of the deck. The guns stood inert, unmanned, and tompions closed their muzzles. Most of the gun crews were sleeping soundly in their gently swaying hammocks. It had been a long, grueling day. The mid watch was on duty, but went about their business with the lassitude of stress, insufficient training, and the sheer newness of it all. Lookouts were posted, but there was no sense of urgency. Nothing more would happen this night. The chase would continue, but there would surely be no action until tomorrow. Indeed, action was unlikely even then. And so it was on the other four ships of Dubordieu's squadron. They were theoretically sailing in support of one another, but they might as well have been a thousand miles apart.

Augustain had his night glass out and thought he saw something approaching. He hailed the masthead lookout. "Lookout, do you see anything, fine off the starboard quarter?" Augustain shouted through his speaking trumpet.

The lookout was a lazy man, none too bright, and irritated by this young spark of an officer. He had been half dozing and resented this intrusion. Officers! He would appease this one quickly and then go back to dreaming of home. He looked in the direction of the bow. What he saw shocked him fully awake. *Mon Dieu!* There *was* something out there, and whatever it was it was, it was coming on fast.

The lookout shouted down, "Yes, lieutenant, something approaching. Frigate."

Augustain was puzzled. Frigate? That made no sense. What frigate would that be? The British were miles away. Wait, he knew the Commodore had given orders for Captain Pasquaglio in *Corona* to rejoin the squadron at the earliest possible moment. He had heard that Pasquaglio was a real fire-eater, even though he was Italian. Word had got around that he was eager for retribution after the punishment *Cerberus* had inflicted. Perhaps he had achieved the impossible and bullied the dockyard workers into completing a speedy refit.

Should he call the captain on deck, or deal with the situation himself? The captain had spoken of the need to show initiative. Augustain was young, had only been in the navy a year, and was eager for recognition. He could handle command and not bother his superiors for counsel about every minor matter that presented itself. He would hail the unknown ship. The more he considered it, the more he knew it had to be *Corona*. There was no reason to be alarmed. He merely had to confirm what he knew to be true.

Hoste on *Amphion* had plotted a circuitous course, one that had *Amphion* and *Active* approaching *Favourite* at a ninety-degree angle, which concealed both ships from the rest of the squadron. They were hidden behind the masts of *Favourite*. And so far, no alarm had erupted from *Favourite's* lookouts.

Amphion's helm completed her final course adjustment. She was now parallel with *Favourite*. The bow of *Amphion* closed to four hundred yards from the stern of *Favourite*. *Active* was four hundred yards astern of *Amphion*. The helms of both British ships were on high alert. This was tricky stuff at night: only the most vigilant and skilled ship-handling would keep the possibility of a collision at bay; but if there was one thing both ships had in abundance, it was skilled seamanship.

A high-pitched hail floated through the night. "Ahoy there, what ship are you?" an uncertain, anxious voice demanded in French.

It was heard clearly on *Amphion*. Hoste had anticipated this. He had Lieutenant O'Brien, an experienced French speaker, standing by to answer.

"We are the *Corona*, Captain Pasquaglio. We come with dispatches for Commodore Dubordieu," O'Brien shouted across the decreasing distance.

Augustain breathed a sigh of relief. He had been right! He had also been correct not to bother the Captain. He would proudly convey the information to Captain La Meilliere and the Commodore. They would praise him for handling the situation so smartly. He had real *sang froid*! Perhaps there was even a commendation in it for him.

Amphion's jib-boom passed the edge of *Favourite's* stern. The two ships were half a cable's length apart now, three hundred feet. *Favourite's* men of the mid watch noted with surprise the shape looming out of the night.

Augustain hailed them again. "Do you wish me to send a boat?"

O'Brien's answering hail came back quickly. "That will be unnecessary, monsieur. We thank you for your hospitality, but will provide our own. Please pass the word to the Commodore we have an urgent message to convey. It will be coming directly." O'Brien smiled wolfishly.

"Very good, *Corona*." Augustain shouted back. "We await it and your visit with pleasure."

A strange uneasiness caused La Meilliere to put his paperwork aside and come on deck. He had no idea why, it made no sense, but it was compelling. It was some form of seaman's instinct, and it had never let him down. As he stepped out onto the quarterdeck, he saw with horror a frigate to port! And not one of theirs!

Augustain experienced a similar flash of horror at exactly the same moment. *Merde!* The ship had her gun ports open! It was the *Roastbifs*! It was the last view and thought the unfortunate Lieutenant Augustain had. A second later, he was flayed by flying iron from carronade number two. There was a thunderous roar, and red-orange flame lit up the night with an obscene illumination that blinded, then froze dozens of French faces in gasps of terror.

Eighteen guns and five carronades spoke in deadly earnest, at a mere one hundred yard range. Flying chain and bar shot rapidly engulfed *Favourite* in a typhoon of lead. Three men standing together were all snipped in half by one of the nineteen projectiles. Their legs were hurled to port, their torsos to starboard. Four stunned idlers standing at the ship's waist were decapitated at the shoulders. A ship's boy of ten had his legs cut off at the knees. He lay quietly whimpering for his mother.

In that brief moment, half of the starboard watch died. The scuppers turned into crimson rivers. Bone, hair, flesh, and teeth plastered the bulwarks and rigging. Those who remained alive stumbled on the now slippery deck. After the huge burst of light, the deck was again an inky black. The lazy lookout who'd first spotted *Amphion* could not make his eyes adjust and still saw the gigantic flash.

But execution of the crew was never the main purpose of the attack; the masts and rigging that were the true objectives. These were savaged. Shrieking chain shot gouged huge chunks of wood out of the main and fore masts. The back and fore stays, stout ropes that held them in place, snapped, as if cut by a giant surgeon. The main and fore preventer stays that assisted in keeping the masts erect parted violently with a strange whipping sound. Without anything to counterbalance the enormous weight of the masts, they began to sway, ever so slowly, but ever so dangerously.

The mizzen topmast shattered, then tumbled over the side, dragging the ship. The ship's jib-boom exploded into splinters and the jib sail shredded; the ship would be very hard to control.

Captain La Meilliere slipped on deck planks coated with greasy blood. A fraction of a second later, a pressure wave slammed him onto the quarterdeck. He examined himself quickly and found he was unhurt. The same could not be said of his ship.

Marines maintained a nuisance fire from the poop of *Amphion* as her stern glided past *Favourite's* bow. It kept the survivors heads down. What remained of the mid watch was in a disorganized state of shock.

Amphion sailed on into the blackness. Act One was complete.

Active's bow now closed with *Favourite's* stern. Act Two was about to begin.

Thirty-Two

Gordon watched *Amphion's* engagement with *Favourite* intently. Through his glass, it showed as a short-lived conflagration of fire, light, and booming sound. *Favourite* offered no real resistance; not a shot was fired in retaliation. One more broadside might take her down, two more would for certain. Gordon wanted to slow his ship slightly and ensure time for two.

Active's bow was two hundred yards behind *Favourite's* stern, a cable length from her port side. Gordon ordered the First Officer to shiver the main top sail. Bracing the yard at a certain angle would cause a sail to shiver, flutter impotently, and cease to draw. Unlike backing, or reversing a sail against the wind, which acted like a brake, shivering simply slowed the ship's progress ever so slightly. Only a slight adjustment on the braces was necessary to cause a shivering sail to draw fully again and return the ship to her former speed.

Dashwood passed the word to Haye in charge of the quarterdeck and forecastle guns to prepare for two broadsides in quick succession. Two of the ship's "four L's," Midshipmen Lownes and Llewellyan, acted as messengers and conveyed the orders to Meers and Moore, in charge of the main battery on the deck below. Dashwood dispatched Midshipman Leslie up the ratlines to inform Pennywhistle. *Good,* thought Pennywhistle, *it will give us time to make a thorough job of it.*

When Midshipman Lockhart brought Spottswood the order, he smiled, having similar thoughts.

*****

Chaos reigned on *Favourite*. The deck resembled a madman's workshop of bloody spare body parts, chiefly torsos and appendages, with a few stray heads thrown in for good measure. Tufts of hair clung to rigging. A few barely recognizable human forms writhed in agony. Many sailors stood idle in simple bewilderment. It had all happened so fast.

The volcanic blast of the broadside roused most of the crew, including Dubordieu and LeMere. La Meilliere belatedly beat to quarters and the groggy crew stumbled, rather than raced on deck. Crews sleepwalked to the cannon on the main gun deck. Powder monkeys shambled to bring charges to the cannon. Everything proceeded in slow motion, as if time were a gift they had in abundance. In reality, they had no time.

La Meilliere ordered damage control parties to begin splicing the severed fore and back stays on the main and fore masts. They were in bad shape. Pressure on the masts was at dangerous levels. This was where the arcane knowledge of specialized rope knots came into play, knowing which ones to use in an emergency to quickly restore severed stays. It was a product of experience the crew of *Favourite* did not have. The gore, the brandy, and the lack of practiced repair drill meant their movements were leaden and inefficient, not the crisp, almost balletic movements of a trained crew.

Five minutes had passed since *Amphion's* attack. It seemed a lifetime on the *Favourite*.

LeMere was in heated conversation with Commodore Dubordieu. "Please do not tell me my marines are unnecessary right now, Commodore. I fear another attack. I will order them to assume action stations on the deck, if you will but permit it."

Dubordieu frowned. "I appreciate your zeal; it is most commendable, but they would be much better employed with the damage control parties clearing the deck. At this point, we need manpower to move debris. I am glad they are keen to prove themselves, but right now, I need brute strength and lots of it."

LeMere was not a man to be easily deterred. "Forgive me,

253

Commodore, but I have a growing premonition of tragedy, greater than the one we now witness. We are not done with battle just yet. Allow my marines to form on deck for but thirty minutes. If nothing happens after that, I would be more than happy to have them assist the damage control parties. Please indulge me on this. I beg of you, this gift, this sight, has never failed me. It has been passed on through my family for generations and has allowed me to survive many sanguinary battles unscathed."

Dubordieu was not in a mood to be importuned by LeMere. The man was nothing if not persistent. But perhaps he had a point. If there was no further threat, thirty minutes would make no difference. If there was... "Very well, Captain. Thirty minutes, no more. Parade your men."

*****

On the main gun deck of *Active*, Moore and Meers walked slowly along, stopping to briefly converse with each cannon crew. The battery of 18-pounders here was the ship's main armament. They made sure there were plenty of cartridges, balls, and wadding. Flintlocks for the cannons were inspected, and flints even slightly suspect were replaced. Buckets of water for swabbing the guns were ready and the deck had been carefully covered in a layer of sand to give greater purchase in case the blood flowed too freely. Moore hoped that would not be the case tonight.

The brooding, darkly earnest Lieutenant Haye performed the same ritual with the quarterdeck and forecastle gun crews.

Spottswood talked to each man on the poop, just the way he knew Pennywhistle would have done. He made sure cartridges were dry, flints sound, and weapons properly oiled and functional. Dale and Wainwright did the same with their men. Pennywhistle spoke to the two privates who shared the main fighting top with him. They knew the drill: look for the highest ranking officer.

The seven officers, four midshipman, two hundred and sixty-four sailors, and thirty-nine marines were ready. They were *Active* and *Active* was them—a perfect symbiosis of machine and man. Each gave life to the other. Men took the measure of the ship and the ship took the measure of the men.

LeMere's men took up their positions on the port bulwarks. None had yet had time to reach the fighting tops when the call came.

"Another ship! Fifty yards off the port quarter!" The lookout's shout was frantic, fearful. He had not been paying attention. There was only supposed to be one ship out there!

La Meilliere was stunned. Only one main deck cannon had a full crew. On the deck below, the same could be said of only four cannon.

Fifty yards to go. *Active's* guns were run out, teeth bared. Twenty-four steady hands held lanyards ready. One slight jerk on each and twenty-four flintlocks would spark the entire starboard broadside into illuminating the night sky with red-orange death. But not yet. "Steady boys, steady," said the crew chiefs. "Just a bit more. Wait for the word."

Moore spoke. "Remember, boys, maximum elevation, aim for the rigging. We are firing to cripple, not to kill. The fore and main masts want to fall; let's help them along." The men smiled. It was not much of a jest, but anything to relieve the tension was welcome.

Spottswood spoke in low, hushed tones to his men. "Remember what Captain Pennywhistle said, boys. Fire on the up roll, aim low, and shoot for the buckles on their shoes." The pressure on the enemy would be incessant. Spottswood told every man he wanted at least three good shots. They would reload in quick time for as long as the enemy was in range.

Twenty-five yards now. The men on *Favourite* were transfixed with horror. La Meilliere and Dubordieu shouted at them to shake them back to their duty. The one group who responded well and calmly were LeMere's marines. They were poised and alert as the enemy ship's bow drew amidships of *Favourite*.

Gordon held his breath. He was cutting it close, engaging from pistol shot, point blank range. He slowly and deliberately raised his sword in the air. What little light there was reflected off the blade and gave the impression of writhing glow-worms. It was deadly quiet.

At the Captain's nod, Gunner's Mate Jordan lit the fuses of the two Congreves and they flashed into the night sky. They exploded, and the two ships were bathed in fiery red, flooding light that shocked eyes used to darkness and caused many on *Favourite* to look away, blinded, from the menace that was upon them. Not so, with *Active*. Her men were ready.

Gordon's cutlass flashed down. "Fire!" A broadside of cannons sent their deadly cargo of lead and chains hurtling forward, and the four carronades screamed their lethal blasts of canister. The marines fired, and then were surprised to see what looked like other soldiers facing them thirty yards away.

Pennywhistle had a brief view of an officer frantically exhorting his men. He held his breath and squeezed the trigger of the Ferguson. There was a loud *crack,* and the rapidly spinning projectile bored its way through the forehead of the gallant Captain La Meilliere.

Spottswood's musket shouted at almost the same instant and its lead cargo drilled a neat hole in the throat of the *Favourite's* Master.

Dale's Baker barked its single insult and a French boatswain clutched a ragged hole in his stomach.

Carronade three demolished four men. All were boatswain's mates, critical men needed to repair the rigging.

One sailor was blown into the night sky, riveting everyone's attention. The kinetic energy of the blast caused his charred arms and legs to flail and spin him like a human pinwheel at a county fair. He lacked a head, and a column of fire shot from his neck.

The chain and bar shot smashed into *Favourite's* foremast, which swayed, then began its lonely tumble to the sea. The gaggle of men who stood beneath it, who had been affecting splices on the stays, were smashed into bits of flying bone and gore. A flying head killed one powder monkey when it struck him full in the face. The men on the mast yards were hurled into the sea, along with the lookout who'd failed to notice *Active* until the last minute. None of the men could swim.

Most of the repair parties on deck were batted into bloody rags, as was the crew of the one cannon that stood ready to fire. One minute there were men; the next, bits of men, blood, and agonized cries for help from the few who still lived. But no help came; most of their comrades lay dead.

Chain-shot cut a French carpenter's mate nearly in half at the waist; his spinal column held him together. He fell to the deck in front of a powder monkey. Then a spontaneous muscle contraction caused the body to spring fully up and stand for a fraction of a second, as if it could not accept its own death. It collapsed for good an instant later. The powder monkey fled, screaming in terror.

The chain and bar shot also shredded the poop deck bulwarks, behind which LeMere's men sheltered, killing three of their number. The marines on *Active* followed Spottswood's directive and aimed low. The excitement of the moment and inexperience caused LeMere's people to fire just slightly too high. The British marines' fire was rapid, accurate, and did great execution among their French counterparts. There was huge difference between real marines and imitations of them.

Still, the French held their positions doggedly, returning fire; nobody broke and ran for the imagined safety of the lower decks. A new marine was the only casualty from French fire. A French marine gloated briefly, then perished with a bullet through the heart, as MacLeod avenged the rookie's death.

Pennywhistle fired a second time. This shot penetrated the gorget of a gangly lieutenant, one of the deck officers. He scored low on the G-scale, but when one had little time, one could not be too picky. One more junior officer would never advance in rank.

A second thunderous broadside roared out. Tons of lead ripped into *Favourite's* side at five hundred miles an hour and cut the mainmast cleanly in half. It did not topple in a stately fashion; it was simply blown in half. Huge, lethal splinters flew in every direction. One six-foot long specimen, weighing a hundred pounds, became a giant javelin, and its razor-sharp edge impaled two French sailors hard against the starboard bollards. They looked like specimens on a naturalist's insect board.

A glancing blow from a passing chain shot smashed the gunner's mate's head inside his chest, and what looked like black cherry jam oozed from the stub of a neck.

Spottswood's men pounded away at their counterparts on *Favourite*. They killed ten and wounded the same number. Spottswood had asked for three shots, but his men got off four.

LeMere realized his men were firing slightly too high and ordered them to aim lower. He was losing men, but there was no panic, and they were wonderfully steadfast. Next time, they would do better!

The killer instinct in Gordon wanted to finish the business. The enemy ship only carried a battered mizzenmast and was un-maneuverable. Gordon had no way of knowing her captain was dead, but he observed that the ship seemed under no coherent direction. The soldiers on her deck maintained a brisk, annoying fire, but most of the sailors had been swept away. One officer in an odd bearskin shako appeared to be the only one on deck giving orders. Gordon desperately wanted to take the ship, but had his orders. There were four other un-bloodied ships out there. He had done his job and crippled the enemy, now it was time to run.

"Set the courses, Mr. Dashwood. Let's get out of here." The disappointment in Gordon's voice was evident.

Pennywhistle sighted the Ferguson on the man in the shako directing what appeared to be French marines. Could that be the officer from Groa? Spottswood had told him a French officer in an Imperial Guard shako had tried to kill him, but he, Spottswood, had shot first. Obviously, Spottswood's shot had not been fatal.

At that moment, *Active* lurched as the courses fully engaged the wind. The wheel spun round and the ship heeled over to gain her new course. The resulting stagger, increased speed, and mast sway spoiled Pennywhistle's aim. He put down the Ferguson. He would do no more tonight. He had the feeling he would have that officer in his sights again.

Dubordieu regained consciousness slowly. He had been knocked out by a glancing blow from a flying wooden block. He had a bad headache, but was otherwise unharmed. His deck was a shambles. God damn Hoste! He had had enough. It was time to hit back, and do as Hoste had done to him. Strike at his base! But for now, *Favourite* was thoroughly crippled and wasn't going anywhere.

Mr. Green, Master of *Active*, set a course south by southeast toward the British base of Lissa. The ship answered her helm with smooth alacrity. *Active* gracefully glided off into the night.

Thirty-Three

Pennywhistle sat, calmly perched on the terrace of an old Venetian nobleman's hunting lodge five hundred feet above the harbour of Port St. George. He had established his headquarters in the rambling stone structure because it gave a fine view of the harbour and would enable him to easily spot any approaching French ships. An old artist's smock protected his coat and a wide brimmed straw hat did the same for his head. Easel and watercolours at the ready, he struggled to decide the precise colour of the tiled roof of the town hall. Umber or sienna? He pondered, then decided it had to be umber. Yes, the roofs of the rest of the town were sienna, but the town hall was definitely umber. He smiled to himself. After the drama of the night battle three weeks ago, it was truly laughable that the biggest decision he had to make was the paint selection for what would probably turn out to be an accurate but uninspired watercolour of an unremarkable Mediterranean town.

He found painting soothing to the soul, relaxing to the body, and stimulating to the mind. It allowed the creative side of his nature a free, if temporary, reign; the destructive side had had quite a good run of late. As his mind focused on the scene below, it became a calm sea upon which thoughts and ideas appeared like beautiful ships bent not on war, but voyages of discovery. It was the same with men who fished avidly. It was less about the activity than the state of mind it induced.

The aesthete within regarded the warrior with distaste and suspicion. The warrior regarded the aesthete with a prideful condescension born of professionalism and success. He certainly was a much harder and more morally coarse man than newly commissioned Pennywhistle of 1802 would have ever dreamed possible.

Each painting served as a vivid reminder that he commanded the tiny garrison defending Lissa, the British island toehold on a coast controlled by the French and, south of Corfu, by the Turks. Lissa was a small island of thirty-four square miles, mountainous, rocky, with many vineyards. A typical island of the Dalmation Coast, there was nothing particularly special about it, save it had a good deep-water harbour at Port St. George. The British had established a small dockyard there, and it was the place to which they brought prize ships, preparatory to sending them on to the main British base at Malta. Six prize ships were currently anchored.

He had selected the scene below not just for its beauty, but as part of an orderly and detailed survey of the defensibility of the port. Each building and town feature his brush placed on the artist's board was sorted and examined from multiple mental angles to best determine if, or how, it could be defended. The painting became a visual catalogue of key points of attack and defense. His tutor, Major Justin du Motier, an émigré who had fled *The Terror,* had trained him to draw as an engineer rather than an artist, and French military engineers were reckoned the best in the world. Still, a deep part of him wished his work would be something more than an accounting of details. It was silly and fanciful, but he wanted to be an artist, not a mere technician.

He currently fielded thirty marines. Ten were from *Active* and knew him well. Ten were from *Amphion* and were familiar with him from Groa. Ten were new recruits brought from Malta when *Cerberus* rejoined the squadron and knew him not at all. The lot from *Cerberus* were almost entirely untrained, and two of the men, Soames and Tilson, struck him as hardcore malcontents and skulkers. They would have to be watched.

He had thirty sailors under his command as well, but these were mostly dockworkers and specialists. They would be of marginal value in a pitched battle. The marines would have to do the heavy work.

The squadron itself cruised up and down the coast, snapping up prizes with a pleasing regularity. Lieutenant Spottswood now had command of *Active's* marine contingent; Pennywhistle remembered the pride in the lieutenant's face when he'd told him he was ready for independent command. When prizes appeared in port, Pennywhistle conferred with the prize masters, and in so doing, obtained updated bulletins of the squadron's position and activities.

Hoste gambled that Dubordieu was sufficiently cowed after the night encounter and the destruction of his powder to want to rest, refit, and regroup. Hoste figured that he would have a free and unopposed hand for the next few weeks to bedevil the French by taking prizes—wolves among a fold unprotected by any guard dogs.

He left Pennywhistle in charge on the understanding that, although it was extremely unlikely Lissa would be attacked, Pennywhistle was the man best equipped to secure victory with meagre resources. Pennywhistle suggested to Hoste that the garrison should be increased, but Hoste wanted as many men with the squadron as possible. He accepted Hoste's decision, but it left him uneasy. He felt it depended entirely too much on the French doing exactly what Hoste expected. Nelson had faced an uncertain and vacillating commander, Admiral Villeneuve. Commodore Dubordieu did not fit that bill. It was fanciful to assume such a man would just stand idle, particularly after receiving a bloody nose instead of capturing a frigate. Besides, the Emperor was not a man of compassion when it came to failure.

Meanwhile, he had evolved a routine. Up at dawn, he started the day with two large cups of stout coffee, taken black, and a steaming bowl of thick oatmeal porridge, generously laden with sugar. Two slices of toast followed, smothered in plenty of local strawberry perseveres. Manton procured a steady supply of brown eggs, which Pennywhistle enjoyed fried or gently poached. He accompanied the eggs with either gammon steak from the island's wild hogs or locally caught kippers. He concluded the meal with a whole tomato, properly stewed. He always left breakfast wonderfully fortified for the active day ahead.

He read Guibert's *Essai Generale* with breakfast, seeking insights into his opponent's cast of mind. He then walked briskly in the hills for an hour to clear his head, elevate his pulse, and welcome any inspirations from his subconscious.

After that, he simply followed his agenda. Morning parade and drill with the marines. Inspection of the town and its defenses. Confer with the masters of any new prizes and gently solicit useful information. Meet with any local officials or town mandarins who had concerns. Check stores, then fill out reams of requisitions in triplicate. Review French newspapers for intelligence information. Talk to Baron Rondo, a displaced aristocrat of uncertain national origin and equally uncertain loyalties and discover what local secrets a guinea a week retainer might buy. Squeeze in an hour of cutlass work with Senor Tripolini, a local fencing master. Dine at the local tavern. Speak with Dale about any routine matters of discipline or punishments to be handed down. More drill with the marines in the afternoon, this time with marksmanship training; a prize of a golden guinea awarded to the marine with the best cumulative scores for the week.

In matters military, his quest for perfection took the form of re-examining basic tenets of marine training. He studied the craft of the marine with the same passion for exactitude with which he pursued his other interests. His approach to training was detailed, orderly, and systematic. He treated it as he would any experiment in natural philosophy: read, observe, record, analyze, hypothesize, test, adjust, and test again.

Many officers learned the rudiments of drill, but left the actual training to the sergeants, opining that a king's commission meant they should lead, not teach. The manual of arms listed 45 separate verbal commands and 109 discrete motions to carry them out. The average officer knew only about half of them. It was the philosophy of British gentleman amateurs.

Pennywhistle thought they had it backwards. An officer's first job was to teach, then lead. Heroic leadership was all very fine, but it worked better if one bothered to wring maximum benefits from even the smallest particulars of training.

Lt. Colonel MacKenzie had stressed marksmanship and "the little things" when Pennywhistle went through Shorncliffe. MacKenzie had told his young cousin that he had heard Bonaparte himself once said, "Genius is the infinite capacity for taking infinite pains," and that it was a trenchant observation worth embracing. Pennywhistle knew he was no genius, but considered attention to battlefield minutiae the true hallmark of the professional.

It troubled him that he had seen British army privates not even seat the butt of their weapon hard against their shoulders. That resulted in bruises from the kick and the shot flying heaven knows where. Others held the piece correctly but kept their heads upright, instead of bending necks, shutting the left eye, and sighting the piece. Still others flinched during the split second between ignition of the pan and main charge, causing them to shoot high. Once identified, those behaviours could be corrected. Even marines sometimes evinced these faults, so he extended training to the marines who had never served under him, and reviewed it in detail for those who had. Repetition and review had their merits when it came to drill.

The British military training budget only allowed for thirty-five blank rounds and sixty live ones per man per year; far too few to achieve any degree of live fire skill or marksmanship. It was more practice than Continental armies allowed their soldiers, but it was simply not good enough for him. Frequent, demanding practice was the only way to develop excellence in any endeavour. The best practioners of every art knew that skill atrophied without exercise. Pennywhistle remedied the problem by investing some of his prize money in powder and shot. He found a supplier who could furnish both. It was a considerable expenditure, but he cared little for accumulating money, and greatly about building a superior unit.

He also decided to improve the general fitness of the men, borrowing an idea from Colonel Coote Manningham. When Shornecliffe began, Manningham found himself burdened with a number of portly officers. They were brave and eager, but their poor physical condition was hardly consonant with the idea of light infantry as vigorous, active fellows. Manningham instituted a mandatory half hour run along the beach before breakfast. Initially regarded as peculiar, burdensome, and somehow ungentlemanly, this had occasioned much grumbling; but in the end, it had paid handsome dividends. Pennywhistle would, of course, run with his men.

The new marines from *Cerberus* were skeptical an officer would take a personal interest in their marksmanship, let alone treat them as anything other than anonymous "other ranks." Dale told a surprised private that Pennywhistle not only wanted to know everyone's names, but wanted an exact assessment of their martial skills.

Pennywhistle addressed the men briefly on the first day of training. He did not bellow or thunder, but spoke confidently and plainly in conversational tones. His first statement was the most radical and unexpected of all, and its frankness instantly commanded their attention. He gave the lie to the dread secret.

"Good morning, my lads! My task is to train you to do two things: achieve victory and stay alive. It is not to train you to never feel fear. Fear is meant to keep you alive. I feel it always when bullets fly, and any man who does not is unlikely to survive long." He saw the confusion on their faces; fear was a thing often whispered of privately but *never* spoken of openly, even among rankers. Officers were supposed to have ice water in their veins. Pennywhistle had a reputation as a stout fighter, yet now he preached heresy.

He laughed boldly, which further startled them. "Yes, you all heard me correctly; I will never attempt to beguile you that fear is felt only by cowards. Do not mistake a bold face and a stern posture for the absence of fear. Those few officers who claim fearlessness are either stupid and unbalanced, or bloodthirsty liars whose overweening hunger for martial acclaim causes them to promulgate a dangerous myth. I prefer to deal with reality, since I have a great eagerness to live. Any soldier who lacks that eagerness endangers his mates." He stared slowly and carefully down their ranks and saw both respect and surprise in their eyes. They knew his reputation as an officer who always led from the front, and they hardly expected his ridicule of the *sans peur et sans reproche* ideal.

"I firmly believe that, with training, fear can be made to serve a good end. By removing the cloak of silence, we can rob fear of its power over us and harness its energy for our protection. I would ask you to consider this: do you wish to deny you are afraid, or do you wish channel the energy of that fear to defeat the French?" He paused and let the meaning of his words sink in.

"Fear is normal!" he said, boldly summing up his thoughts in an easily remembered phrase the men would repeat. A giant collective expulsion of air rather than anything articulate greeted his observation. Men nodded, knowing once and for all they were not weak, lily-livered, running dogs for being afraid.

"Are you with me?"

"Aye, aye, sir!" yelled one inspired marine with the fervour of an atheist who had suddenly found God. An instant later another seconded him, and then the assembled voices erupted into an approving chorus. He had them!

Pennywhistle smiled broadly and unabashedly. "People react in battle according to how they are trained. Success in battle is far less about gallantry than it is about training and drill. I intend to make your training as rigorous and realistic as possible. I have invested some of my prize money in a large supply of extra powder and shot, so we will never engage in dry firing or the shooting of blanks. We will fire at targets resembling men, since you are unlikely to be attacked by paper bulleyes."

He pointed to a six-foot tall scarecrow dressed in an old French uniform fifty yards away. "Meet Pierre. You will be getting to know him well in the weeks ahead." The chest was stuffed heavily with straw and gave a good approximation of the dimensions of a man. A bright red circle had been placed over the heart. A nasty, snarling face had been carved into the gourd that acted as the head, and an imposing mustache of soot applied. A battered old shako squatted atop the gourd. The men laughed, for suddenly training sounded like it might be rather fun.

"In the third hour of battle, when your ears scream, your eyes sting, your vision tunnels, your fingers grow clumsy and your mind turns blank, it is the *training* your body will remember," Pennywhistle explained. "You will react on instinct, but it will be trained instinct. Instead of flinching or freezing, you will pour destruction on the French! I would far prefer to fight alongside ten trained professionals than one hundred untrained amateurs." He was pleased to see a general nodding of heads.

Surprise turned to wonder when actual shooting began. A recruit with only a month's service on *Cerberus* fired a shot that went very wide of the target. Pennywhistle calmly and quietly, without a word of reproach, marched over and took his musket. He reloaded it quickly and easily, as if he could have done so in his sleep. He placed it firmly against his shoulder, sighted it almost instantly, fired, and scored a direct hit on the heart. Mercury barked loudly in approval, to the vast amusement of the men.

"That's how it is done, marines," he said. "And with practice, there is no reason you can't all do the same thing."

Dale smiled as he watched astonishment spread like a ripple over their faces, followed by a variety of pleased grins.

After demonstrating marksmanship from the classic standing position, Pennywhistle showed the men how to shoot accurately from a wide variety of stances, from prone, to kneeling, to crouching. He stressed speed in reloading, but said accuracy was important. He told them shortcuts, like omitting ramming, were understandable but very unwise. As fouling accumulated in battle, balls could jam midway down, creating dangerous pressures that might explode the barrel.

He cautioned them against the expedient of holding a ball in their mouth and simply spitting it down the barrel. He said that in the confusing thunder of battle a man who did that was as likely to send the ball down his gullet as the barrel.

He told them to always replace their ramrod in the stock channel and make sure it was accounted for; new recruits sometimes fired them accidentally at the enemy. Others stuck them in the dirt for easy access, then lost them during fast maneuvering.

He patiently explained the idea of a bullet's parabola in simple terms they could understand. Bullets had a tendency to rise in an arc upon leaving the musket, then drop as the distance increased. "Think of a rainbow," he said. Pennywhistle went on to explain that the closer a man came, the more likely aiming at the classic target, the midsection, would send the round high. Aiming at the shoe buckles at very close range was no mere turn of phrase, but very practical advice. Leveling a piece vaguely at the enemy and not factoring in distance, elevation, or terrain meant that, firing uphill or downhill, or on the up-roll or down-roll at sea, many shots simply went wild.

"Bullets don't fly in a straight line? Whoever would have thought it?" whispered a surprised Soames to Tilson. Neither of the grumbling malingerers had ever met an officer willing to take the time to give direct instruction to the men. Pennywhistle's directness riveted the men.

"Aim every shot. Conserve ammunition and be mindful at all times of how many rounds you possess. Never engage in long distance firefights. They are pointless; they decide nothing. Unaimed firing takes hundreds of rounds to hit a soldier beyond a hundred yards, a man's weight in lead to kill one. Reserve your fire until you see the enemy mustaches clearly. One well-aimed volley fired low at close range is worth ten un-aimed ones delivered at distance. Follow that quickly with a loud cheer and a determined bayonet charge, and you will break any enemy!"

Against his will, Tilson left drill that day with Pennywhistle's voice echoing in his head. "Hold fire until thirty yards for best results," rang through Tilson's thoughts and even made an appearance in his dreams. *That is mighty, mighty close range*, he reflected.

"Take your time and get it right," was Pennywhistle's favourite axiom. He repeated it so often that the men could almost say it in their sleep. The marines chuckled about it privately, but they were exceedingly pleased an officer would be so thorough about their training. They knew it increased their chances of survival in real battle considerably.

As the weeks passed, three disparate groups gradually merged into one cohesive corps, and the marines felt part of something elite. Soames, against his will, grew less cynical by the day, and as a joke coined the term "Pennywhistle's Pack." It was eagerly embraced by the unit.

Marine spirits soared further when prize money from recent captures arrived. Pennywhistle knew they would spend freely and enjoy themselves. Most avidly pursued the traditional and time-honoured interests of wine, women, and cards. MacLeod and Chance invested in good watches; portable, showy, practical souvenirs easily resold if ready cash were needed.

Blandon thought he had found true love with Maria, the sturdily attractive but dim daughter of a local wine merchant. His eyes blazed with puppy-dog passion when he asked his officer's permission to marry.

Pennywhistle knew it unwise and impulsive, but avoided a direct no. He told Blandon to ask him again in four weeks to see if their love "endured." Wartime romance was usually fleeting.

He expected the marines to show up ship-shape and Bristol fashion for morning drill and parade and woe betide he who did not; but off duty he was content to let marines be, well, marines. He merely told them to avoid anything destructive to either buildings or the local citizenry. He did not need, want, or expect saints or angels. He saw his marines as good men, and he did not particularly care if they were God-fearing and pious off duty. He had never discovered any special relation between faith and fighting, but had noted some of the best soldiers displayed a distinct lack of religious devotion. He considered "blue light" evangelical notions of tending to the spiritual welfare of the men laughable and offensive. He wanted men who would fight hard, tenaciously, and skillfully. He wanted resourceful men who could use their initiative when all else failed, not whipped, unthinking curs terrified by threats of hellfire or the discipline of the cat. He felt that a combination of sound, realistic training, unremitting but fair discipline, decent food, rewards and distinctions, and free evenings out of sight of their officers' gaze was a highly effective program to achieve success.

He had his own program for the evenings, and her name was Carlotta Ruzzini. She was an anomaly: a fiercely independent tradeswoman in a world dominated by men. She had worked hard to achieve her position, guarded it with spirit, and occasionally defended it with venom. She was Venetian in heritage and had all of the mercantile acumen associated with that ancient republic. She could charm a customer when need be, but oftentimes displayed a prickly demeanor to let people know she was in charge, not just a figurehead. She had mastered the arts of tailoring with ease and skill; yet, because of her appearance, brusque personality, and lack of any visible male in support, she was regarded with uncertainty by the town. They respected her, but they simply had no proper frame of reference for her.

All allowed that she was a beautiful woman, but her height intimidated. She was an even six feet tall, superbly proportioned, with slim legs that went on to the end of time itself. She wore slippers to reduce the number of inches she towered over most men. She walked with brisk efficiency, always a woman with a purpose. She dressed in colourful skirts of calico and white blouses that showcased her spectacular figure, but her commanding, sometimes dismissive manner made most men fearful to do much more than merely look and lust. Her generous bosom and the rhythmic swaying of her wide hips said, "come hither"; her quick, dismissive speech said "go-to-hell." She valued her independence. One marriage had been quite enough for her.

Pennywhistle lost his breath when he thought of her. She was crowned with a beautiful mane of silken hair that was the colour of a fire burning out of control that cascaded with searing, flamboyant triumph to just below her shoulders. Her skin was pure alabaster, tinged with faint pink on the cheeks, with none of the freckles common to redheads. She was exotic, unapproachable, and challenging—a far cry from women he had known in England.

She had an oval, patrician face, high, intelligent forehead, and piercing, cat-like green eyes. She had long lashes, a lovely petite nose, and full crimson lips. Her uncompromising jaw set itself against anyone foolish enough to oppose her will. It was a face that radiated awareness and intelligence. She would have made an excellent model for Phidias's Pallas Athena. It was easy to visualize her as a warrior goddess defending the Acropolis.

Carlotta had inherited the tailor's shop from an older husband who had been as superb a tailor as he was inept as a businessman and lover. When she took over, she proved an excellent and hard-nosed businesswoman, careful about granting credit and energetic in demanding payment. She was frugal in her ways and used the rapidly increasing profits to expand what had been a two-person shop into one now employing four other tailors. She had two children, ten and twelve, who did some of the piecework. She charged reasonable prices, used the best quality wool—mostly British now, thanks to Hoste's squadron—and always delivered on time.

When the British squadron first moved in, officers sought laundresses to do their laundry, then seamstresses to keep their uniforms in repair. Townspeople naturally directed some of the officers to Carlotta. She haughtily informed them she was no seamstress; she was a tailor and a good one. She would brook no condescension. Her beauty might have attracted the initial attention, but it was her skills with cloth, needle, and thread that retained it.

Several officers, dazzled by her beauty, made overtures to her in none too subtle ways. The gallant Lieutenant Boxley, 3rd Lieutenant of *Cerberus,* flattered her with flowery romantic compliments. Dashing Lieutenant Dunn, *Amphion's* Number One, wanted to know if she got lonely of evenings, since her husband had passed. The elegant, sophisticated, and immaculately groomed Lieutenant Moore simply wanted to know if some sort of financial arrangement could be worked out whereby he might acquire a place to call home when the ship was in port. The first received a bored look that said, "How tiresome"; the second a frosty smile and a bitter, "Lonely for the likes of you, young sir? Hardly!" The third received a hard slap across his cheek that stung for the rest of the day.

The rebuff of the three young sparks cemented her reputation. All stayed clear of the woman officers called "the Amazon," but only in a romantic sense. Business boomed. The quality of her work cornered most of the squadron's business.

So, when Pennywhistle received a share of his prize money and looked at the sorry state of his replacement uniform, it was natural to seek the best tailor in the area.

The honey-tongued, voluptuary James Moore recommended Carlotta, partly for good reasons and partly to see if Pennywhistle might succeed where he had failed. He was still puzzled as to why she had not succumbed to his easy-going manners and languidly handsome looks, but he put it down to the peculiarities of foreign women.

There had been an amused conspiracy of officers not to forewarn Pennywhistle about either Carlotta's looks or her temperament.

He walked wearily into her establishment one afternoon, after an especially grueling and unrewarding drill with his marines, as they and he had been off their games. They had been uncharacteristically clumsy, and he had been unwontedly short with them. He regretted this, but decided he would banish the day from memory and start fresh tomorrow. Now he was hot, sweaty, and thoroughly out of sorts. He had meant to attend to the problem of his uniform many times before, but things always seemed to get in the way. He'd decided at the last minute to see to it today; one more onerous task in a day that already seemed burdensome.

Active's sailmaker had done his best fashioning a replacement uniform, but Pennywhistle found it an embarrassment. It did not fit well through the shoulders, the dye was cheap, the fabric thin, and, horror of horrors, the button cuffs on his sleeves were nonfunctional. It looked like what a pimp from a cheap Shoreditch knocking shop would think of as gentleman's attire. It was high time and past time for a proper kit. The men appreciated being commanded by a gentleman of quality whose clothing proclaimed him so. It was about appearance and perception. Good clothing paradoxically got men to pay attention to the man underneath, rather than his attire.

"*Scusi, buon giorno*, Signora Ruzzini, isn't it? My name is Captain Thomas Pennywhistle and I am in sore need of a new uniform. Can you do a marine?" He addressed his words to a red-headed woman sitting in a chair with her back to him. He suppressed his free-floating discontentment and forced his voice to be pleasant, businesslike, and direct. She was probably a fine, decent woman and certainly did not deserve his ire. An instant later, the unintended *double entendre* of his words hit him. He really was tired! "Sorry, ma'am, I meant can you copy a marine officer's uniform? My present one is wholly inadequate to my needs and tastes."

Carlotta had not heard the stranger enter, for her eyes were cast down and her mind and quill pen locked in battle with a long column of figures in her ledger book. It was late in the afternoon and she was attending to her least favourite part of the business. She was as weary as Pennywhistle and just as frustrated with her day. His very soothing baritone voice sliced through her boredom like a refreshing zephyr on a hot day.

She stood up, faced him after his first words, started to summon her best professional smile, and then utterly froze. It was something about the voice, which had a decidedly sensual, seductive edge to it, hypnotic in a friendly, masculine sort of way. It caressed her very soul, causing her fatigue to instantly disappear. It was pleasantly deep, cultured, scholarly, and induced a state of easy, relaxed trust.

"Excuse me, ma'am, are you all right?" She noted that the stranger's face wore an expression of pleasant puzzlement; hers, amazement. The owner of the lovely voice was a handsome man actually taller than she! Her eyes locked with his, her breath caught in her throat, and her voice would not come. Time stopped.

Thirty-Four

It was just sunrise when Pennywhistle awoke.

He had not slept much. He looked at the beautiful red tresses in passionate disarray on the pillow next to him. Carlotta had lovely deep-set green eyes, now closed, and full, sensual lips across which she touched her tongue in languid sleep. When she turned, the valley between her generous breasts deepened and the morning light caught the tuft between her ballerina's legs and made it glow a beautiful orange-red. He wanted to kiss her from head to toe. They had made love three times the previous night. He'd thought he was thoroughly sated, but looking at her, he felt the familiar tingling in the loins.

God, it made no sense! He told himself it was just because he had not been with anyone for some time. A body deprived of such a basic need naturally sought to restore balance when an opportunity presented itself. He had only been seeing her for a week. But damn, he wanted her madly, in defiance of all of the reason he prized so highly. Perhaps he could stay just a bit longer.

No! He had a city to defend, duties to perform, and men awaiting his direction and guidance. He had to set an example. It would not do for him to be seen as less than perfectly zealous in the performance of his command. His loyalty was to Mars, not Venus.

"Discipline, sir, discipline," his conscience lectured. "Duty comes first! Nothing must interfere!" But the captain of his mind was overruled by the colonel of his nether regions. Colonel Sensual demanded he come to attention and brooked no mutiny.

The colonel quietly, gently issued his orders. They had to be obeyed and they were; delightfully so.

He shaved and dressed hurriedly. As he gently lifted the door latch, he heard a sweet, full-throated voice say in heavily accented English, "You will return this evening, *cara mia*, will you not?" It was infused with superb carnality as well as kindly concern.

"As surely as night follows day, I shall return, my dear," Pennywhistle said gallantly, then wondered why he had called her, "my dear." It had come so naturally. Alarming!

"Then, I am content," replied Carlotta, in a voice rippling with the soft vowels of Italianate sensuality. She rolled slowly and languidly onto her side, revealing her six luxuriant feet of perfectly formed nudity. She leaned casually on her elbow, insouciantly brushed back a lock of renegade flame hair, and smiled with lovely mischief. It was all meant to capture Pennywhistle's full attention and it emphatically did. He had trouble tearing himself away. He shut the door slowly and headed down the stairs with great reluctance. He focused his mind on his command, or tried to.

He walked not with his usual brisk, efficient stride but sauntered with an uncharacteristically relaxed, easy gait. Life looked amazingly good this morning and Providence seemed to say, *Why not enjoy it?* He had seen plenty of death, wasn't it time to relish real life? But, unbidden, a frightening question battered his serenity. *Are you falling for her?* The questioning voice was insistent, but he was loath to answer.

Carlotta had done a magnificent job on his uniform and it put a confident bounce into his step. The white silk shirt underneath the coat felt light and comfortable, and the black silk stock around his neck fit fashionably close, yet was soft and un-constricting. The double-breasted, scarlet tailcoat, cinched tightly at the waist and fitted closely to his athletic physique, was of the finest Cotswold wool and made his shoulders look broad and his waist small. He wore the upper buttons unfastened to reveal the coat's splendid navy blue facings. There were ten gold buttons in pairs on each lapel, one at each side of the starched, blue collar, and four on each blue cuff and pocket flap. Each button bore raised anchors framed with laurel branches, with ROYAL MARINES emblazoned above. All of the buttonholes were functional and there was gold bullion, not mere gilt, in the fringed epaulettes.

Marine captains wore two epaulettes rather than the one that regular army captains sported. The general design of their jackets had been revised in 1802, when they had been designated "Royal." The new coats had been copied from the 1st Foot Guard's uniforms, and officers of that elite regiment always merited a pair since they guarded the sovereign.

The coat's vestigial swallow tails were hooked back to reveal white linings and two embroidered hearts. The hearts were traditional military symbols, but they caused him to smile at the double meaning. His luxuriant sash was of the finest, thickest crimson silk. Cherry red braces supported the slate grey, high-waist trousers; grey had recently become fashionable among marine officers rather than the traditional white. The trousers were uncommonly comfortable, yet fashionably tight, fitting him like a second skin. His tasseled, well-blacked Hessian boots and exquisitely polished gold gorget complimented the clothing perfectly. He felt a military version of a Mayfair dandy. He thought the uniform every bit as good as whatever Gieves had ever done for him or his father. Passion could inspire amazing efforts!

Carlotta wanted "her man" to look perfect; she already thought of him as hers. She pronounced him a splendid specimen of manhood, although it sounded like "a sploondeed spacey man of mun'odd" when she said it.

Her uncertain forays into English both amused and enchanted him. She spoke serviceable English, but her French was much better and they mostly conversed in that tongue. He admitted that while English might be more efficient, French was better suited for love.

Neither of them had meant for this to happen. The attraction each felt was warm and immediate, but they were both reserved, disciplined people who prepared, planned, and carried out their lives with intelligence and foresight. Each had a public persona that was a winning mix of forthrightness and reserve, directness and charm. In navy parlance, they both kept an even keel. They each had to manage men, and masks were a necessary concomitant of that. It was as if they both kept some ineffable, unspeakable creature of wild debauch locked in a dungeon deep in their soul. Both feared the release of the creature—unbridled, monstrously powerful, careening lust. Its essence was spontaneous, mad passion that was the enemy of all that was ordered in their lives, all that was reasonable. They feared being vulnerable, discredited, losing command of their destinies.

It had started simply enough. She asked him to stand still while she walked around him several times, assessing his outfit. Her expression was neutral but her eyes were deadly serious and her concentration deep. When she finished she said simply, "Yes, sir, we can do better!" Then a joyful smile broke out that transformed her and lit up the room. "Oh yes! Much, much better!"

They spoke to each other with the exaggerated courtesy of two people trying to pretend a business transaction was just that, a business transaction, studiously ignoring the undertones of mutual attraction. She showed him various grades and weights of wool appropriate for uniforms. With her advice and counsel, he made his selection. As they examined the bolts of fabric, each stole delighted little glances that each hoped went unnoticed. On a conscious level, they went unacknowledged, but on the subconscious level, they registered. Two conversations proceeded simultaneously. One was of the voice, crisp and efficient, all business. The other of the body, passionate, slow, and sensual.

Pennywhistle agreed to come back the next afternoon to have the proper measurements taken. When he left the shop, his evil mood was gone and he felt better than he had for a long time. He very much looked forward to the next afternoon.

For her part, Carlotta thought the next twenty-four hours could not pass swiftly enough. She could not ignore the delightful quivering she felt whenever she pictured his face, which was often.

Their conscious minds would admit nothing but, deep down, both knew exactly what was happening. Their unspeakable creatures had wrecked the locks on their cages and were about to come forth in full cry. Yet on the surface everything appeared serene and civilized.

Pennywhistle returned the next day. They had a leisurely, eminently civilized tea and chatted pleasantly about trifles. She then began the labourious process of the first measurements. Ordinarily, two male apprentices always performed the actual measuring under her guidance, lest male customers become uneasy, but she told them to take the day off.

It surprised him that she was going to do the actual measurements herself, but he put it down to her independent cast of mind. He could muster no objections to being touched by a beautiful woman. He stood still, as she requested, but he found it difficult to remain so when she moved close. He inhaled a delightful lavender scent that he could not recall smelling yesterday, but then they had not been separated by scant inches. Today's dress revealed rather more of her ample bosom than the sedate frock she had worn the day before.

She moved with experienced efficiency, measuring tape and notebook in hand, taking the requisite measurements, but as she touched him, she found it increasingly difficult to concentrate. She tried to think as a tailor, but his muscles felt hard and firm. It was a mistake not to have had her male assistants do this, but a deep part of her subconscious was glad she had dismissed them. This was a client, she told herself, no different from any other. Your job, her conscience lectured firmly, is to make him look good and have him leave with a uniform of which he can be proud. No more, no less.

Pennywhistle reminded himself this was business, no more, no less. The woman was a perfectionist; that was all. She refused to trust even a small detail to an underling, the mark of the true artist in any profession. He appreciated the attention to minutiae; it was just what he did with his battle preparations. It was ridiculous to read anything else into her attentions. He was getting good value for his money and that was it. He tried to push other thoughts away. She was so close he noticed beads of sweat on her brow. What was that, concentration? Then he noticed he was sweating too.

When she was measuring his waist, nature finally won its contest with reason. Pennywhistle lost his valiant battle to control his manhood. It asserted itself fully and dramatically.She had been looking down at his waist, measuring tape in hand, and noticed it immediately. It startled her but some part of her knew she had wished for it all along. She looked up into his eyes.

In that second, a cavalcade of emotions flashed through their eyes: shock, desire, and finally, pure blind lust. It was as if Eros had fired a starter's pistol. Every bond of traditional morality vanished in an unexamined instant. Pennywhistle locked his arms round her waist as she reached up and savagely kissed his lips; long, slow, exquisite. He returned her kiss with the abandon of a man who had been at sea for months. He felt himself drowning in her splendour.

She savoured his lips with the unabashed delight of child unexpectedly being given a sweet. She could barely breathe.

They literally tore the clothes from each other's bodies and made love on the floor of the shop. It was fierce, yet somehow powerfully *right*, the action of two souls who wanted each other and demanded to be listened to. It was molten passion beyond the heat of any Vesuvius, and it utterly consumed them. They each seemed to instinctively know how to pleasure each other. Like most fires, it burned quickly, and was over in minutes. It left them breathless, exhausted, soaked in sweat, but very, very satisfied. They lay naked, stared up at the ceiling, then looked at each other and laughed in sheer joy and shared merriment.

Pennywhistle had certainly known his share of women, but his encounters had generally been carefully and discreetly planned. While satisfying, he had never utterly lost his reason as he had just now. He felt completely an animal, thinking not of duty, career, or honour, but only of having his way with this magnificent woman.

Carlotta, for her part, had been in an arranged marriage with a kind, older man, who, while sincere, had never satisfied her. Sex had been a wifely duty she had borne with grace, but what had happened just now was pleasure beyond imagining.

They gazed at each other and touched gently. Pennywhistle's other brain seized control and his body presented a bold salute. Carlotta smiled in pleasure, sinuously moved on top and gently eased him inside of herself. She proceeded to ride with the passion of a skilled horsewoman. It seemed impossible, but the second explosion was even more powerful than the first.

They talked for hours after, but he had duties to attend to and finally had to bid her *au revoir*. He promised to return tomorrow for the first fitting, and Carlotta said she would work all night to translate the measurements into the initial shell of a coat. He knew she would be as good as her word.

"But Carlotta, this will actually be the second fitting. I have just had the first one, and I must say, you are a splendid fit!" He smiled broadly.

Carlotta smiled back, but then turned serious. "Truly that was something grand, Thomas, if I may call you that. I must see you again. I have had all of these silly little roosters strutting to get my attention, and in walks a man who wants nothing but a new uniform. He is calm, courteous; a thorough-going English gentleman. He listens closely to everything I say, treats me like a duchess, then shows me, how is it you English say, 'still waters run deep.' There is much more to you than meets the eye. You do not try at all; perhaps that is your secret. Act charming and let the ladies seduce you."

Pennywhistle smiled. "I assure you, I came to the shop merely because of recommendations, and I was much impressed by the quality of work you had done for others. I confess I immediately thought that I had never met a tailor so lovely! But it was your voice, your grace, your ladylike deportment that compelled my attention. And when I returned today, I sensed a passion that had long gone unrequited and yearned to breathe freely. I think you sensed the same in me. I would say we each liberated the other because we are of a breed. I think we gave fully to each other, and that is not something either of us does easily.

"I know little about you, nor you much about me, but I believe our souls took a peek at each other and liked what they saw. I believe that is what spurred our bodies to become so well and happily acquainted. I cannot say how long I will be here; the life of a marine can be unpredictable as well as short, but I should be very, very sad if I did not see you again. To not touch you again would bring the greatest pain imaginable!" It surprised him that he had real emotion in his voice. Most of the women he had been with had been amusing, some even rollicking good fun; but, in general, it had not bothered him much when the ship sailed and he left them behind. This woman had a mixture of lust, heart, and stately presence that he found endearing and compelling.

He pushed his very pleasant reminiscences away when he reached the parade ground. He put on his mask of command. He was no longer a lover. He was back to being a bringer of death and a destroyer of worlds who would train others to do the same.

Thirty-Five

Pennywhistle was well satisfied with the morning drill. The men were more proficient each passing day. Marksmanship had improved greatly, morale had surged, and the unit could now operate as a platoon, in small clusters, or as individuals. The men had come to know they could utterly depend on each other and their officer. They knew that when others ran, they would stand fast.

The ten new recruits from *Cerberus* lost most of their awkwardness and executed drills with a fair degree of quality. Even the two malcontents, Soames and Tilson, grumbled less and less each day. Soames actually smiled when Pennywhistle said his drill was "smartly done."

Tilson was old by marine standards and set in his ways. He had served twenty years in the army and had found civilian life much harder than he expected. He had impulsively succumbed to the strong drink and large enlistment bounty offered by a passing marine recruiting party.

He had a back full of scars from the cat and had never been in a military unit where men were not flogged regularly for the smallest infraction. It puzzled him that this Pennywhistle fellow did not train men like spaniels—by the stick—and had forbidden the use of the cat-o-nine tails. Punishment in his new unit took the form of extra drill or running exercises with small weights fastened to the legs. It finally penetrated Tilson's none-too-agile brain that his officer was interested in physically toughening and training men, not breaking them and wrecking their spirits.

Pennywhistle's men were ready, but the central problem remained the same; he simply had too few marines to defend the island if it were attacked. He painted the harbour each afternoon following dinner, each day from a different angle; and while the quality of the pictures improved, the situation they depicted did not. Each time he painted, he thought of the problem and possible outcomes. No matter how clever the expedients he devised, the marines always ended up on the losing side.

He finally settled on a Fabian defense. Late each night, he reviewed Vauban's ideas on fortification and tried to remember everything du Motier had taught him about military engineering. He could not increase the number of men, but he could increase their effectiveness by putting them behind earthworks. He drew his ideas on artist's board and decided to show the five best sketches to the men so that they might better understand what they were building.

The marines were skeptical at first. The extensive manual labour in his scheme sounded like something fit only for the riff-raff sent to Botany Bay. But after Pennywhistle showed them his drawings and patiently explained his plans in detail, they nodded their heads and murmured approval. Their officer was clearly of a mind to preserve them, not hazard their lives recklessly. By the end of the first day, the marines were very much into the spirit of the enterprise.

To say it was exhausting work was to grossly understate the case, but Pennywhistle enjoined repeatedly, "An ounce of prevention is worth a pound of blood." The marines liked that, and whenever a ranker became dispirited, his mate would repeat that phrase with a knowing smile. If a marine bungled something, the rest of the men would intone, in a faux-derisive chorus, Pennywhistle's other favoured aphorism: "Take your time and get it right."

When Soames grumbled, saying, "Why, we are no better than Jamaican field hands on a sugar plantation," Blandon spoke for the rest of the marines. "Shut up, you lazy bugger, and put your back into it. What we are doing, you fool, will double our chances of coming out alive from the next scrape."

His marines dug trenches, assembled great piles of dirt, and wove large wicker baskets called gabions. They filled the gabions with dirt to make the skeletons for earthen forts. They covered the baskets with thick walls of earth, hewed pointed wooden spikes, and rolled barrels of gunpowder up steep inclines. Yet they still managed to sandwich in a bit of drill promptly at two each afternoon. They worked sunup until sundown for three weeks; on the last day, they worked into the night, continuing by the light of torches soaked in pitch.

Pennywhistle knew the inexperienced French would have to land their boats on the one large beach west of town. It was a mile long; there were no odd currents, shoals, or rip tides to its front. The obvious targets were the prize ships, the dockyard, the powder reserves, and the town beyond. The town itself was small, much tinier than Groa. His marines constructed three small earthen s at blocking points on the only road from the dockyard. The walls were six feet high, three feet thick, and embedded with a line of *fraises* halfway up: sharpened wooden stakes meant to impale anyone climbing quickly.

The walls of the square-shaped fortifications zigzagged every yard for enfilade fire. A long fire step on the inside of each wall allowed marines to step down to reload and step up to fire. Five-foot tall *chevaux de frise* positioned two feet in front of each wall provided obstacles to any approach. Each *chevaux* was a series of sharp wooden pikes in the shape of x's radiating from a central core of stout pine, free standing filters to any attack, designed to break the integrity of an approaching line of battle. They had to either be hacked apart or climbed over slowly. His idea was not to man all of the redoubts simultaneously, that would have been impossible with his small numbers, but to man them in succession, retreating as each one became untenable. It was a classic Fabian strategy: delay and wear down, and it would be a running battle, not a static one. The French would rely on force and surprise, the British on preparedness and guile.

He wished he could have armed the redoubts with cannon, but he could only muster one operable twelve-pounder. There were other cannons around the harbour, but they were hopelessly rusted pieces from the early seventeenth century. He would probably only get two rounds out of the twelve-pounder before they would be forced to retreat, and it would have to be abandoned. He'd had a local blacksmith fashion a steel spike that could be driven through the venthole to disable the piece. The French would not turn it against his men.

There was one thing the British had in abundance, which the French were surely short of after his own recent activities: gunpowder. A large cave among the vineyards in the hills, which had been the site of ancient worship, its interior covered with strange petro-glyphs, stood empty. He saw to it that all of the powder was moved there. It was hard work, rolling barrel after barrel uphill, but it would be equally hard for the French to find them. He was uncertain of his ability to safeguard the ships, but quite confident he could protect the squadron's powder reserves.

As the barrels were being rolled uphill, it occurred to him how much easier it would be to send them careening downhill. If he fitted a few with fuses they could be turned into giant hand grenades. It would be a game of bowls, and Frenchman would be the pins. With that in mind, Pennywhistle ordered his men to dig two lines of trenches, one midway up the hill behind the town, another at the crest. They would hold the lower trenches as long as possible then retire to the summit. Each trench line had fifteen barrels of powder with fuses.

Tuesday afternoon found him above the town in his usual perch, easel and watercolours deployed. But this time he was not alone. Carlotta was dressed in a charcoal-coloured taffeta skirt and a shamrock green silk blouse that matched her eyes and set off her flame-red hair nicely. A bone-white shawl of delicate French lace encircled her shoulders, and a small gold locket adorned her neck. She tried to appear casual, but the look was actually studied and had taken long to prepare. She wanted to please Pennywhistle. From the way he looked at her, she knew she had succeeded.

"You see? It does not hurt to smile! You should do it more often, Thomas; it becomes you." She pronounced his name "Toe mahs."

From anyone else it would have sounded silly, but from her it was charm personified.

"You smile much in the bedroom, Thomas, but seldom when you are among people. I wonder if you believe it a crime against nature to smile or laugh. Perhaps you worry that if you are something less than completely stern and purposeful that your men will not take you seriously. I know your men worship you, but I heard Private Tilson refer to you as 'old sobersides.' I think it is wonderful to embrace the joy of life and revel in its surprises." She laughed merrily.

Pennywhistle frowned slightly, not realizing his expression confirmed her point. "That's not true, Carlotta. I do smile and laugh. I value a good joke and a droll story as much as the next man."

"Oh?" She said with an expression of friendly mockery. "Prove it to me! Tell me a joke or a funny story. Make me laugh."

Pennywhistle's brow furrowed. His expression of fierce concentration seemed completely at odds with a man trying to devise something humorous.

A minute later he smiled. "I remembered two jokes that made me laugh. What animal goes bow wow and makes tic tock noises?"

Carlotta shrugged. "I do not know."

"A watchdog." Pennywhistle chuckled, but Carlotta merely looked puzzled.

Pennywhistle rallied. "All right then, here is a better one. Why do lions have a hard time apologizing?"

Carlotta sighed, anticipating this joke would be a dud as well. "I did not know lions spoke, but tell me."

"Because they are full of pride." This time Pennywhistle burst forth with a loud laugh. He cut the laugh short when he saw Carlotta was not laughing.

"I do not understand at all, Thomas. Where is the humour? Is it something special understood only by people from your country?"

"It's a pun, my dear. A band of lions is known as a pride." He looked slightly crestfallen. "Perhaps both jokes lose something when they are rendered in French." He rubbed his chin several times and looked skyward, as if a deity might convey humorous inspiration.

"All right, I do have two shipboard stories I find funny. Both involve a Parrot named Bob."

"A parrot?" said Carlotta with hope. "I have never seen one, but I have heard they are very amusing."

"My first captain was a fine man and a good officer, but he had something of a stuttering problem. On a cruise to the Caribbean he acquired a beautiful red and green parrot he named Bob. He taught the bird to talk and was very proud of it, but unfortunately he passed on his stutter. He would have Bob perform after dinner and all of the ship's officers had a very hard time suppressing their laughter. The bird's usual opening line was, "Polly wanna cra...cra.. crak... biscuit."

Carlotta laughed unreservedly. "That must have been hilarious."

Pennywhistle continued with a smile. "What the bird did really well was imitate the sounds of the boatswain's whistle. On a ship, many commands are given with it. One day a very old admiral afflicted with the gout was being heaved up to the entry port in a bosun's chair. That's a contraption used to bring persons aboard, landlubbers mostly, and ladies of course, who cannot climb the steep entry port steps. The men were heaving mightily on ropes and the chair was almost up to the entry port when Bob trilled the command for 'release.' The sailors were used to following orders and simply let go of the rope. The chair and the admiral both plunged into the sea. The Captain had a hard time explaining that one to the Admiral."

Carlotta laughed loudly. "That is funny. There is hope for you, Thomas! Why not try unbending a bit and telling stories like that more often. We Venetians have always believed a hero with a sense of humour is better than a hero without one."

She walked over to his watercolour of the town and examined it approvingly. "Your work is very good, Thomas. I think you have hidden talents that can bring joy to people. Someday you should hold an exhibition, like those artists in London. Who is that one you like so well? J. M.W...?"

"Turner," said Pennywhistle, now grinning broadly. Carlotta was right. He did not laugh enough, and sharing laughter with her brought a simple joy that all of his responsibilities had caused him to forget. She had also given him a peace and contentment that he had never really known. He enjoyed talking with her about subjects both trivial and profound, but he was equally happy to walk silently with her, just holding her hand. During such quiet moments their souls conversed with delight. A feeling grew that his soul had been searching for just such a woman all of his life, even though it had declined to inform his conscious mind.

She had once accused him of being a compulsive over-planner, a good thing for a soldier but not in a lover. She'd said he should be more spontaneous. Now he felt like a teenager experiencing first love and decided to grant her wish.

He took her in his arms, began humming a tune, and they started to dance. He led her in a dance of sheer exuberant joy. She looked puzzled at first; he realized she had never seen the dance they were doing, but she followed his guidance easily and her expression soon changed to one of great delight. He held her close and they whirled, twirled, and glided. They looked into each other's eyes and each saw laughter there. The dance lasted only five minutes, but it was five minutes of soaring, unbridled, perfectly silly pleasure. They were smiling broadly when it ended.

"What was that, Thomas?" Carlotta demanded breathlessly. "It was marvelous, but very different from a minuet or reel."

"It's called a waltz, my dear. It's a very new and somewhat scandalous dance from Austria. Some older folk have complained it is but lovemaking set to music. I saw it done in London, liked it, and took the trouble to learn it. I may not tell jokes skillfully, but I fancy I dance reasonably well. Dancing and drawing have always been part of an officer's education. I practice a great deal with the blade, and it seems to me that dancing is very similar to movements learned during fencing. I love to dance and think a world without dance would be a world not worth living in."

"You are full of surprises, Thomas." Carlotta walked back over to the watercolour on the easel and examined it closely. "*Che bello!* A warrior who can paint well and dance too! *Che meraviglia!*"

"Thank you, my dear. I am just an amateur dabbler in art, but I flatter myself I continue to improve. I paint what I see. I hope that, as I continue, my vision will come less from my eyes and more from my soul. That is how the great artists see. I tell myself it is like the manual of arms. The more you perform it, the better you get. So I come here daily and perform drill with a brush instead of a gun." He looked deep into Carlotta's eyes. She had the most bewitching feline eyes he had ever seen. He was having trouble concentrating.

"I think you worry too much, Thomas. I know that after I fall asleep in your arms, you slip away and study into the long reaches of the night. I have seen your books all about the art of fortification. Last night, I tiptoed downstairs and saw you reading intently. I thought to kiss you back to bed, but I realized you would fret more the next day if you did not continue to study, so I left you alone. I think you are doing everything you can to keep your men and this town safe. I know you come here to think and meditate as much as to paint, because you need respite from responsibility. Something violent and terrible may be on the horizon, but it is not yet here. I understand your duty, but please grant me a little time to love you."

She smiled gently with a brilliance that eclipsed a thousand suns, but Pennywhistle caught the hint of sadness in the smile. Whatever they had, whatever was developing, had a limited life expectancy. The war was an ever present spectre. He could be killed; even if he were not, the squadron would eventually depart. He could not prolong their time together, but he could try his best to live fully in the moment. She was right, he had done his duty.

It was the first time she had used the word *love*, he realized. He knew she meant much more than the physical act. The physical attraction was strong, but it was only an aspect of the deeply emotional natures they both seldom indulged. He told himself to be sensible, that perhaps all he had was an acute, delayed case of puppy love. He was no better than a love-drunk swain in a bad novel. But the lecture of his head failed to make any inroads on his heart. He was well and truly smitten.

"If for no other reason than it pleases you, I will accept your words as truth. But I confess, your beauty distracts me from my watercolour. The landscape below cannot match the landscape of your hair, you eyes, your smile, and the loveliness of your form. So, I will bow to necessity. Let me paint you just as you are. Permit me to apprehend this moment in time. Whatever happens, I want to be able to look at you in the painting and remember the day I painted it and all the glorious feelings of the day. Perhaps you will be the muse that inspires a mediocre artist to surpass himself." Pennywhistle took down the artist's board he had been working on and replaced it with a blank. He pivoted the easel so its back faced Carlotta.

"That would be wonderful, Thomas, I should like that very much. How do you wish me to sit, or would you rather have me stand? What of my hair? Perhaps I should wear it up for a portrait. Perhaps—"

His laugh cut off her chatter. "Trust me. You are beautiful as you are. Any pose will be wonderful, but the relaxed one you are in at present will serve very well."

He painted in silent focus for the next hour. He captured her beauty, but he liked to think he captured some of the tempestuous passion and generous soul which informed her personality. When he finished, he knew he had passed a milestone. He was no longer a mere illustrator—he was an artist.

She gazed with awe at the finished work. "But you have made me look beautiful, Thomas. I am not nearly so lovely as the woman in the painting. I think your heart got in the way of your sight. But thank you, this is wonderful. No one ever wanted a painting of me before."

He smiled. "You have it wrong. Whatever my best efforts, the woman in the painting is inferior to the real article. But I am pleased you like it." He thought for a moment; he could not express his thoughts in the casual French in which they conversed.

He switched to English, which alerted Carlotta he was about to say something personal. "You make me feel like the best artist in the world; someone who has risen far above the modest talents with which he has been gifted by nature. You make me feel the same way, as a man."

290

Carlotta smiled slowly and licked her lips. "But you are an accomplished artist of another kind already; it has been my pleasure to observe your technique. You have finished one work of passion. Perhaps it is time to begin another."

Pennywhistle smiled back, moved slowly toward her, helped her up, and drew her to him. The sun was setting as they kissed. They caressed and lost track of time, saying nothing but feeling everything. The hours passed with an easy grace and beauty. Long after midnight, they made slow, dreamy love in the open under the Milky Way.

Thirty-Six

Pennywhistle left Carlotta sleeping peacefully in his bed in the hunting lodge. The twin bouts of lovemaking had been quite spectacular, but he awoke at dawn feeling troubled and expectant. A sense of foreboding flooded his being and grew in strength and insistence. He recognized it as battlefield intuition: a mixture of reason, experience, and sensibility that conspired together for the express purpose of keeping him alive. Whatever he called it, whatever it was, it had served him infallibly in the past.

He dressed and breakfasted quickly. The presentiment of danger would not leave him. He spoke to his servant, Manton.

"Manton, I leave Carlotta in your charge. Let her sleep, and when she wakes tell her I said it was imperative that she fetch her children here. I fear danger is imminent. She will trust my instincts. Go with her, and once everyone is here, let no one leave under any circumstance. This place is the safest in town. Is that clear?" Worried and impatient, he spoke more forcefully than was his wont.

His servant blanched; this was not like his master at all. But then, who would not want to protect such a beautiful and gracious lady? "Of course, sir. You may trust me. I will not let her out of my sight. But I do wish I could be alongside you if something happens. I want to fight and I want to win glory!" Manton spoke with the eagerness of extreme youth, of one who had never heard the whine of bullets, tasted the bitter grit of gunpowder, choked on stinking thunderheads of battle smoke or the rising stench of blood and loosened bowels, or listened to the heart-rending cries of men dying obscene deaths. He had spent the sea battle with *Favourite* deep in the hanging magazine, making cartridges.

Pennywhistle wondered if he had ever been that young and that naive. "I commend your zeal, Manton, but you would serve me best by remaining here. It will quiet my mind greatly to know Carlotta is safe. Battle is about winning; some parts are less glorious than others, but those supporting parts are *indispensible* to victory," he emphasized. "You have a part to play today that you may think lacks importance, but I tell you it is most important. I charge you upon your very life to do your utmost to protect my lady. I repose complete confidence in you. I trust I am not mistaken?"

The boy brightened. "Oh no, sir. Not at all. She will be safe with me!"

Pennywhistle smiled. Manton was a month shy of seventeen, but for a moment he seemed mature beyond his years. He had given this young man responsibility, and he had accepted it. The boy was an orphan from the London slums, but he had great eagerness and bore watching. Pennywhistle knew worthiness when he saw it.

*****

The fortifications were as complete as he could make them. Today, the marines would exercise and drill. He would make today's sessions shorter and easier than usual. He wanted to maintain their fighting trim but he did not want them worn out for the battle he felt sure lay ahead. He visited the innermost recesses of memory and asked himself if there was anything he had forgotten. He did not think so.

Just a quarter before noon, the harbour lookouts descried the Crapauds. Pennywhistle tensely watched the stately entrance of the French into the bay of Port St. George an hour later. While he observed, he made sure rations were distributed. Not just ordinary rations, but rations with plenty of extra meat from five pigs he had purchased the week before. He had ordered them slaughtered and dressed that morning when he'd had his first presentiment that a battle lay ahead. He wanted his men well fed. Battle was exhausting work and burned energy like no other activity.

He walked unobtrusively among the marines and quietly spoke words of confident encouragement, mostly about trusting their training. He saw the determined looks on their faces and knew they were as prepared as any troops could ever be. It was a pity there were so few of them.

"I'm ready, sir," said MacLeod confidently. "We will give the frogs a thrashing they won't soon forget."

"We will show them, sir!" declared Corporal Chance. "We will make them howl so loud Boney will hear them in Paris!"

The four French frigates placed themselves parallel to the beach at half a mile's distance. Their seamanship was coarse and rudimentary, but functional. Pennywhistle's gravest concern was that, once they landed, the French would prove to be the seasoned troops who had conquered so much of Europe for their Emperor. If this were the case, his Royal Marines had their work cut out for them, and this could be the day that saw them all die.

The ships opened a thunderous bombardment on the beach, aimed at the phantom soldiers that might be there; Pennywhistle felt it was intended more for the encouragement of their own forces. The sound and fury of a sustained naval bombardment was a mightily impressive thing. Troops might well think nothing could stand before such a heavy fusillade; but the truth was, the denizens mainly frightened were the local sand crabs, who earnestly sought their holes.

Pennywhistle's troops assembled behind the stone parapets of the small three-gun harbour battery. The crescent shaped demi lune had been built three centuries earlier but its limestone walls gave protection nearly as good as that of the three earthen redoubts. Two of the guns were corroded almost beyond recognition, but the one 12-pounder stood primed and ready. The marines enjoyed the sound and light show. It amused them that the flashes and thunder caused them no harm whatsoever.

Blandon and Addison laughed openly at the French wasting ammunition, something Mr. Pennywhistle had cautioned them to never do. The bombardment lasted for the better part of an hour.

Pennywhistle offered no direct resistance on the beach. He had no blank check on lives; the loss of even one marine was significant. He would keep them down and out of sight until the last possible moment. He also wanted to assess the strength and skill of the French landing force. The French never wanted for bravery, but they had sometimes suffered from a want of training as newer soldiers replaced the veterans of the European campaigns. He wondered if he faced anything like marines, or merely sea-going soldiers of little experience. He would wait and observe.

LeMere's troops had been well trained to fight on shipboard, but no one had taught them the basics of disembarking into smaller boats or landing. When numbers of inexperienced men descend small rope ladders down a frigate's steep tumblehome into wildly bobbing boats, it is a sure bet there will be confusion and a great deal of disruption. Men in too much of a hurry, perhaps inspired too much by LeMere's oratory, stepped on heads, hands, and feet, missed toe holds, and occasionally fell into the sea, amidst shouts, curses, and sometimes laughter.

One chubby corporal slipped on the last rung and grabbed for anything. He succeeded in grasping the hand of a thin private behind him, pulling him into the sea as well. They had to be fished out with long boathooks. Sodden and chagrined, they rejoined their comrades, the cartridges in their boxes rendered useless by seawater.

Pennywhistle watched the spectacle through his glass and permitted himself a smile that relieved his earlier anxiety. Their behaviour was amateurish and unskilled. It took the men a solid hour to gain the boats. British marines would have done it in a fraction of the time, and in disciplined silence. Corporal Chance, promoted for his exploit at Groa, remarked with astonishment, "That's the best they can do?"

The men in the boats rowed steadily toward the shore. At least their rowing looked rhythmic and orderly. Most of the soldiers were seated, but a few stalwarts stood with muskets advanced. One boat, far in the lead and going much too fast, slammed into the beach, knocking several soldiers off their feet and into the surf.

Pennywhistle had made a rough estimate of the troops during their embarkation. Half a battalion at least. Bad news, but no real surprise. He had expected to be outnumbered. He waited to see how they disembarked and formed up. Would it be haphazard or orderly? That would tell him a great deal about their discipline, and something about how they would fight. He wondered who was in command.

The remaining boats beached more cautiously. What Pennywhistle took to be skirmishers cautiously advanced in a widening arc from the beach, expecting resistance but finding none. Several boldly advanced in front of the rest, obviously scouts. Soldiers splashed clumsily ashore. Officers shouted commands, drums pounded, and bugles blared. The men formed up in a disciplined, orderly column; the fastest way to move troops. Clearly, these people had been training.

His question about who was in charge was answered when a command was shouted and the column came to attention, in perfect unison. The front, back, and sides of the column were razor straight lines. There was no hesitation, no shuffling, and no confusion. A tall man with the bearskin shako and splendid mustache of the Imperial Guard stepped forward. He was out of earshot, but appeared to be giving some kind of speech to the troops. Whatever he was saying appeared to have an electrifying effect on the soldiers. They stood more erect and puffed out their chests. At certain points, when the Guardsman paused, the men responded with loud and hearty cheering. It all seemed very theatrical, as if the Guardsman were a director and the soldiers his players in some battlefield drama. Pennywhistle had never had much truck with battlefield oratory, but the Guardsman obviously belonged to the flamboyant school of inspirational leadership.

Pennywhistle looked closely at the tall officer with the solitary gold earring. Was this the man Spottswood had described to him, the one who had tried to kill him at Groa? If so, he was a resourceful and brave antagonist, but what of it? Pennywhistle steeled his resolve. He had beaten this man once; he could and would do so again. Nevertheless, a careful part of his mind warned him that the Guardsman would make few mistakes and would be quick to take advantage of any he or his men made.

He thought of Carlotta momentarily. It surprised him how much he worried for her safety. But, he could not permit himself the luxury of personal concerns at this moment. Manton would take care of her. He could best defend her by making sure the French never came anywhere near. He wondered for a moment about the name of the officer he opposed, then dismissed the question as irrelevant. He fought the man's experience and ability; the name hardly mattered. "A rose by any other name..." No, a thorn by any other name drew just as much blood.

*****

LeMere finished his address to the troops. They had encountered no opposition, which was so unexpected, so unusual, he wondered at first if the island had been abandoned by the British. They generally liked to dispute things at the earliest opportunity. But no, that could not be the case. He could see the masts of the prize ships soaring above the dockyard in the distance. He had decided on the landward approach because there was no point to seizing the dockyard before any supporting troops were first neutralized. Then he wondered who was in command. Could it be the man he had almost killed at Groa, the one with the odd name that recalled a child's toy? He had been crafty, that one, and determined: a warrior in the ancient sense of the word. This departure from the obvious seemed... characteristic.

LeMere's mission was simple. Brush aside any opposition and secure the prize ships for prize crews that Dubordieu would send later, and cause as much damage to the dockyard as possible, paying special attention to the destruction of British powder reserves. Hurt the British as badly as possible, deprive them of their much anticipated prize money, withdraw in an orderly fashion to the boats, and sail away with a triumph to report to the Emperor, long before Hoste knew what had happened. A noble endeavor, and all that stood between him and achieving it was a man named Pennywhistle. It had to be him. The British would only select their best for such an important post. Good! A Guardsman deserved a worthy antagonist.

The first scouts he had sent out returned. They reported that the British were indeed out there, several hundred yards ahead, in uncertain numbers, posted behind an ancient fortification with several pieces of heavy ordinance. LeMere would have to drive them. He welcomed the challenge. Their numbers could not be large if they had failed to prevent his landing.

It was time to begin. He ordered a change in the column to present a one hundred and twenty foot front. The French did it seamlessly. He deployed a thin line of skirmishers to the front and sides of the column. Amidst bugles and flapping banners, the column began to move. Officers on all sides of the column, led by two newly minted lieutenants, shouted words of encouragement.

The men began chants of "Death to the English!" A few shouted the exceedingly vulgar *"Nique ta mere!"* in the direction of the British. Miscellaneous bellows, yells, and yips of defiance resounded from the column.

Private Des Barres, an eighteen-year-old from Tours, felt pleased that he outshouted all of the men in his file. He was sure his earnest maledictions had sent real shivers into the British.

Hundreds of French took up the chorus: *"Vive la France! Vive la France! Vive la France!"* The movement and noise displaced flocks of seagulls which rose with angry squawks and circled above the column.

Pennywhistle watched closely. British officers tended to keep their men quiet. They held their fighting frenzy under tight control, to be unleashed at the decisive moment, usually in conjunction with a bayonet charge. It seemed reckless to Pennywhistle to squander that enthusiasm at the beginning, in one grand gamble. If things went against your side after the first push, nothing was left to sustain you and men quickly lost heart.

His had ordered his men at the twelve-pounder to welcome the French to their island with two double rounds of canister, then dash from their position to redoubt number one. He unslung the well-oiled Ferguson and sighted it. Both Lord Wellington and Sir John Moore had stated it was not the business of officers to kill enemy commanders, but they were neither marines nor in command here.

With great responsibility came greatly increased risk. The French officer in the imposing bearskin shako had tried to shoot Pennywhistle; it was time to return the favour.

Luck deserted the marine. At the moment he fired, some foretaste of danger caused LeMere to move his head ever so slightly. The Guardsman felt a rush of air and heard a whine close to his face, but the bullet went an inch wide of its mark. LeMere noted it briefly, dismissed it, then moved to the rear of the column. He wanted to make sure it was properly dressed before advancing.

Pennywhistle cursed under his breath. He no longer had a shot. But he would again; he could wait.

The column began to move.

Ba bum, ba bum, ba bum bum bum, the drums rattled the sound of the advance.

"Vive la France! Vive la France! Vive la France!"

"Vive l'Empereur! Vive l'Empereur! Vive l'Empereur!"

Skirmishers kept up a steady fire, which had the desired effect of keeping marine heads down. Unlike at Groa, this fire was well and intelligently aimed. MacLeod went down, shot in the head. Blast! Pennywhistle felt a sharp pang of loss. Young Corporal Chance, hit in the chest, dropped his musket, and the light left his eyes. Pennywhistle was down to twenty-eight men, and the engagement had hardly begun.

The skirmishers handled themselves so well that the marines were compelled to ignore the column and focus on them. Pennywhistle ordered the marines to return the skirmishers' fire. The marksmanship training now came into play, and five skirmishers were felled before the rest sought cover. Meanwhile, the column continued to advance. The marines reloaded and began to direct a steady, galling fire at them.

Pennywhistle accounted for two more skirmishers and wounded several others, but the French bobbed, weaved, and ducked effectively, so that hitting them was a challenge to his marksmanship. He then shifted his aim a bit and killed one of the officers at the head of the column. But, the French ignored the deaths and tramped steadily, inexorably, intimidatingly on.

LeMere was pleased. The column did not flinch under fire. They moved with the momentum of a juggernaut. He had taught his men the safest course was not to fret over deaths or wounds, but keep everything focused on the objective immediately ahead. Far more men died in retreat than advance. The men were obeying his instructions perfectly, and the British were in for a harsh lesson today.

The column was close enough to Pennywhistle's position that the skirmishers moved aside and let the column take centre stage. Soon the marines would have to retreat. Pennywhistle told his men to halt their individual firing and wait ten seconds. The column was now less than forty yards away. "Steady, my lads, steady! Wait until you can see the warts on their faces," said Pennywhistle in a low, yet firm voice. A few smiled. "Aim low!"

To Dale, the officers prancing and flourishing their swords looked like they thought war was no different from a minuet. The sergeant chimed in, "Come on, lads, let's spoil their dancing!" Soames and Tilson laughed out loud for a brief second. Mercury crouched and growled.

Pennywhistle held his breath, his hand on the lanyard of the double-shotted cannon. He was counting on the devastation it would unleash to give his surviving marines the chance to retreat.

"Fire!" yelled Pennywhistle as he gave the lanyard a smart jerk. The cannon belched a sheet of crimson fire and legions of lead balls shot toward the French.

High up in the hills, Carlotta heard the report of the cannon. She knew what it meant, and it scared her.

Thirty-Seven

The double dose of canister punched the head of the French column like a chainmail fist. Twenty-eight musket balls followed a second later. The column staggered, then stopped, as if it were a living serpent suddenly slammed on the snout with a stout oaken club. Like a beast, it was dazed and unable to think. Screams, shouts, and blasphemies echoed skyward. Men fell, others stumbled, wounded, crazed with pain, but nobody broke and nobody ran. Training asserted itself. Thinking stopped, but discipline held. The drums continued their insistent beat and sergeants kept the men in line.

The chubby corporal who had fallen boarding the boats actually quickened his advance. He was eager to expunge his earlier embarrassment and was not in the least clumsy on dry land. He performed his evolutions beautifully.

LeMere shouted at the top of his lungs and the men heeded him. He moved about the column quickly, like a sheep dog moving his flock forward. The first shock had passed. He was pleased the men had weathered it well.

The dread chanting resumed. *"Vive la France! Vive la France! Vive la France!"*

Pennywhistle was impressed. These men were nothing like the ones his men had beaten at Groa. They obeyed their officers and NCOs and closed ranks quickly over the dead and wounded. They were a real unit, with true cohesion, not a mere aggregation of individuals. He was in for a tough fight. Damn Hoste! He needed more men!

Pennywhistle caught a glimpse of LeMere, but the man was moving too fast for him to sight properly. The marines fired a second volley, and few shots missed. Pennywhistle himself helped reload the cannon. It belched its second torrent of flame and lead. More men in the column died, or fell writhing in agony. The two newly minted lieutenants who had cheered so heartily moments before were among them. Still, the column kept its integrity and again closed ranks over the dead and wounded.

LeMere's training showed brightly. The drums beat out the command to shift formation. The column neatly followed the rhythmic orders and reformed into a three rank deep line that delivered a coordinated volley.

This time, all of their muskets were brought to bear. This time, the French did not shoot high. The small cannon embrasure behind which the marines sheltered intercepted most of the bullets, but two of Pennywhistle's men, Walker and Armstrong, eighteen-year-olds from *Cerberus* who had responded brilliantly to his training, went down; twenty-six left. A French charge would easily overrun their position.

The French line fired another volley, the front rank kneeling. Poorly trained troops often froze, reluctant to leave the imaginary protection of the kneeling position once they had discharged their weapons. This front rank rose decisively, but did not reload. With astonishing parade ground precision, they swiftly brought their weapons to the "charge bayonet" position, leveled for business. It was the signal they were going to charge and decide things not with lead, but with steel. The drummer beat the advance at the double quick, one hundred and twenty paces per minute.

Excellent move! They were going to make their superior numbers count. Pennywhistle's professional self appreciated sound tactics, even if they were displayed by an enemy. The cannon could do no more good; he was out of time to reload. He reluctantly pounded the steel spike into the venthole.

He hated giving the order to retreat, but it was the only sensible course. The usual method would be to affect a fighting retreat as a body of men, slowly yielding ground and obeying the first rule of defense against a predator: never show him your backside. Sensible normally, but speed mattered now, so he told the men to make for the first fort in the fastest dash they could manage. They would run in pairs, each watching out for the other. Less disciplined troops would break and scatter and not stop running until they were well out of danger. Pennywhistle's men knew a solidly defensible rally point awaited.

Redoubt number one was a quarter mile inland, and it was not unoccupied. Pennywhistle had rounded up every sailor he could scrounge. Sailors were better at deck fighting with cutlasses, but they did not lack for martial spirit. They could certainly give covering fire as the retreating marines entered the redoubt. Each of the thirty sailors inside had two loaded muskets ready at hand.

"*Attaquez, mes enfants, attaquez!*" shouted LeMere.

"*Hourra! Hourra! Hourra!*" A thunderous ululation arose from hundreds of French throats. The fast battle step shifted into a slow run. The onrushing soldiers gripped their muskets tight and thrust the bayonets forward, eager for blood.

"Go!" yelled Pennywhistle to Dale. Mercury led the way with a fast, graceful lope. The marines ran as ordered, Stratton and McCarthy the first pair to depart. Every pair obeyed Pennywhistle's order to zigzag. A running man was hard to hit, a weaving one nearly impossible.

The sailors opened a covering fire as soon they saw the marines running toward them. At this distance it was inaccurate, nuisance fire, but it checked, ever so slightly, the French advance and bought the retreating marines precious seconds to make good their escape.

Pennywhistle stood defiantly alone. His mind filtered out the din of shouting, screaming, running men, the discordant bugle calls, and throbbing drums. He had no way to stop the French, but as long as his men were safe, he could not resist the temptation to pour in a few last shots. He fired, methodically reloaded, and fired again.

His job was to command, not engage in personal duels, but his blood was up and, for once, it got in the way of his judgment. He should have evacuated with the marines. Personal martyrdom was illogical, foolish, and unproductive, but he was so focused on killing the French that he waited too long.

One French soldier scrambled over the parapet and made a savage thrust with his bayonet. Pennywhistle parried it aside easily, then jabbed the Ferguson's bayonet into the man's mouth. "Eat this!" he shouted with an anger that startled him. The man blinked, gurgled red froth, then slumped forward. Pennywhistle felt rather than heard another soldier behind him and to the right. He snapped the gun backward as he withdrew the blade and let the rearward momentum continue toward the source of the sound. There was a sold *thunk* as the butt of the rifle collided with the man's jaw, shattering it. Pennywhistle spun round and broke into the fastest rug his long legs could manage.

Bullets kicked up dirt and stones as he ran. Marines in the redoubt opened a covering fire. Sailors and marines shouted cheers at the top of their lungs. Soames found himself unaccountably yelling like a crazy man. "Come on, sir, come on! You can make it!"

Buzzing and whining attacked Pennywhistle's ears, as if he had fallen into a nest of hornets. He felt rushes of air pass his head. Something tugged at his shoulder. Damn it! That was a new epaulette!

The sight of a running officer tempted nearly every French soldier coming over the parapet to try his luck. But the Briton moved fast, and even the marines trained by LeMere in marksmanship had trouble with an erratically moving, small target. This was no barrel in the water. They cursed him and their luck, then gathered at the abandoned redoubt to savour their triumph. They had driven the vaunted British from a solid, fixed position!

Pennywhistle was counting on that reaction. When troops without battle experience captured a position, they often stopped to enjoy their good fortune instead of immediately pressing on to a more important objective. The French had just captured empty real estate, but he knew it did not seem that way to them; meanwhile, he now had a respite to consolidate his position.

At the demi-lune, LeMere congratulated his men. They had done well, very well, but the *Roastbifs* must not be allowed to get away. He stormed at them, shouted they must not lose time, yet they simply would not be moved. He reluctantly acknowledged they needed to rest and gloat. Men laughed, cheered, and clapped each other on the backs in soldierly fellowship.

"Form up, form up, form up," bellowed LeMere. Officers like Lieutenant Flaubert took up his call and hectored their men. Flaubert was a former tailor and old for his rank at thirty-five, but he was LeMere's most enthusiastic acolyte. The *Grande Armée* had given Flaubert status such as he had never even dreamed of as a mere craftsman in Royalist France. There was nothing he would not do for the Emperor, who rewarded merit, who had broken the chains of tyranny held by hereditary aristocrats. Too many times, lords had ordered suits made of the finest damasks and silks, then refused to pay; and if he'd dared demand settlement of the account, they'd had him beaten. Now he was an *officer*, by *le bon dieu*, and the new France of *egalité, liberté, and fraternité* that allowed him to be a man, was what he would live for, fight for, die for if need be. And if the other soldiers forgot their purpose, he would remind them! Finally, the men reformed into a column and began to move up the hill.

LeMere chose to not follow the retreating British directly, but took a side street in an effort to achieve surprise by flanking them.

*****

When Pennywhistle caught up with his marines, the men hailed him with delight. He was greeted with the greatest enthusiasm, oddly enough, by Private Tilson. Maybe he had been a skulker before, but by God, now he was a real veteran! Captain Pennywhistle's training had paid off.

Pennywhistle stripped off his uniform coat and checked the right epaulette. Some of the gold bullion fringe was missing, but that could be repaired. He wondered for a split second if Carlotta was well, then forced his mind back to the pressing matters at hand. It was after three o'clock; less than three hours left of daylight. There were two more redoubts behind this one, but after the second one fell, the dockyard with the prize ships would be vulnerable.

He had fifty-seven men, counting himself, and the French still outnumbered them at least eight to one. Time to repeat the hat trick. It might not work for long, if the French officer remembered and recognized it, but every minute it bought meant lives preserved. Forty spare marine hats were placed on sticks so that their crowns and plumes showed just above the parapet.

Pennywhistle's force was tightly packed in the small earthen redoubt and the smell of battle sweat made the air rank and fetid. He had wisely had butts of water laid in. The men took their turns in an orderly fashion and drank their fill, then assumed their positions behind the solid walls of earth and waited.

LeMere's men advanced. No skirmishers now, as it would have been pointless in the narrow street. Lacking good maps and intelligence, LeMere proceeded with a caution at odds with his customary *élan* and dash. The column moved to the beat of drums, slow, steady, and determined.

With the curve of the streets, Pennywhistle heard the column before he saw it. Indirect approach, flanking movement, exactly what he would have done.

When the head of the column emerged from a side street onto the small square, it quickly halted, as did the throbbing drums. Standing silent, it was almost as if the column gave an audible sigh when they saw the second redoubt. The British had not fled and dispersed; they were posted behind robust earthworks.

Pennywhistle ordered one file of short sailors to march from the rear entrance of the fort to the front, with bayonets fixed and held high so that only the weapons could be seen above the walls. He then ordered them to halt, ground their muskets, wait three minutes, break ranks, then reassemble outside the entrance, and repeat the same maneuver four times. By this artifice, he hoped to fool his opponent into thinking he was receiving a steady stream of reinforcements.

*****

Dubordieu saw something of the fight from *Uranie* through his glass. He decided a triumph was close at hand and it was time to land the sailors he had designated as prize crews. LeMere's men might be able to capture the ships, but they could not sail them. He sent enough men to lightly crew six ships under the most able petty officers he had. It pleased him that he would be able to take back something Hoste had stolen. He also dispatched a special detail under Chief Gunner Bovary with orders to find the powder magazine and blow it and the entire dockyard into oblivion.

*****

LeMere unhurriedly walked to the head of the column to see what had caused the halt and murmurs of dismay. He projected an air of nonchalance and absolute confidence. He unfurled his glass and surveyed the redoubt carefully. The fort was well built and he could see round hats inside. There were more marines here than he'd expected, and new troops were arriving. Deception, or strategic reserve?

It was a strong position, but it was also a small one. He had the advantage of numbers, so he would deploy skirmishers to occupy the defenders, then send a column of files around the right flank to take it from the rear. He looked up at the sky and worried. It would have to be done quickly. It would be very hard to perform the maneuver in darkness.

Pennywhistle watched the French through his glass. Skirmishers started to deploy and spread out. This time they had no cover; the square was devoid of shelter and gave the men in the redoubt a good field of fire. He told his men to conserve their ammunition and aim carefully, since the skirmishers clearly were not the main attack. The marines fired at will at targets of opportunity and Pennywhistle instructed the sailors to load muskets and hand them to the marines.

Leicester's firing was typical. He had won several marksmanship prizes in training, and did not disappoint in combat. He would not be rushed. He zeroed his targets expertly, tracked their progress with studied care, and fired only when he had a clear shot.

*****

Miles away, in the calm, late afternoon breeze, the three ships of Hoste's squadron were homeward bound for Lissa, bringing with them an impressive haul of prizes. Gordon felt bad that Pennywhistle had been cursed with the thankless task of harbour defense, but he was clearly the best man for the job. At least Pennywhistle would share in the prize money. In all probability, nothing of interest had happened. He was probably at that moment enjoying a well-earned rest and communing with his watercolours.

*****

From her commanding view high above the harbour, Carlotta could not make out individual men, but could observe the movements of large masses of colour. The blue of the French and the red of the British showed their relative positions. She heard the reports of cannon and knew the battle had begun, but she knew nothing of Pennywhistle's fate and it ate at her. She wanted to rush down, cast caution to the winds, and be at his side. It was insanity, but then love was insane if it was anything. Manton patiently explained to her his orders and the captain's desire. Her reason made a late, if unwelcome, comeback. She knew he would send word at the earliest moment. She exhaled deeply, then returned to sewing a shirt for him of the finest Indian cotton. It gave her something on which to focus her anxious energies.

*****

LeMere watched closely. Skirmishers were dying, but such was the nature of war. They were doing their jobs well, keeping the British occupied. The British fire was accurate and deadly, but the column was untouched and was slowly working round to the right. It was only a matter of time before the British position became untenable.

Thirty-Eight

Pennywhistle cursed, then wracked his mind for some way to forestall the eventual success of the flanking movement. He could think of none. The redoubt would have held the square if the French had been of the same calibre as those at Groa, but these men were disciplined enough to maneuver their way to victory.

His men were taking a respectable toll on the skirmishers. A skirmisher would clutch an arm, leg, his chest, or head, then fall to the ground. He noted Private Sheffield executed an exquisite tracking shot that killed a gallant . Some of the shots travelled beyond the skirmishers and took down men of the column, but each time this happened, soldiers stepped over their fallen comrades, closed ranks, and slogged inexorably on.

Pennywhistle had never seen his men reload so quickly after each shot, yet they fired with great care and precision. He continued his usual policy of aiming at officers. When none of those presented themselves, he went for NCOs. Two senior sergeants were among his victims. But LeMere's files kept active, kept maneuvering, always to the right.

The column of files halted. The men moved their weapons to the support arms position.

The steady maneuvering of the French had distracted Pennywhistle from the passing of time. It was after five now, and the long shadows of evening told him it was time to move to the work directly in front of the dockyard. Nightfall was a friend to the British, and it approached quickly. The move had to be timed well. The men would move in pairs again, each man responsible for the

309

safety of his mate. The pairs had been numbered off, so when the time came, Pennywhistle could call out the numbers.

LeMere moved up and down the long file, encouraging and directing his men. They were eager to take the earthwork. Corpses littered the square and men continued to fall, but LeMere was pleased that these losses strengthened, rather than diminished, their determination. Truly, French *élan* was an amazing thing! They had tasted victory today, and it was as sweet and addictive as opium.

Pennywhistle ordered the withdrawal, and the men responded instantly. They fired a rolling volley, then each hurled a smoking, hissing grenade. The volley disoriented the French files, but did no appreciable damage. The rolling grenades, however, exploded at ground level, sending jagged shards of metal into legs and knees. The files recoiled; ten men collapsed as their legs failed them. In the brief interval of their dismay and confusion, the British withdrew. Blandon and Sheffield were the last rankers to leave the redoubt, and they fired two final shots of defiance before starting to run. Pennywhistle was the last to leave, as before. This time he was prudent and dispensed with any personal parting shots.

Hampered by the sudden shortage of officers and sergeants, LeMere managed to organize a swift, disciplined advance. He was impatient to gain the interior of the work that had slowed his efforts—slowed, but not baffled—and put an end once and for all to these troublesome defenders. Reaching the entrance, he cursed. The fort stood empty. He had more than half expected this, but it still angered him. His opponent's strategy was to engage, delay, and retire. It was proving effective, but it also indicated to LeMere that his opponent was substantially weaker in numbers, always a useful thing for a commander to know. He wondered to where the British had retired. Was there another point of defense between him and the dockyard entrance? Or was the way to the dockyards wide open, the ships ripe for the taking?

LeMere pointed his glass toward the ships in harbour and saw several lower boats. The prize crews were on their way. He decided to wait on the arrival of the sailors so they could all advance to the ships together, much as he chaffed at delay. An hour passed, and he grew restless. Then it struck him that, even if there were another point of defense between them and their destination, he would not have to capture the next fort. He merely had to occupy the defenders, which would allow the sailors to walk on unopposed. The target, after all, was not the British troops, but the dockyard and the prize ships.

It took the sailors time to form into a small column and march forward with the peculiar rolling gait of sailors unused to land. They observed the signs of fighting with some alarm, but since nothing barred their way, they assumed fortune had favoured the Tricolour.

The sunlight was almost gone. LeMere did not relish the confusion of a night action. When the men smiled and joked about their triumph, he upbraided them with a harangue about time growing short. He harped on how they must proceed to the dock with one glorious rush. There would be no subtle tactics, just courage and gallantry. They would not waste time softening up the British if they encountered them, but would gamble everything on one knockout blow.

"Do you wish for a triumph?" he demanded with the practiced cunning of the orator who can shape exactly the response he desires. "*Hourra!*" the men answered.

"Do you wish for glory?" LeMere yelled, daring them to answer in the affirmative. "*Hourra!*" came the response.

"Do you wish for prize money?" He saved the best for last. "*Hourra!*" It brought the loudest shouts of all. LeMere knew how to manipulate. But much of command was about exactly that, working the men round to become an extension of your will.

The column of sailors came trudging up at last. Their leader eyed LeMere uncertainly, afraid to disrupt his oratory, then made his decision and moved boldly forward.

"Chief Petty Officer LeBatt reporting, sir. My orders are to secure the prizes and get them out to sea as quickly as possible. I gather your efforts have gone well, sir."

LeMere burst into a rare full-throated laugh. "I am delighted to see you, LeBatt. You could not have arrived at a more propitious moment. Our efforts have indeed gone very well, but some resistance remains. I believe your people can provide us very substantial help."

LeBatt liked this officer's enthusiasm. "We would be happy to assist; pray tell us exactly in what manner." He listened closely as LeMere discoursed with his usual enthusiasm.

LeMere felt the exigencies of time and was unusually terse, at least for him. He explained his plan in less than five minutes. "So you see, Chief," he concluded, "we will assault and block, as we have been blocked, and you and your men will take care of the yard. We will act as your shields, but you must move as soon as you see we are fully engaged. It is almost dark and time is of the essence."

LeMere then turned to address the Gunner. "Bovary, as Chief Gunner, I hold you responsible for the fate of the dockyard. At all hazards, find the magazine and blow the whole supply back to Creation!" The fierce look on LeMere's face was formidable and brooked no argument.

LeBatt and Bovary saluted. "I understand perfectly, Captain," said Lebatt. "And my men are truly grateful for your protection."

Pennywhistle inspected the troops in redoubt number two. He was down to twenty-four marines and twenty-six sailors. His force was diminished, but his objective of trading space for time was working. Most of the men inserted new flints. Some cleared the fouling in their muskets by relieving their bladders down the barrel. Most of them each had about thirty rounds left, having already expended a similar number.

Morale was high. The men knew they had done well. But the expressions on their faces were grim. They were too experienced to delude themselves as to what was coming, or their likely fate. Nevertheless, they would fight, and fight to the last extremity. "We will smash them up!" Blandon assured Addison.

Pennywhistle's men jumped to attention at the sound of the drums and the muffled *tramp, tramp, tramp* of shoes on flagstones. Troops were not yet visible because of the sinuosity of the streets. No one had to tell the marines what the sound meant; they were at their posts in a trice. Pennywhistle balanced his Ferguson on the parapet, while Leicester, Soames, and the others did the same with their muskets. He repeated his warning to conserve ammunition and make every shot count. As darkness settled and concealed the shapes of men, they would aim at muzzle flashes.

The head of the long file emerged from a side street. This square was larger, and the file began to expertly resolve itself into a three rank deep line, just out of range of Pennywhistle's men. That alone told Pennywhistle his opposite had done his research and directed this maneuver. The French performed the maneuver to perfection, as they had done their other evolutions this day. When they finished, an uncharacteristic silence descended on the French ranks. Officers went up and down the lines and checked the dressing of the men with their swords. The lines were straight as arrows. Gritty faces beamed with pride.

The spectacle impressed Pennywhistle, but he was undaunted. He told his men to prepare to fend off an assault. They made one last check of cartridges and bayonets. Each looked at his two grenades. They made sure the fuses were properly seated.

LeMere strutted slowly down the front line in an inspirational show of pride and bravado. Mentally, he was daring the British to shoot at him, knowing it would impress the men. He also knew no shots would be forthcoming. The British commander would want to conserve ammunition and wait until he was sure of the range. The British work lay one hundred and twenty yards ahead. He knew he should close further before ordering a charge, but his men looked so eager, he could restrain himself no longer. He should have waited.

LeMere ringingly gave the command, "Charge bayonets." Bugles blared. He deployed a line of eight sappers armed with axes to deal with any wooden obstacles. The men thrust their bayonets level and eagerly awaited the word that would release them. This time there was no cheering. The lines grew deadly quiet. This was the moment his men had lived for, trained for, set their minds and hearts for: final success! He felt a towering surge of pride. "Charge!" bellowed LeMere, with all the fury and gusto he could muster, and the men, unleashed, broke forth. This was no fast battle step, this was a flat out run, the product of martial exuberance. Now the charging men yelled all manner of battle cries which merged into a giant "*YAAAAAAAHHHHH!*"

If they had held off until full darkness, the night would have protected them. As it was, the dying sun was at their backs, making them perfectly illuminated targets. At thirty yards, Pennywhistle yelled, "Fire!" and a mighty whip of red-orange flame cracked above the parapet. Nearly every bullet told. Soames remembered Pennywhistle saying it was the best range, and by God, he was right!

A score of Frenchmen died in that first volley, but it was like swatting gnats. Numbers mattered and nothing could stop the crazed French momentum. LeMere had ordered them not to halt or return fire, but to simply keep barreling forward. This was about sheer smashing power.

The French tide stopped briefly when it broke upon the *chevaux de frise*. Sappers frantically chopped away at the long wooden impediment. The marines focused their fire on them and killed two immediately, but the rest courageously continued to hack away. Soldiers struggled through the wooden teeth in small clumps, oblivious to the deaths of their fellows. It was slow going and the British poured relentless volleys into them while they were perfect targets. Finally the sappers cut a real opening. The French poured through and began clawing their way up the walls like a sea of carpenter ants attacking decayed wood. Now the line of *fraises* acted as giant porcupine quills. Three Frenchmen became impaled upon them because of the frenzied pushing and shoving from the rear.

The crest of the parapet became a sparkling necklace of red-orange flame. Muskets reported and men screamed. Most devastating of all were the grenades, which Pennywhistle's men lit and simply dropped on the heads of the French.

This was point blank range. The marines could not miss, and Frenchmen died in droves. But, numbers were firmly on their side. They had leadership, confidence, and the pure fury of battle was upon them. No amount of bravery or cleverness could prevent them gaining the parapet. They swarmed the parapet like bees on a honeycomb and jumped down inside. Des Barres was the first into the redoubt, only to die at the point of Sheffield's bayonet.

It was fully dark now. The fighting became hand-to-hand: bayonets, blades, and reversed muskets. Screams, shouts, curses, sobs, and noises more animal than human filled the brimstone-laden air. Men stabbed, slashed, clubbed, kicked, punched, and even bit each other. No quarter was asked and none given. Fighting in a tight, confined space with no place to run or hide brought out the monster in every man. It came down to sheer collective will. The French meant to take the redoubt; the British were unwilling to yield an inch.

It was hard to reload muskets in the tightly packed space, but some managed; they thrust their piece into the nearest stomach and pulled the trigger. Many of the men who fell to gunfire had powder burns, so close was the action. It was hard to tell friend from foe and many lashed out at whatever face appeared in front of them. Some men actually died by the hands of comrades in arms.

Blandon muttered absent-mindedly what many of his mates were thinking, "Madness, madness!" A young man hardly more than a boy thrust at him with a bayonet. Blandon recognized with horror Ducot, the blond drummer boy Pennywhistle had rescued at Groa. The boy had apparently decided to become a fighting man. Blandon nearly retched but did his duty and thrust his own bayonet through the boy's chest. Choking back bile, he surged forward to guard his commander.

A Frenchman slammed his bayonet toward Pennywhistle, just as he faced round toward him. The bayonet should have gutted him, but at the last second Blandon interposed himself and struck the Frenchman in the abdomen with his own bayonet. As the Frenchman went down, his bayonet ripped a gash and laid bare Blandon's intestines.

Pennywhistle saw his men were overwhelmed and knew they could not hold. Soames and Tilson died gallantly in front of his eyes under an avalanche of bayonets; a large pile of blue-clad bodies lay in front of their corpses.

A tall French corporal sought to skewer Dale in the back as the sergeant struggled against a French officer. Dale had no idea of the danger, but Mercury did. The huge dog growled, jumped, and flew through the air. The impact of one hundred eighty pounds of canine flesh was like a hammer propelled by a hurricane and it knocked the French corporal sprawling. Mercury snapped his jaws around the man's neck, crushed it like a twig, then shook the corpse as if it were a rag doll.

In seconds a score of bayonets plunged furiously into the dog's neck. The dog gave a short, loud howl and died. The lament alerted Dale, who turned quickly. Tears filled his eyes when he saw what had happened.

Other marines saw it too. A general cry went up. "They killed Mercury! Get the bastards!" The marines had fought fiercely before, but now they fought like berserkers. They cut, slashed, and impaled, not like men but demons from hell. Frenchmen died by the score, but there were simply too many of them.

A tall French sergeant slashed out with his musket's bayonet. He hated the English who had killed his brother in Spain, and the tall English officer made a fine target. Pennywhistle ducked, kicked him in the knee, and then delivered a vicious sideswipe with the butt of the Ferguson to the man's jaw. A private fired his Charleville and missed Pennywhistle's head by an inch. No one had taught him that the bullet arced in flight. Pennywhistle responded with an angry riposte which put his bayonet into the man's throat. He rammed it home with vigor.

A voltigeur corporal sought to run Pennywhistle through from the rear. Instead, he looked down with stunned curiousity and found a bayonet tip protruding from his own stomach. Dale muttered under his breath, "That's for Mercury, you damned rat."

The French sailors who had followed the column took advantage of the confusion and made their dash for the dockyard. They smashed the gate away with gleeful efficiency and headed toward the ships. Upon boarding, they discovered that the British kept the ships in good order and well ballasted. It would be an easy task to get them ready and out to sea. They felt it high time they got prize money, even if it was for reclaiming their own.

Bovary located the powder magazine without difficulty, but got a nasty surprise when he entered. It was completely empty. He was frustrated beyond measure. He had no way to destroy anything.

Pennywhistle fought furiously, but even amidst the mayhem, he noticed the passage of men streaming by. The dockyard was breeched. He had failed. He had done everything he could, but it had not been enough. He had no time for recriminations. He was too busy fending off a sword thrust from a young sergeant. The man was good, but Pennywhistle was better. He deflected the sword aside, then rammed the bayonet upwards under the sternum and punctured the heart.

One of the grenades ignited a fire in a nearby house that blazed up viciously and gave a creepy, dancing, malevolent illumination to the confined gore in the fort's centre. It was like something Hieronymous Bosch might have painted if he had been addicted to opium. Men's faces twisted, stretched, and contorted in hellish expressions of fear, glee, bloodlust, rage, and hatred. Dale in particular, the fury of battle upon him, wore the face of a male Gorgon. It was as if demons had decided to assume parodies of the human form and stage a street carnival for the sole delight of the Prince of Darkness. If it had been a painting, Pennywhistle would have titled it "Satan's Slaughter Pit."

Nothing could make things worse, because people simply could not do any worse than this. This was mankind at its most bestial, most savage, most unreasoning. Revulsion flashed through his mind, but he knew every man harboured demons, and sometimes those demons were necessary. This was such a time.

Pennywhistle was about to order a retreat when a tall, mustached French officer with a single gold earring stepped forward out of the shadowy chaos, seemingly appearing from nowhere. He flourished a beautifully balanced saber.

The two men locked eyes, and the French officer uttered one word with a combination of excitement, admiration, and satisfaction.

"Pennywhistle!" LeMere had found his nemesis.

High up in the hills, for no reason she could pinpoint, Carlotta gave an involuntary shudder.

Thirty-Nine

When LeMere confronted Pennywhistle, animal instincts seized control, not just of the two principals, but of the entire crowd. All fighting stopped, as if a master wizard had cast a powerful spell which held everyone in thrall. It was against logic, training, and reason; some primitive part of their brains told the men on both sides that two powerful tribal shamans were about to contend for dominance, and it was not for them to interfere. Rather than assist, both sides watched. There was a weirdly theatrical air to it, like a duel between gladiators. The fort formed a tiny Coliseum. What was wagered on the outcome was not money, but soldiers' lives.

Neither Pennywhistle nor LeMere had sought this, but both recognized and welcomed it. Their paths had crossed, almost fatally so, twice before, and had generated in each a curiousity and a certain sneaking admiration for the other. Pennywhistle would have found LeMere's rabid atheism and unremitting loyalty to the Corsican Tyrant distasteful. LeMere would have regarded Pennywhistle's belief in a deity and his unexamined fealty to the insane King George as peculiar. Yet these differences were minor.

In most respects, the men were eerily alike. They were both estranged from their families, both wanting familial approval and scorning it. Both were rationalists. Both had extraordinary powers of concentration and were consumed by a fiery obsession to be the best in their profession. Both had participated in famous battles, Pennywhistle at sea and LeMere on land. Each knew much of the language, culture, and fighting prowess of his adversary's country and felt no hatred for his cause. Pennywhistle's tutor had been a

319

French engineering officer; LeMere had attended St. Paul's School in London, having fled *La Terreur* with his father. Pennywhistle was less pompous and prolix, but was every bit as good, if less devious, at convincing superiors to adopt his plans. Pennywhistle was somewhat more cerebral, but both were wedded to notions of gallantry, courtesy, and honour, in an occupation where it was easy to lose sight of common humanity. For all of that, the most important thing they shared was a killer instinct, a ruthlessness when it came to achieving victory.

"No, don't kill him!" Warning cries went up on both sides and were perfectly understood by all of the warriors involved. "Don't fire!" echoed in French and English. Then everything went utterly silent.

Pennywhistle handed the Ferguson to Dale and placed his hand on the hilt of his cutlass. He wound the attached gold and crimson swordknot slowly and carefully around his wrist, a precaution against losing the weapon in case his grip was broken. The weapon slid swiftly and silently into his hand. The fine, blued steelpoint danced with razor-sharp, firefly glee as it reflected the malevolent light of surrounding small fires. He felt heat flood his face, a slight flutter in his stomach, and unnaturally dry lips; good signs: the body read the situation correctly. His pulse rate increased then steadied. His nostrils flared and his pupils widened. His mind overrode everything with a detached, reptilian-cold eagerness to kill his opponent in the swiftest manner possible.

The lurid arabesques of flame cast odd shadows. In the dancing light, Pennywhistle was surprised to see in LeMere's face a mirror image of his own: the same determined crimson flush. They were the visages of twins, demons separated at birth.

Pennywhistle went easily to the formal *en garde* position. He breathed deeply several times and tightened his grip on the hilt of his cutlass. The cutlass felt solid and its weight reassuringly familiar. His practiced eye methodically assessed his opponent head to foot, looking for clues to his strengths, weaknesses, and style of fighting. He saw with surprise that the other had weapons in both hands; his right held a beautifully proportioned and balanced dragon-pommeled cavalry saber of forty inches, his left a basket-hilted parrying dagger. He could strike with one hand, block with the other, and both hands would have the capacity to cut and wound. It was an older style of fighting, one Pennywhistle had thought died the century before.

The man was strong, Pennywhistle realized. He flicked the heavy saber through the air in quick, easy circles. His touch was light and deft. His effortlessness made the heavy Chattelerault blade seem as if it were made of paper. He was loosening up, commanding his muscles to be as supple and flexible as possible.

Pennywhistle performed the same ritual with his cutlass. It was a lighter piece with a narrower blade, but he had made sure it was exactly balanced. Wilkinson's in London had fitted the grip to his hand like a tailored glove. What the cutlass lacked in length and bulk, it made up for in the speed with which it could be wielded. He had always thought speed of maneuver much more important than raw strength. But in the end, the blade mattered much less than the skill of the man wielding it. An expert could do great damage with the poorest of weapons, an amateur little even with the best.

His cutlass was ten inches shorter than his opponent's saber, a shipboard weapon designed for close-in fighting. The Wilkinson blade was designed for quick thrusts with the point. LeMere's weapon was designed for slashing, the long, deadly edge the principal killing surface. The contest would be point versus edge. Pennywhistle's sword was a precision instrument, LeMere's one of power.

LeMere was a tall man, only an inch shorter than Pennywhistle. With the same reach and a longer blade, he would use distance to his advantage. The situation was similar to that of two boxers; one with a long, leisurely right cross, the other with a quick, powerful jab.

Pennywhistle had no constraining notions about fair play. The start position might be formal, but this was a fight where any move that brought victory would count. The outcome would depend on the skilled use of the usual elements: footwork, arm movement, coordination, grip, aim, focus, timing, and follow-through, and all of these an expression of willpower.

"Before I kill you, Captain, honour me with your name. You have the advantage of me in that regard." Pennywhistle spoke loudly and briskly, surprised at himself for asking such a question. His tone was courteous, even scholarly, as if he merely wanted to confirm the species of a particular specimen of butterfly for his mounting board. Even in moments of danger, his curiousity was ever present.

LeMere was startled, then a hint of amused satisfaction played at the corners of his mouth, but it did not reach his eyes. The man's French had been excellent: Parisian. A cheeky, if reasonable question. Of course he would answer; his ego would not permit him otherwise.

"Captain Rene LeMere of the Emperor's Imperial Guard," he bowed briefly, then smiled with lupine satisfaction, "at your service! A distinct pleasure to make your acquaintance at long last, Captain Pennywhistle." The response was combative, menacing, despite the silken merriment in the voice. A very long minute passed. The men watching nodded: the *dramatis personae* had been named.

Now it was Pennywhistle's turn to be startled. The man's English sounded as if were from the Court of St. James! He responded, "Your English is excellent, Captain. If you will but see reason, and surrender yourself, I promise you, I will provide you opportunities to speak it freely and in genteel circumstances in my own country. Give your parole and I promise you honoured residence at my brother's estate until properly exchanged. You will have comfort and freedom!" That was duty and courtly courtesy speaking. A darker part of him was glad LeMere would never accept. He wanted the combat, wanted to match his skill against this man.

LeMere grinned coldly and responded with exaggerated courtesy. "How very civilized and chivalrous of you! I was about to offer you the same choice. But let us be frank and honest gentlemen. Neither of us will endure captivity and both want to test our blades. Let us proceed with what our natures demand!" He paused for a wistful moment. "It is a shame a gallant man like you must die, merely for having picked the wrong master! And now, Captain, let the match begin!"

They both went to the formal *en garde* position; weight on the rear foot, trunk thrust slightly forward. Their eyes locked for a brief second, challenged, then narrowed in fierce concentration.

*****

The French sailors in the dockyard went about their business methodically and paid little attention to the fire burning in the town. The illumination helped their work somewhat, but the luminous full moon helped much more. Ropes, shrouds, fore and back stays and sails were all checked. The fastest way to get to sea was to set jib, maintop, and driver and simply cut the anchor cables. The wind was light and against them, but by properly bracing the sails round, they could manage a slow departure. The prize crews were small, skeleton crews, but that would be enough. The weather was clear and there was no opposition. They would be at sea in a matter of hours. The Commodore would be pleased.

Just now, the Commodore was not pleased. He was alarmed. "So you believe it was Hoste's squadron you spotted?" He looked directly at the young Lieutenant Dumanoir making the report.

"Yes, Commodore, we spotted them at dawn. Three ships, frigates, with seven prizes. I do not believe they saw us. The *Gaspe* is a small ship, and an exceedingly fast one. I cracked on all possible sail. I felt it critical you should know."

"I am sorry, Lieutenant. I do not mean to seem angry with you or ungrateful for your excellent initiative, but you have brought me news that is most unwelcome. I wish to meet Hoste, but at a time and place of my own choosing. From their course, speed, and location, they will arrive here around dawn. I wish to be gone before then. We shall have to advance our timetable."

*****

High above the town, Carlotta and Manton engaged in a heated argument. Rather, Carlotta argued and Manton sought to patiently listen, explain, calm, and restrain.

"Miss Carlotta, I know you care for the captain and want to help, but there is really nothing you can do. It will help him most if you stay here and remain safe." Manton tried to be tactful yet firm, but the woman's fiery passion was wearing him down.

"Manton, you can see as well as I that something has gone wrong. A fire burns near the dockyard, a fire that has no business being there. It can only have one cause. The British have had to retreat." Then she jabbed her finger violently in the direction of the dockyard. "And see there, lanterns are being hoisted on the masts of ships in the yards. The British would have no reason to do that, but the French would if they had captured the prize ships and had nothing to fear."

"All that you say is probably true, ma'am, but if the captain can't stop 'em, what can we do?" Manton was frustrated. He was young, vigorous, and aspired to be much more than a servant someday.

Carlotta had no experience of warfare, but she was an intelligent woman and a remarkably quick study. She searched her mind for ways to help, then remembered what Pennywhistle had said of his preparations. An inspiration came to her.

"Those barrels Thomas stored here and lower down. Those are bombs! Giant hand grenades. We could at least cause a diversion."

"But ma'am, roll them against whom? Captain intended to roll them against targets at fairly close range. And anyway, it's just you and me, ma'am."

Carlotta responded fiercely, "Not just you and me; my sons Nico and Marko are young, but strong. They will help as well. Isn't that so, boys?"

The two boys took after their mother and were tall for their years. They were at an age when they still respected their elders, but were fully capable of doing tasks without constant supervision. Nicko said earnestly, "The captain taught me how to shoot and has been like a father to me! We have to help!" Marko chimed in, "We can't just leave him hanging, mother."

"You see, Manton?" said Carlotta. "Even the children know we must do something. You remember how Thomas always says 'Lose not a minute?' We must act now!"

Her determination was persuasive; love under stress produced extraordinary results. Manton picked up Pennywhistle's night glass and surveyed the town. She was right. He knew the captain had doubts about his ability to hold for long. He looked at the barrels several hundred yards away. The barrels had fuses set to detonate quickly. They were the instruments of a last ditch defense. They would explode long before they reached the town. Impractical.

But... and then Manton smiled. The powder barrels on the defenses much lower on the ridgeline had far longer fuses. He saw through the glass that the paths the barrels would follow would take them immediately to the rear of where the fire burned in town. He had heard the captain say in the wardroom that the best way to disrupt the enemy was not to hit him in the front, but to smash him in the rear. He said men did fine against an enemy they could see, but not nearly so well against an unexpected attack from a quarter they could not see. Barrels just appearing out of the night and exploding would answer that well.

Manton asked himself: what would the captain do if he were in my situation and had my orders? Would he be obedient, sit here, do nothing, and simply trust to hope and Providence? No! He would act! To hell with his orders! He felt very bold, almost like his captain.

"Ma'am, you are right!" he exclaimed.

Carlotta looked relieved and muttered, *Grazie a Dio*" under her breath. Manton then launched into a quick explanation of what would work.

When Manton finished, out of breath, Carlotta swiftly replied, "Then let us not stand here talking. We have everything but time!" In half a minute, Carlotta, Manton, Nico, and Marko were racing down the hill into the night. They ran like people possessed, which was actually not far wrong. It was lucky they knew the path.

*****

LeMere wasted no time. Directly after he finished his introduction, his saber flashed swiftly toward Pennywhistle's head. The cut was delivered from well over the shoulder; the weight of the saber increased the speed and force of the blow. Pennywhistle recognized the maneuver, called a *moulane*, and a flick of his wrist slammed his cutlass forward from the classic low guard position. The two swords collided violently in mid air amidst an outpouring of sparks that seemed a shower of blue raindrops and a loud resounding *klaaaannnng*. He knocked the saber aside.

LeMere jumped back. When the marine followed, LeMere feinted at his head then lunged at his belly. Pennywhistle jumped back, his hanging parry stopping LeMere's blade a fraction of an inch from his navel. LeMere feinted a second belly stroke, then cut at the head. Pennywhistle anticipated this and a straight vertical block shoved it swiftly aside. LeMere slashed with the blade of the parrying dagger and drew blood from Pennywhistle's shoulder. Two more swift attacks by LeMere followed, each deflected by quick movements of Pennywhistle's wrist, but the flickering dagger forced him to keep his distance instead of pressing in.

The wound was trifling, but the pain sped up his already quick thinking. LeMere was good: fast, light on his feet, aggressive. But his moves were too studied, too obviously choreographed, stolen directly from Angelo's *L'ecole des Armes*; no unconventional variations, no surprises. They were moves of the fencing salon, not the battlefield, all slashing arcs and circles. LeMere's blows pulsed with enormous energy, but they traveled slowly enough that Pennywhistle was able to use the lighter cutlass to move inside and block so that his parries were a split second ahead of LeMere's cuts and thrusts.

LeMere feinted retreat, as if to regroup, then lunged at Pennywhistle's chest. He parried deftly. LeMere cut twice at his head; again he parried expertly. He riposted with a cut to LeMere's belly, which was turned aside. LeMere slashed at his bleeding shoulder with the dagger, but this time Pennywhistle shot the clam shell guard of the cutlass upward and rammed it full force against LeMere's wrist. The dagger flew off into space. LeMere cursed, attacked again, feinting at head, but cutting at the belly. Pennywhistle deflected and cut at LeMere's head, only to have the strike parried flawlessly.

To the awed spectators, the blades danced with such fast, deadly grace that they appeared living entities, independent of their owners. They spat streams of sparks. They rose, dipped, slashed, lunged, blocked, and thrust in quick succession, back and forth, back and forth, lock, separate, lock, separate.

There were two schools of thought in fencing: those who favoured quick, elaborate footwork and those who favoured the less showy, but faster primacy of the wrist. One used large, elaborately choreographed moves, all about maneuvering, to set up the single killing slash or thrust. The other taught that standing your ground with small, nimble adjustments of the wrist in a semicircle pattern would win the day. Ideally, the two should be combined, but each school had its devotees who advocated forcefully for the inherent superiority of their technique alone. LeMere clearly favoured the first school, Pennywhistle the second, because of the confined spaces on a ship. LeMere moved with panther-like speed and force, but Pennywhistle's wrist was lightning.

Pennywhistle believed each fight had a distinctive beat, rhythm, and flow; it was a martial ballet with two composers. Grasp the instinctive cadence of your opponent and you could confidently anticipate his moves. His intuition had deciphered LeMere's.

LeMere cut at Pennywhistle's head, blocked. Cut at his belly, neatly parried. Side slash to his ribs, expertly deflected. Pennywhistle flowed with his opponent's rhythm, stood his ground, moved his feet not an inch. Pennywhistle's lighter cutlass and fast flicks of the wrist stopped LeMere's heavier blade each time. He cut at LeMere's head and belly; one cut opened a long, shallow gash on his chest.

The unfolding duel transfixed the men of both sides. They were completely quiet, the only cheering done with facial expressions. Dale, as experienced a combat hand as the Royal Navy possessed, knew they were viewing something extraordinary that rarely happened in warfare: anachronistic single combat, each side having its own champion.

LeMere was puzzled. His repeated feints, cuts, thrusts, and lunges had only caused one small wound. He was loath to admit it, but he was tiring. He sweated heavily, his palm grew greasy, and the hot breath of defeat whispered down his neck. These were disagreeable sensations. He had never lost a match in training salon, field of honour, or combat. He was not about to do so now. It was time to throw in his reserves of strength and launch a driving, relentless push against which no opponent could stand.

LeMere had great natural ability; he was well trained and experienced in combat, but he had neglected one crucial element that his marine opponent had not: constant, demanding practice. LeMere was good, but he was no perfectionist. Even great skill atrophied without constant attention. Pennywhistle's obsession with the blade paid off in endurance, timing, and intuition burnished to a brilliantly fine edge.

The Englishman's mind felt clear and vibrant. There was a pang of pleasure; it functioned so adroitly, and his body answered admirably, as it had been schooled to do, like a sound ship conned by a good captain. He formulated a strategy. He would use LeMere's aggression against him. The battle so far had been staid and conventional. It was time to change that. Surprise was the greatest weapon of all. He knew LeMere's pattern, but LeMere did not know the steps were about to change, violently.

*****

Carlotta, Manton, Nico, and Marko were covered in sweat. They had taken an hour to line up fifteen barrels of gunpowder in a row, held in place by spare ship's blocks attached to ropes. The blocks acted as chocks and held the barrels immobile. The plan was to light the fuses, pull the ropes from the side to jerk the blocks away, and let the force of gravity do the rest. None of them had any knowledge of the fuses' burn time, but they trusted that Pennywhistle had known what he was about. The incline was steep and the barrels would gather speed quickly.

Manton guessed they were maybe a third of a mile from the second redoubt. Manton took a deep breath, said a silent prayer, and lit the first barrel with a flint and striker. Nico and Marko pulled the blocks out on one side, Carlotta on the other. The fuse hissed into life, the barrel hung in the air for a fraction of a second, then slowly began its journey down the hill towards a hoped for, but ultimately uncertain destination. The four watched it gather momentum, then quickly began the same process on the second barrel. Only fourteen more to go.

*****

The first two prize ships cleared Lissa and stood out to sea. The other four would soon follow. It had been easy because the British had done most of the work. The French would reap all of the profit.

Dubordieu would count the mission a complete success as soon as all of the prizes were in his possession and sailing for Ancona. He had been dismayed when he'd received a signal that the powder magazine was empty and the dockyard could not be destroyed. Someone on the British side had real foresight. Still, it was a raid, not an invasion, and systematic destruction was only the secondary objective. He would soon sound the recall for LeMere and his marines, reembark them, sail away, then proudly write the dispatches, which he knew the Emperor would have reprinted verbatim in *Le Moniteur*. It would be a significant strategic victory and a propaganda coup of the first order. He would be generous with praise to all, particularly LeMere. The man lived for recognition and praise, and he would receive it from the highest quarters. Dubordieu would be exalted and Hoste would be mortified. Dubordieu might be promoted; Hoste might be relieved of command. Only a few more hours now.

LeMere summoned his deepest reserves of strength and slashed at Pennywhistle's head. *Merde!* He had to win soon! Pennywhistle parried, but to LeMere's practiced eye, the parry was slower than before. Pennywhistle fell back and LeMere lunged with a thrust to the sternum, which was barely cast aside.

It is definite, LeMere thought, *my opponent is tired.* The emboldened Frenchman launched a quick series of slashing attacks to the head, chest, and belly. Pennywhistle parried them enough to prevent harm, but each time seemed to do so with less efficiency. LeMere, the predator, sensed his prey was ripe for the kill. Pennywhistle grimaced and touched his wounded shoulder as if in pain. His sword was at the low guard position, but sagged, as if the weight of it was becoming too much.

He is almost spent! Time to trust to his exquisite sense of combat timing and gamble everything on a killing blow. "You are finished," hissed LeMere with a mixture of triumph and anger.

Amateur! Thought Pennywhistle. *He's never spoken until now. It's a tell. Here it comes!*

LeMere drew his blade back full from the shoulder and shoved all of his reserve energy into a mighty downward slash at Pennywhistle's head.

In a fraction of a second that made an eye blink seem an eternity, everything changed. The gravely wounded animal came fully alive and shot his blade upward against the predator's thrust, not only blocking it, but sending his opponent's sword arm high above his head.

At the moment of LeMere's greatest exposure, Pennywhistle snapped a swift, vicious kick to LeMere's knee. The heel of the Hessian boot connected solidly with LeMere's kneecap and crushed it utterly. It was a technique not from fencing but from Savate, a street fighting system his tutor, du Motier, had said was an improvement on mere boxing. It was definitely not in any catalogue of approved dueling techniques.

LeMere stood transfixed for a second, then dropped like a man whose bones had suddenly turned to dust. As he fell, Pennywhistle shot a short, fast jab at his jaw with the brass clamshell guard of his cutlass. LeMere was out cold by the time he hit the ground.

What happened next was foolish, but a reflexive action. Pennywhistle pinned the prostrate form with his left boot and held the tip of his cutlass to LeMere's throat. He was not so ungallant as to kill an enemy unable to respond, but the animal gesture of dominance came naturally. He wanted to scream his triumph to the heavens, a primal cry of victory, but he could not spare the energy.

His breath came in laboured gasps, his heart thudded, adrenaline-laced blood thundered through his veins, and his mind flooded with the strange, soaring, cruel joy of the conquering warrior. He savoured the moment for what seemed an eternity, although in actual time it was a matter of seconds.

He heard cheers. Something that sounded like a mad jumble of a thousand voices assaulted his hearing; then a huge invisible hand from God-knew-where hurled him to the ground. He heard a thunderclap half a second later; followed immediately by wind and noise.Explosions; where had they come from? Close; very, very close. *Boom, boom, boom!* Not one big one, but many little ones.

Like the kiss from a prince, the explosions broke the trance into which the crowd had fallen. Men recovered themselves and remembered who they were and what they were about. The French seemed uncertain and awaited orders from LeMere that never came. They searched for someone to assume command. The British, however, sprang into action. They had orders and knew what to do.

Dale grabbed the dazed Pennywhistle. "Come on, sir. You won. Let's get out of here. The men are headed to the rally point at redoubt number three."

Pennywhistle saw French soldiers pick LeMere up and gently carry him to safety. His men cared for him and he had made a gallant fight of it. He should have killed him on the spot, he reflected. The man would be back to plague him in the future. Men like that never gave up. But, right now, he had done enough. He slowly followed Dale toward the final rally point. He would reassemble the men and find out who was left. He needed to know the butcher's bill for the night.

Lieutenant Chevalier assumed command and decided withdrawal was the prudent course. He did not know the source of the explosions, but he thought they might well be evidence of more troops hidden and ready to attack. The explosions had come from the rear, perhaps their line of retreat was compromised. LeMere would have known how to proceed, but he did not. At any rate, their mission was accomplished. The dockyard had been captured and the prizes reclaimed. They had done more than they had ever done before and had covered themselves in glory. It was enough for one evening. He reformed the men and marched them back to the boats that had brought them.

Dubordieu congratulated the marines as they reboarded *Uranie*. They had taken heavy losses—forty killed and a slightly greater number wounded. Regrettable, yet the Emperor would see the heavy casualties as evidence of fighting spirit. He had the unconscious LeMere taken to the great cabin. The surgeon set the knee, but it was badly damaged and there was a real danger that gangrene could set in. It would have to be watched, and smelled. Gangrene emitted a foul odor that, once encountered, was never forgotten. At the first sign of gangrene, the leg would have to be amputated. Even if the leg was saved, LeMere would walk with a pronounced limp.

Dubordieu got the squadron underway. By midnight, the four ships, now accompanied by six fine prizes, were clear of Lissa and on their way back to Ancona. They had beaten Hoste at his own game. Dubordieu knew matters between him and Hoste were far from settled, but he had stolen the initiative, and he was not about to yield it.

Forty

Defeat tastes bitter, thought a depressed Pennywhistle. He had done his best; he'd had no right to expect a different outcome, but he had failed. He had never experienced that side of battle before. It left him with a curiously powerful feeling of inadequacy. Still, he would never let it show, and he would maintain an outward face of confidence for the men. At least they had done well.

It was after 10 p.m. Exhaustion showed in the haggard, sunken eyes, grey lips, and powder-blackened faces of the marines and sailors who had determinedly slogged their way back to redoubt number three. Men lay slumped against the walls in various positions of fatigue. They were tired, but not dispirited. Pennywhistle issued them a well-deserved tot of grog, and some sausage, cheese, and bread to go with it. They consumed it hungrily enough, but at the leaden pace of the exhausted.

Pennywhistle and Dale conducted an informal roll call. Out of the sixty who began the fight, forty-five now reported for duty. Ten of those who answered were wounded. Eight would probably recover, but two had wounds that were almost certainly mortal; Blandon with a bayonet cut that lay bare his gently throbbing grey intestines and the excitable Barnes with a bullet wound to the same region. Even the most inexperienced recruit quickly learned that few survived such injuries.

Blandon and Barnes did not cry out, ask for their mothers, or curse God. Barnes bore his wounds in stoical silence. Blandon whispered, "Maria, Maria, Maria," every few minutes. Only the grimaces on their faces betrayed their pain.

The fifteen who had not returned were certainly dead. In the days to come, Pennywhistle would discover their bodies, give them a decent burial, auction any meagre goods they left behind, and forward the funds to any relatives. He would put "DD" after their names on the official rolls; discharged, dead. But Pennywhistle's immediate task was to attend the ones who could be helped.

There was no surgeon to dress their wounds, and the only man present with any knowledge of anatomy was Pennywhistle himself. He had seen the surgeon in action a few times, and his memory of the dissections in Edinburgh was excellent. Seeing to the men gave him a task to perform and moved his mind away from self-recrimination.

The men were grateful.

To Pennywhistle, tending the wounded was concomitant to his duties as an officer and a gentleman who looked after his men. He did it because he was a thoroughly decent chap and he had knowledge no one else possessed. But on a deeper level, the whole thing was an artistic and intellectual challenge to the surgeon he might have been. He had always wondered how things might have worked out but for the duel.

The men were surprised to see another side of the captain they so admired. As a temporary surgeon, he was thorough, methodical, and gentle. While his dressings were a bit on the crude side, they were effective. The men found him as good a doctor as he was a soldier.

The saddest of the wounded was Blandon. Blandon, like MacLeod, had been with Pennywhistle since he came aboard *Active*. He had stayed with his lady, Maria, even though Pennywhistle had been skeptical their love would last. More than that, he lay gravely wounded because he had interposed himself to save Pennywhistle's life. That touched Pennywhistle deeply.

Blandon held his sausage-like, red-grey intestines in with his right hand, his face contorted with the ghastly pallor of fast approaching death. He moaned quietly from time to time, but spoke no words other than to repeat Maria's name. Pennywhistle examined the wound. An idea struck him. If the intestines could be pushed back and the skin sewn up, Blandon might live. It would be like sewing a garment. Perhaps, after all, he might be able to return Blandon's life-giving favour! What an extraordinary and pleasing thing that would be! He had failed today, but by God, maybe he could redeem at least a little of his lost honour.

Carlotta! She had the tools, and there was no particular reason why skin could not be joined together in the manner of a sleeve being attached to a jacket. Granted, it would be grisly, bloody work, but Carlotta was a woman of resolve and grit. He had the anatomist's eye, she the tailor's hands. Damn! It was a fantastic idea, but together, they could do it! But time was short; Blandon was fading. He had to find her and fast. He explained the situation to the ever reliable Dale, who volunteered to bring her. He hoped she had followed his instructions and stayed put at the hunting lodge.

*****

Gordon willed *Active* to go faster. Logically, he realized his wish could have no effect on what was a complex amalgamation of wood, rope, cordage, and canvas. But Gordon was, at heart, a confirmed sentimentalist and saw the ship as *she*. He loved *Active* and mentally whispered to her in the way a man might address a sweetheart. He hoped she was listening. For a second, he had a vision of his own beloved, Lydia, in England.

As if Nature herself lent an ear, the wind began to increase. What had been a light breeze began to deepen into a respectable zephyr. The studding sails would have to be taken in lest they tear, but the other sails drew strongly and fully. Their speed should increase by at least a knot, perhaps two.

Gordon's anxiety did not abate as the journey progressed; rather the reverse, his sense of unease growing stronger as Lissa drew closer. He scanned the horizon with his night glass. Even in the dark, Lissa should be visible any time now as a solid mass against the horizon.

*****

Carlotta and Manton had watched the explosions with satisfaction.

It was hard to tell what damage they had caused. The night was silent now. No more flashes of red stained the moonlit sky. They began cautiously walking toward the town. The moon was full and bright and made things much easier than they would have been on a cloudy night.

They had not proceeded far when they ran into Dale. Dale, infused with the urgency of his message, had left the redoubt at a run. He saw four figures ahead and wondered who might be out on a night like this. Most of the townspeople had taken refuge in homes and cellars. As he closed the distance, he recognized a tall woman and knew the familiar, gangly shape of Manton. He smiled. Luck was with him this night.

Carlotta grabbed Dale in a bear hug of an embrace. She was five inches taller and nearly smothered him. "I am so glad to see you, sergeant! I must have news! My Thomas, is he alive, unhurt?" She was breathless with worry.

Dale was a brave man, but this flummoxed him. The captain's lady hugging him, why it was just not done! But then it came to him. Italians; they were emotional, and they always seemed to want to touch, embrace, or kiss.

"Yes, ma'am," he answered sturdily. "He is unhurt and well. He don't kill easy, ma'am, although plenty of folks have tried. One big French feller tried to best him with a sword tonight. Not a wise idea with Mr. Pennywhistle. But ma'am, he needs you now, real urgent like." He launched into a quick summary of the situation with Private Blandon. "He says he can't do it without you," Dale concluded dramatically.

Carlotta's eyes widened slowly, like rings from a pebble cast into a pond. The whole thing sounded repulsive. But her Thomas needed her and a man's life hung in the balance. It would be a challenge to her stomach, but being of a practical bent, she realized it would be no great test of her skills. She mentally began to detach herself from the unpleasant aspects and reset her mind to view a belly as a torn garment that needed mending. She began to consider what needle, thread, and stitching would work best. Silk thread was expensive, but it was strong, soft, and, most importantly, smooth: easy to remove once the wound had healed. She had heard somewhere that surgeons used it to tie off arteries during amputations. She used it only on the most expensive garments. Even the humblest man's life, however, was worth far more than the most resplendent coat she had ever produced. That had been for Count Belgrano, a mean, conceited man who surely would disapprove of the same quality silk that graced his coat being used to save the life of a mere soldier. Pampered aristocrats with no regard for anyone not in their own class disgusted her.

Dale, Manton, Carlotta, Nico, and Marco lost no time in getting to her shop. She gave quick and specific orders to her children to fetch soft, unbleached cloth and silk thread, and occupied herself with selecting a supply of needles. She had four different sizes, for both coarse and fine work. She was not sure which one was appropriate, but she would find that out soon enough. Before long, she had a large carpetbag filled.

It was time to go. She sent her children down the block to her sister's home. This was something they did not need to see. She was terrified. She prided herself on her skill as a tailor, but that was a matter of professionalism and reputation, never life and death. She thought of her Thomas and relaxed a bit. He would help her. He would know what to do. He always did.

*****

Pennywhistle ate the bread and sausage mindlessly. He could not remember when he'd felt so low. He was too tired to care about food, but he knew the furnace needed fuel. He ate with one hand and used the other to keep pressure on Blandon's stomach to reduce the bleeding. Blandon faded in and out of consciousness, but his condition seemed no worse. Men had been taking turns with the gruesome duty, and he felt it was important for him to take his place in the rotation. He'd held his men together tonight; now he was literally holding a man together.

He pushed aside his despair at the evening's failure and refocused his mind on what lay ahead. He reviewed the dissections from university and pictured the pages from his anatomy text, quietly turning over in his mind. The intestines would have to be placed in their former position and held there before the sewing could begin. He would do that while Carlotta sewed. There was one piece of luck: the intestines were prolapsed, but unpunctured. Blandon had been raked by a bayonet, but the blade had not gone deep enough to tear the intestine. If he survived the operation, absent infection, he might actually recover.

Pennywhistle wondered how to deal with the pain factor. He could try knocking Blandon out with a pistol butt to the head, or give him extra grog until he was insensate, or simply hope he slipped into unconsciousness on his own. An idea occurred to him, but sadly, he lacked the wherewithal to execute it. He wished he had some of the nitrous oxide from Ancona. It would be the perfect solution. He briefly wondered why no one had ever thought of using it as anesthetic.

The men revived somewhat after the food and drink. Stratton and McCarty engaged in a quiet chat about their sweethearts back in Portsmouth. Leicester and Sheffield talked of how they would spend prize money. Pennywhistle knew the mundane small talk was a good sign. Others fixed their attention on Pennywhistle in silent amazement. Most officers would never have bothered with Blandon. They would have just made him comfortable and let the inevitable happen. The men were skeptical of surgeons in general, calling them drunken butchers, which was not far wrong in many cases, but they had an almost superstitious faith in their captain. No matter the predicament, any situation to which he set his hand seemed graced with success.

He saw their expressions and guessed the meaning. He wished he shared their confidence. He marveled at their continued trust in him, given that he had failed them utterly this evening. He told himself Blandon had nothing to lose, but he was nervous, nevertheless. He calmed himself by repeatedly viewing sets of intestines in his mind's eye; position, cant, alignment with other organs.

"Thomas, I am here!" It was the joyful shout of Carlotta, her lilting voice calling him out of his doldrums. She raced towards him with open arms and they embraced with passion, relief, and devotion obvious to all who beheld them. Pennywhistle felt joy and confidence flow into him. But he had a nagging doubt: *Will I save Blandon, or will I kill him?*

Carlotta had exactly the same thought.

Forty-One

Thread, needles, scissors, sheers, awl, and clean unbleached muslin were spread neatly on a white cotton sheet. All tools of the tailor's trade, they were now to be used in performance of the surgeon's art. Unlike most surgeon's tools, the metal implements had been scrubbed clean before use. Carlotta did that because it was simply her habit. Dirty tools sullied expensive fabric. She washed her hands thoroughly as well. Her customers expected beautiful clothing beautifully presented; even a speck of dirt was unacceptable.

She did not know it, but she had already given Blandon a better chance than he would have had at a typical field hospital. Knives and saws were used without cleaning between operations. They might be rinsed with water from time to time or be scraped to free them of clinging gore, but that was it.

Pennywhistle had heard the story that Lord Nelson complained of cold instruments when his shattered arm was amputated after Teneriffe. He'd ordered henceforward that all saws used in amputation be first heated. Remembering this, Pennywhistle heated all of Carlotta's instruments over the fire the soldiers had started. He did not know it, but it had the effect of sterilizing all of her tools. Blandon's chances for survival went up another notch.

Carlotta always thoroughly waxed her thread to facilitate entrance to the needle head. Most surgeons typically used their own saliva, thus introducing a gumbo of bacteria into a wound. The muslin that would be wrapped around Blandon's stomach after the stitches were in place was pristine and spotless. Surgeons in field hospitals routinely reused old cloth from dead patients. Yet another point in

Blandon's favour.

The marines tore a door from a nearby house. They placed it horizontally and gingerly laid Blandon upon it. The door was smooth and finished, far better than the usual field operating table made of recently cut logs. Blandon faced no danger of splinters in his backside. Marines then heaped more wood on the fire so that it blazed higher, a bonfire rather than a campfire. Pennywhistle wanted it as large as possible. Other than the moonlight, it would be the only illumination he and Carlotta would have. The dancing flames bathed the grave assemblage of patient, tailor, officer, and marines in a strange eldritch, flickering light whose eerie glimmers belonged more to the realm of old Norse myth than their own era.

The marines formed a circle around Carlotta, Pennywhistle, and Blandon. The air was heavy with tension, the anxiety almost palpable. Yet there was an air of excitement too, as if they were watching a sporting event. Blandon was like the long shot horse in the Derby at Epsom: not likely to win, but the sentimental favourite of the crowd.

Pennywhistle poured a tiny jot of hundred-fifty proof rum down Blandon's throat. He was only half awake, so it took little of the fiery stuff to send him drifting into complete unconsciousness. Lucky for him, too, that his captain was so moderate. Pennywhistle knew that too much rum given to a person in his condition might induce a sleep from which he would never awaken. As soon as he was out, Pennywhistle stripped off Blandon's shirt. The marine exerting downward pressure on the stomach had to let go.

"Oooohhhhhhhhhhhhh!" the crowd murmured as the wound was fully visible. The jagged gash looked terrible in the murky firelight. The ropey, sausage-like intestines shone with a morbid, grey-red sheen. They pulsated slightly with hopeful life. No stink, no gangrene; a good sign. There was no dirt on the wound. Pennywhistle sprinkled a liberal dose of rum on it to discourage sepsis.

Carlotta's face turned white. She rose, hand to mouth, and raced out of the circle.

Pennywhistle sympathized. The effects of battle were a sight beyond the most wretched imaginings. Poets wrote odes to the glory of battle, but their pens were traitorously silent about the costs.

Carlotta wretched violently for a full minute. As the paroxysms subsided, an insistent voice spoke in her head. "You can do this," it said. "You must do this! Thomas needs you, just follow his instructions. He told you it is a garment to mend, something you are good at. Believe him. You are proud of your craftsmanship. Trust it. Think of flesh as just a piece of fine English wool. Now be about your business!"

Pennywhistle studied her expression as she returned to the circle with a slow, measured tread, the walk of someone who has an unpleasant task ahead, but who is determined to see it through. Her face was white, but it had a fierce resolve.

His voice was gentle. "Carlotta, don't worry about that. It was your body reacting, getting ready. This is new to you, unsettling. Your body merely let you know that. I have seen men wet themselves in battle, yet go on to do their duty. Fear is normal, and it is by our deeds we are judged, not our body's reactions."

The marines nodded, and there were murmurs of approval. They knew it was extraordinary for a woman to be here, even more extraordinary that she was going to try to save one of their mates.

He took Carlotta's hands in his. He squeezed them in a gesture of both affection and reassurance. Their eyes met. He quietly said, "I trust you. We can save this man. Are you ready?"

The words were spoken not much above a whisper, but they were heard by everyone. The men leaned slightly forward to hear her response.

"Yes." She said it calmly and simply. She looked into her man's deep-set green eyes. She thought his angular face handsome, but it was more than that; he radiated calmness and quiet assurance. No wonder the men would follow him anywhere. She knew she could do anything if this fine, deep man believed in her.

"Good," he said. "Let us begin." He had sent two marines to the smithy, hard by the second redoubt, and they had returned with a variety of implements. Pennywhistle selected what he thought best.

They were not quite the Hale's forceps used by Surgeon Swayne, but they were close enough.

He knelt, forceps in his left hand. Private Coldwater pushed the intestines back into place, following his captain's instructions. Pennywhistle hooked the forceps' curved edge on the skin flap and pulled part of it back, so it would not get in the way of the area Carlotta was about to work on. The gash itself was eight inches long, two inches below the navel.

She looked at her hand. It was steady. A marine offered her a cup of wine. She said no, but thanked him. She was afraid but Thomas was right. Fear was natural and could be put aside. She needed no assistance from alcohol. She assessed the wound. She blocked the slowly suppurating blood from her mind. She became a tailor.

She would do the operation in two parts. Pennywhistle would hold the second four-inch section away, while she worked on the first. A Venetian cross stitch would give the greatest strength. She would use her heaviest needles to pin the flesh in place. She had brought an awl as a precaution. She had never worked on human flesh, but she had worked on leather, which was after all, tanned animal skin. If a needle failed to penetrate, she would use the awl. She checked the needles to make sure they were properly waxed to facilitate easy passage.

She said a silent prayer and inserted the first needle. It penetrated easily. Flesh was actually easier to work with than heavy wool. She inserted three more, at one inch intervals. The flesh was joined. Now she had to sew it up. She worked with quiet, methodical precision. She filtered out the rest of the world. Her world was a small patch of flesh, four inches wide. The men watched with awe. Pennywhistle recognized the near-trance state of the deeply focused.

Her stitches were small masterworks of her art: clean, strong, efficient. Her long hands moved back and forth, back and forth, in swift, precise, graceful movements. Following their movements closely, the marine audience were as hypnotised. Time seemed to slow down, but it was actually only a few minutes before she finished the first section. Her practiced, professional eye assessed her work. Very good!

Pennywhistle smiled gently. This was going to work. She smiled back. A wealth of silent communication flashed between them. He released the forceps, and she started work on the second section of the wound. She finished in ten minutes. The stitches held firm, no blood visible. There was no change in Blandon's breathing.

It remained to protect the stitching with a bandage. Two marines lifted Blandon, then Pennywhistle and Carlotta gently wrapped several layers of unbleached muslin around his stomach in a six-inch wide layer, almost as if he were a mummy. The marines laid him quietly on the improvised table.

A collective *ahhhhhhhhhhhhhhh* rose from the crowd. Even the most fatigued managed at least the hint of a smile. The job was done. The next few days would provide the final verdict but, for now, it looked like the patient would survive. A man near death might live to have grandchildren.

Four marines carried the door with Blandon on it to a quiet corner to let him recover. Pennywhistle posted two sentries and ordered the others to get some sleep. He and Carlotta slumped down against the far wall. He put his arm around her and her head rested affectionately on his shoulder. Her eyes fluttered, she smiled, and a second later, was sound asleep. A minute later, Pennywhistle followed.

He had pleasant dreams of sunlit afternoons fishing for trout and salmon on the banks of the River Tweed in Scotland. He was thirteen again, and worried only about his haul of fish for the day. He had a friendly rivalry with his companion, Jackson Gunn, the only son of the chief ghillie on his grandfather's estate. Gunn had his father's unerring instincts for finding the best fishing grounds. Try though he might, he was never quite able to top Gunn's daily catch. He sometimes caught a bigger trout than Gunn, but never as many. Gunn was from a different class than he, technically a servant, but ghillies had a special status on Scots' estates. Not quite family, but much more than ordinary servants, their expert knowledge of hunting, fishing, and stalking game was valued and treated with great respect.

"Hold on tight, Tom, you've got yourself a monster," shouted Gunn.

He had hooked a salmon. It was a big one, and it was putting up jolly fine fight. He felt shaking and was being pulled forward. This one would be quite a prize.

"Sir, Captain Pennywhistle! Wake up! Please, wake up! Pennywhistle awoke with a start to find Spottswood gently shaking his shoulders. He looked anxious. The sun was just peeking over the horizon. He guessed it was after seven. He had slept for a while, and felt noticeably better. The depression had retreated. Carlotta was still asleep. He gently eased her to the ground and let her repose continue.

"I am fearful sorry to disturb you, sir, most sorry! I have orders from the captain to find you and bring you on board. The squadron's in. Let me tell you, everyone is in state of powerful upset. The captain talked to the commodore and he was so upset and mortified that, well, I heard the captain say, tears actually formed in Hoste's eyes. He did not cry really, but he is in quite a bad way. The captain told me to find you at all hazards and bring you aboard directly. He said if any man knows what happened, it would be you. I said I hoped you were still alive. The captain laughed and said Pennywhistle is a deuced hard man to kill—the Devil just isn't ready for him yet. He said just follow the path of destruction and you will find Pennywhistle at the end. I did, and here I am." Spottswood smiled, then his voice filled with real concern. "You are all right, aren't you, sir?"

Pennywhistle nodded. "No more than the usual harvest of cuts, dents, and bruises, Lieutenant. I wish I could say the same for our cause at the moment. We gave them a bloody nose last night, but the truth is, they took the prizes and got clean away. The men and I did our best, but it just wasn't enough. Come on, Lieutenant. Let's go tell the captain the whole sad story."

Forty-Two

Hoste put down the dispatch and began to think. Weeks had passed and the squadron was refreshed and repaired. He had been assigned an extra ship, HMS *Volage*. It was high time something be done. The French had been left to roam free long enough. He would assemble a council of war. He would call it that only in his mind, simply inviting his captains to a relaxed, jovial dinner, but they would understand what it signified. A general design had already begun to form in his head, but he wanted the ideas of his captains. He also was exceedingly curious about the new captain, Phipps Hornsby, and wanted to make the proper introductions. The squadron worked well because there was mutual confidence and trust among the captains. He would let Hornsby learn over dinner what it meant to be part of a band of brothers.

*****

Pennywhistle had reviewed the attack on Lissa many times since it happened. His depression faded as he gradually came to the realization that defeat itself was part of a tempering process every officer had to endure. Sometimes even with the best preparation, a certain outcome was inevitable. What you did with it and how you confronted the future was a test of character. Excessive self-recrimination was both illogical and destructive. But, by God, he wanted another go at the French!

His duties had been light since the raid. He did the routine paperwork, filled out rosters, requisitions, and requests. He conducted daily inspections and drills. He dealt with small infractions of discipline and resumed his earlier routine.

His free time was devoted to two major projects. One was official and had the strong support of Gordon and Hoste. The other was personal and enjoyed the strong support of Pennywhistle's heart. He spent his afternoons sketching the dockyard from various angles and perspectives with a view to devising a plan for future fortifications. He was the closest thing the squadron had to a military engineer, and his drawing talents were well known. Whether the fortifications ever got built and manned was a matter out of his hands, but Pennywhistle enjoyed the challenge to his mental and artistic faculties.

It also conferred the added benefit of allowing him to sleep ashore at the Hunting Lodge. He reported for duty early in the morning, but afternoons were free for his project, and evenings for Carlotta. The lodge became a studio and repository for formal sketches based on the informal ones drawn at the yard, but it also became a place of passion in the evenings and long into the night.

Gordon knew the situation, although he never officially took note of it. Pennywhistle needed the time and space for a vital defense project. He felt that Pennywhistle was a gentleman and whatever a gentleman did with his spare time was his own business, as long as it was done with discretion and did not interfere with duty. The idea of Sea Service officers keeping mistresses was hardly a novelty.

A ship was a small community and a difficult place to keep secrets. The men knew, and rather than resenting or envying Pennywhistle, they admired his taste in beauty and character. The story of Carlotta saving Blandon's life spread like wildfire throughout the ship and earned her a special place in the men's hearts. Plenty of civilians thought sailors and marines the detritus of society, thoroughgoing reprobates who, while useful, were to be avoided whenever possible. Many civilians only interacted with sailors to bubble them out of their cash. "Spending like a drunken sailor," was not an idle phrase. Sailors did not often have cash and coin but when they did, they usually did not have it for long. For all of their roughness and bravery, sailors and marines were like small children in many ways. Gestures like Carlotta's touched them deeply, because they were so rare. Any man on the ship who spoke ill of Carlotta—but none did—would have found himself facing an angry mob very quickly.

Carlotta and Pennywhistle's passion for each other grew. Love-making was sometimes frenzied and impetuous, but more often was long, deep, and leisurely. Lust gradually began to take second place to an emotion they cheerfully deluded themselves into believing was merely a general accretion of affection, care, and sentiment. Neither dared speak the real word, lest uttering it burst the fragile spell they had woven for themselves. Love frightened them. It seemed to both that love was like ghosts and saints: lots of people talked about them, but no one had personally met them.

Carlotta had had a stable but passionless marriage, and her husband had been the only partner she had ever known before himself. Pennywhistle understood the powerful feelings she had for him were as new to her as they were to him. He had enjoyed his share of ladies, and while it could be said he had some feelings for all of them, none had really touched his heart. Women were beautiful but confusing creatures with strange moods that shifted like unpredictable tides; full of capricious demands, some of them unvoiced, to a man's greater confusion, and enough emotional baggage to fill the hold of a ship of the line.

Carlotta was different. Nothing seemed forced, studied, or planned. Everything about her was natural, easy, and direct, which outflanked every emotional defense in Pennywhistle's heart. She seemed to anticipate his thoughts, words, and needs with a facility that both startled and amused him. She had even gotten him to smile more, although he continued to be hopeless at telling jokes.

She was ten years older than he, with two children and a business of her own. She had roots on the island. He was a sea-going gypsy, a warrior of the waves, and never long in one place. Unlike his brother, who had a family and children in their ancestral home in Berwick, Pennywhistle was not sure if he was ready for an anchored life. Part of him rebelled against the prospect, yet a certain portion of him craved the emotional security it promised.

A shadow hung over their romance. A battle was coming, a

decisive one which might see his end. Even if he survived, the war would eventually move on, leaving Lissa behind. Part of him wanted the battle very badly; another part wished his time with Carlotta would continue forever. But whatever his personal conflicts, he knew that, until Bonaparte was overthrown, his first duty was to his country.

They tried to avoid discussing the future of their romance. When hints of uncertain shoals ahead surfaced in conversation, it usually led in short order to frenzied and desperate lovemaking, as if passion could make the world stand still. Or even better, drive it away entirely.

*****

Hoste's dinner for the new captain was a splendid success. Phipps Hornsby was young, voluble, and eager, with a singular wit and a quick mind. He laughed with Gordon and charmed even the taciturn Whitby. He had a gift for the elegant phrase, but like Hoste, could speak plainly and bluntly when circumstances dictated. Two hours of a wonderful dinner of turkey, ham, and sea pie transformed him from an outsider into a full-fledged member of the band of brothers, as if he had always been there and always would.

At the end of the meal, Hoste addressed his officers. "Gentleman, I fear I must now veer away from the agreeable matters upon which we have discoursed these last very pleasant hours and set a course to matters professional. I have a proposal to make. I think you will find it bold, and it is not without elements of risk, but I do not think it foolhardy. Let me explain it, then I would trouble you for your comments and recommendations."

The three captains, spirits boosted by generous amounts of spirits, said, almost in unison, "Hear, hear!" They knew the dinner was merely a sumptuous prelude to the real event of the day, and here it was.

"Gentlemen," said Hoste with a weary sincerity, "I am heartily sorry for the debacle of the dockyard. I can do nothing to change the past, but I can direct the future. A reverse should not make us timid;

nay, it should serve to fuel our boldness. Our opponent expects us to mope and assume a cautious course of action. We must do the opposite. Now that I have four ships, I am prepared to risk a decisive battle. But I want Dubordieu to believe that the battle is his choice, not ours.

"What I propose is this. We split our forces to perplex him. I know it seems folly to divide inferior forces in the face of a superior one, but it is the best use of our resources. *Amphion* and *Volage* will seek future prizes in the Gulf of Trieste, while *Active* and *Cerberus* take back some of the prizes we lost. Four of the prizes are in Pestichi. They are defended, but only against large ships.

I propose a night cutting out expedition, using only the boats from *Active* and *Cerberus*. If a moonless night is chosen and the oars are muffled, we can achieve surprise and be back at sea before they muster. It would redeem much of the humiliation we have suffered, and it would anger Dubordieu. Four ships, two seizing new prizes and two reclaiming old, will push him. He will steer for Lissa, but this time he will not come after our base, he will come after our ships. I am guessing Bonaparte will have given him reinforcements after his recent success. He will think himself ready. But we will also be ready. This time when he comes, we will be there to give him a proper reception." Hoste stopped and looked at the faces at the table. All three were silent, all making calculations about the plan and their ship's role in it.

After a long minute of silence, Gordon opined, "It has its risks, Commodore, but in general, I think it is an excellent plan. My only question is, when would the divided squadron reassemble at Lissa?"

Hoste replied, "Three weeks to the day after we sail. That should give us plenty of time to take prizes and enough time to let our depredations fully impress themselves on the mind of our esteemed opponent."

The reserved, studious Whitby asked, "When would you want our ships ready to sail?"

Hoste answered decisively, "In one week's time."

Forty-Three

The dark grey sea was surly. Hills of water rose sharply. Dense banks of cloud and a persistent, low-hanging canopy of fog blotted out the moon and stars. An annoying mist dampened everything it touched and extinguished the last hint of light. The cutters rolled precipitously as mountainous waves threatened to overwhelm them—a bad night to be out for those with queasy stomachs and a regard for personal safety. The perfect night for a cutting out expedition.

Pennywhistle gingerly negotiated the rope ladder down *Active's* hull. The tumblehome of the hull was steep, and spray made the steps slippery. It would be easy to lose one's footing and fall into the cold, clutching water. That would not only be dangerous, it would be a blow to his dignity. The cutter showed a lantern, which would be extinguished directly when they put to sea. He looked over his shoulder as he descended, using the glowing lantern as his destination. As the commanding officer of the expedition, he was the last to board.

The men waited patiently, silently. They had been well and carefully briefed about targets, tactics, schedules, passwords, and countersigns. Danger lay ahead, but so did the prospect of good prize money. Moreover, revenge was always sweet. They would steal back from Johnny Crapaud what Johnny Crapaud had stolen back from them.

The men had the usual sort of pre-battle thoughts. A boatswain's mate mentally rehearsed his drill with the boarding pike. An experienced able seaman worried about the heavy chop. A very new recruit, still classed as a landsman, had never seen action and wondered how he would bear up.

Four boats assembled from *Active*. Another four would join from *Cerberus*. Eight boats targeted against four ships; two boats for each ship. One boat would approach starboard side aft; its companion, larboard side forward. The plan was to create a crossfire if circumstances permitted, cut the anchor cables, bow and stern, then swiftly put to sea. The hearty breeze would facilitate their exit. Surprise was their best ally; no one would be expecting action on a filthy night like this.

The four ships, *Harfleur*, *Valmy*, *Marie et Jeanne*, and *Frere Francois*, lay four miles distant. It was unlikely they would be heavily manned, but they lay under the guns of shore batteries mounting 12-pounders. However, on a night like this, the weather would mute most noise, and even if they were detected, a solid target would be difficult for the gunners to locate.

As an added precaution, to keep the silhouette of the boats low, no sails would be used. The way out would all be done by rowing, then the empty boats would be towed back by the prizes. To keep sailors fresh, rowers would be changed halfway. The boarders needed to be active and quick. The plan was for *Cerberus* to target *Harfleur* and *Valmy*, while *Active's* boats aimed for *Marie et Jeanne* and *Frere Francois*.

Pennywhistle commanded one cutter, Spottswood the second, Moore the third, and Meers the fourth. Each contained eighteen men, giving thirty-six to man each prize. As Pennywhistle assumed his position near the tiller, lanterns on the boats from *Cerberus* several hundred yards to port, uncovered, then covered, three times in quick succession. The boats from *Active* responded with a similar signal. Then all of the lanterns were doused. The course had been worked out in advance. They would steer by compass since the night cloaked all reference points. Pennywhistle ordered a weapons check. He wanted to ensure muskets stayed unloaded, lest an accidental discharge give the alarm. Cutlasses and bayonets would be the weapons of choice. In case the boats got separated, the password and countersign were reviewed; "Britannia," being the first, "Caledonia," the second.

"Shove off! Oars out! Give way all!" Pennywhistle issued the commands and the mission got underway. The sailors rowed in steady, familiar rhythm, although the rough, heaving seas made that difficult. The landsman mentally reassured himself; *You can do this, calm down, Mr. Pennywhistle knows what he is about. He believes in you.*

This was Pennywhistle's first action since Lissa, and it felt good to be back adventuring against the French. He reviewed his plans, then allowed his mind to drift back two weeks to his final night with Carlotta.

*****

Their love-making had been poignant and languorous, as if it might be their final tryst. They savoured each other in the manner you would the last bite of a fine soufflé, if you knew you might never have another. They had only a few hours until dawn before he had to report to the ship. He told Carlotta no details of the upcoming mission and made light of it, but his very attempt at levity told Carlotta the situation was serious. She wished he would stop trying to shield her from danger, from knowledge.

"You will take care of yourself, Thomas, not take any unnecessary risk, will you promise me that?" she asked plaintively.

"I promise you, I will be the most cautious man in Christendom," he said with a somewhat forced joviality. Carlotta noticed he had switched from his usual French back to English. That always told her he was worried.

"But now you mock me, Thomas. I think that I should make no demands, but I want you to come back to me. I have had you for so little time, I could not stand to lose you. I fear to look too deeply into the distant future. But I want what we have to continue as long as possible." Her expression was one of naked earnestness.

Pennywhistle turned serious. "I would never mock you, my dear, I just do not want you to be consumed with worry. I will take care of myself, that I promise; but I would never do anything that would compromise the safety of the ship, my men, or my duty. I could tell you otherwise, but you know me too well to believe that lie. The immutable fact is my business is about risk and danger. I sometimes have to hazard my own life to protect the lives of those I care about. If I suddenly became the comfortable shop keeper, the safe, solid citizen, I should cease to be the man with whom you have fallen in love." A second after he said it, he regretted it. He had uttered the dread word: love.

Carlotta sighed and tears formed at the corner of her eyes. "Yes," she said in a whisper, "I do love you."

Pennywhistle frowned. Now he had done it! This was not a conversation he wanted to be having the night before shipping out on an important mission. He needed his mind clear and unfettered by *affaires de coeur,* since *affaires de guerre* demanded all of his mental and emotional resources. But as he looked at her sad face, the steel portcullis that guarded the doorway to his heart unexpectedly retracted with blinding speed as if it had never been there at all. He was naked. His brain froze in confusion and shouted, *What happened?* No answer came, but he didn't care.

Instead, he felt a torrent of warmth flood his heart, his brain, and the very fibre of his being. He had no prior experience with the emotion of love, but whatever he was feeling was glorious. The best he could do was hark back to his university days, reading Shakespeare's sonnets; that was a great poet's musings, the realm of intellect and the mere echo of passion; this was reality. Beautiful, passionate, soaring, illogical, messy reality. He had been infatuated with his first woman, felt affection and lust for many of the ladies he had known carnally, but nothing like this. This was deeper and more passionate, and at the same time, kinder, gentler, graced with real spiritual beauty. To his analytical mind, it made absolutely no sense. But exactly because his mind could not dissect and catalog it, his heart eagerly embraced it with the totality of its being. This was the ecstacy and exaltation of love, the thing poets spoke about. He who prided himself on his cold rationality felt this rush of irrationality make his heart quiver with joy and his mind quiver with fear. It also made his tongue unnaturally brave.

He realized he had been lost in thought and internal debate for some minutes. Carlotta's cheeks were covered with silent tears. She looked at him with anxious expectancy. He made his decision and said calmly, "I love you, too. I think I have known for some time, but I could never voice it until now. Your actions over the past few weeks have been so selfless, they caused me to accept something I never could before; that real love from a woman does actually exist and just might have a place in my life."

His green eyes were radiant, not with their usual fire, but with a gentle reassuring glow akin to a comforting beacon from an emotional lighthouse. Carlotta felt a great wave of peace wash over her as she looked into them. She knew safe harbour lay ahead.

"How could I not love you?" he said with quiet passion. "Sending the barrels down the hill saved my life and those of many of my men. But more than that, after we lost the prize ships, I began to doubt myself. I simply could not accept defeat. I had never been beaten. I felt the approach of the 'black dog' that was the curse of my father. I sensed benighted heredity calling forth melancholia to destroy my soul.

"You did not run, as so many women would have. You were my Gibraltar. You pitted love against sadness, knowing love was stronger. You comforted me, soothed me, and took away my pain. You listened in a way no one else ever had. You filled up the empty spaces in my spirit and brought me back from a very dark place. You redeemed me with your body and your grace. You were…" he groped for the right words, then smiled, "an angel sent by heaven." He gently took her hands in his.

Carlotta smiled an uncertain smile, as if she heard something she wished for deeply but could not quite credit. "Thomas, I have longed to hear you say 'I love you' since our first night together. But are you sure? You are not just saying this to comfort me when you must go to sea?"

"No, my dear," said Pennywhistle with deliberation. "I have never said those words to anyone, never expected to say them. I am not even sure why I said them just now. My own heart has always been a mystery to me. But I have never been more sincere in my life."

She slowly smiled a profound expression of joy that lit the predawn sky like a bursting supernova. "That is wonderful, wonderful, Thomas! But what shall we do? What is to become of us?"

He smiled. "If I could answer that in detail, I would be adjudged the greatest philosopher and seer in Europe. I know you care for me, but you must acknowledge I am hardly that!"

She turned serious and spoke with quiet resolve, "*Cara mia*, I will not burden you now with talk of the future, since you have enough to worry about. I do not want you to be distracted and make a mistake. I just need to know we will speak of it when you return. Please notice, I said *when* you return, not *if*. I cannot believe that whatever God rules in Heaven would be so uncaring and uncharitable as to frown on and cut short our love."

He took her in his arms and kissed her slowly. He pulled slowly back and looked into her deep green eyes. "I will return to you, my dear. I treat those words as a sacred oath."

Carlotta cried tears of joy. She threw her arms around him, and they held each other, never wanting to let go.

*****

A strong wave assaulted the bow and jolted Pennywhistle back to reality. He mentally batted away thoughts of peace and love and reminded himself he was on a mission of war. Happiness lay hundreds of miles away over the horizon; the mission, two miles dead ahead.

He checked his compass and mentally reviewed the course. "Helm, a point to larboard." The helmsman nodded and silently complied. "Rowers, second watch." New rowers took over the oars while the old ones made preparations for boarding.

The cutters glided swiftly and silently through the waves. The fog began to dissipate. He took up his night glass and found he could at least discern vague shapes up ahead, including the masts of four ships. They were carelessly anchored in line ahead formation. His recognized his target, *Marie et Jeanne,* by its rig and position in line. Spottswood's *Frere Francois* was two hundred yards directly astern.

Spottswood, in cutter two, was excited. This was his first cutting out expedition. His wished his father could see him. His father, for all of his gambling on various fanciful shipping enterprises, had never been willing to hazard a farthing on his own son. Captain Pennywhistle was willing to trust him with his life, and the responsibilities of an officer.

He decided then and there that life offers you two families: the one into which you are born and the one your choices in life select for you. One was hereditary, of unpredictable merit, without choice. The other sprang from an affinity of spirit, the attraction of merit, and the conscious exercise of free will. One was passive, one active. Nelson had wanted a band of brothers. Spottswood liked that. Pennywhistle had become the older brother he never had.

The cutters ploughed on through the night seas in relentless purpose. The whitecaps subsided, as did the chop, and the breeze dropped slightly. Three quarters of a mile to go to target. Pennywhistle made final preparations.

Forty-Four

Pennywhistle heaved a sigh of relief when the fog vanished entirely as the boats approached their targets. The bulk of each ship stood out as a muted silhouette against night sky. Small lanterns shone at the stern of each ship for navigational safety, as the ships were bunched closely together. None would have been lit had an attack been anticipated. They were very useful to the cutters as homing beacons.

The ropes binding the boats together were retracted. Each cutter altered course for its attack station. Sailors checked grappling hooks, rope ladders, cutlasses, and bayonets. Seamen readied boathooks and ropes.

Boathooks would be used to grab the hull of the ship and pull the cutters alongside, ropes would be used to lash the cutters to the ship. Once the boats were secured, the climb up the tumblehome would begin. With luck, it would be in stealth. Without, it would be in naked exposure. Once the climb began, the British were committed. There would be no going back. "Victory or death," was a hackneyed, overblown phrase, but sometimes completely applicable. This was one of those times.

The boats from *Cerberus* increased their rowing speed and passed those of *Active*, as their targets lay astern. Pennywhistle's cutter made for the larboard side of forecastle, while its companion, under Moore, steered for the larboard side aft, the ship's quarterdeck its target. Spottswood's and Meer's boats continued on to the next ship, *Frere Francois*, and would use the same tactical plan.

Pennywhistle was by far the tallest man in the cutter, with the longest reach. He would heave the grapnels—not normally an officer's task, but his practicality outweighed any adherence to established protocol. When all was said and done, only success counted.

No alarm had been sounded. If someone was on lookout, he was lackadaisical. The oars were retraced and the boat glided the last hundred yards, sylph-like and silent. An able seaman extended the boathook and held it steady. Thirty feet to go. A sailor stood by with binding ropes.

Twenty feet. Pennywhistle made sure his cutlass and scabbard were secure. They hung from a frog worn on a shoulder strap, rather than around the waist. It would keep the weapon tight against his body, free his hands, and ensure the scabbard did not interfere with his legs; an admirable arrangement for climbing.

Ten feet. The mass of the ship loomed like a leviathan out of the darkness. The coxswain held the tiller steady.

Thunk! The boathook thudded into the hull. A well-muscled sailor gave a mighty tug and the cutter was pulled hard against *Marie et Jeanne*. Two sailors lashed the cutter to her side with a grapnel and rope. The cutter bobbed slightly, but was as steady as she would ever be.

Pennywhistle seized the first grapnel and focused on the forecastle ten feet straight up. He aimed for a spot just abaft of the cathead and whipped the iron-spiked rope in quick circular motions to build momentum. Now! He let it fly.

The grapnel's iron-fluked head arced over the boarding nettings and landed on the deck with a slight *kerchunk*. Pennywhistle pulled hard on it and the iron head hooked itself firmly against the ship's hull. The line was taut. He repeated the process with the second grapnel and was rewarded with equal success.

He cupped his palms firmly on the rope and began the climb. Dale began a similar climb on the second rope: slow, steady, hand over hand, legs twined around the rope, bunching upwards like human caterpillars.

The men watched intently. Their progress seemed agonizingly

slow to the sailors in the cutter, but Pennywhistle and Dale actually moved with the speed of strength.

A foot to go. Pennywhistle paused for a second and listened. No noise, no alarm. Good. He continued. His hands gripped the boarding netting, and he curled himself onto the deck. He stood, drew his cutlass, and scanned the deck. He had no customers for his blade, at least not yet. Dale joined him seconds later. Pennywhistle removed the rope ladder he had strapped to his back. He anchored it firmly on the deck, then threw it over the side. The force of gravity did the rest. Sailors gratefully grabbed the ladder and began to climb.

The new landsman was surprised at his own eagerness and was first out of the cutter. He moved faster than he ever would have believed himself capable and was well pleased with how it was all working out.

Pennywhistle waited in suspense as the men climbed. This was the most exposed part of the mission. Men climbing were supremely vulnerable to attack. If they could just gain the deck! Fortune smiled. The men ascended the deck without incident. Lieutenant Moore arrived with the port boarding party. They were secure aboard.

"*Allors, allors!*" Drunken shouts came from the waist of the ship. A few confused, sleepy looking French sailors shambled uncertainly onto the deck. Someone had given the alarm. There were not more than twenty of them and they appeared to be under no coherent control. They wielded boarding pikes and cutlasses, but from the way they held them, Pennywhistle could tell they were not schooled in their use. They could be disposed of quickly.

Pennywhistle's topmen scurried up the fore and mizzen ratlines like a pack of crazed spiders. Two veteran topmen, old for their jobs at thirty, gleefully raced each other skyward, piles of prize money dancing in their imaginations. Groups of topmen moved quickly sideways along the footropes, cut the gaskets holding fore and main top sails to the yards and allowed the force of gravity to drop them toward the deck. Sailors on the deck sheeted the sails home, hauling back on ropes at the edges of the sails to secure them to wooden deck bollards.

Two burly sailors from Pennywhistle's party chopped through the forward anchor cable with tomahawks. Two others from Moore's boat did the same on the rear anchor cable. The ship drifted with the current for a moment, then the sails caught and the ship started to make real headway.

"Marines, cold steel, charge!" yelled Pennywhistle. He was pleased to see a fully recovered Blandon in the front rank, running full tilt at the enemy. The marines screamed like demons and made straight for the disorganized French, who did what any sensible people would do when faced by a dark line of angry men with hungry bayonets: they threw down their weapons and surrendered. The marines converted their death charge to a flank-and-seize maneuver and quickly hustled them below decks. Dale posted Stratton and McCarthy as guards. These French would cause no further trouble tonight. Later, they would be enticed to join the British Navy. There was a distinct possibility some would accept. These were merchant sailors, after all, not sailors from the regular French navy, bound by oaths of loyalty. Because crews were much smaller, merchant sailors' duties were often much more onerous than those in the regular navy.

With the French crew under control, Pennywhistle took the wheel himself, alongside the quartermaster. It pleased him to practice skills he had read about. He steered a course back the way they had come. A fine action with no casualties; he would use the word "uneventful" in his report. He hoped the same was true on the other ships.

But it had not been the same on *Frere Francois.* Peter Spottswood was in the fight of his life.

Unlike *Marie et Jeanne,* the Captain of *Frere Francois* was an ex-Navy officer who took words like "security," "lookout," and "safety" seriously. His lookout spied Spottswood's boat before it came alongside and frantically rang the ship's bell.

With surprise gone and the enemy roused, Spottswood would have been well within the dictates of reason and command judgment to sheer off and abandon his attack. A roused, combative, fully-armed crew firing downward on men precariously gripping ropes would be many sailors' idea of suicide. Spottswood entertained the idea of retreat briefly. He was flat out scared, not just for himself, but for his men. Pennywhistle had taught him to never hazard their lives unwisely. Was this a calculated risk, or a reckless one? He asked himself what Pennywhistle would do.

Spottswood remembered his remark that a bad decision immediately taken was still better than a good one long after the situation had spun out of control. Spottswood banked on two things, the speed and ferocity of his attack, and the fact that he was not alone: the other boat was about to assault the French from the rear. The French were alerted, but it was still hard to see at night. The sailors would be fast moving, indistinct shapes.

"Heave the grapnels!" Spottswood leaped from the boat, thudded against the side, and scrambled frantically upward, using the handholds on the entry port steps. The grapnels took hold and he grabbed a rope. Bullets whizzed past his nose, sweat streamed down his face, and angry men shouted at him. This was chaos, but real command; leading from the front, utterly alone and exposed. Damn, his blood was up and racing!

He targeted a French pikeman above and turned the energy of fright into the energy of the climb. Adrenaline increased his coordination and his limbs moved in perfect synchronization. He rocketed up the rope like a starving monkey assaulting a coconut tree. There was no time to unfurl the rope ladder on his back. Sailors and marines followed directly beneath, knowing their one chance was to get aboard as rapidly as possible. Hesitation meant death. Bullets hit one sailor in the chest and one marine in the head. They dropped into the sea with cries that ended with splashes that swallowed their voices. They were ignored. The frenzied climb continued.

Spottswood's fingers scrabbled a hold on the chains, but he found himself staring up at an angry six-foot sailor with a boarding pike aimed at the top of his head. The powerful arms raised the pike to strike. Spottswood grabbed the sailor's ankle with his right hand, the only portion of body he could reach. He gripped the ankle with the strength of a hungry dog seizing a new bone and yanked with all his strength. The violent motion upended the man, who landed heavily on his back. The kinetic energy actually caused him to bounce up and over Spottswood into the sea.

Spottswood hoisted himself roughly aboard the chain-plates, stood up, and drew his sword. "Come on!" he yelled, and waved the men upward. If he could just hold the chains long enough for his men to get aboard, they had a chance. A French sailor thrust a cutlass at Spottswood's chest, so close he could smell a fetid odor emanating from the man's trousers. God, the man's bowels had let fly! It put strange heart into him; the man was far more terrified then he was!

Spottswood moved sideways a fraction of an inch and the blade shot by. Spottswood thrust his own cutlass into a sailor's belly. He wrenched the blade free, then parried another cut by a second sailor. With his left hand, he yanked a pistol from his sash and smashed the heavy calibre piece directly into the sailor's nose, breaking cartilage. Spottswood pulled the trigger. The man's face exploded, leaving a smoking black abyss that was unrecognizable as human, and he fell backwards into the night.

More men joined him on the chains. The fight grew more equal. It was cutlass against cutlass, cutlass against bayonet, cutlass against boarding pike. There was no art to this; this was close range, toe-to-toe butchery. It was slash, cut, thrust in rapid succession, and then again, and again. There was no retreat, no quarter. A sailor of *Active* severed the arm of a sailor from *Frere Francois* with his cutlass. A seaman of *Frere Francois* buried his tomahawk in the stomach of a marine of *Active*. Another marine blocked a boarding pike and rammed his bayonet through the chest of a snarling sailor.

Men became berserkers, maddened by primitive bloodlust run amok. Men died ghastly deaths on both sides, arms severed, guts disemboweled, faces slashed, but Spottswood finally made it to the main deck. "Follow me!" he yelled. Marines and sailors did just that.

The French retreated, but slowly. A tall, horse-faced officer slashed at Spottswood, who parried it aside. He had no way of knowing it was former *Capitaine de frigate* DuTeil of the French Navy. DuTeil recovered quickly and made an expert thrust at Spottswood's head, missing narrowly. Spottswood quickly noted from the speed and angle of the thrust that this man was an expert swordsman. Spottswood was brave, but had no great skill with the blade. He was outmatched and would lose unless he acted quickly. Pennywhistle's voice flashed through his skull: *Do the unexpected; don't worry about pleasing your fencing master.*

Spottswood's blade slashed down. He did not aim at the chest, belly, or thigh, but thrust his blade directly through the man's shoe. It penetrated fully and temporarily pinned DuTeil to the deck. The Frenchman cried out in agony, bent over, and lurched forward. At that moment, a roll of the deck caused his good foot to lose his balance and he fell forward.

"Huzzah, Huzzah! Huzzah!" Three mighty cheers arose at the stern of the ship. It was the other boarding party. Meers was late, but most welcome. Men with cutlasses and boarding pikes surged forward. The rear attack completely unmanned the French. The battle had hung in the balance, but this new attack tipped it entirely in favour of the British. In an instant, armed resistance changed to supine surrender.

Spottswood took a good look at the epaulettes of the officer he had knocked down. It had to be the Captain. The Frenchman's face was a mixture of disbelief and confusion. Spottswood held his blade a fraction of an inch from the officer's throat.

"The play, sir, is over. Surrender, monsieur."

The officer looked up with an expression of great fatigue. "I am Captain DuTeil and regret to say, my sword is yours, monsieur." A moment after he finished, he lapsed into unconsciousness.

Spottswood picked up the sword gingerly and marveled at the elaborate gold and silver inlay in its hilt. The sword was priceless to him, not because of precious metals, but because of what it symbolized.

He was elated. He had gambled with everything, but he had made the right choice. In a moment of crisis, he had not hesitated and the men had followed him. Pennywhistle had been right. Men wanted leadership above all else. He felt a justifiable surge of pride. He had the greatest prize of all: command. The ship was his!

Forty-Five

Hoste threw away his pen in anger and frustration and abandoned the letter to his father. Try as he might, he could not paint an optimistic picture of the situation. Oh, he could dress it up enough to fool the Parson, but he was really writing the letter to the surrogate father who existed in his head: Nelson. Given his record, many would have thought he should be proud and content. His superiors were pleased. In the four months since the destruction of the powder at Ancona, Hoste's squadron had continued to take prizes, make night raids on enemy shore installations, and acted a plague on French interests in the Adriatic.

But Hoste was dejected, puzzled, and uncertain. He felt his achievements superficial. True, the French were constantly off balance, but he had not yet provoked the decisive battle he so earnestly sought. He thought he had the measure of Dubordieu, a brave antagonist who responded to provocations; why had he not come again? The general engagement should have happened weeks ago. How much more would it take to push him over the edge?

Hoste knew Dubordieu's target. What he did not know was from what direction Dubordieu would appear, and in what strength. He despaired of his strategy of insistent provocation ever bearing fruit. He had no idea what else to try. He could only wait and maintain a vigilant lookout.

His squadron was at peak efficiency. The crews were battle-tested and had absolute confidence in their officers and Hoste. The captains worked well together. Not only was each ship a model of teamwork, so was the squadron as a whole. He could not have asked for a better group of men or ships to command. He had a sentimental streak, like Nelson, and each time he reflected on the deep honour he had been vouchsafed, his eyes moistened ever so slightly. His men were worthy, his ships sound, his cause just. The only problem at present was *Cerberus*. Her crew had been siphoned off to man several prizes, and she was ninety men under full compliment. Whitby adapted, but Hoste hoped replacements would arrive soon.

He crumpled the letter and decided to go on deck. It was a beautiful, sunny day and it seemed a shame to squander it fretting about matters he could not change. Besides, it did his spirit good to see the ship and her crew going about their business. It reinforced his confidence about the final result of any future engagement.

Hoste's assessment of Dubordieu was more accurate than he could have known. Dubordieu was indeed planning an attack, and the target was Lissa. Unforeseen developments in Paris had conspired to delay the start of Dubordieu's attack, which had frustrated him considerably. His exasperation, however, had been appeased when a sudden, massive increase in men, cannon, and ships was put at his command.

Napoleon had decided to invade Russia. This was a closely guarded secret, save to his closest confidants. It would be the greatest, most logistically complicated invasion in history, but Napoleon was determined to extend his empire eastwards, and he had his eye out for anything that could threaten his grand campaign. He repeatedly said soldiers could always fight men, but never empty stomachs. If those stomachs were kept empty by interrupted victuals, the whole design of the campaign would be disrupted, perhaps fatally so. The British in the Adriatic were perfectly positioned to execute spoiling expeditions against exposed supply lines stretching back to Paris. The Adriatic was no longer a sideshow theatre, but a critical one.

It puzzled Dubordieu that Paris was suddenly so eager to help, but he was grateful. He knew Napoleon wanted a victory, and badly, that was nothing new; but this time, everything necessary for a victory was suddenly forthcoming. There was no foot dragging, no delays, and no incessant demands for tedious reports. He had but to ask and it was given. He decided it was pointless to try to guess Napoleon's intentions; the man was as smart as a scholar, as cunning as a fox, and as devious as a snake.

He decided he would take extra time to get things absolutely right. He wanted this blow to fall with the force of Thor's hammer. He restrained his urge to strike quickly and went meticulously about bringing his forces to a high standard of efficiency. He understood Hoste's provocations, but decided delay would actually work to increase Hoste's uncertainty. Let the Englishman worry and wonder!

Dubordieu would be thorough. This time the result would be decisive and permanent. This time he and his men would return covered in laurels and glory.

He was pleased by his promotion. He liked to think it was for merit, but he knew his subtle manipulation of LeMere, who had Napoleon's ear, had facilitated it. On the other hand, LeMere had been advanced two ranks to colonel, which only inflamed LeMere's already outsize ambitions.

Colonel Marcus Gifflinga had recently arrived at Ancona with a full battalion of troops. They came accompanied by a large and impressive artillery train. They would form the garrison of Lissa after the naval victory and discourage any future British attempts to retake the place.

Gifflinga, a battled-scarred veteran, was not pleased when Dubordeiu informed him his troops were to be employed as sea-going infantry until Lissa had been captured. Gifflinga and his men had no knowledge or experience of salt water. Gifflinga felt it beneath their dignity and said they should be preserved as a unit for the greater task of providing an unassailable garrison.

But, newly minted Colonel LeMere, now back to duty but with a marked limp, convinced Gifflinga to see things Dubordieu's way. Since he was now Gifflinga's equal in rank, he held nothing back. He used his best oratorical appeals to patriotism, glory, and honour to prevail. He strongly implied that since the naval victory was a virtual certainty, it would be a shame for Gifflinga's men not to share in the glory. LeMere said they would be French versions of the

English Henry V spoke of in his Crispin's Day speech: "Gentlemen in England now abed shall think themselves accursed they were not here."

LeMere reposed much greater confidence in his trained marines than in Gifflinga's men, but this was to be a knockout blow and anything that added to the strength of the punch was welcome. LeMere was even more eager for a victory than Dubordieu. The British had lamed him; he detested being referred to as a "gimp." The leg pained him greatly, but he masked the pain, lest his men see weakness. He had some measure of revenge: promotion to colonel. But he needed real revenge: a great victory due in great part to his efforts. It would be LeMere's personal Last Judgment against the British in general, and that man Pennywhistle in particular. His thoughts were uncharacteristically bitter, and he realized he had lost objectivity. It was personal now. He would make his own pain their pain, Pennywhistle's pain.

Dubordieu decided that, rather than give the British patrols an opportunity to spot him by sailing directly to Lissa, he would use the island of Lisessa, twenty miles distant from Lissa, as the staging area from which he would launch his final attack. The island had a harbour large enough to shelter his fleet and, best of all, gun emplacements that commanded the anchorage and would make any British attack extremely costly.

He reviewed his armada from the quarterdeck of *Favourite*. It was formidable, consisting of seven major ships and several smaller gunboats and xebecs. The squadron encompassed two hundred and eighty-four guns and two thousand and seven hundred men. Careful reconnaissance informed him he was opposed by four major ships, with one hundred and fifty-six guns and nine hundred men. Napoleon's largesse meant Dubordieu would enjoy a nearly two to one advantage over the perfidious British.

The squadron was divided into two divisions, because Dubordieu intended a bold repeat of the line-breaking tactics Nelson had used at Trafalgar. Dubordieu wanted no temporizing, no hedging of bets. He intended to go all out and set a new standard of boldness for the

French Navy. He thought it curious that a dead Englishman should have such an impact on both navies.

Contre-Amiral Dubordieu, for that was now his title, hoisted his flag in *Favourite*, 44, Captain Le Martin, which led the first division. It was followed by the *Flore*, 44, Captain Villon; *Bellona*, 32, Captain Duodo; and the *Principessa Augusta*, 16, Captain Perignon. The second division was headed by a new arrival, *Danae*, 44, Captain Peridier. *Danae* was followed in line by *Carolina*, 32, Captain Baratovich; and *Corona*, 44, Captain Pasquaglio. Pasquaglio was particularly keen to get back at the British after the way *Cerberus* and a storm had nearly wrecked his ship months earlier. *Corona* was refitted fully and had four new guns added.

The squadron sailed in two stately parallel lines. The wind was fair for Lisessa: the speed was seven knots.

*****

Gordon was holding a splendid late supper in the great cabin of *Active*. He had managed to procure a case of *Veuve Clicquot* from one of the prizes, and tonight it flowed freely. Carlotta was the honoured guest, and Gordon the picture of manly chivalry. He felt it a stain on the ship's honour that her life-saving efforts had not been officially recognized. It was not just with his compliments that she was invited, but with those of the entire ship.

Pennywhistle was proud of her and delighted to publicly proclaim her his lady. He was aware rumours had begun to spread that his connection might soon become more permanent. He was not sure he was ready for that, yet the thought did not bother him.

She made the cabin positively glow. Her beauty dazzled the officers, her spirit won their hearts, and her amusing and voluble English provoked their gentle smiles. She proved a poor card player, she liked whist even less than Pennywhistle did, but she was an excellent a cappella singer with a sweet contralto voice. She sang sad, nostalgic, wistful island ballads that affected him greatly and made the unsentimental, unmusical Dashwood look as if he might burst into tears. Even the brooding enigma, Lieutenant Haye, smiled

370

for a fraction of a second. The party broke up at a quarter to three.

Pennywhistle intended to escort her back to shore in the captain's gig. Her green eyes sparkled and her face was flushed and bright. It had been a wonderful evening and she had come to know more of his world. The ship was cruising two miles northeast of the island, so it would take a while for a small boat crew and Pennywhistle to convey her ashore.

She thought it marvelous to be here and make such a night journey under the stars. The brilliance of the sky was a perfect reflection of the state of transcendent happiness she felt at this moment. She could not think of any place she would rather be. She was with her man in his element. She rejected the offer of a boatswain's chair, refused to be lowered into the boat like a rank landlubber, and instead chose to brave the rigors of the rope ladder used by the men. She was being helped to the first rung when it happened.

"Deck there! Sail ho, fine of the port bow!" It was the masthead lookout. His tone was surprised, urgent. Haye, officer of the deck, noted the urgency. "What sail?" he shouted up.

Pennywhistle froze. "Wait!" he peremptorily yelled to Carlotta.

A minute of suspense passed as the lookout unfurled his glass and carefully counted. "Seven sail, two lines. Lying hove-to, dead ahead, two miles." He said nothing about nationality. That many ships left but one conclusion.

Haye grabbed one of the midshipman on watch that night: Lownes, a skinny boy of fourteen, whose voice still squeaked. "Mr. Lownes, my respects to the Captain, and would he please come on deck immediately. The French have arrived." Haye spoke with a calm that was completely at odds with his racing heart.

Pennywhistle knew what this meant. "Carlotta, I hate to say this, but you must stay here. The French have stolen a march on us, and I haven't time to get you ashore. I would not wish this upon you for all of the jewels of Araby, but it appears you are stuck with us. You will be safest in the orlop where the surgeon works. It's dark, but it's the safest, best protected, part of the ship."

"Thomas, I would rather be with you through whatever lies ahead than be safely tucked away ashore and be worried sick for your safety. I wish to be at your side, but I realize that I might distract you from your duty. I would not want you to worry for a second about me. But allow me to help. Perhaps I can assist your surgeon. I sewed up a man once and I can do it again. They say anything is easier the second time."

Pennywhistle kissed her and did not care if anyone saw. "My dear, I warn you. You will see unspeakable horrors in the surgery, but if you can stand it, I know Mr. Swayne would welcome your help. He is short-handed. Moreover, the men trust you. Some men will undoubtedly depart this life today, and if their last sight is of a beautiful, kind woman..." He laughed. "It certainly beats Mr. Swayne's grim visage."

"Mr. Lewellyn!" Pennywhistle hailed the other midshipman on duty.

"Yes, Captain?" The midshipman inquired uncertainly.

"Please escort the lady to the orlop and introduce her to Surgeon Swayne."

"Yes, sir!" The midshipman responded with alacrity. Fifteen-year-old males were highly susceptible to the charms of beautiful women. Mr. Lewellyn was a King's Officer in training, but he was still an adolescent beset with raging, untested emotions. His trousers suddenly felt very cramped and very small. "Please come this way, ma'am!" He tried hard to lower his voice two octaves. Carlotta smiled knowingly at Pennywhistle and followed the boy's lead.

Gordon stormed onto the deck. "Damn and blast, how could *Volage* have missed this show?"

Pennywhistle responded, "Not sure, Captain. I know *Volage* had patrol tonight. But captain, we have been making our patrols on the assumption the French would come directly from Ancona. Just suppose the French came indirectly, and purposely staged from another point?"

"Lisessa?" Gordon spoke as if he could scarcely credit the French with that much cleverness.

"My guess, sir," said Pennywhistle.

Gordon sighed and regained his composure. He spoke with his customary rapidity and decision. "Well, Tom, whatever the truth of our guesses, the enemy is here and means to strike us. I believe Commodore Hoste has his wish!"

It was 3 a.m., the hour of the wolf; the dark, secret time before dawn when a man's responses were at their lowest ebb.

Forty-Six

"And if they can see us? So much the better! Let them give the alarm and tell the world, for all I care." LeMere spoke to Dubordieu with arrogant derision. Dubordieu had just received word that a British frigate had been spotted, and had informed LeMere. "The sooner this engagement begins, the better!"

Dubordieu looked at LeMere with an expression of great forbearance. He knew a colonelcy was not enough for this ambitious man, and that he aimed for the big prize: the gold baton of a Marshal of France. A man like LeMere was never satisfied. He would always push, intrigue, and agitate for the rank just over the horizon of ambition. He would never be content to play the role of subordinate for long. He hoped the man's arrogance was not contagious.

He was tired of tactfully coddling the Guardsman's boundless self-importance, but he consoled himself, knowing today would be the time when his careful maneuvering of LeMere paid its most important dividends.

"I appreciate your eagerness," he told LeMere. "I, too, feel certain of victory. I would pursue the British ships, but there is no need for the unnecessary risk of a night action. They will be there at daybreak waiting for us. There is nothing recondite about Hoste's strategy. I do, however, think it is time for you to depart for *Corona*. I believe the Venetians could use your inspirational leadership, and you will find Captain Pasquaglio a man very eager to fight; just your type, I should think.

"You will lead the marines of the second division. Colonel Gifflinga will command those of the first. I know you do not like someone else in command of your marines, but since we will pierce the British line in two places, the second division is an equal post of honour with the first. I would suggest you depart immediately. Battle cannot be more than a few hours away. I wish you *bon chance,* Colonel!"

LeMere saluted. "This will be a day poets will commemorate. Our epic contest with the British is at an end. The deeds of the next few hours will echo through the centuries."

Dubordieu smiled pleasantly. Typical bombast, but to be expected.

Never one to believe he would be consigned to a footnote of history, LeMere felt his great day of glory had finally arrived. He found it ironic that, because of his actions, Dubordieu would end up being remembered as something he hardly deserved: a great commander. He limped off, leaning heavily on his gold-headed walking stick, but his eyes blazed bright and his chest thrust proudly forward. His head was full of detailed tactical plans for the next few hours. He was darkly impatient, but he could stand to wait a few more hours for his appointment with destiny.

*****

Active's helmsman put her helm hard over and tacked back toward Port St. George. Mr. Lockhart, the signals midshipman, hoisted the night signals for *"enemy in sight"*; two lanterns hung from the cap on the maintop mast. The night was clear. Hoste would see them.

Gordon's standing orders were to rendezvous with the squadron off the harbour mouth. They would have several hours to assemble. The French were poor night sailors, so he discounted the risk of a night attack.

Active's lanterns were seen and the news was quickly conveyed to Hoste in his sleeping cabin. He dressed swiftly and was soon on deck. He had long prepared for this moment and was greatly relieved it had finally arrived. Three lanterns were placed in the cap on the mizzen, signaling to *Active* her message had been received. Two more were placed on the cap of the main top to relay *Active's* news to *Volage* and *Cerberus.*

The efficiency of the British squadron was never better demonstrated by what came next. In three hours, the squadron assembled, organized itself, and formed up in textbook line ahead formation, all in the dark. By the first pink tendrils of dawn, the British squadron was standing out to sea toward the French. *Amphion* first, followed by *Active*, *Volage*, and *Cerberus*.

Hoste watched the French squadron grow gradually larger in his spyglass. The French were approaching at a ninety degree angle. Hoste always felt chagrin at having missed Trafalgar; his ship had been on resupply port call. Now it appeared he was going to have his own, small scale Trafalgar, but with the positions reversed.

Hoste made his counter move. The way to stop a line being penetrated was to make it close and tight as a finely fitted leather glove. He hoisted the signal for *"close up formation."* The *"acknowledge"* signal quickly shot up on the masts of the other ships. The evolutions were carried out in short order.

Hoste's poop deck was so close to *Active* he could see Gordon clearly. He took out his speaking trumpet, leaned over the taffrail, and hailed him. "I say, Jim, pass the word to keep the flying jib-boom over the taffrail, for we must not let those rascals break our line."

The ships moved even closer; the jib-boom of each ship literally hung over the poop deck of the ship ahead. It was a fine piece of delicate and constant maneuvering, one quite beyond French seamanship.

Almost in unison, beat to quarters sounded on each British ship. The marine drummers rat-tat-tatted the command with precision and enthusiasm. The pre-battle ritual commenced. Hundreds of feet moved with practiced celerity to their appointed posts.

All of the collapsible partitions on *Active* disappeared and all of the furniture was unsecured from their eyebolts and quickly stowed. Sailors doused the galley fire and herded all of the livestock aboard the ships boats, which were lowered and towed astern. Petty officers made sure all hammocks and bed rolls were stowed in the net racks around the poop, quarterdeck, waist, and forecastle and covered with moistened canvas; good protection against musket balls. Sailors wetted the decks to kill stray sparks, then sanded them to provide secure footing when the decks turned slick with rivers of blood.

Gunner's mates filled shot racks, and a stream of powder monkeys hurriedly hauled cartridge boxes from the magazines below to the gun captains above. Carpenter's mates laid out plenty of greased wooden shot plugs to fill holes below the waterline. The Boatswain and his minions methodically checked tackle ropes on all of the guns, then rigged the overhead netting on the quarterdeck to shield the crew from falling wooden debris.

Petty officers distributed leather fire buckets to the gun captains, and gunner's mates hung wet screens in the passageways connecting to the powder magazines. Gun crews filled the blue buckets next to each cannon with water for swabbing. Sailors topped off the large deck scuttlebutts. The scuttlebutts would be a source of drinking water, but also an emergency reservoir in case of fire.

Captain Gordon's servant laid out his finest silk shirt and best dress uniform. Silk, unlike cotton or wool, generally caused no infection if carried into a wound, which was why men who fought duels habitually wore shirts of that fabric. Men would look to him today for inspiration and it was important that his uniform be as splendid as his conduct. His navy blue tailcoat, made by Hawkes of Savile Row, was of the finest, heaviest broadcloth. The gold in the coat's buttons, lace, and epaulettes was thick and impressive. His bone-white breeches were of comfortable buckskin and fit tightly. He wore slippers instead of boots since he had found slippers gave him better purchase on a blood-slicked deck.

Once dressed, he placed his black *chapeau de bras,* worn in a fore and aft rig, on his head and adjusted it slightly. He looked at himself in the mirror the servant held up. Yes, just right. He was ready for battle.

Gordon ordered the lowest sails, the courses, taken in as safety precautions. *Active,* like all of the British ships, would enter battle under topsails, topgallants, and jibs. The sails were wetted as well. Not just as a safety precaution against fire; wetted sails drew wind more efficiently.

Haye commanded the guns on the quarterdeck and forecastle. Meers and Moore commanded the cannon on the main gun deck, one deck below. Although it was unnecessary, these officers called out the loading procedure. One more repetition, practiced in silence: one more drill to be absolutely sure that engrained habit would hold men's wills in the midst of carnage, confusion, and death. Once the battle began, most signals would be by hand, drum, or whistle. Voices would not be heard above the thunderous tumult of battle.

Haye, Meers, and Moore made sure all of *Active's* guns were double-shotted. Today it would be a combination of one solid shot and one load of canister: one round for the ship, one for the crew. This practice increased the lethality of the first broadside. The French were much more reluctant to double shot their cannon; their guns simply were not as resistant to the increased pressures. British metallurgy was the most advanced in the Western world, and it enabled the British to hurl more lead through the air. British gun powder was also noticeably more potent than the French, thanks to the purity of Bengal saltpetre.

The British enjoyed an additional advantage over the French because their ordinance was fitted with gunlocks, flintlock mechanisms triggered via a lanyard. Gunlocks were far more reliable ignition devices than slow matches. More importantly, a gunlock enabled the gunner to stand directly behind his piece and sight it properly, as well as time things just right to allow for the pitching and rolling of the deck. The French slow matches meant the gunner had to stand beside his piece to ignite it, much to the detriment of accuracy.

Pennywhistle divided his men so that Spottswood took charge of the marines on the rear quarterdeck; Dale, those on the forecastle. Pennywhistle himself would command the main group on the quarterdeck and waist. Much as it would have been satisfying to fire from the tops, his place was on the main deck. Today they would be outnumbered, and there was a very good chance the French would attempt to board. He would make sure not one French boot touched

Active's deck.

Deep in the belly of the ship, fear enfolded Carlotta. The orlop was a place filled with dark, eerie, shifting shadows, lit only by a few feeble, swinging lanterns. The damp, musty, fetid air reeked of death. She would have vehemently disagreed with Pennywhistle at this moment about fear being an ally. The surgeon and his mates had formed crude tables by placing boards between sea chests. She gasped when he laid out his tools. They looked like they belonged to a carpenter. They did not look to be implements suitable for use on human beings. The idea of those cutting into men was... Carlotta cut that thought off at the knees—appropriate for the situation. She choked back an urge to vomit. No, she had done that once, and it had been quite enough.

Surgeon Swayne was grateful for her help. He had a number of loblolly boys, but no assistant surgeon. He provided her with plenty of needles and thread. In battle, a surgeon was overworked and everything depended on speed. If he could just patch them, and let her finish the work, he could handle many more patients. Most of his work would be amputations. He said he could have an arm or leg off in ninety seconds, a feat of which he was quite proud. He would cut, tie off ligatures, and cauterize; she would deal with the coverings. In case of bullet wounds, he would probe and extract; she would sew them up. It was an equitable, if grisly, arrangement.

Carlotta paced back and forth. Her Thomas was right. Waiting was the hardest part. It was even more difficult when you could see and hear nothing of what was happening outside. She now knew what it must be like being cast into a dungeon. Something brushed past her foot, something sleek and furry. It was a rat, not an uncommon presence on a ship. She jumped back, then heard a yowl from behind. It was Sparkle, the ship's large, grey coon cat, whom she had seen majestically prowling the quarterdeck earlier as if he, and not James Gordon, were the real captain of the ship. Hissing, Sparkle jumped forward and seized the hapless rodent in his eager jaws with a snap that broke the rat's back, cutting short its shriek of pain. Becoming bored with his unresponsive new toy,

Sparkle rubbed himself about Carlotta's legs and purred lovingly. Carlotta, who hated rats, especially in a place where men would bleed and suffer, realized she had a new friend. In this dark and lonely sinkhole, any friend was welcome, even a feline one. She bent down to stroke the cat's arching back.

Pennywhistle unshipped his glass and noted large numbers of soldiers on the enemy decks, in addition to the expected sailors; plenty of work for his marines! Four ships in one group, line ahead, apparently intending to penetrate between *Amphion* and *Active*. The second group of three ships was aimed to cut between the stern of the *Volage* and the bow of *Cerberus*. He did not see how that would be possible. The British line was buttoned up tight. He wondered if the French would veer off.

Doubts assailed Dubordieu at the same moment. It had never factored in his planning that a line could be so tight and seamanship so fine. "Perhaps I have been too rash," he murmured out loud, to no one in particular. "However, courage!"

Colonel Gifflinga, new to sea fights, turned to Capitain LeMartin."Captain, would it not have been better to have taken an extra hour and formed one line?" LeMartin looked distressed, as if instinct wanted to agree, but duty forbade it. "You must have patience, Colonel. The plan is sound. The Admiral knows his business." Inwardly he asked himself, *Does he?*

Hoste watched the range closing. He turned to his first officer, the gallantly reliable Lieutenant Dunn. "Mr. Dunn, I think it's about time we let our French friends know we bid them welcome. Let's try a ranging shot with one of the eighteen-pounders."

"Very good, sir!" acknowledged Dunn. A few seconds later, an 18-pound ball whistled through the air and plopped into the sea a foot in front of *Favourite's* bowsprit. Spray showered the forward seamen adjusting the jib.

Not quite, thought Hoste, *but almost in range.* The British waited.

Forty-Seven

Hoste gave an order to the signals midshipman, and the signal flags raced up the halyards. Home Popham's system made it easy to communicate, and to this squadron, these two words were charged with magnificent inspiration. They would move the sailors to extraordinary deeds, well beyond the limits of duty and endurance. Tears formed in Hoste's eyes.

The signal simply said, "*Remember Nelson.*"

The reaction started as a low, rumbling chorus of human voices that quickly swelled to rolling thunder that echoed across the water. It was the full-throated cheering of four ships: hundreds of men, their voices raised in celebration, a salute to the man who, more than anyone, had made decisive victory the sole property of the Royal Navy. It proclaimed a mighty confidence in themselves and their ships. They knew with certainty they were about to add one more grand laurel to that tradition.

Gordon, caught up in the spirit of the moment, ordered the ship's small band to strike up "Rule Britannia." They played with a fervour and inspiration that warmed the hearts of all the sailors. Even the aggressively unmusical Dashwood felt his heart beat a little faster.

The taciturn Captain Whitby on *Cerberus* was not immune. He knew what lay ahead would be sanguinary, but he had no doubt of the outcome. He thought nothing showed on his face, but any slight alteration in his trademark wooden countenance was noted by his men.

Captain Hornsby on the *Volage*, the smallest of the four ships, spoke to his First Lieutenant, voicing an emotion common to all of the officers of the fleet. "Never again, Number One, so long as I shall live, shall I see so interesting and glorious a moment."

Pennywhistle's blood stirred. Had he heard Hornsby, he would have agreed fully. This was to be a battle between two squadrons of frigates, something that almost never happened. Fleet actions occurred from time to time, but they were usually between ships of the line, lumbering leviathans designed as gigantic, floating artillery platforms. This would be a fight between ships designed as scouts, raiders, and escorts, fast ships built for speed and maneuverability; a dogfight of the greyhounds of the sea.

He savoured the moment, frozen in time, before the bullets, balls, grape, and canister began their deadly work. He looked at his men, poised and eager. These were the last few minutes of life for some, and the scuppers would soon run red with blood, but for right now, this was honour, this was pride, this was achievement. He thought himself a rationalist, but he felt a powerful jolt of pure, soaring emotion. He remembered at the height of a battle that Nelson had once remarked, "This is warm work, but mind you, I would not be anywhere else for a king's ransom." Pennywhistle understood completely.

Deep in the orlop, Carlotta heard the cheers and wondered what they meant. But, she concluded, British cheers must be a good thing. Another sleek furry thing brushed past her ankle. She cringed, and then angrily kicked it aside. She was adjusting.

Spottswood cheered as lustily as his men. He was a young man, after all, and young men were full of passion. Besides, it felt good to expel some of the fear he was feeling in a good, ringing shout. He was now a King's Officer, proud of it, and today was his birthday. What an amazing party he was about to have! He would celebrate by blowing out quite a few French candles. He had reached the ripe old age of twenty-one. He hoped he would see twenty-two.

On the gun deck, the elegant Mr. Moore's eyes glowed with predatory eagerness. He liked this hunt; the foxes were about to savage the hounds! Meers did not feel his usual fluttery stomach today, so overcome was he with the emotions of the occasion.

The cheering floated across the rapidly shortening distance to the French flagship. It unnerved the French sailors and caused murmurs of fear. What did it mean? Why did the British cheer so? Did they have some secret knowledge the French were not privy to? After the silence, the cheers were an unpleasant reminder of what was about to happen. But this time the outcome would be different, they assured themselves. Victory lay close at hand.

Hoste's tight line sailed westward, in the direction of Lissa. He cut across the path of the two French lines at right angles. In naval parlance, he was "crossing the T." It was the classic maneuver, enabling the party performing the action to bring far more guns to bear than his opponent.

Dubordieu was determined to copy Nelson at Trafalgar, but it now dawned on him that two major factors were different. First, Nelson had gambled correctly that during the ninety-degree approach, when only his bow chasers would bear, the slow speed and general inaccuracy of French gunnery would limit the damage. Dubordieu faced an opponent whose greatest strengths were their gunnery speed and accuracy. Second, the French line at Trafalgar had had gaps. The British line directly ahead had none. A vulgar thought assailed Dubordieu's mind. An officer standing near had the same thought and absentmindedly voiced it, "That line is as tight as a virgin's hymen!"

*****

Whitby and Hornsby held their fire. *Danae*, leading the second French column, was not yet in range.

"I think the time is right, Mr. Dunn, you may open fire." Hoste said matter-of-factly to his first officer. On *Active*, Gordon made it a joyous bellow. "Fire!"

BOOOOOOOOOOOOOOOM! BOOOOOOOOOOM! The broadsides sounded like giant, deep, extended belches from Neptune himself. Tongues of hot, orange flame licked out simultaneously from *Amphion* and *Active* in perfect synchronization. Flying iron balls from thirty-seven cannons punched, crashed, bored, and splintered their way into the bow of *Favourite*. Scores of men died on the forecastle, and her jib-boom was shot away. That made her hard to control. Scuppers turned into racing streams of blood.

Bang! The single bow chaser on *Favourite* spat a feeble reply.

BOOOOOOOOOM! BOOOOOOOOM! The British fired again, a mere ninety seconds later. Smoky thunderheads cloaked the decks of both ships. Huge chunks of wood flew off *Favourite's* head rails and British iron smashed her female figurehead into kindling. Superstitious sailors always felt the loss of the figurehead a bad omen.

A few short minutes before, Dubordieu had told Captain Le Martin, "This will be the most glorious day of my life." Now, he was beset by doubts. They were taking a terrible pounding. The British fire was fast and accurate. Quite a number of his ship's guns were knocked out of action, and men were falling rapidly. The distance to the British was closing, but *Favourite* was almost defenseless. She would be a smoking ruin when she reached the British line. And there were simply no gaps in it for her to go through.

BOOOOOOOOOM! BOOOOOOOM! Active's and *Amphion's* broadsides thundered again. More orange tongues darted out, and more shards of wood flew off *Favourite*. More men died, most impaled by flying splinters.

At the moment of greatest risk, Dubordieu lost his nerve and hoisted signals for both lines of ships to sheer off. He ordered both lines of ships to wear and come parallel to the British line, where their guns would bear. There would be no second Trafalgar.

His ships slowly began the execution of the maneuver. Captains saw the signals with a mixture of disappointment and relief. At least they would now be able to hit back.

Dubordieu thought quickly. The one thing he had in excess was men. He had well-trained marines, land soldiers, and sailors. He decided that rather than risk a slugging match with British cannon, he would close the range as rapidly as possible and attempt to board.

That, of course, was predicated on Hoste doing exactly what was expected. With Hoste, that was an unwise assumption.

The ships were now on parallel tracks, sailing toward the Island of Lissa. A line of breakers, marking the rocky shore, loomed closer and closer. Both sides ignored the precarious navigational problem and focused on the combat. The British fired a fourth broadside that carried away *Favourite's* foretop mast stay sail. The French finally managed a slow and not terribly effective broadside, which mainly succeeded in ripping the stays holding *Amphion's* jib sail. The jib sail flapped helplessly in the breeze. The French cheered. At least they had done some damage.

Dubordieu frantically assembled a large group of boarders in the bow of the ship. Then he made a fateful decision. He was a personally courageous man, a man of real honour. He wanted to inspire his men and lead from the front. He would head the boarding party himself. Logic dictated he would better exercise his true responsibility to the squadron by remaining on the quarterdeck and delegating the leadership to junior officers, but his blood was up and gallantry prevailed over reason.

Lissa's breakers were in clear sight; the rocks drew ever closer and eagerly awaited the chance to gut a ship. Quartermasters on both sides ignored them and kept their attention focused on the wooden enemy. The heat of battle blanked out nautical common sense and no one sheared off.

Hoste ceased firing. *Favourite* was close enough for him to see the huge group of borders assembled in the bow. From her course, he guessed she was aiming what was left of her bowsprit at *Amphion's* poop deck. *Favourite* would entangle and lash the two ships together, then board over the bowsprit. Hoste knew numbers would tell, if he permitted it. *Favourite* had at least double the number of men.

But Hoste would not permit it. He had a surprise for the boarders that would do more than even the odds, it would tip them decisively in his favour. It was something that had no business being on a ship. No one could recall where Hoste had procured it, but the rumour was it was a gift from a friend in the Royal Artillery.

It was a gleaming five and a half inch howitzer, a land-based weapon, for which Hoste had ordered his carpenters to build a special sea-going carriage. Five and a half inches was the diameter of its front aperture; a howitzer could manage steeper arcs of fire than conventional cannon. Hoste crammed it with an unbelievably lethal dose of canister: seven hundred and fifty musket balls. Giant shotguns were great weapons if you were not fussy about blood.

Hoste wanted *Favourite* at point blank range, even closer than pistol shot. He wanted them on the verge of boarding: confident, eager, and completely exposed. He wanted this one shot to finish *Favourite* as a threat. Dubordieu had lost his nerve, if not his courage. This would test Hoste's resolve to the limit.

Dubordieu stood at the head of the boarders in the bow of *Favourite*. He was eager, yet he wondered why the British had ceased firing. One hundred yards, very close, and still the British held their fire. The French marines began a desultory fire at *Amphion's* main deck.

Hoste ordered his men to lie down and wait.

The seconds plodded by like hours and tension and tempers rose to the breaking point on *Favourite*. *Amphion* was only ten yards away. The men could clearly see each other's faces. In a second, the French would begin to hurl boarding grapnels.

Hoste picked out an officer, whom by his ornate uniform he judged to be Dubordieu. He had wondered what his opposite looked like. His curiousity was satisfied.

Ten yards: just right. Hoste said the simple word, "Fire."

Boom! The slightly tenor report was quickly drowned out by screams. The discharge was one of the most unbelievably destructive in the history of naval warfare. The entire boarding party, hundreds of men, vanished like smoke in the teeth of a hurricane. Gore and body parts littered what was left of the rigging and red human scraps and oddments flew in every direction. The smell of roasting flesh hung in the air, along with a fine crimson mist. It all drifted toward *Amphion*.

Dubordieu died with his men. A swarm of balls ripped his head and shoulders from his torso. It could be said he died a hero's death, but there was nothing heroic about the situation he left behind. The blast from *Amphion* killed all of the ship's officers. The few sailors left alive stood paralyzed. The earlier loss of the jib-boom and bowsprit caused the bow of *Favourite* to swing slightly away from *Amphion*. She was under poor control and extremely difficult to steer.

Colonel Gifflinga was miraculously untouched, but he knew nothing of the sea or ships. The only one left alive to issue orders was a young midshipman of fifteen. His training was limited, his seamanship elementary. Moreover, the destructiveness of the blast left him in a state of shocked speechlessness. He stared impotently into space.

"Rocks!" A frantic shout went up from the lookout. A line of breakers loomed ahead and close. *Favourite* needed to alter course, immediately. With the jib-boom and bow spirit shot away, quick maneuvering of the ship was almost impossible. But no one gave any orders. *Favourite* sailed on.

Hoste saw the danger. "All hands wear ship!" he bellowed. Men scurried up the yards. The helm was sluggish and fought the quartermasters. With the jib sail flapping feebly, *Amphion* might well perish on the rocks. The captain of the foretop saw the danger. On his own initiative, he raced aloft and rove the shattered lines through a block. The safety of the ship came down to the actions of one man. It was a crude rig, but the jib billowed and the helm began to answer. The bow swung away from the rocks at the last second and toward the open sea.

Favourite was not nearly so lucky. With a shattering crash of timber, her hull smashed solidly into the rocks. A huge gash split open her underbelly and water blasted in. She was hopelessly aground and out of the battle.

Forty-Eight

The rocks retreated as *Amphion* clawed her way out to sea. The rest of the British ships followed Hoste's command signal and all wore a safe course away from the danger; viewed from the clouds, this resembled bees doing figure eights. The maneuver placed the British in open sea, headed northeast, away from Lissa.

Captain Villon, commanding *Flore*, immediately astern of *Favourite*, watched her destruction in horror. It fascinated him in a morbid way, as if he were viewing the slow motion journey of a horse and carriage to the edge of a cliff, the driver confidently expecting a bridge across the chasm but having no idea that recent rains had washed it away. There was no way to warn. Beyond a certain point, the laws of physics propelled the trip to its inevitable and terrible conclusion.

Villon's ship was intact, all officers at their posts, and he had time to avoid *Favourite's* fatal mistake. *Flore* wore ship and steered toward *Amphion*. *Bellona*, Captain Duodo, directly behind, performed the same evolution, as did the little *Principessa Augusta*, bringing up the rear of the line.

Villon's line came round to the same direction as the British. Villon was in command now, and he would fight in the spirit of Dubordieu. He would attack and try to double on *Amphion*. *Flore* would rake the starboard quarterdeck and stern of the *Amphion*, while *Bellona* opened fire on its larboard side. They planned to put *Amphion* in a box and subject her to a lethal cross fire.

Gordon, now ahead of *Amphion*, saw the danger. But there was danger ahead of him as well.

When *Cerberus* wore ship, a lucky shot from *Danae*, leading the second French line, jammed her rudder. *Cerberus* completed the maneuver, but could not hold the new course; she strayed out of line and away from the battle. Whitby's carpenters frantically puffed and strained to fix the problem and restore steering.

A gap in the line opened. *Volage*, the smallest ship, became vulnerable. Captain Peridier had a powerful ship in *Danae* and his logical target would have been *Active*. But, like a predator seeking an easy kill, he pointedly ignored *Active* and made directly for what he perceived as a much weaker prey, *Volage*. Peridier hoped to pound *Volage* to dust before even considering *Active*.

Two hundred men, including Colonel Gifflinga, managed to get into the wrecked *Favourite's* boats and head toward the shore. A few minutes later, a tremendous explosion shattered the air as sparks reached *Favourite's* powder magazine. Gifflinga had decided to make sure there was no possibility the British would salvage the ship. Masts, spars, and chunks of wood and bodies shot skyward in a thunderous spectacle which ordinarily would have commanded attention, but now went unremarked.

Flore closed on *Amphion's* stern. Hoste could not avoid being raked, but he could save men. "Lie down!" he shouted through his trumpet. The men complied with alacrity. The broadside did significant damage to *Amphion*, but very few men were killed. A minute later, *Bellona* ranged alongside and fired a ragged broadside into her port bulwarks. *Amphion* was under fire from two directions. It put a huge strain on her gun crews, because there were only enough men to man the guns on one side at any given moment.

Nevertheless, Hoste replied with a broadside to *Bellona*. Then he brought *Amphion* slowly round; the crews raced to the starboard side guns, and two minutes later discharged a highly effective broadside into the *Flore*. *Amphion* held her own, thanks to the unflappability of Hoste and the superb training of the crew.

The overconfident Peridier now closed on *Volage*. He planned to enjoy this. He would wait until he was at half a musket shot range, where his larger calibre and greater number of guns should be decisive. He wanted his first broadside to be devastating and needed to get close enough so his inexperienced gunners could not possibly miss.

But a surprise awaited him. The *Volage*, while small, was part of a group of experimental frigates armed entirely with carronades. *Volage* had almost no hitting power at a distance, but at close range her thirty-two-pound carronades could throw far more metal than any opponent could reasonably expect.

Peridier fired. Masts were hit, stays and shrouds severed, and a few men died. But much of the fire went high and did little damage to the guns or men on the deck.

Hornsby held his response for thirty seconds, then his return fire broadside was murderous. Eleven thirty-two-carronades double-shotted with canister, rather than ball, shot enormous jets of red-orange flame and slammed backward on their slides. The gigantic wallop of lead laid low a sixth of *Danae's* crew. The blood rushing in the scuppers slapped at Perdier's ankle. Hornsby had fired to kill the crew, Peridier to cripple the ship. The French were slow to reload, the British were not. Eighty seconds later, *Volage's* carronades roared again. Another sixth of the crew died.

The battle was going against *Danae*. Peridier realized with horror that his opponent had a freakish armament exactly suited to close-in fighting. He quickly disengaged, swinging away from *Volage* and out to sea.

Cheers erupted on *Volage*; the men thought the enemy had turned tail. Hornsby silenced them and ordered them to prepare for the next round of engagement. The French, he knew, were only finding the distance that would be more advantageous to themselves. He observed through his glass as Peridier took *Danae* out of carronade range, then began the slow turn back toward *Volage*.

Cerberus fixed its errant rudder and was tacking back in the direction of *Volage* when it was pounced upon by *Corona*. Captain Pasquaglio, hungry for revenge, opened an effective and determined fire, to which the British quickly responded. *Cerberus* normally would have had no problem discharging three to four broadsides for every two of the enemy's, but she was ninety men short of complement. As the slug fest wore on, the shortage began to tell. Her fire was accurate, but the volume fell off as men died and could not be replaced. She was barely holding her own, and taking a severe pounding.

Once he was confident of his range, Peridier gave the order to fire. His heavy guns lashed out and their iron occupants connected heavily with *Volage*. *Volage* returned fire, but her shots dropped harmlessly into the sea hundreds of yards in front of *Danae*. Peridier smiled grimly; he had the British ship exactly where he wanted it. It was just a matter of time now.

Pasquaglo was pleased with his ship and his men, but he was violently angry too. Where was *Carolina*? What the devil was Captain Baratovich playing at? *Carolina* had been behind him in line; if she would just join the fight, move to close quarters, together they could finish *Cerberus*! But Baratovich stood away and seemed content to lob occasional shots at extreme distance. His fire was merely an annoyance when it should have been decisive.

Baratovich was playing a waiting game. He was happy to be in on the kill, but was loath to enter a free-for-all firefight. He came from a Pre-Revolution school which held that a ship was a valuable creation and should always be preserved to fight again another day. It was a mindset that Dubordieu had worked hard to extirpate, but Baratovich had not been under his command long enough to be converted.

Gordon faced a grave decision, the most difficult of his career. His was the only British ship largely undamaged. His colleagues were in serious jeopardy. He could not save everyone. Who needed him most? If he made the wrong decision, the battle would in all probability be lost.

Looking astern, he saw Hoste pulling ahead of *Bellona* and *Flore*. Their fire appeared to be slackening and less effective. He had confidence Hoste would prevail. It was a calculated risk, but Hoste was Nelson's disciple. If anyone could weather double fire and survive, Hoste was the man to do it. *Cerberus* was holding her own, if just barely. Her hull was damaged, but she fought on. *Volage*, on the other hand, was taking a severe beating. Hornsby was resolute, but Gordon knew without help his ship would soon be a lifeless hulk. Peridier was just outside of the range of her carronades and continued to send wave after wave of broadsides into her port quarter.

On *Volage*, Hornsby tried a desperate expedient by increasing the powder charges in the carronades in the hope it might increase their range. The gamble failed. The increased powder charges only caused the breeching ropes to break, dismounting the carronade barrels from their carriages. *Volage* was helpless. Her hull was shattered and her rigging hung in pieces.

Gordon made his decision. "Mr. Dashwood, unfurl and wet the fore and main courses. We need some extra speed. Steer for *Volage*. Captain Hornsby will owe me a case of port for this!" His words and voice sounded cheerful, but his face looked grim.

Bellona and *Flore* blazed away at *Amphion's* starboard and port quarters for twenty minutes, with more determination than skill. *Amphion* finally surged ahead and out of the French kill box. By taking skillful advantage of the wind, *Amphion* deftly pivoted, took a position off *Flore's* bow, and poured in three broadsides in quick and deadly succession. It under fifteen minutes, that contest was over. *Flore* struck her flag.

The *Principessa Augusta* fired a few shots at *Amphion* from some distance, but sheered off when *Amphion* fired a pair of eighteen-pound bow chasers in her direction.

Bellona came up on *Amphion's* stern from starboard and attempted to rake her deck, but *Amphion* expertly swung away at the last minute. *Bellona's* shots missed, and some of them arched over *Amphion* and hit *Flore*. An officer on *Flore* angrily waved a French flag in *Bellona's* direction, indicating her nationality and that she had been struck. Hoste neatly sidestepped *Bellona's* attack and instead spun *Amphion* round to bring her port broadside to bear on the *Bellona's* bow. Two accurate, overwhelming broadsides in rapid succession reduced *Bellona* to an immovable ruin. She hauled down her flag.

Flore had taken advantage of *Amphion's* occupation with *Bellona* to do something disgraceful. Surrender was a serious matter of honour; gravely given and meticulously observed, it was never subject to reconsideration or recantation. But Captain Villon did just that. He used *Bellona's* fight as cover to escape and bore off rapidly to the east.

"It's a damned disgrace!" shouted an enraged Hoste. But he had no way to pursue. Instead, he sent officers in the ships repair punt to *Bellona*, to ensure she did not attempt the same underhanded trick.

Lieutenant Donat O'Brien boarded *Bellona*. It was a shambles; dead men lay in heaps everywhere and the decks ran red with blood. O'Brien was escorted to the captain's cabin where he found Captain Duodo lying on his back, clutching his stomach, from which protruded a long sliver of wood.

They had a brief conversation, during which Duodo asked O'Brien to do all he could for his men, particularly the wounded. O'Brien, being a gentleman, of course agreed.

"And, Captain, we will do everything in our power to help you personally. I will summon a surgeon." O'Brien could afford to be gracious.

"I only ask that you look after my ship and my men; do not trouble yourselves about me." Duodo spoke with a fatalism based on experience. Many times before he had seen the type of wound he had, and he knew he had only a few hours to live.

O'Brien saw something odd in Duodo's eye: a glimmer of latent triumph. It puzzled him. Just then, a midshipman approached.

"My respects, Mr. O Brien, and might I have a word in private with you?" Seventeen-year old, beanpole-thin Midshipman Hanks seemed alarmed.

"Certainly, Mr. Hanks." They stepped out onto the quarterdeck.

"Sir, the whole ship is rigged to blow. Duodo has fuses set all over the place. He planned to blow the ship's bottom out and take us all down with him; go out in a blaze of glory. I am sure some sailors will attempt to light the fuses the second our backs are turned."

"That is indeed disquieting, Mr. Hanks. I had no idea these

Venetians were the glory-in-death types. Get some sailors to set about the ship with buckets of water and kill the fuses. We will turn the powder into a sticky muck that won't light in a million years. Post guards on all of the barrels of powder." Outright perfidy puzzled O'Brien. Perhaps the wisest course of all was to presume nothing of your opponent and verify everything.

Meanwhile, Gordon cracked on all of the sail he dared and closed quickly on *Volage*.

The sight of *Active*, an undamaged, resolute ship tearing down on him, caused Peridier's nerve to break. He signaled *"disengage"* to *Corona* and *Carolina*. *Corona* had been badly knocked about, but Baratovich had showed no heart and had been only lightly engaged.

The French ships piled on sail and fled. *Carolina* led the escape, followed by *Danae*. *Corona* brought up the rear and kept up a steady, long-distance cannonade on *Active's* bow with a single stern chaser. It did little substantial damage, beyond fraying Gordon's normally sanguine temper.

Gordon was determined to bag *Corona*, and with luck, *Carolina* and *Danae* as well. He knew where they were headed. They sought cowardly shelter under the guns of Lisessa, now twelve miles away. *Corona* was almost in range of *Active's* guns. It was time for the French to feel *Active's* wrath.

Forty-Nine

"Sir, why will you not stand and fight? What is it you fear? I have men with the training, spirit, and enterprise to bring victory and glory to our arms. Why will you deprive them of the chance to redeem our cause? I grow tired of expostulating with you, sir. You seem to forget, sir, I have been promoted colonel by the Emperor himself for my part in damaging the British. Do not condescend to me, sir, I am your equal in rank!" LeMere leaned precariously on his gold-headed walking stick, as if his insolence had physically unbalanced him.

Pasquaglio, feet planted and firmly anchored on the rolling deck of *Corona*, wore a look of angry exasperation. "Colonel, your talk crosses the border from the merely insulting to the patently insubordinate. As I have told you, it is not my decision to make. I was ordered, *ordered*, mind you, by your own Captain Peridier to make best speed to Lisessa and protect our rear. I was, and am, eager to fight. The Admiral commanded you and your marines to sail on my ship instead of his own because, deep down, he feared Italians lack spirit. In the present situation, the irony is overwhelming! You seem to insinuate cowardice, sir, a deadly accusation, but if you must make it, I suggest you direct it to the right man: your own naval officer. I am a proud descendent of a line of Doges of Venice, sir, so do not seek to lecture me about honour and duty.

"But let us end this discussion, sir, which is as jejune as it is pointless. You will probably get your wish anyway, regardless of orders. The British are almost in upon us. If battle is joined, I assure you, my men with fight with the utmost heart and gallantry. You will

395

have to prove to me that your men will do the same."

LeMere physically winced at the verbal jab. Then he summoned up the lofty dignity of an officer of the Imperial Guard. "I assure you, sir, you will not be disappointed. I only pray your men observe carefully, so they may learn from us. At any rate, allow me to depart. I must prepare."

Arrogant son-of-a-bitch, thought Pasguaglio.

Active came up smartly and swiftly closed to within four hundred yards of *Corona*. She maneuvered within hailing distance of *Corona's* port quarter, just abaft of the quarterdeck. Not close enough, thought Gordon. Three hundred yards was acceptable, but one hundred yards would be much better.

It was time to relieve the tension. "Piper McLaren! Do your duty! Give us 'Hearts of Oak'!" McLaren nodded and began to play. The high keening notes carried easily over the entire ship. Gordon smiled with pride.

Pasquaglio maneuvered with skill and precision. He weaved and danced away from *Active*, spoiling the chance for a critical broadside. He pivoted his ship, trying to cross the T on *Active* and bring his port broadside to bear on *Active's* bow. Gordon was too skillful to permit that and slipped the trap with consummate grace. They were like two wary, experienced boxers circling, watching, and waiting for an opening to land a knockout punch. It was move, countermove, point, counter-point, all in slow motion.

From the air, the two ships seemed locked in a gradually narrowing zigzag pattern. Each time they wove back and forth, they edged closer, each captain heedless of the narrowing distance and focused only on lining up the perfect shot. One of them would make a mistake, sooner or later. The ships were now only eighty yards apart.

LeMere's marines held their fire, although it was with the greatest reluctance. Pennywhistle's marines held their fire, awaiting Captain Gordon's command.

A slight reduction of wind made *Corona* slow, ever so slightly. She did not yaw quite enough. It was minor, but the pattern was broken. It was not really a mistake, just the caprice of the wind, but it was enough. Gordon had the shot, a clear one at the port quarterdeck, range: thirty yards. His patience rewarded, he took it with gusto.

"Fire!" he bellowed through his speaking trumpet. Cannons and carronades thundered into life. Shot, grape, and canister tore into the *Corona's* side at two hundred meters per second and swept across the deck. At the same time, Spotswood's, Pennywhistle's, and Dale's marines fired, their muskets sounding like a swarm of angry bees. The marines sent a deadly rain of lead from *Active's* fighting tops. Pasquaglio's first officer, Lieutenant Drogo, fell as a musket ball penetrated his right epaulette and continued downward to his spine.

Pasquaglio gave the order to fire his own broadside. It was heavier than *Active's* and crashed solidly into the oak scantlings on the starboard side. Long, jagged splinters flew in every direction, one impaling two men on cannon number five.

LeMere's men fired a well-aimed volley directly at Pennywhistle's marines. The two British marines who had done so well against the snipers in Groa were hit, Scorsby in the thigh and Lemon in the shoulder. Pennywhistle's men responded with a volley that killed three French marines outright.

Pennywhistle realized his opponent had training, but lacked experience firing from a rolling deck. That took seasoning and a directing officer with an intuitive and exquisite sense of timing. Ropes were being hit and severed just above his head, which indicated they were firing just a tad too high. The shots were lower than in the night battle with *Favourite*, but were missing heads by a quarter inch. Close, but not good enough. Pennywhistle's men, as usual, aimed for the shoe buckles.

Amidst all of the thunder, the thrilling skirl of McLaren's pipes playing "Lilibolero" could be faintly heard.

Numbers one and three carronades smashed into pulp the crews of cannons two and four on *Corona*. The two cannon barrels broke free and tumbled along like gigantic kitchen rolling pins. Several thousand pounds of unsecured cylindrical iron made formidable deck-clearing implements. Five men were not just killed, but squashed into pancakes.

Pennywhistle fired his Ferguson rapidly. He was certain that at least three of his shots hit home but, as the battle continued, clouds of greasy gun smoke severely limited his vision. A ball shredded the top of his hat plume and one tugged at the hem of his jacket, but he was unscathed. He heard the *zip, zip, zip,* of bullets past his ear, felt the attendant rush of air, and heard thuds around him as casualties dropped to the deck. Everything was wreathed in smoke, so he ordered his men to aim for the muzzle flashes on the enemy deck. It was a shooting gallery where only tiny fragments of the targets were visible for intermittent seconds. Cannon fire appeared as sudden, popping flashes of ball lightning in a pea soup fog. The incessant short bursts of light from the cannon played havoc with vision.

Active poured broadsides into the *Corona* at point blank range. The two ships were so close that with the cannon barrels fully run out, they almost touched. Neither side even attempted to maneuver. They were like two boxers on the ropes locked in a fatal embrace, pummeling each other with as many jabs as their energy would permit. There was no need to aim, no need for precision. This was about delivering smashing hammer blows as fast as possible. The ships were two angry, living entities opposed to each other with a will and a destiny beyond the lives of their crews.

After forty minutes, the superior gunnery of the British began to tell. Half of *Corona's* guns were out of action, and the same percentage of her crew killed or wounded. The remaining cannon were down to half size crews, which severely limited the speed of reloading.

A puff of wind cleared the smoke for a few seconds. LeMere spotted a marine officer on the poop shouting orders and fired. The ball tore into Peter Spottswood's left shoulder. The impact spun him around like a top, before he pitched forward onto the deck. His men watched in horror, but remembered his orders and their duty and continued to fire.

The same gust of wind gave Pennywhistle a brief glimpse of the officer whom he had bested at Port St. George. "Damn," he snarled to a startled marine, "that man just will not go away. I spared him once because he was defenseless. I will not make that mistake again." In a blinding flash of anger, speed, and skill, he swung the Ferguson to present, sighted, and squeezed the trigger.

A momentary roll of the deck spoiled Pennywhistle's shot so that it grazed LeMere's shako without penetrating. The impact propelled him forward. Forward, almost into the path of a cannonball that passed within an inch of his nose. LeMere was untouched. Nevertheless, he fell forward, and by the time he struck the deck, he was stone dead. The concussive air blast had killed him, leaving his body unwounded, but his face black and blue.

Wave after wave of cannon balls pounded *Corona* relentlessly. The ships were now so close that sparks from the cannon barrels actually singed the wood of their opponent's bulwarks. "*Fuoco, fuoco, fuoco!*" Frantic shouts arose from the deck of the deck of *Corona*. A flaming wad from one of *Active's* cannon had ignited her rigging, and the fire was spreading. Rope, oiled with tar, was extremely congenial to fire.

It was too much. Pasquaglio had had enough. "We strike, we strike, we strike!" he yelled frantically across at Gordon, or where he thought Gordon should be. The billowing clouds of choking smoke made it hard to see much of anything. The Venetian flag fluttered despondently down the halyards.

Dashwood glimpsed its descent briefly. "Captain!" The usually bland, laconic First Lieutenant was actually excited. "The enemy has struck!"

"Cease fire, cease fire, cease fire!" shouted Gordon through his speaking trumpet. Drums beat out his command, and boatswain's whistles trilled it. McLaren heard and changed his tune to *Amazing Grace.* He had forgotten in his eagerness that the evangelical piece was not a favourite of Captain Gordon.

The firing stopped. After the oppressive din of battle, the silence seemed eerie and peculiar. The only sound was the mournful, almost requiem-like tones of the pipes. Then Gordon saw the flames crawling up the mizzen and maintop shrouds. All seamen understood the threat.

Once combat ceased, the iron law of the sea took effect. It was the duty of any ship at sea to help another in distress. *Corona* was no longer an enemy, but a ship under British protection and in dire threat.

"Captain!" shouted Gordon across the short interval between ships, "we see you require assistance! I am sending men over to help you fight the flames!"

"*Si, Si! Grazie! Grazie!*" Pasquaglio many not have understood the words, but he grasped their meaning. If the positions had been reversed, he would have done the same.

"Mr. Dashwood, take charge of the boarding party. Take possession of *Corona*, but first, put out that fire!"

"Aye, aye, sir!" crowed a triumphant Dashwood. Grappling hooks were quickly thrown from both *Active* and *Corona,* and extra spars were laid down to produce bridges between the ships. Men from *Active* hurried across the gap.

Dashwood and Pasquaglo, British and Venetian seaman, stood together against the flames. Enmity was forgotten; survival was the only thing that counted. It was death for all of them if they could not subdue the flames. The scorching heat melted the skin from the skulls of two wounded sailors who had been missed in the confusion and were unable to crawl clear of the flames. *Corona's* fire engine, linked to the ship's pumps, frantically sprayed jets of seawater on the fire. It was a long way from out, but its progress was arrested. Seamen loaded fire buckets from the deck scuttlebutts and cast their contents onto the flames. They passed them in relays, irrespective of rank or nationality.

Pennywhistle's men brought him to Spottswood, who was unconscious, breathing slowly and heavily. He bent down and examined the wound. He could see the gash where the bullet had entered, but no exit wound. The shoulder was badly damaged. Whether the arm could be saved was problematic and beyond his expertise. He hoped surgeon Swayne was as good as he believed himself to be.

He reluctantly gave the order he dreaded above all others. "Take him to the orlop." Four marines gently picked up Spottswood and carried him toward the aft companionway. He decided he would go with them. He had to know.

In the orlop, Surgeon Swayne and Carlotta were already busy.

Fifty

Hoste had hoisted the signal, "*make general chase*," after he saw *Active* pursue *Corona*, *Danae*, and *Carolina* into the distance, but in truth, he knew it more of a heroic gesture than a realistic one, something Nelson would have done. *Amphion*, having fought three ships, was in a bad way. Two of her lower masts had been shot through and stayed aloft precariously. Replacements were needed, and soon. The larboard main yard was smashed, as was the mizzen top mast. Hoste was loath to admit it, but *Amphion* needed greater repair than was available locally or even at the dockyard in Malta. The ship could be sailed, but it would have to return to England.

She had fifteen killed and wounded forty-five. Hoste's face had been scorched by musket cartridges exploded by a stray shot, and he also had a "small" splinter in his left arm—less than twelve inches long. Nevertheless, he refused to list himself among the injured. Dunn, his Number One, had suffered rather more severe facial burns from the same cartridge explosion.

Hoste was still greatly angered by the disgraceful flouting of surrender conventions by *Flore* and would demand her return. He realized that such a demand, while justified, was unlikely to be honoured by Bonaparte's government. Bonaparte had no sentimental feelings for ships and demonstrably negligible respect for antique courtesies of war. Each French ship that remained in play was one more implement in his grand design for victory, and woe betide the commander who was foolish enough to surrender one to the British over something so trifling as honour.

Volage and *Cerberus* were severely damaged as well. *Volage* had her main yard and foretopgallant mast destroyed, and her rigging hung in ribbons. Her port side was peppered with shot holes. Thirteen lay dead and thirty-three wounded out of her crew of one hundred and seventy-five.

Cerberus's hull was riddled with shot and her mizzen topsail yard had been shot away. Thirteen of her crew of one hundred and sixty were dead, forty-five wounded. *Cerberus*, unlike *Volage*, was able to make some headway and came up behind *Active*. She even managed to send a boat and sailors under her resourceful First Lieutenant Clive Dickson to help combat the fire on the *Corona*. But she was not going to be fighting any battles in the near future.

The blaze on *Corona* was persistent. Not only did personnel from *Cerberus* pitch in, but Gordon was forced to send an additional boarding party under Haye and lend *Active's* own fire engine. The fire proved a crafty, almost human, opponent, flaring up in unexpected places just when everyone thought it beaten. *Corona's* foremast, already shot through, was charred badly. Haye almost singlehandedly maneuvered the fire engine and put out that fire. His reward was a singed face and badly burned hands. Once the fire finally surrendered its last bit of life, *Corona* fell in beside *Active* and *Cerberus* and slowly tacked in the direction of Port St. George.

Pasquaglo boarded *Active* and offered his sword to Gordon, addressing him in Italian. The third officer of *Corona* spoke something almost discernible as English and interpreted. "Captain Pasquaglo offers his respects, Captain Gordon, and wishes you to accept his sword in honour of the very skilled, spirited, and gallant fight you have made against *Corona*." Lieutenant Paolo spoke with sincerity. Pasquaglio looked as dignified as a man can be who had just lost his ship.

Gordon smiled graciously. "Please tell Captain Pasquaglio that the defense of his ship was able and admirable. I cannot in good conscience accept his sword, but I would be very gratified to accept his hand in friendship." Gordon extended his right palm.

Paolo smiled and quickly translated. Pasquaglio looked thunderstruck, but smiled and executed a sweeping bow. He extended his hand to Gordon's and shook it firmly several times.

Gordon spoke with lofty sincerity, "I apologize for the state of my ship, Captain, but I would be most honoured if you and Lieutenant Paolo would join me in my cabin. We have much to discuss and I think it would be better if we did it in more convivial surroundings. I have a supply of a beverage from my native land. I am not sure if Captain Pasquaglio is familiar with it, but I believe he will find it soothing, smooth, and agreeable. It's called Scotch. Glen Garioch Single Malt; the best!"

Lieutenant Paolo translated. Pasquaglo laughed and spoke in rapid-fire Italian. "The captain would be delighted to join you in your cabin, Captain Gordon. He says he is familiar with the smooth fire you describe, but it is exceedingly hard to find in the Mediterranean. He says that kind of fire is welcome, unlike the one we have been fighting."

Gordon spoke with genuine delight. "Excellent! Even in war, men of honour need not treat each other like barbarians. Now, Captain, Lieutenant, if you will please come along." Gordon headed toward the hatchway and the great cabin.

Pasquaglio and Paolo followed, Pasquaglio repeating "Come along, come along." He had decided he needed to learn English, and that phrase was as good a place to start as any. Over the next few days, he would repeat it endlessly, to the immense amusement of officers and men. His nickname on the ship quickly became "Come Along Pasquaglio."

In the orlop, a much less civilized drama was unfolding. Twenty-four men lay in the dark, close confines. The place stank of fear and sweat, and low moaning noises echoed off the wooden beams. Swayne had done ten amputations already and extracted five bullets from others, and Carlotta had sewn them up. Nine men still awaited attention.

Carlotta was proving equal to the task. Her heart was rent by the suffering of these men, but the pain was mitigated by the knowledge that her efforts might save some of those moaning and mewling men. It was hard at first, but each time she performed a task, it got just a little bit easier. She could never quite manage to think of the men as garments needing mending, but she was able to block out their cries enough to function competently. She thought her efforts barely adequate, but Surgeon Swayne was both impressed and grateful.

Marines gently laid Spottswood upon an operating table, and Surgeon Swayne examined him carefully. Carlotta and Pennywhistle held their breath. The surgeon probed the wound for a minute or two. Spottswood emitted low, animal groans, but mercifully did not regain consciousness as the probe plotted a course though ribbons of flesh and muscle. It seemed hours before Swayne spoke. "We should amputate," he said laconically.

Spontaneously and in unison, "No!" sprang forth from the mouths of both Pennywhistle and Carlotta. They looked at each other in surprise. The surgeon was equally stunned. He was unaccustomed to others gainsaying his medical pronouncements.

Pennywhistle reached down inside himself, below the depths of fatigue, and summoned his most tactful and diplomatic manner. "Doctor, surely there is some way to extract the bullet and save the arm?" He favoured the surgeon with a title merited only by a higher order of healer, a physician.

The surgeon cast doubtful and grave looks at him; just as his lips began to form a word, something caused him to stop. He seemed lost in thought for a full minute. "The bullet is lodged in the axillary nerve. It is close to the point where the arm and shoulder intersect. I could extract it, but there will be a grave risk of sepsis if I do. Even if I can extract the bullet, it will be delicate. If the nerve is damaged, even nicked, he will not have much use of the arm, perhaps none at all. As I said, amputation is the safest course to pursue. That is my best judgment."

Pennywhistle's idetic memory went hyperactive. He saw in his mind's eye the splayed shoulder of the criminal's corpse on the Edinburgh dissection table. He saw the bone, sinew, and muscles with absolute clarity. He saw the axillary nerve, buried deep amongst the musculature. It would indeed be difficult to reach. The musket ball that hit Spottswood would have flattened, but it might also have splintered. Removing one piece would be difficult; extracting multiple pieces almost impossible. First things first.

"Dr. Swayne, when you probed, did the bullet," Pennywhistle paused for emphasis, "did it appear to be in one piece?"

"It did, Mr. Pennywhistle, but I will not know for certain unless I pull it out and examine it."

"That is a good and promising sign," said Pennywhistle. "As I understand it then, if the bullet is got out, it would be a matter of sewing, splinting, and waiting to see if gangrene sets in and if he recovers use of the arm?"

"You are correct, Mr. Pennywhistle, but it involves a legion of 'ifs' and far too many imponderables for my taste. Amputation is still the best course. I can do it in ninety seconds."

Pennywhistle's temper flared at Swayne's fixation with amputation and he tried to keep the rising irritation out of his voice. This was a moment for tact and cleverness, not bile and venom. "Think of this as a test of your skills. You are good at amputation, your skills recognized, your reputation deserved. You could rest on your laurels and still have the gratitude of every man on this ship. But you have before you a most worthy young officer. If he could speak, he would ask you the same question I ask you now. How good are you? How good are you, really and truly? Are you something more than a simple butcher? Are you an artist, a healer, a skilled and gifted surgeon? You can run from an answer to that question, many men do, content to live with a fantasy instead of discovering the real truth of their abilities. I suggest to you that the test of your career and your life is at hand this very moment. How will you answer, sir? How will you answer?" Pennywhistle was a courageous man, but was frightened for Spottswood, who had become a better brother to him than his own back in Berwick.

He always frets more about his men than himself, thought Carlotta. It was part of why she loved him.

Surgeon Swayne's face wore a troubled expression. He stood

transfixed for a long moment. Then he picked up the hollow cupped probe. "Very well," he said. "Let's find out!"

Swayne gently inserted the probe into Spottswood's shoulder; the half cups at the end of the scissor-like instrument slightly open. He knew where the ball was, but because of the delicacy of its placement, he searched gently and with great care. Beads of perspiration formed on his brow. He felt soft lead. Very, very slowly, he spread the halves of the probe. He pushed forward slightly, little by little, then brought the two halves of the probe back together. The ball seemed firmly locked in. He withdrew the probe in the same way, slowly, gingerly, and with great care and patience. When the probe came free, he held it up to the slow swinging lantern. Carlotta and Pennywhistle leaned forward intently.

Swayne opened the probe. The ball was there. Wide, deformed, barely spherical, but intact. Swayne looked at the ball with almost a jeweler's eye to be sure nothing was missing. A piece of scarlet cloth was wrapped round the ball. Bits of clothing were often the chief sources of infection.

Pennywhistle and Carlotta realized they had been holding their breath and inhaled deeply. They laughed. It was not the laugh of mirth, but of sheer relief. It remained to be seen whether infection would be a problem, and whether Spottswood would be able to use his arm, but the first hurdle had been successfully negotiated.

Carlotta sewed up Spottswood's arm in short order. Blandon, Manton, Spottswood's servant Smithers, and Pennywhistle used Spottswood's unwrapped sash as a sling to move him up several companionways to his quarters near the wardroom. Pennywhistle then ordered Smithers and Manton to keep a close eye on him and to immediately notify him when Spottswood regained consciousness. When he came to, Pennywhistle advised them, he would be ravenously hungry, and thirsty enough to drink the contents of the nearest two scuttlebutts of water, but moderation was the wiser course, because the cravings of the body usually exceeded its ability to absorb succor. The best guarantee of recovery was not any of the ministrations of the art of medicine, but the enormous, inherent, recuperative powers of the body and the steadfast reserves of the human spirit. The wise physician knew this and would simply step aside and allow the body to heal itself. There were medications, potions, elixirs, powders, leeches, and pills galore, but rest was still the simplest and best prescription.

Pennywhistle urged Manton and Smithers to trust their noses most. If that dread scent of gangrene reached their nostrils, death lay a very short time in the future, and swift amputation would be Spottswood's last hope.

Five hours later, a soft, croaking voice floated up from Spottswood's tiny cabin: "I'm thirsty." Outside, Manton and Smithers heard it with surprise and joy. He was awake!

Fifty-One

"Gentlemen, to absent friends." Hoste stood to attention in *Active's* great cabin and solemnly raised his glass in salute.

The remaining twelve officers at the long table rose to their feet and gravely chorused, "Absent friends." Pennywhistle decided: superstition be damned! For these men here, thirteen was a lucky number.

It was a common enough toast at naval dinners, but today, a week after Lissa, it had a special poignancy. All present were grateful to God, Fate, Destiny, or whatever power had spared them, but they all had friends and crew upon whom those entities had frowned. Tears rose in many eyes as each man pictured fallen comrades and thought of merry voices forever stilled. Pampered civilians might have found the raw emotions distasteful, but this was an age where tears were reckoned manly. Nelson had sometimes wept openly over lost comrades. Each of the four ships had survived, but each of the four ships also died a little that day. A debt of honour was owed to the fallen, and the toast was one very small way of paying it. Nothing important was achieved without a price, and the profession of arms demands a very steep one.

Pennywhistle was not immune. A solitary tear slowly wound its way down his cheek. He thought sadly of the other toast, the ugly, sardonic one, often proposed at the start of a war, regarding prospects for promotion: "A bloody war and a sickly season." Tomorrow, he would be writing eight sad letters home.

There was silence after the toast was drunk. Normally loquacious officers like James Gordon were simply overwhelmed by the gravity of the moment. All were resplendent in full dress uniforms, a sea of blue and gold with two islands of scarlet. The formality underscored the dignity of the proceedings. Death was propitiated and sacrifice commemorated. Some faces were grave, some meditative, some downcast.

For that brief eternity, the great cabin resembled a gloomy, rustic banqueting hall out of the brooding world of *Beowulf.* The warriors present wore no chainmail, no iron gauntlets or horned helmets, and flourished no flagons of bitter, dark ale, yet their heavy hearts summoned forth ancient racial memories. Death grinned in the background. Servants stood behind each officer, motionless and silent.

It had taken a week of hard work to make basic repairs. The cessation of battle brought no cessation of work. Ships required constant maintenance, never more so than after a battle. It took days of unremitting labour just to remove the bloodstains and reeking body parts. The decks were scrubbed and holystoned relentlessly to remove the last hint of red. Shot holes had to be plugged, masts had to be fished, ropes had to be spliced, shrouds and stays had to be mended. The carpenter, boatswain, and their mates were very busy.

Pennywhistle remembered the five dead near cannon number four. They had lain in odd positions where they had fallen, all with their eyes still open. Blood had oozed slowly from them and rivulets of red had found their way between the deck planks, creating a strange, striped effect. The final disposal of the dead had been the saddest duty of all. The dead men's hammocks were transformed into canvas burial shrouds. Two round shots were placed at the feet of each, to be sewn inside along with the corpse. A brief service was read, with comforting phrases like "looking for the resurrection of the body when the sea shall give up her dead," then the bodies were pushed out the entry port to wend their way to Davy Jones' locker.

The sailors were not especially religious, but they appreciated giving their mates some kind of ceremony. When the shroud containing his messmate went over the side, one Able Seaman had simply said, "We were mates, Bill. I done what I could for you and can't do no more. Bless you and good bye."

In the heat of battle, some corpses had been unceremoniously pitched over the sides. It was the harsh necessity of clearing impediments, and the sailors accepted that out of sheer practicality. A respect for the dead could not be allowed to jeopardize the chances of the living.

"Thunder and confusion to the French!" Captain Hornsby raised his glass. Smiles slowly blossomed on thirteen faces. The mood was broken. Mourning was good and proper, but it should not spoil what promised to be a wonderful dinner. The meal was, after all, a celebratory one. The British had won a great and remarkable victory.

The meal was indeed splendid. Food was served on the ship's best Adams blue china with intricately festooned scenes of life in Canton, and wine was poured into glasses of the finest Waterford crystal. The first course, terrapin soup, had been a great success. Distinctive local white Chianti complimented it well. Pennywhistle was no longer downcast and introspective, but was warming to the celebration.

The servants cleared the table and put an array of foods on the sideboard to which guests might help themselves. There was something for every fancy and appetite: boiled duck, roast goose, fricasseed chicken, and peppered Albacore tuna. Potatoes, French beans, cabbages, and carrots complemented the main dishes. Guests helped themselves liberally. Servants hovered patiently about the guests and poured wine frequently—white, of course, to favour poultry. The local wines were tart; the stuff brought from prizes was much sweeter. Either way, not a glass remained empty for long. Faces reddened, tongues relaxed, and conversation flowed.

Pennywhistle untied and removed his gorget, then loosened his stock. Formality faded as the meal progressed. After sampling the goose and tuna, each with a different local wine, one bold, one muted, he decided on the duck bathed in a tart cherry sauce. It was excellent, particularly with a subtle Beaujolais that accentuated its gamey, earthy flavor. His normally restrained appetite declared a holiday, as did his normally restrained tongue. He felt expansive and

411

giddy; a very pleasant relief after the last few weeks.

Guests ate heartily. The sideboard was cleared, and sea pie, mutton steak, and roast beef were presented to the increasingly jolly guests. These were accompanied by tarts, sweet fritters, and three kinds of puddings. Bottles of merlot and Bordeaux were opened to do honour to the red meat.

Gordon snapped his fingers and seamen trundled in a case of *Veuve Clicquot*. The bottles were smothered in cold crystals—amazing, since ice was much harder to come by than even superior champagne. General applause greeted the popping of the first cork, and hours passed with an easy grace. The normally bland Dashwood actually displayed sparks of real humour. Moore enthralled the slightly tipsy guests with his fox-hunting exploits. Meers talked eagerly of his fondness for cricket.

Haye, recovering from burned hands, had trouble holding his glass, but that did not prevent him from happily sampling quite a few of the available wines, which rendered him talkative. He rippled on fondly about his parents and sister on the Isle of Man. Pennywhistle was stunned to discover that Hayes, the brooding enigma, was actually a rank sentimentalist.

Gordon launched into a jovial, champagne-fueled disquisition on why bagpipes were actually the most difficult instruments in the world to play. Dunn listened with puzzlement, but each succeeding glass of *Veuve Clicquot* increased his interest in Gordon's talk.

Pennywhistle considered the figgy pudding, but rejected it as too heavy after all he had eaten. He instead chose the vanilla, which was lighter, smoother, and creamier. He complimented it with a glass of champagne, ice crystals sparkling on its brim.

The sideboard was cleared quickly and discreetly, and dessert appeared as if by magic. It featured a bewildering array of cheeses: Stilton, cheddar, and Gloucester from England, as well as Gorgonzola, Tellegio, and Pecora from the Italian Coast. Even Dutch Gouda and Illyrian Feta were in evidence. Apples, pears, and peaches were set out in large silver bowls. Almonds, Brazil nuts, and cashews accompanied the cheese and fruit. For those with an excitable sweet tooth, there were hot pumpkin and apple pies. Locally produced strawberries and cream made appearances as well, fresh and brimming with flavor. Two varieties of coffee flowed from gleaming silver pots: one a sweet Brazilian, the other West Indian, with a robust, nutty flavor.

Pennywhistle chose the pumpkin pie and added some local cream to it. He decided on the Brazilian coffee with some of the same cream atop. Like Hoste, he was an abstemious man, but there were rare occasions, such as this one, where self-imposed restrictions were put aside. He would have a sore head in the morning, but the meal was a fine one, and, in its way, would help to heal some of the stresses of battle. It was a kind of medicine; a salute to honour, an homage to duty, and a memorial to brave deeds, heroic souls, and a battle whose like men would never see again.

He sipped his coffee slowly, savouring it. It was rich, piping hot, and luxurious with the fresh cream. It steadied him. He looked across at Spottswood, arm in a sling. His face was beet red and he was obviously feeling no pain at all; quite a pleasant change from the intense suffering of the first few days after the musket ball had been removed. Gangrene had not appeared, and after a week was unlikely to. It remained to be seen what use he would have of the arm. His servant, Smithers, cut his meat throughout the meal.

Spottswood thought, *Whatever lies ahead, I will never forget this evening or what we have accomplished. These men are my friends, my comrades, and will always live in my mind. I can't even recall the names of my so-called friends back in Cork. They were nothing; these men are everything.*

A spoon tapped gently against a Waterford crystal tumbler produced a distinctive *ting, ting, ting* which immediately caused everyone to look toward Hoste at the head of the long table. His face looked battered and his cheeks were badly singed. "Gentleman, if I might have your attention please." He spoke more slowly and deliberately than usual. "I am truly gratified to have you here, to have one last glorious dinner with my band of brothers."

Nods of agreement and cries of "Hear! Hear!" rose from the table.

413

Hoste's voice caught a little when he spoke next. "I thought a dinner a convivial and practical way to let everyone know what lies ahead. As some of you probably have heard, *Amphion* needs a complete and thorough refit, and that can only be done in Portsmouth. We have her jury-rigged and ready to sail for England. We will depart with the tide tomorrow morning."

Groans arose from the table. Tears formed in Hoste's eyes. "I will miss you all. It has been the greatest honour of my life to serve with you."

Tears appeared unbidden in many eyes, including Pennywhistle's, but then Spottswood, revealing a surprisingly strong tenor voice, launched boldly into "For He's a Jolly Good Fellow." He had not gotten far before the rest of the table joined him. The singing was loud, boisterous, and a bit off key, but Pennywhistle thought it as grand as the King's College Choir performing Handel's *Messiah*.

When the singing concluded, Hoste simply said, "Gentlemen, that means more to me than any medal or any amount of prize money. Thank you!" He brushed aside tears and struggled to regain his equanimity. "Now, gentlemen, let me continue, before I am again attacked by a broadside of emotion."

The table was silent. They leaned forward in their chairs. Manton poured Pennywhistle another cup of coffee.

"Gentleman, *Cerberus* and *Volage* need repair as well. But I believe their requirements are well within the abilities of the Malta Dockyard. Captain Gordon, this means that after Friday, *Active* will be the only British ship in the Northern Adriatic. I know it is a grave responsibility, but I am confident of your ability to handle it and handle it well. I have received intelligence that what little remains of the French squadron is cowering—cowering, mind you—in Trieste Harbour, like a pack of beaten hounds, incapable of offering any mischief to anyone. You should have a free and unhindered hand at intercepting any hostile merchant shipping you choose."

Gordon spoke in a voice thick with emotion, "I thank you for the confidence you repose in me, but might I inquire how long it will be before replacements arrive?"

"It will be several months at least," replied Hoste seriously, "but reinforcements will come. *Alceste*, *Unite*, and *Acorn* have been assigned to this theatre. Two are strong fifth rates, *Acorn* a small sixth rate. Captain Maxwell of the *Alceste* is an old friend, I believe."

Gordon smiled. "Maxwell is a very dear friend. We served together in the West Indies and in Spain. He and I share a love of writing perfectly dreadful poetry." The table laughed. Gordon's unskilled efforts as a whimsical poet were well known.

"And now, gentlemen," said Hoste with a broad smile, "I know our waists are all bulging, so might I suggest we all repair to the quarterdeck and walk some of this meal off? I understand Captain Gordon has assembled quite a capable ship's band, which stands ready to serenade us. Isn't that right, Captain Gordon?"

"Indeed it is, Commodore. They have been practicing rigorously and are most anxious to show off their achievements. The band leader is a German named Anschluss. I understand he was once the kappelmeister of a small duchy along the Rhine. At least he claims that. But whatever the truth of his boast, he is a very fine musician, and I feel our little band is the equivalent of anything you might hear in Vauxhall." He spoke with evident pride.

It was a beautiful evening on deck. Pennywhistle was almost moved enough to seek his paints. The sea was a glassy aquamarine, unusually gentle, and a friend to mariners. *Active* rode easily at anchor. The sky was filled with stratus clouds tinged a reddish gold. It was the red sky poets said was the delight of sailors. He looked out to sea and contemplatively sipped the last of his coffee. He experienced a rare emotion, real serenity, the calm after the storm. He felt good, whole, and fully alive, a feeling that things had turned out exactly as Fate had intended. He had been a part, an important part, of something much greater than himself. The guilt he felt from the earlier land battle at Lissa was finally banished. He had killed, yes, but he also realized many were alive today because of his leadership. It was not a life he would have chosen if he had planned things to coincide perfectly with his highest nature, yet, at this moment, he felt a perfect contentment with the choices he had made. It was a moment to be savoured and remembered, for, unlike the happy endings extolled by poets, he knew it would not last. A chapter was finished, but he knew more battles loomed ahead as long as Bonaparte ruled.

The band played beautifully, as advertised. "Heart of Oak," "Roast Beef of Old England," "Lilibolero," "Greensleves," "Rule Brittannia," and "Spanish Ladies" were among the traditional tunes and airs they played. Pennywhistle enjoyed the performance and was careful to let the musicians know he was pleased. He liked music, had a good ear, but had absolutely no skill in creating it.

But his mind was not really on the music or the loveliness of the evening. It was occupied with Carlotta and their future together. She had shown more resolve, pluck, and bravery than any woman he had ever met. She had gone through fire and darkness for him. She had a heart of gold and a soul of steel. She had comforted him when his soul ached. She had never flinched during a crisis, but had instead stood steadfastly alongside her man. She had won not only his heart, but that of every sailor on the ship. With her help, he might even learn to competently tell a joke someday.

Right now, it was too much to think about. He was tired and too fuddled with alcohol to consider it with the rationality on which he prided himself. Or perhaps he needed to discard reason entirely and just embrace the demands of his heart. Now, however, it was time to surrender to the ministrations of Morpheus. He left the quarterdeck, lost in thought, and walked slowly to his cabin where the trusty Manton waited. Manton patiently helped him disrobe and gently bundled him into his swinging cot. He lay his head heavily on the musty pillow and instantly dropped into a deep and dreamless sleep.

Fifty-Two

Pennywhistle needed to think. He needed to be alone. He was in his usual perch, far above the harbour of Port St. George. He was here on matters of the heart, not matters of the sword. He was alarmed and needed to puzzle things out. It was misting slightly, but he did not care. The mist was entirely appropriate to his thoughts about the future. Everything was softly veiled and slightly out of focus. Love had changed Pennywhistle's paradigm of life and he was uncertain whether to welcome it or fear it.

In matters of the heart, he felt like a child wandering a lonely midnight forest beset with strange and outlandish creatures. He liked to feel he was in control of his destiny and make decisions that, while honourable, were based on a logical and rational self-interest. Facing the dangerous prospect of real love, he did what he had never done in war. He hesitated, temporized, and prevaricated.

In the past, women had always seemed to him beautiful but baffling creatures of unknowable intent, complicated motivation, and unpredictably volatile emotions. They were best handled like violently combustible chemicals or gunpowder in a magazine: kept in safe, distant storage, insulated and handled with extreme circumspection and care, only brought into direct employment when they served a useful purpose.

It was easy for him to keep relationships in a neat box, the same way he carefully arranged and packed items into his sea chest. It was logical, it was orderly, and made it easy to transfer from one relationship to another. Relationships with women should be like the partitions that separated the cabins off the wardroom: they should be light, easily dismantled, and easily stowed at a moment's notice.

So far, that approach had worked splendidly. He had satiated his desires, and he had never been lonely when he desired not to be. But deep down, a feeling had lurked and whispered with a soft but insistent voice, "The adequate and convenient are not enough. There is something deeper, more important, and more valuable. You must give it a chance. Lower your defenses, allow the unexpected, embrace the unpredictable."

Carlotta's presence compelled him to think, not as Tom Pennywhistle, but as part of a couple. He had never thought of himself as selfish. He cared for his men, took great pains for their welfare, and never risked their lives unnecessarily. He considered himself an independent gentleman, a self-contained entity, and it had never before occurred to him that what might be good for him might not necessarily be good for a couple. Now he found himself, will-he-nill-he, thinking about a family. Carlotta had two children. If vows were ever spoken, he would have two stepsons. Was he ready for that? His carnal longing for Carlotta practically guaranteed children of his own. Was he ready for that as well?

He thought briefly about continuing what they had and keeping her as a long-term mistress. It was not an uncommon choice among Sea Service officers. The Service had a saying that east of Gibraltar, marriage vows were cancelled, and every officer became a carefree bachelor. He had enough money, military reputation, and social cachet to present the world with a damn-your-eyes, I-dare-you-to-protest demand that she be acknowledged his lady without virtue of a ring. But that felt unseemly, even sordid. He had no wish to cast the two of them as social rebels. If children were involved, they were entitled to a name of which they could be proud. Carlotta had captured his heart and she deserved the best.

His current reflections on marriage were part of a pattern that often placed him mentally on the outside of society. He had been packed off to university at Edinburgh because of his strong, demanding, and insatiable curiosity. He'd asked too many questions, voiced too many independent observations, and left too many conventional thinkers puzzled and uncomfortable. The fire within him burned so brightly as to scorch those who approached too closely. Great intelligence often provokes fear in lesser minds.

As the years wore on, he had learned to mask his intelligence with a studied, gentlemanly reserve and pleasant, polished speech. Safety lay in being observant and blending in; letting others reveal themselves and giving people just enough information so that in their imaginations he became whatever they needed him to be. Carlotta intuitively saw past his mask, looked deep into his soul, and seemed well pleased.

His father had appreciated his aggressive intelligence and realized university provided a fine niche for all manner of eccentrics with unusual casts of mind. Then he had mucked everything up with an ill-considered duel over the honour of a woman he barely knew. He had been a damned fool, allowing a woman in distress to unbalance his carefully ordered universe. Was he being a damned fool again?

He sighed deeply and shook his head. It seemed illogical to him that a lifetime commitment should be entered into without the deepest, most mature reflection. The alleged wisdom of his caste proclaimed marriage to be about securing property, advancing social position, producing heirs, and preventing people of different classes from ever joining in wedlock. For all of his devotion to reason, it seemed wrong to reduce marriage to a cold mathematical algorithm, an equation of the mind, rather than a song from the heart. For men of his class, marriages were arranged, and Love was regarded as merely a lucky accident. Carnal passion was supposed to be explored only after marriage, at least for the women—an incredibly unwise prescription. No one would attempt to walk through life with a pair of new boots before first making sure the fit was a good one.

He had no liking for the sort of marriage his brother enjoyed: safe, genteel, dull and absolutely predictable. It was a solid marriage, as polite society reckoned things, devoted to marginally principled money-grubbing, social bootlicking, and a drab, conventional seeking after a life of luxurious ease. It was an eminently sensible alliance that joined two good families, but it was absolutely devoid

419

of adventure.

Whatever he wanted personally, his family would never approve of Carlotta. To their conventional world, she presented too many drawbacks. She was older than the fashionable maidens men of his class courted, had children, and was not of the proper station. Marriage to her would secure him no financial or social advantage. She was involved in trade, she worked directly with her hands, and was the sort of person who used the rear entrance. She had a dangerously independent cast of mind. Why, she wasn't even British, and was perhaps, horror of horrors, a Catholic! Her heart, intelligence, resourcefulness, and courage simply would not be factors in his family's assessment.

He also knew her striking beauty would make the women back home look like shriveled old beanpoles by comparison. The mere glimpse of her face and voluptuous figure at a party, no matter how disguised in the most conservative of dresses, would make many apparently contented husbands think instantly of infidelity. The men would envy him; the women would hate him for bringing such a creature to England. Gossip about her would be viscious and unending. And yet, and yet... he had trouble thinking of his life ahead without Carlotta in it.

In the four months since Hoste's departure and Captain Maxwell's arrival with three new ships, he had spent a great deal of time with Carlotta, save when *Active* was out on patrol. He was often ashore, having been designated the squadron's engineer officer by default. He spent much of his time supervising the construction and arming of Fort Hoste on a small island at the harbour entrance to discourage return visits by the French. The work was satisfying. It gratified him that he would leave something of permanence behind when he left this island.

He had not seen any real action, save for *Active's* part in the capture of a twenty-eight-ship convoy, which made clear the ripple effects of Lissa. After an anemic attempt to evade *Active* in a maze of Dalmation coast islands, the unescorted convoy surrendered en masse and offered not even token resistance. The crews all loudly cursed the want of French military support. For want of enough men for prize crews, all but ten of the ships had been burned.

That morning, Gordon had summoned him to dicuss problems with the prize court in Malta. They had sat down in the cabin's Windsor chairs, facing the slanting stern windows, overlooking a sea filled with whitecaps.

"Rest easy, Tom," Gordon had said. "Do have a cup of this Green Tea. We took it off one of the prizes. It's from the Japans and quite potent stuff. Superior I think, to Darjeeling."

Pennywhistle took a sip. Gordon was right, it was strong stuff; not a drink for the ladies. Still, he'd thought, even the best tea was inferior to coffee. Carlotta would probably like it. It was hard to get her out of his mind.

"Captain, it is delicious, but I gather you did not summon me here so we could have a learned discussion on the merits of exotic varieties of tea. You mentioned something about the prize court in Malta."

"Well, Tom, I hate to be the bearer of bad tidings, but some serious problems have developed which are delaying the payment of our prize money. I fear the prize court in Malta is hopelessly corrupt. You have heard, no doubt, of the problems Lord Cochrane had with the court adjudicating his prizes. The court officials charged double, and even triple fees, for their services. In addition, some of the prizes were sold to specially favoured merchants at less than expected prices. Cochrane actually filed suit against them.

"I received a note yesterday from the squadron's prize agent, Alexander Davis. He is requesting we send an officer from the squadron to help him expedite the payment of the funds due us. He felt that it might be useful to let the prize court know that our squadron feels the matter urgent enough that it sends a..." Gordon searched for the right comparison, "well, watchdog."

"I would be more than happy to look into it, Captain, but might I ask, why me?"

"First and foremost, you are honest, and you have a good head for figures. But I also thought, you among us have the most immediate and pressing need for prize money. I don't like gossip, but it is silly to deny the rumour that is on every jack's tongue, that you and the lady will soon be married." Gordon looked chagrined, as if he had just blurted out a state secret. "Forgive my impudence in saying that, Tom."

"That's quite all right, Captain. I doubt there is a living soul on the island who does not know. I have not formally proposed, and I confess the prospect of marriage frightens me. Let me just say the matter is under serious consideration," he replied thoughtfully.

Gordon coughed discreetly, as if to buy time while he marshaled his thoughts. "There is a packet ship leaving the harbour tomorrow morning for Malta. I have booked you passage on it; you and your... wife." He hesitated. "I booked a double cabin."

Pennywhistle smiled. "Captain, that is most generous of you. Carlotta would love a sea voyage that does not involve gunfire, and I know that she has never been to Malta. It's quite a beautiful place. It will charm her."

Gordon cocked an eyebrow. "It occurred to me that the captain of the packet will simply assume you are married. You are a British officer, after all, and he would never have the gall to question you on the matter. I thought it might be a time to test the idea of marriage. I, of course, am a strong proponent of it. Might be just the thing to help you make up your mind: a voyage at sea without the responsibilities of command.

"You know," he continued, a faraway look in his eye, "I look forward to the day when Lydia and I will be joined. I have a wonderful little manor house in Hampshire picked out. I think my prize money on this cruise will be enough to purchase it. Not a day goes by that I do not think eagerly of our wedding. I fervently hope, no, I *know* it will happen when this cruise is finished. It will be the happiest day of my life." Gordon's puppy-dog joy radiated so brightly it made Pennywhistle instinctively smile.

He was genuinely touched. "That is most kind, Captain. Throughout this cruise you have always shown great consideration for my welfare. I consider myself a lucky man to be on your ship."

Gordon's smile changed to a more serious expression. "You are family, Tom. Don't ever forget that. And the lady may soon be joining that family, so I am concerned for her too. Besides, speaking as the captain and on behalf of the entire ship, we owe Carlotta a debt. She saved lives, and that will never be forgotten."

The talk of family, marriage, and the earnestness of Gordon's concern for Carlotta caused Pennywhistle's eyes to moisten slightly. He hated being so obviously emotional, but perhaps that was one of the concomitants of love. He would just have to learn to deal with it.

He gradually came back to himself. It was now early evening. Port St. George looked beautiful and peaceful. Hours had passed, but it seemed to him he had only just arrived. The mist was clearing. Out of the pale rays of the slowly fading sunlight, Carlotta appeared. He wondered how long she had been there, patiently watching, unwilling to disturb his concentration. He gathered she had guessed where he would be, and also guessed what he had come there to think about. She knew him better than he knew himself.

He told her the news about Malta and she literally jumped for joy. "But this is wonderful, Thomas, wonderful. A sea voyage with you will be so romantic. I will pack my best dresses so I do you credit as your lady. I have never been East of Corfu!"

Pennywhistle spoke with concern. "Can you make arrangements for the children to be cared for? I apologize for giving you so little notice."

Carlotta laughed. "I have three sisters on the island. Trust me, they will all want to take the children. My only problem is deciding which one gets the privilege."

"That is a relief. I would have understood if you demurred because you could not make arrangements, but I would have had to go anyway. And a month without you would be very difficult."

"We shall not be parted, my dear Thomas! But tell me about your errand. All of the talk of prize money is confusing. I understand the general idea, but not the way it works."

Pennywhistle explained it patiently, and Carlotta listened in amazement. "It is almost as if you make war for profit, with everyone getting money from ships you capture," she said at last.

Pennywhistle nodded. "Not exactly, but I can see how you might think that. Let's just say it gives our captains an added incentive to sweep French shipping from the seas. The faster and better we do it, the greater the financial reward. Money works much better than medals. The men love the system. Every sailor receives a share proportionate to his rank from the sale of a prize, so it's a great way to bind a crew together. Captain Gordon's sailors have accumulated quite tidy sums of prize money. They need it more than I do, which is a good reason to go to Malta and speed up the payment process."

Carlotta looked surprised. "But Thomas, you act as if you do not care about your own share!"

"I am a bachelor; my financial needs are modest. I have no estate, no fancy stables to maintain, no pack of foxhounds to fund. Mostly, I bank my prize money with Coutts in London and forget about it. Beyond that, I just I draw drafts from time to time, for things such as," he smiled, "new uniforms; but in general, I don't think much about my balance. I do this job for many reasons, but lust for money is not one of them. If you want to talk about lust for money, you need to speak to my half-brother."

Carlotta fixed him with a deeply soulful gaze. "Why do you do this job, Thomas? You have told me how you came to be in the marines, but have never told me why you remain. I think you are very good at your job, yet not entirely comfortable with your profession. As I have come to love you, I have seen so many conflicting eddies and currents in the river of your soul that it unsettles me. I... my French fails me," she said with a look of exasperation. "*Manachel! Figilio en cane!*" she sputtered in Italian, then rallied and continued in English. "I am sorry I do not speak the English as she is meant to be spoke, but it will have to do. My soul knows you to be a man of invention, scholarship, and healing, yet I see you engaged in struggle with the warrior, the peace-killer, and the destroyer for control of your destiny. Those dark portions are part of you, necessary in some ways, but my love, they do not define you. I believe your heart to be a bright light, and I have implored Our Savior that you will come to realize this."

He had never seen her lovely face look more earnest. He gazed skyward, as if some heavenly agency could supply a satisfactory answer to her question.

"Why do I do this job? 'Why' is the ultimate question in all matters, isn't it? I wish I could give you a good answer, but for all the thinking I have done about it, I am not really sure myself. Maybe it's the fact that I am needed, that I make a difference, and that I can do things most men cannot. What I do gives me purpose, something many gentlemen lack. I have seen too many squander their lives and fortunes at horses and cards. I flatter myself, I know, but part of me wonders if the job would get done were I not here. I want to see this thing through to the finish. And I will not deny that I find the adventure stimulating, nor that my curiousity demands I discover what lies over the most distant horizons." He gazed out over the darkening sea as he said this, and his hand clenched involuntarily. Carlotta, seeing this, nodded slowly.

"But in the end, I think it's about family and belonging. The ship and her men are close to me in a way that's hard to explain. They trust me with their lives, and I happily return the favour. I have never felt closer to anyone." He smiled thoughtfully. "Present company excluded. Your coming into my life has caused me to consider new possibilities about family."

Carlotta flushed with a passion equal parts love and desire. She slowly extended her long, graceful hands to Pennywhistle. He stepped forward and impulsively kissed her, long and slow. He drew back and spoke in soft, kind tones, "My attitude toward money is changing, though. I am thinking I may soon have some very delightful ways to spend it. Money can never buy love, but it can provide plenty of ways to make sure that it flourishes."

"*Cara mia,*" she said softly, in a voice rich with smoky sensuality. "I want you! Come to me!" Her husky voice radiated raw passion, yet it was laced with a curiously child-like innocence. Pennywhistle saw her visage through waves of shimmering heat. Her breath pulsed with intensity as she whispered, "I will never love any man the way

I love you. If I were to die at this moment, I would still reckon myself the luckiest woman to have ever lived."

She touched his cheek with a gentle, kind hand and her fingertips danced with incendiary magic. Her bright red hair glowed and her nipples hardened against the transparent, rain-soaked fabric of her blouse. Her eyes widened and her breath come in short, hard gasps.

He had never wanted anyone so much in his life. He was filled to bursting and needed her now and forever. The rest of the world meant nothing and could fry in its madness. England, ship, and duty suddenly seemed mere chimeras.

"I love you," he husked, and gathered her into his arms. His mind switched off as a torrent of lust overwhelmed him, a force of nature as powerful as the sea itself. He kissed her hard as time stopped and the world went away. There was only Carlotta and love and fire.

They clawed at each other with the frantic passion of shipwrecked sailors clutching a floating spar and shed most of their clothing well before they reached the bed in the hunting lodge. They loved, laughed, and caressed long into the night.

As the first rays of dawn crossed the horizon, he and Carlotta lay in naked, uncompromised alliance, covered in sweat. It was the quiet peaceful afterglow of two souls merged into one. Pennywhistle had never been happier. And yet, a nagging voice insisted it was too perfect to last. All things changed, decayed, and eventually died. Entropy was the nature of the universe. He would have railed against reason and nature, but just now, he was far too relaxed. Nature and reason would have to wait their turn.

Fifty-Three

Whitecaps raced across the heaving sea. Dark, angry thunderheads discharged rippling sheets of cold rain down on Lissa Harbour. It was boisterous, inhospitable weather, perilous for the amateur. Most landsmen would have called it a good day to stay indoors.

Gordon watched the tumult through the stern windows of the great cabin of Captain Maxwell's ship, *Alceste*, which was riding at anchor in the harbour. They had just finished a dessert of Stilton cheese, Brazil nuts and almonds, and smooth coffee topped with some local cream. The ship transmuted the violence of wind and waves to a rhythmic rocking, accompanied by the creaks and groans of straining timbers that, to the ears of men long accustomed to life aboard ship, was almost a lullaby. He compared the interior of the cabin to the storm outside. Here, everything was measured, orderly, and tranquil. The dinner had been excellent.

Gordon knew Maxwell. A fine dinner was always a prelude to something important. The more urgent the business, the more Maxwell strove to appear the perfectly nonchalant, civilized host. Maxwell realized there was a war on but the blood and gore simply made him more determined not to recognize it, socially.

Gordon looked up. "Murray, why did you really call me here? The more the invitation seems purely social, the more I know it is purely business."

Murray sighed. "And I thought my preparations so cunning. You know me too well! I needed time to consider some new intelligence; to digest it. Now that I have, it's time to put you in the picture. I had a visit, several hours ago, from Lieutenant

427

Samuel Pasco, skipper of a small Navy cutter, HMS *Surly*."
"What did he report?" asked Gordon.

"He said that three days ago, through sheets of pounding rain, he glimpsed what he thought were three frigates. They were at a great distance, even through his glass, bearing northeast. What we have then, are three unknown ships, possibly frigates, and if so, definitely hostile. What I have been pondering the last few hours over our very pleasant repast is their destination, intentions, and our best course of action. You are a valued colleague as well as an old friend. You have been in these waters much longer than I. I should very much welcome any insights you might have." Maxwell looked at Gordon expectantly.

Gordon was silent for a full minute, absent-mindedly staring out over the tempestuous waters as he focused his thoughts. "The French have not been up to any tricks recently," he said slowly. "That in itself is cause for alarm. Boney is nothing if not an active leader. We may have thoroughly trounced the French at Lissa, but it seems to me he might well try something because he would expect us to be resting complacently on our laurels."

Maxwell responded. "Where do you think they are headed?"

"My guess is Trieste. The tattered remains of Dubordieu's squadron have been lurking there for months, licking their wounds and, at a guess, attempting to rebuild their shattered morale. It makes sense Boney would be sending them some reinforcements. They are in poor shape, but they are the only French naval forces of any consequence left in the theatre," Gordon concluded with conviction.

"Exactly what do you think the nature of these reinforcements would be?"

"If I were Bonaparte," answered Gordon, "I would be sending supplies. I would send the one thing that is indispensable to a wartime navy and that is nearly impossible to procure in this theatre—cannon, and lots of them. The Trieste squadron must want them badly. Two new ships would be a godsend, but I think they may well be merely powerful escorts for a large supply ship with valuable cargo. But," Gordon looked wistful, "I am not General Bonaparte, and sad to say,

I can only guess at his intent."

Maxwell slowly poured himself another cup of coffee and took another bite of the apple pie he had been picking at during the conversation. Gordon could see the furrows on his forehead deepen and the active blue eyes glaze over in deep thought.

The only sound in the cabin was the steady *swoosh, swoosh, swoosh* of waves slapping the stern.

The silence was finally broken by Maxwell's voice. No longer droll and urbane, it was alert and decisive. "I do believe you are right, Jim. It makes perfect sense; two powerful frigates escorting a heavily laden stores ship. But even if you are wrong, we must to put to sea and investigate. I hate to do so in such beastly weather, but we must lose not a minute.

"Will you take the entire squadron?" asked Gordon.

"No, I will not leave Lissa undefended. I will leave *Acorn* behind to deal with any French marauders, and I believe each ship can spare a few marines to man Fort Hoste and discourage unauthorized entrance to the harbour."

Gordon queried, "Do you think there is any possibility they might be headed here?"

"No," said Maxwell, "the force is too small to be bound here, and anyway the course they were on is contrary to one they would take if this were their destination."

"I agree," said Gordon, "but we will need to act with dispatch. Even if we put to sea forthwith, it will take time to find them. The weather won't make that easy."

"Then I suppose we must conclude this very pleasant meal and be about our business. We shall put to sea with the evening tide. The wind is with us. We shall have to post vigilant lookouts to see through this muck, and post lanterns on the mastheads and maintain visual contact, hull down over the horizon."

"Good luck to you, Murray, and to your ship," Gordon said graciously.

"And to you, Jim. Let us make this a final blow to French hopes in the Adriatic."

John M. Danielski

*****

Carlotta and Pennywhistle had endured an unpleasant night together in their cabin on the packet ship *Carlyle*. The rough seas would have tested the stomach of even an experienced sailor, which Carlotta most certainly was not. Pennywhistle took the foul seas literally in stride, but Carlotta spent most of the night moaning and retching into a bucket. Her red hair clung limply, framing the sickly green pallor of her face. She stirred uneasily, groaned from time to time, and slept for short periods only, between agonizing bouts of nauseous wakefulness. She had been drunk only a few times in her life; this was far more severe than the worst hangover.

Carlotta knew that some of her sickness was not entirely of the sea's making. She had been ill several mornings before the voyage started. That, coupled with missed periods, meant but one thing: she was carrying Tom Pennywhistle's child. She had rehearsed how she would tell him, thinking a sea voyage might be just the setting. Now, she decided she would wait until Malta, when they were again on dry land.

Pennywhistle played not the lover, but the nurse. It was an inauspicious beginning to what should have been a romantic journey, but it would take her awhile to get her sea legs in such weather. How long a person took to acclimate to the motion of the ship was unpredictable and varied widely. He'd never had a problem, even in his first days at sea, whereas Nelson himself had been seasick for a week every time he returned to sea after an extended period on land. He made sure that Carlotta drank lots of water and tea. Most of the pain of seasickness was caused by the early stages of dehydration.

Close to dawn, Carlotta finally fell into an exhausted sleep. Pennywhistle gently eased her head down on the pillow. He hated seeing her in pain, and it made him think about the kind of life he had chosen and the impact it had on the uninitiated. He noticed the rolling was beginning to subside. The weather must be moderating. He dressed in his foul weather oilskins and went on deck.

He was greeted by a hazy sunrise, grey being gradually edged out by gold. The wind was still strong, but the rain had subsided to a slight drizzle. The waves were no longer mountainous, the whitecaps fewer in number, and the sky was beginning to clear. He had nothing else to occupy him and decided to stroll the ship. The Captain was just coming on deck, noticed him, and walked toward him.

"Ah, Captain Pennywhistle, you are looking well. I see by your face and your gait that you are an experienced sailor. The same cannot be said of the other passengers. Last night was miserable." Captain Barclay had the solid pink face, calloused hands, and rolling stride of a man who had spent his life at sea.

"It was indeed a bad night, but the day promises fair. These Adriatic storms are violent, but of no great duration," Pennywhistle remarked.

"Deck there! Sail ho," shouted the masthead lookout. "Three points off the starboard quarter."

Pennywhistle froze and listened intently. On a ship of war in a hostile theatre, those words often presaged dramatic developments. He had to remind himself that this was a merchant ship, not a ship of war, and he was a mere passenger.

Captain Barclay yelled up to the masthead. "What do you see, lookout?"

"Three sail, sir, bearing north northeast, maybe ten miles. Hard to tell through the mist, but they don't look like any merchant ships I know."

Pennywhistle's pulse began to race, although his face retained its calm expression. Passenger or no passenger, Pennywhistle was still a King's Officer and needed to see what was out there. "Captain Barclay, do you mind if I climb and take a look for myself? I confess it is difficult for me to regard myself as a gentleman of leisure when sailing through hostile waters. I should like to have a look at those ships through my glass."

"Be my guest, Captain Pennywhistle. I was once a Sea Service officer myself long ago, and the ingrained habits of years of training are hard to ignore."

"Thank you, Captain. I shall do so directly." He began his long climb up the ratlines. When he reached the top, he braced himself against the mast and unfurled his glass. He scanned the horizon for a full minute before he spied them.

There were indeed three ships. They were French and, unmistakably, frigates. And they were bearing directly for the *Carlyle*.

Fifty-Four

Pennywhistle raced down the ratlines from the maintop to convey the unwelcome news of the French presence.

"I appeal to your sense of duty as a former officer of King George, sir. We shall have to run, of course; the French have no aversion to grabbing an easy prize that presents itself, whatever else their mission is. This ship is only armed with eight four-pounders; pop guns compared to the big stuff on those frigates. We would be reduced to kindling in one broadside, no matter how gallant our conduct."

Barclay nodded. His guns were for defense against local privateers, not warships. Even if the French fired from great distance the thin scantlings on his ships would be sliced through like tissue paper. He had his life savings invested in this ship and did not want to lose her.

"Captain, our best option is to cram on all possible sail and turn in the direction of Lissa. We must, not just to save ourselves, but to warn Captain Maxwell's squadron. I have no idea if Maxwell has any intelligence at all of these vessels. If he does, he may have already put to sea. We may be able to intercept him. Even if we fail, we need to try. We have one advantage; I don't believe the French have detected us."

Barclay replied, "I may just be the civilian skipper of a small packet ship, but, by God, I am still a patriot. Schedule and port calls be damned. We need to help our brave tars. I am happy to do my part to put a roadblock in General Bonaparte's way. Excuse me, Captain, I shall attend to it forthwith."

Barclay picked up his speaking trumpet and began issuing orders. To Pennywhistle's surprise, they were obeyed and executed almost as quickly and smartly as if by the crew of *Active*. Barclay had a small crew, but they had been well trained. The ship altered course, tacked expertly, paid off, and swung in the direction of Lissa.

*****

The French ships from which the *Carlyle* fled were *Pauline*, 40, Commodore Montfort; *Pomone*, 40, Captain Rosamel; and *Persanne*, Captain Satie. The first two were warships; the third had been built as a frigate, but most of its guns had been removed and it was now a heavily laden transport. They were bound from Corfu to Trieste and expected to rendezvous with the Trieste ships at sea. *Persanne* carried a valuable gift from the Emperor: enough heavy cannon to arm an armada of ships, enough cannon to alter the balance of power in the Adriatic and perhaps reverse the results of the battle of Lissa.

The meet up with the Trieste fleet was eagerly anticipated, but no exact longitude and latitude had been designated. It was to be in the general area north and west of Trieste. This was another example of the careless planning that characterized the French navy. The British would have designated exact coordinates for the rendezvous.

Montfort posted six lookouts with glasses to sweep the horizon in hope of spotting their compatriots. Eventually, one of the lookouts espied a small merchantman on the distant horizon. The news was passed to Montfort. "No!" said Montfort to his first officer. "Let it go; it is of no importance. I will not be distracted from our mission. Our task is to deliver the guns as quickly as possible, not go haring off in search of prizes. Tell the lookouts not to bother me any further with reports of merchant ships. They need to search for warships, warships! Any we find will be French! Is that clear? The Trieste squadron will be at sea and we must find them as quickly as possible."

"Yes, sir!" replied First Officer Dulpy. He disliked the Commodore and thought he was overbearing, even arrogant. He was too experienced and well trained in his duties to voice his objections, but it bothered him that Montfort seemed unwilling to consider that the British might also be at sea.

*****

Three hours of skillful sailing and helpful winds left the French Squadron miles astern of *Carlyle*. Pennywhistle breathed a sigh of relief and began to calculate possible positions for the British squadron. *Carlyle* was bound for Lissa, but if the information could be conveyed to the British without having to traverse the entire distance, odds of a successful interception would increase. The question was, were the British at sea, or were they still back in harbour?

Carlotta appeared on deck. She still looked a bit green, but somewhat better. She lurched uncertainly across the mildly rolling deck, and used the bitts supporting the ship's ropes as wooden way stations on her journey to Pennywhistle, standing just in front of the mainmast. She almost lost her footing several times, but finally managed the last few steps and stumbled into Pennywhistle's arms.

"How are you feeling, my dear?" he inquired gently.

"I feel terrible!" she said, with dramatic emphasis. She showed just the barest hint of a smile. "But somewhat less terrible than I did last night. I woke up and I heard the noises of running feet and lots of activity. What has happened?"

He briefly recapitulated the events of the last few hours. She looked downcast. "So the French have conspired yet again to spoil our happiness. And I will not get to see Malta!"

Pennywhistle replied, "My dear, it is like so much in life. The phrase is, 'subject to the requirements of the service.' It saddens me you must pay the same price as I."

"But what will happen now, Thomas?" A few hours ago the future had seemed settled and hopeful. Now it was obscured and uncertain.

"My job is to warn the British. If we encounter the squadron at sea, I wish for you to remain here, out of danger. Captain Barclay has assured me he will guard you as if you were his daughter. If we must return to Lissa, I will put you ashore. I value your safety above all things. Staying close to me is a dangerous proposition.

You have already been through one sea battle; more than enough for a lifetime."

Carlotta flushed red, angry and defiant. "No, Thomas, I will not leave you. I am not some dainty little girl that you must protect from the world. I will not cower distant from you when you are facing death. The worry I would feel being separated would be far worse than any danger from being near you. I have seen death and suffering, and I have endured. I can be of use to you and your shipmates. It is so much better to be of use than useless and consumed by the wildest fears of the imagination. And," she paused for emphasis, "no one can ever know how long we will have together. If it is to end soon, I want to savour every last moment and be with you when it is over. I fear to even utter the word, but my greatest horror would be that you died alone, without comfort. Couples stand together when danger threatens!"

She started to sob gently. She stopped herself when Pennywhistle hugged her. She looked him in the eye and said decisively, "Do not attempt to argue with me! My mind is made up! Once I decide, my decision is unshakable."

Pennywhistle knew her well enough to know this was true. She was a remarkable woman, as splendid of spirit and character as she was of body. Her steel core of will was unshakeable. He contemplated her with just the faintest tinge of awe. She would indeed be useful. And she was right. Couples stood together against danger, drew strength from each other's love and proximity. Truth be told, he himself would worry less about her if she were nearby. The orlop was safe and well protected.

"Sail ho! Fine off the port bow!" the masthead lookout shouted. The words electrified the ship.

"How many sail?" shouted Barclay. Pennywhistle listened intently for the response.

"One... two..." the lookout was counting. "Three, sir! I can just make out the Union flag on the first one!"

Pennywhistle's heart leapt. The Union Jack! It was indeed the squadron from Lissa. He raced aloft with his glass and trained it on the lead ship. By God! It was *Active*! He descended the ratlines even faster than he had climbed up and made straight for Barclay.

"So, Captain, I will trouble you for the loan of your gig and several of your men to row me and my lady to *Active*. It is imperative I convey this information to Captain Gordon at the earliest possible moment."

"I quite understand, and I will have it called away immediately. Will your lady require the use of the Bosun's chair?"

"No," said Pennywhistle, proudly. "She is quite capable of negotiating a rope ladder."

"I thought as much!" replied Barclay.

An hour later Pennywhistle stood on *Active's* quarterdeck in animated conversation with Captain Gordon. Gordon allowed Carlotta the use of his daybed when he saw the ravages of her recent bout with seasickness. She had no shortage of men willing to escort her to the cabin and look after her every need. It was not because of lust; they regarded her in an almost reverential way. They viewed her as something of a good luck talisman, both for the crew and the ship. Because seamen were a superstitious lot, she was very safe on a ship full of lonely sailors.

"Well, Tom, I am damned sorry the French spoiled your pleasure cruise but, selfishly, it is a great stroke of luck for me and the squadron." Gordon laughed joyfully and launched into a recount of his conversation with Maxwell on the previous afternoon. He then grilled Pennywhistle on the French squadron's course and heading. He knew Pennywhistle had a fine memory and he wanted to be certain he extracted every last detail. "Very good, Tom. I will signal Maxwell, then alter course a few degrees to starboard. If our mutual suspicions are correct, we should encounter the French in a matter of hours."

"We gamble on their course, but I think it is a reasonable gamble. Now, Captain, if you will excuse me, I need to see to my marines. And thank you for understanding about Carlotta. She would simply not hear of being left on *Carlyle*. I can fight the French or I can fight her, but I cannot do both!" He looked slightly chagrined.

"On the contrary, Tom, I am glad to have her aboard. I, too, care for her safety and believe she will be safest aboard this vessel. Besides, nothing inspires men to fight harder than doing so under the eyes of a beautiful woman whom they believe brings good fortune to the ship." Gordon clapped Pennywhistle on the shoulder. "You and I are entirely too rational, Tom! Perhaps she really does bring good luck."

Carlotta lay in Gordon's daybed and waited. She was not sure what she waited for, but the hours dragged by at the stately pace of a sleepy snail. Her stomach improved as the pangs of seasickness retreated, but butterflies of anxiety took their place. She had a feeling a decisive moment was fast approaching, not just for the ship but for her and Pennywhistle. She wondered whether she should tell him about his child now, or wait. She decided it was better to wait. He already worried terribly about her; there was no point in making him worry about another. She could neither see the near future nor direct it, but something lay ahead that unsettled her. Try as she might, she could not identify it. Then a shout came that caused her to sit up abruptly. "Sail ho!"

Fifty-Five

Captain Gordon yelled up at the masthead lookout through his speaking trumpet. "What do you make of them?"

The reply came back quickly. "Frigates, sir, definitely French by the rig of them. Five miles distance and closing. They are in line ahead and making straight for us."

Gordon thought that strange. Why would they be steering straight for the British? It was not the usual French style. Dispense with maneuver and go straight at 'em was a purely British tactic. The French were more likely to evade, fight briefly and fiercely, then depart quickly to live to fight again another day. This direct approach was most odd. But, Gordon needed to let Maxwell and Captain Chamberlayne of *Unite* know.

"*Enemy in sight.*" Signal flags shot up the masts to be seen clearly on *Alceste* and *Unite*.

*****

Montfort in the *Pauline* was relieved. At last, the Trieste squadron was in sight! He instructed the quartermasters to steer directly for them. Montfort hoisted the standard recognition signals, a sort of flag handshake to establish *bona fides*. After several minutes of suspense, he realized no response was forthcoming. A jolt of adrenaline shot through him. No, it could not be! He trained his glass on the ships ahead. He gasped as he saw the ships run up red British Naval ensigns. He had just made an extremely serious mistake. But there was still time to remedy it.

"*Monsieur* Dulpy, those are Englishmen out there!" He tried to keep the alarm out of his voice. This was a re-supply mission, not a hunt for enemy vessels. "Alter course, north northwest, toward the island of Pelagosa. Crack on everything we have, including studding sails. Signal *Pomone* and *Persanne* to do the same."

Burdened with a cargo of more cannon than Napoleon had used at the Battle of Wagram, *Pesanne* was exceedingly sluggish and wagon-like. She simply could not keep up with *Pauline* and *Pomone*, and so Captain Satie altered course away from the other two frigates to the northeast. *At least I can divide the pursuit, give the other ships a better chance*, thought Satie.

*****

The British ships cleared for action. Maxwell, in command of the squadron, hoisted the signal *"general chase."* The British matched the French with an equal press of sail. The British ships had the weather gauge and quickly began to gather speed. When one of the ships, slower than the others, changed direction, *Active* set out in hot pursuit. She hoisted all the sail she could carry.

Active slashed through the waves like Ophiotaurus of Greek myth; part sea serpent, part bull. Her fine sailing qualities had never been more evident. If *Pesanne* was a wagon, *Active* was a chariot. Gordon's blood was up and he was in full thrall to the thrill of the chase. *Active* was closing fast on *Pesanne* when *"recall"* shot to the top of *Alceste*'s main mast. Gordon said a quiet "Damn!" under his breath, but he understood. Maxwell wanted *Active* along with his own vessel to take on the two French frigates. It was a matter of sailing qualities: *Active* and *Alceste* were much faster ships than Captain Chamberlyne's *Unite*, but *Unite* was still quite a bit faster than *Persanne*. It was logical that *Unite* take over Gordon's pursuit. He ordered *"acknowledge"* hoisted and watched the change in the ship's wake as it altered course. Behind them, *Unite* angled off to intercept the fleeing French.

Unite's sailors were experienced in every trick of wringing the most use out of wind, so they were able to close on *Persanne* and engage her with bow chasers. One of *Unite*'s twelve-pounders tore a solid chunk out of *Persanne's* taffrail. The fading thunder of cannon fire boomed across the water as *Persanne* continued steering off to the east, replying with her own stern chasers. Gordon followed the cannon flashes through his glass as the ships headed off toward the horizon.

Maxwell's plan was to briefly engage *Pomone*, slow her down, and let *Active* deal with her. *Alceste* would then continue on to overtake *Pauline*. *Alceste* surged boldly ahead of *Active* and fired a shot that ripped splinters from *Pomone's* stern quarter.

To Maxwell's astonishment, *Pomone* tacked expertly, denying him the easy shots down her vulnerable stern, then reversed direction and bore down directly toward *Alceste*. He heard drums, whistles, and a loud creaking noise as gun ports opened and cannon wheels rolled forward. *Pomone* brought her starboard battery to bear on *Alceste's* port quarter. Instead of making the usual French mistake of firing too soon, she displayed excellent battle discipline and held her fire as the range closed. Maxwell believed he knew the French, but today he was dead wrong. *Pomone* was an unpleasant anomaly: a French ship whose gunnery training was a match for the British.

Captain Rosamel had drilled his crew extensively. He was a stout-hearted, aggressive leader who positively welcomed a fight. *Booooooooom!* *Pomone* opened with a devastating broadside expertly fired on the down-roll at one hundred yards' range. It instantly knocked two cannons out of action and killed twenty men. Huge chunks flew from *Alceste's* hull.

Maxwell was stunned.

"Fire!" he shouted. *Alceste's* cannon crashed out a second later. She scored solid hits on *Pomone's* poop and forecastle, but failed to disable any guns. Choking clouds of gritty, grey gun-smoke made men cough and wheeze.

Rosamel's men slammed rounds into their cannons and poured broadside after broadside into the British. The men of *Pomone* worked like demons, confident that they were going to prevail over the arrogant British.

Alceste's men fired back with determination. No Frenchman was going to beat them!

The battle blasted on, two ships mauling each other at close range. Maxwell was worried. Not only did *Pomone* match his rate of fire, their shooting was actually more accurate. Men were blown apart, the scuppers ran red, and the air was thick with the choking smells of smoke and blood and worse, rent with the cries and screams of the dying. At the same time, *Pauline,* in the near distance, was reversing course and reducing speed, preparatory to altering her course back to her compatriot and also engaging *Alceste.*

Then *Pomone* hit *Alceste's* main top gallant mast with a well-placed shot and splintered it. Rosamel saw the damage and told his gunners to direct their fire toward it to bring it down. Three broadsides later, the mast, ropes, and sails went over the side and acted as a giant drogues and anchors. The tangled mess slowed *Alceste* to a crawl, then a full stop.

Maxwell knew his ship was in real trouble. He had ax men chopping frantically to sever the mast, but the work was slow. Rosamel's men could not have asked for an easier target. Broadsides poured into the crippled *Alceste.*

Pomone moved ahead of *Alceste*, fired one last broadside, and surged toward *Pauline.* With *Alceste* immobile, Rosamel thought he would rendezvous with *Pauline,* then the two of them would turn back on *Alceste.* Rosamel probably could finish the business on his own, but two on one was a good way to be sure.

Derisive shouts of *"Vive l' Empereur!"* floated from her wake toward *Alceste.* Maxwell felt it the most humiliating moment of his life. *Alceste* was badly damaged and rolling heavily. He needed help.

Gordon saw the danger and knew he had to act immediately. He did not hesitate. "Helm! Come left two points to starboard, bear directly for the Frenchmen!" *Pomone* had to be stopped before she caught up with *Pauline.* Gordon looked at the faces of his men and saw their eagerness. They knew *Alceste* had been roughly handled and it was up to them to save her.

Pennywhistle checked the action on his Ferguson. He applied more beeswax to the breech-screw so that it moved easily and fluidly. His men were in position and would open fire directly after the first salvo from *Active*.

Spottswood made one last inspection of his men on the quarterdeck. He was trying to be as thorough as he knew Pennywhistle would. He had discarded his usual fusil and had a Baker rifle, procured through Dale's extensive network of NCOs. He had been practicing on targets, but was eager to see how it would perform in real battle.

Dale inspected the marines on the forecastle. They were as ready as they would ever be.

Active reduced sail for battle, but still raced over the waves. She was making fine speed and the distance to *Pomone* closed quickly. *Active's* jib-boom surged toward the bow of *Pomone*, yet *Pomone* withheld fire. *Excellent fire discipline*, thought Pennywhistle. *That captain is good, very good!*

Active continued forward. Soon she was directly alongside *Pomone* at one hundred twenty yards' range, just a little too far for effective musketry. Still, the French did not fire.

Rosamel and Gordon were of a pair and had the same idea. Close the distance just a bit more. Patience, patience! Steady, steady, wait for it! The distance narrowed to eighty yards. Both captains judged the moment right.

"Fire!" Both ships discharged tremendous, well aimed broadsides at the same instant. Under the onslaught of iron, masts, scantlings, and yards splintered, sending deadly shafts in every direction. Pennywhistle saw four marines near him go down; Wainright, Whelen, Parker, and Addison. The four no longer resembled anything human, just four ruined, bleeding heaps of tortured red muscle.

Pennywhistle gave the order to fire, as did Spottswood and Dale. Most of the marines scored hits. Spottswood's Baker accounted for one of the senior deck lieutenants. He was immensely pleased. Swayne's surgery had worked!

Pennywhistle and his men kept up a rolling fire that efficiently winnowed out the crew of *Pomone*. Dale did the same from the forecastle and Spottswood from the poop, and *Active* slammed a steady stream of cannon balls traveling at six hundred feet per second into *Pomone*'s hull. Huge hunks of wood were gouged away each time a broadside discharged. The crew of *Pomone* replied in kind. Twenty minutes of this pounding left plenty of holes in each hull.

At this point, training alone was outmatched by training plus experience. Captain Rosamel had prepared his men, but this was their first naval battle. They were cheered by their fight with *Alceste*, but it had also left them fatigued. The *Active*'s were fresh and had fought before as a well-appointed team under a battle-hardened leader. Whereas men on the *Pomone* paused to mourn their fallen comrades, casualties on the *Active* slowed her crew's exertions not a whit. Tears and sadness were for later. They merely closed ranks, worked around the casualties, and did their jobs.

The mounting list of casualties and attendant horror conspired to reduce the rate and accuracy of *Pomone*'s fire. Each time another man fell, each time the hull was hollowed just a little more by enemy shot, *Pomone*'s fire slackened ever so slightly. Eventually, *Pomone* was only firing two broadsides for every three of the *Active*. But battle was not all about statistics, training, and equations. Just when things seemed headed toward an inevitable outcome, Lady Luck chose to intervene. She was fickle and changeable, but not entirely devoid of reason, and sometimes attached herself to the side that showed heart, preparation, and skill. *Active* certainly displayed those quailites. But sometimes Lady Luck showed a fondness for the underdog, and the crew of the *Pomone* emphatically was that, and today the Lady decided to smile upon them.

The next broadside fired from *Pomone* was not especially destructive to the ship or men, but it was hugely injurious to the command structure on *Active*. A solid twelve-pound shot hit a port carronade, ricocheted off, took the arm of a seaman, bounded forward and smashed the knee joint of Captain Gordon, stationed just forward of the capstan. He went down as if tripped by some invisible ghoul. His lower leg was barely attached to the knee, held by only a few sinews and some flesh. Gordon remained conscious and felt little sensation, the effects of shock attenuating what should have been extreme pain.

He noticed a seaman standing over him, real concern in his face. He searched his memory. It was Winston, a malingering sailor who had earlier sought to be excused from duty because he claimed he had injured his left hand. Winston bent down and gently supported the captain. "Glad to see your hand is working Winston; wish my leg were," Gordon said with gentle sarcasm. He struggled to stay awake. He retained just enough presence of mind to calmly say, "Take over, Mr. Dashwood," before sailors picked him up gently and carried him toward Mr. Swayne's waiting blades in the orlop. Gordon's final thought before he lapsed into blessed unconsciousness was of his beloved Lydia. Could she love a cripple?

Dashwood held command for a grand total of a minute and a half before a passing piece of grape removed his arm at the elbow and pitched him unceremoniously across the deck. Sailors ran to his aid and applied a crude emergency tourniquet, which barely slowed the flow of blood. Haye, the second officer who had been commanding the guns on the quarterdeck, took over and was about to issue his first order when a musket ball caught him in the shoulder and sent him spiraling to the deck.

Pomone's fire was slackening, but still deadly. Another broadside ripped into *Active's* hull and sent giant splinters of a heavy oak knee beam flying onto the gun deck. Meers was hit in the head by a ricocheting fragment of the beam and wore a brief surprised look before flopping to the deck. Another section of the beam, bouncing off the opposite side of the hull, struck Moore in the back, hard as a giant's fist, and knocked him out. Pennywhistle and his men continued firing, unaware of the losses. They had accounted for quite a number of officers: the command structure on *Pomone* was being systematically gutted. The cannon fire thudded on.

Mr. Green, the master and senior warrant officer, urgently sought out Pennywhistle. The redoubtable Mr. Green looked ashen. "Orders, sir?" asked Green. Pennywhistle looked over the quarterdeck and forecastle, and realization hit him like a flying sheet anchor. *My God, all of the commissioned officers must be down!* "Where are

Moore and Meers?"

"They are both out cold, and it don't look like either will be up for a good while," said a flustered Mr. Green.

He was in command. It was a development he'd never expected, never looked for, but one that had to be shouldered, and shouldered immediately. He scanned the deck, thought quickly, then made up his mind.

"Let's finish this damn business. We are going to board. Assemble the boarding parties! We will take the Frenchmen by storm, Mr. Green! Steer straight for her stern quarter. We will board across the jib-boom. When I board, you have the con."

"Aye, aye, sir!" replied Green.

Several members of each cannon crew were designated for boarding parties and despite the tumult and deafening noise, they assembled quickly. Weapons were taken from the chests on deck: pistols, pikes, tomahawks, and swords. The men wore determined expressions, quiet under the control of their petty officers. Dale brought half the marine complement with their muskets. The other half would remain on board under Spottswood and provide covering fire to the boarding party.

Green put the helm over and *Active* swung round a new heading. Propelled by a stiff breeze, she covered the eighty yards to the *Pomone* like a racehorse. *Active's* cannon continued to fire and scored a hit on *Pomone's* foremast, which toppled into the sea. Even without officers, the gun captains knew their business. With a screeching crash of wood upon wood, *Active's* jib-boom ploughed viciously into the stern of *Pomone*. Gigantic, lethal splinters of several hundred pounds flew in every direction. *Active's* sailors used ropes to bind the two ships together. Inaccurate musket fire, mostly aimed too high, whizzed over the heads of the boarding party. Thirty-five sailors and marines crouched in readiness.

The thing had to be done in a rush. Running along a jib-boom was a precarious business, but Pennywhistle told the men it was much safer to risk losing your balance than extend the time you were exposed to gun fire.

Spottswood's marines, concentrated in *Active's* forecastle, blazed away with covering fire. Their volleys kept French heads down and cleared a path in front of the jib-boom. Spottswood, quite taken with the Baker, accounted for two French petty officers. This quite effectively reduced the organization and responsiveness of the French defense.

Pennywhistle drew his cutlass and raised it high above his head. "Follow me!" he shouted with all of the mad fury he could summon, and leaped forward and up onto the round, narrow, spray-slick jib-boom As soon as he did, he became a target for every French sniper who could sight him. Bullets whizzed around him as he advanced at a run. The boom bobbed madly, making it terribly difficult to keep balance, but likewise making him hard to hit. More bullets tore by his head, and one clipped the plume off his hat. Dale, Stratton, McCarthy, and Leicester followed directly, all screaming like Bedlamites. Thirty more marines and sailors joined the onslaught, cheering loudly. Pennywhistle saw the mainmast in front of him sway dizzily. Cannon fire had hit it, but it was not from *Active's* guns. *Alceste* must have rejoined the fight. The last stays on the mast parted and it toppled, groaning, into the sea, the sails falling like shrouds to cover the men below.

He jumped onto the deck and landed heavily. Three determined Frenchmen, not caught by the sails, charged him, cutlasses drawn; brave men, but more than that, brave men who had worked together before; far more lethal than brave men who were strangers.

Time slowed down. The fury and tumult on deck faded into background noise. Pennywhistle took in the face, posture, and sword position of each man and assessed the primacy of the threat each of them posed; in a flash, he knew exactly how he would divide and conquer. The Frenchman on the left was closest, slightly ahead of the other two. The leader he was; fiercely defiant, violet eyes confirmed it. He held his cutlass confidently, with the point aimed at Pennywhistle's stomach. Very professional. He would have to be dealt with first. Kill the leader and knock the heart out of his followers. The second Frenchman, directly ahead, held his cutlass less certainly, his hazel eyes tinged with just a hint of diffidence. Amateur. He could wait.

The third Frenchman, to his right, held his cutlass way too high. Another amateur. But there was something else about this one: his eyes were like dead opals. He'd be very dangerous to a weak man, Pennywhistle realized, but he was also the type who would hang to finish off a fallen enemy—and probably rob the corpse. He would die last.

Pennywhistle became a blur of swift motion. He pivoted quickly to the left, a low crouch with his left knee bent, his cutlass retracted laterally at cheek bone level. It made him a small target, but gave him plenty of space to spring upward and thrust with all the power his well-muscled legs could muster. With his peripheral vision he kept the second Frenchman in sight.

He waited for his opponent to commit.

The sudden crouch startled the leader. He hesitated for a moment, then recovered and aimed a downward thrust at Pennywhistle's head, a small and poor target unless you were a swordsman of the finest calibre.

With great economy of motion, Pennywhistle's wrist easily flicked the blade aside, then he thrust diagonally upward to a point just below the man's trachea. He leapt upwards, all one hundred and eighty pounds of him behind the thrust. The blade ripped through the man's throat, the light faded from his eyes, and he became an upright corpse. There was no time to withdraw the blade, so Pennywhistle spun around and shoved the impaled man violently forward as a human battering ram into the second swordsman. The impact knocked the wind out of him, and he fell back as struggled to regain his balance. Most importantly, he dropped his guard.

It was only for a second, but that was enough for Pennywhistle. He wrenched his blade free, recoiled to the half circle extension stance, and thrust directly for the man's exposed sternum. The man saw with horror what was about to happen, but could do nothing to stop it. The blade smashed through ribs and cartilage, and his heart's blood pumped out in a red, spreading stain.

Pennywhistle pulled his blade free just in time to deflect a head slash from the predatory third man. He had no time for a duel; he needed to push forward to make room for those behind him. With calculated ferocity he executed an efficient wrist-flick riposte, which pierced the man's carotid artery. He deliberately withdrew with a sideways slashing motion to make the cut as lethal as possible. Jets of blood spurted from the dying man's neck as he swayed and gurgled, dropping his weapon and clutching his throat futilely, then toppled to the deck.

"Follow me!" The power of his voice, his bloody sword, and the terrifying expression on his beet-red face galvanized the boarders, even as it unmanned the defenders. The power of a true leader at a tipping point in battle is an amazing thing.

The boarding party surged forward and around him, screaming and bellowing like berserkers. A sailor's cutlass slashed at the onrushing Dale. He ducked slightly and gutted the sailor with his bayonet. A pike-man lunged at him next; he dodged aside, withdrew his bayonet, and skewered the man through the throat. Stratton and Leicester ran along side Dale and charged two French sailors armed with pistols, who were just bringing their weapons to bear. The Englishmen's blades batted the pistols aside and continued on to pierce the Frenchmen's stomachs. *It's just like sticking pigs back at home*, thought Leicester, as he surged on.

The French party detailed to repel boarders backed away in hesitation, then split into small knots of men. They did not run but backed away, like a lion tamer facing a lion that was no longer tame. And they did face a lion of sorts—a British lion. British sailors and marines overflowed the deck like an incoming tide.

The deck vibrated and rolled heavily. Huge shot holes were causing *Pomone* to leak badly; she had six feet of water in the hold. *Active's* guns continued to pour broadsides into her punctured sides. *Alceste* was some distance off, but kept up a steady fire into *Pomone's* bow. Three quarters of *Pomone's* guns were now silent. The concussive thuds of cannon made walking the deck feel like treading an earthquake. With a huge crack, a solid shot pierced the mizzen mast and it toppled. *Pomone* was now a dismasted hulk, bobbing like a cork without the aid of the ship's masts to steady her motion.

A stray piece of grape tore away the gallant Captain Rosamel's jaw and sent him spirling onto the deck. First Officer Arouette noted he was unconscious but alive. He picked up the captain's sword, knowing what he had to do.

Captain's Rosamel's wound and the death of her last mast cast a spell on *Pomone's* crew. There was no prearranged signal, but the fighting suddenly just stopped. They had simply had enough. The ship's First Lieutenant stepped forward and gave voice to what the crew had already decided.

"We surrender!" he shouted. The French tricolour was hauled down from what little remained of the halyards on the stump of the mizzen as the signal to both British and French that the battle was over. The lieutenant, covered in blood, walked slowly forward.

Pennywhistle saluted Pomone's Number One, who returned the gesture crisply. "My captain's sword, sir. He is badly wounded, but he would want you to have what you have so valiantly earned." He offered the classic gesture of capitulation.

"After the gallantry of your crew's conduct today, Lieutenant, I am unable to accept it. Please retain the sword and return it to your captain upon his recovery."

Tears formed in the Lieutenant's lightning-blue eyes. "That is most kind and gracious of you, sir. *Vous avez un grand cœur monsieur. Ce salaud de Montfort n'en a pas! Pauline* abandoned us! That bastard!"

At that moment, *Pauline*, Montfort's ship, was making maximum speed in the opposite direction. She had fired a few desultory broadsides into the damaged *Alceste* and cleared off. Had she come to *Pomone's* aid, the fight might have had a different outcome.

The other ship, *Persanne*, with all of the cannons aboard, was finally overhauled by *Unite*. A short, one-sided fight ensued, easily settled by the appearance on the horizon of *HMS Kingfisher*, 18, attracted to the battle by the concussive vibrations of cannon fire that rippled through the heavy air. Sustained resistance in the face of overwhelming odds was pointless, and Captain Satie surrendered with his honour intact.

No one realized it at the time, but the capture of *Persanne's* cannon ended the French naval threat to the Adriatic once and for all. The French would scheme, intrigue, and launch occasional vexing raids, but they would never again pose a serious naval threat to the British hegemony in the Adriatic.

Fifty-Six

Pennywhistle left a small prize crew aboard *Pomone* and wearily returned to *Active* to find the deck covered with the usual human and material detritus of battle. It was horrid and unpleasant, but in his exhausted state, he barely noticed it, and instead focused his remaining energies on getting the ship back to at least minimum functionality. With all of the ship's officers, save Spottswood, *hors de combat*, he was Captain of *Active* and would continue to be so until such time as a replacement could be found.

Men rested briefly, then began the innumerable activities necessary to bring the ship back to herself. Above all, she had to be kept seaworthy. Sailors energetically manned the pumps, despite the fatigue they felt; no one wanted to go down with a sinking ship. They spliced severed ropes using marling spikes; carpenters plugged shot holes; and the boatswain inspected the foremast rigging, which hung in shreds, like tattered garments on a clothesline after a hurricane. Battle was a hurricane, a force of nature beyond control and no respecter of property or persons.

The wounded were brought to the orlop. The dead were sewn into their canvas shrouds. It looked as if Pennywhistle would be reading the final service. He disliked having to play the role of spiritual leader, but someone had to speak reverential words on behalf of the ship to honour the dead. It was important for Jack Tar to hear the name of his dead mates spoken aloud. No man wanted to die an unremembered cipher. The words might seem hollow comfort to Pennywhistle, but they were not to the men. Routine and ritual were the sinews of the ship, and this was one.

452

Active would need a thorough refit, and that could only be done in England. Well, at least he would get to Malta, where he and Carlotta had been bound in the first place. Some pleasure cruise!

Carlotta was an angel of mercy in the orlop. She not only sewed men up, she comforted the dying with her gentle touch. She listened to their final words, stroked their brows, and held their hands as they began their last journey. She calmed the fearful ones by asking them to tell her about their homes. They burbled and babbled, and finally faded peacefully out. A beautiful woman who listened with compassion was not an unpleasant last vision of life.

It was she who had stitched up the Captain's amputated leg, directly after it was sealed off with turpentine and hot tar. She had squeezed his hand in comfort after, steadfastly standing in for his distant sweetheart. Gordon had woken briefly, and said, "God bless you, Carlotta. You will be one of Lydia's bridesmaids." Carlotta reflexively touched her belly and thought of the child within.

Before the battle, her anxiety had overpowered her and she had felt the need to talk to someone about the secret. Lieutenant Spottswood had dropped by to thank her again for her efforts in saving his arm. He was kind, intelligent, and obviously Pennywhistle's protégé. On impulse, she asked him if he could keep a secret. It was foolish of her, but she needed to apprehend some idea of how Pennywhistle would react when she told him the news. Spottswood reacted with shock, then a smile of great pleasure. He assured her Pennywhistle would be awed and delighted. When she wept gentle tears of joy, Spottswood told her not to worry. He was discretion itself and would say nothing to Pennywhistle. She told him she would enlighten Pennywhistle when they reached Malta.

But, in the midst of all the blood and suffering in the orlop, she changed her mind. It was the perfect time to tell her beloved Thomas about his child; new life in the midst of death. She would give him the news as soon as she came on deck.

Pennywhistle was imagining what would happen when he brought Carlotta to England. With the battle damage, Malta was merely a stopover point. He would be granted leave to visit his only family: his dull, upstanding brother, Peter, and equally stifling wife and children. They would be stunned meeting Carlotta, but his passion and conviction would bring them round to his point of view. He would hear the usual lectures about finance and commerce, but this time, he would respond with a lecture of his own about the wonderful healing power of love. Pure sentimentality, but he didn't give a damn.

He would make things work out, if necessary by sheer willpower. Peter, for all of his failings, realized that family was family, blood was blood, and nothing was more important. The house in Berwick had mixed and bittersweet memories, but it was the nearest thing he had to a home. Standing amid all of the relics of death on deck, he felt it was high time family rifts be healed and emotional chasms be bridged.

There would be a month at Berwick, then he would report back to Stonehouse Barracks in Plymouth for reassignment to a new ship. It would mean a new commanding officer, and new adventures. *Active* had been home for nearly two years, and the men and her officers had become his real family. It was painful to contemplate how battle had decimated them. Moore and Meers had severe concussions, Haye and Dashwood had each lost an arm, and Captain Gordon's leg was gone. The carnage brought a tear to his eye, but it vanished when he thought of Gordon's love for his fiancée. Love was a powerful thing. He knew Gordon would do anything to walk down the aisle with Lydia, even if he had to do it on a peg leg. It certainly would not preclude him walking a quarterdeck again. Thank God, at least Spottswood remained untouched.

Four of his marines were dead. He would not forget them. The stupid but earnest Wainwright, the eager messenger, Addison, who had wanted a marine career, the fast-talking Irishman Whelen, and the superb marksman Parker. They were men in his mind, never "other ranks."

Active had taken his measure and he hers. Both were well satisfied. Their cruise together had been successful and profitable. He would not have believed he could be so sentimental, but he had come to share Gordon's belief that she was not just a ship, but a living being; a grand lady who brought adventure, honour, and distinction to those who walked her decks. Women had come and gone, but she had been the enduring lady in his life.

But now he had Carlotta. What was to become of their love? He had no idea just now. His mind had too many details to which to attend.

"Thomas!" He was startled to hear her voice, but it was a beautiful, lilting, comforting sound. He had no way of knowing it was overflowing with joy because of the wonderful news she was about to tell him.

He turned and saw she was standing just in front of the uncertainly upright mizzen mast. She smiled gloriously, even though she wore a blood-soaked surgeon's apron. Strangely, she looked beautiful, but in a dark, ancient way; as if she were some primal, long forgotten, warrior goddess who defended hearth and home with all of the blood-curdling ferocity of a lioness protecting her cubs. *Active* was her hearth, the crew her cubs. She had fought death today in surgery, and many sailors were alive because of it. She was the *Active's* figurehead come to life, a symbolic protector of the entire ship. She was a Queen Boadicea of the waves, a woman triumphant. She was Yin, Gaia, the Life Force itself. Amidst all of the death and destruction, he thought he had never seen such a luminous sight.

His heart jumped insanely and he knew with complete certainty, in a glorious instant, the step he had been so frightened to take, that ultimate and irrevocable step, was now the right, obvious, and easy one. A bolt of insight shattered the barriers in his heart, and the simple words, "I do," no longer held any terror. She was what had been intended for him all along! God, Fate, Destiny—call it what you will—was boldly making his future clear; odd it should be in the presence of so much death.

He wanted to give himself fully, freely, and without reservation to her, now and for all the rest of the days of his life. He had an instantaneous vision of all of the wonderful children they would have together! They would know real love, so different from his own

455

childhood. At that moment, he cared nothing for career, or social standing, or what lay ahead. He simply *knew*, and it transfixed him.

Because he was transfixed by her beauty, his observant eye failed to heed something he normally would have spied instantly. One of the fore stays on the mizzen mast, under enormous pressure and dangerously frayed because of battle damage, parted like a shot. When it gave way, it released an attached pulley called a block. The block was very heavy, carved of dense wood, and it came speeding forward on its rope toward the deck like a deadly pendulum. The block headed directly for Pennywhistle's head.

Carlotta saw she had no time to warn him; impulsively she jumped forward and shoved him out of the way. It was pure instinct, pure selflessness, pure love. However, she was not quite quick enough, and the block slammed brutally into the side of her head, even as Pennywhistle hit the deck.

He sat up, dazed, then saw what had befallen.

"NOOOOOOOOOOOOOOOOOOOOOOOOOOOOO!"

The cry was wrung from his heart. He staggered towards her, trembling with disbelief, and knelt down. He cradled her gently in his arms and willed her to wake up. "Please, God, not this!" he begged aloud, even as the cynical part of his mind knew that his pleas would fall on deaf ears. She still had a smile on her lips, but no breath escaped them. Her beautiful green eyes stared up at the sky, without seeing. He put his hand on her carotid artery. There was no pulse.

He cradled her in his arms and kept murmuring, "No, no, no!" It was impossible, it could not be. He stared blankly into space; the same hopeless, resigned stare he had seen in wounded men who realized their wound was mortal. But even in such a state, a part of his intellect began to make plans. Carlotta would want Nico and Marko looked after. He made a firm vow in his mind to do just that. He would bring them to England and see that they were given a proper education. He had no idea how to be a father, but knew his brother would be eager to provide guidance and precepts. The boys were his responsibility now, a living link to his beloved.

In this moment of death, he realized how much a part she had become of his life, how much she had changed him, humanized him, made him fully whole. She had traded her life for his willingly, without hesitation, and she had done it on instinct. The measured reason he prized so highly played no part; the purity of her selflessness awed him. He had always thought love a chimera and a cheat, but she had just shown it was the strongest force in the Universe. And now she was gone. It was not just his heart which screamed, but his very soul. He felt so empty!

He began to sob; slowly at first, then convulsively. He held her close, as if he would never let go, and wept until no more tears would come. He so wanted to let her know he had finally mastered a joke that would make her laugh. The men on deck stopped their work and gathered round in protective sympathy.

McCarthy wept freely as well; he would never forget the miracle she performed on Blandon. Even the reserved Mr. Green felt wetness on his cheeks. Stoical Sergeant Dale shed no tears, but was glad he had had a chance to know Carlotta, even briefly. She was pure of heart. The woman he had loved had played a double game with him and abetted his betrayal to the authorities. Carlotta had given her life to save her man. Remarkable!

Manton watched his master's grief with a deeply pained helplessness. Being an orphan, he had come to regard Miss Carlotta as a wonderful surrogate for the mother who had died so long ago. She had shown him so many kindnesses he would never forget. More than that, her courage had given him the strength to take actions that he liked to believe had saved Captain Pennywhistle's life. He thought he could hold back his feelings, but tears proved stronger than will. They coursed freely down his face.

Spottswood came upon the scene and saw with horror what had happened. He stood beside his captain quietly, and debated whether to tell Pennywhistle about Carlotta's pregnancy. He weighed the matter carefully before deciding. Telling Pennywhistle would be cruelty itself; it would change nothing, only magnify the captain's pain and grief, perhaps beyond his ability to cope. It was the act of a brother shielding his sibling. He had told Carlotta he was discretion itself. He would be exactly that.

He looked with deep sadness at the weeping man who had done so much to give his own life purpose. But for Pennywhistle, he might now be an angry, friendless drunk. He had been a wastrel boy when he stepped aboard, a mere military apprentice with a commission; now he was a man and master of his soldierly craft. Pennywhistle had granted him a dignity and redemption he would have never believed possible. Why was this man, who so deserved love, being denied it? There was no answer.

Pennywhistle's chest heaved and his shoulders shook silently, and the weight of the world thudded down upon his heart. Time slowed to an agonizing crawl. Hell was not fiery, but dark, cold, and empty. But then the Master's words abruptly jerked him back from his slide into perdition

"Orders, Captain?" asked Mr. Green. "Nightfall is comin' on and the wind is shifting. We may be in for a strong blow. We have two bad holes below the waterline and six feet of water in the hold."

The words pierced his grief like ice water thrown into his face. The "black dog," which had started to bay, was silenced. He put his grief aside. He shoved his sorrow into his mental sea chest. He would deal with it all later. He had never hated the word "duty" so much in his life! Carlotta sacrificed her life so he could command and help the men who were his true family. God, Carlotta's death tore at him, but damn it! His other lady was still there. *Active* needed help; without it, she, too, might die. The sea was relentless, unforgiving, and cared not a jot for his plight. Grief and mourning were "subject to the requirements of the service." The men on deck looked at him with sympathy, but he saw in their eyes they still needed someone to lead them. They were children, they needed a parent. This was the bitter loneliness of command.

Active surged forward through the night, into contrary winds and uncertain seas.

Spottswood walked over to him, his expression one of quiet understanding. "Tom, let me help. You are not alone."

He spoke in the soothing tones of a parent talking to a distraught child. "It's all right, you can let go now. We will see to her." He bent down and gently untangled Carlotta's body from Pennywhistle's grip. He laid her lovingly on the deck. Dale quietly covered the body with sailcloth. Spottswood saw bewilderment in Pennywhistle's eyes slowly change to gratitude. He stood up and reached down to Pennywhistle. "You saved this arm, now take my hand."

Pennywhistle squeezed his palm in deep fellowship and felt himself gently helped to his feet. The kindness did not stop the pain, but it temporarily stanched his soul's bleeding. He would carry on.

He pulled himself determinedly to his full height and adjusted his rumpled uniform. He wiped his bloodshot eyes with his sleeve, shoved a mental ramrod up his backside, and screwed his face back to an imitation of equanimity. He took a deep breath. "Steady as she goes, Mr. Green." He began to issue orders. His command voice quivered slightly, his iron resolve not at all. His lady was dead, but his other love would not die today. He would bring her home.

Tom Pennywhistle will return in *The King's Scarlet*.

COMING SOON!

The King's Scarlet
By John M. Danielski

The Peninsular War in Spain is moving toward a climax. Captain Thomas Pennywhistle of the Royal Marines is trapped behind enemy lines carrying vital dispatches for Lord Wellington. His mission will lead him inexorably toward the decisive Battle of Salamanca.

Pennywhistle violates orders to save a lovely stranger and sets in motion a train of events which transform a less than straightforward assignment into a confusing maelstrom of treachery, betrayal, and uncertain alliances. The French want him badly for something beyond the dispatches he carries and are prepared to stage a huge manhunt to capture him. His Spanish allies prove less than helpful. The woman turns out to be much more complicated than expected.

His assets are few; the odds against him, daunting. The only things he can trust completely are his sergeant, his servant, and his Ferguson Rifle. He will face hard fighting, wilderness survival, and even torture, but he is a difficult man to kill and just too damn stubborn to ever admit defeat.

Visit: *http://www.tompennywhistle.com*

About the Author

John Danielski spent four years working his way through college as an interpreter at historic Fort Snelling. He played a soldier of 1827; wore the uniform, did the drill, fired the weapons, and ate the food of the period. He particularly enjoyed serving on the cannon crew of the Fort's 12 pounder. He is a phi beta kappa, magna cum laude graduate of the University of Minnesota and has worked as a high school history teacher and small town newspaper editor.

He has a black belt in tae kwon do and enjoys sailing, cross country skiing, and hockey. He is a master of the board game Diplomacy, a determined if abyssal chess player, and is proud to say he has never played Halo. He lives with his closest advisor, Sparkle, the wonder cat.

For the Finest in Nautical and Historical Fiction and Non-Fiction

www.FireshipPress.com

Interesting • Informative • Authoritative

All Fireship Press and Cortaro Publishing books are available through FireshipPress.com, Amazon.com and via leading wholesalers and bookstores.

CPSIA information can be obtained at www.ICGtesting.com
Printed in the USA
LVOW10s1542070616

491590LV00016B/1153/P